Rough Seas Ahead

A Novel

by

Anne Higgins Petz

This book is a work of fiction. The characters and events in their lives are products of the author's imagination. The historical occurrences and figures described are factual.

ISBN-13: 978-1502449740

ISBN-10: 1502449749

Bekan Press

www.annepetz.weebly.com

DEDICATION

For my parents, Thomas Joseph Higgins and Anne Marie
Geoghegan Higgins. They instilled in their five children a
love for the old country, which my father left behind,
but could never forget.

ACKNOWLEDGEMENTS

Thomas Higgins, my cousin, a retired school teacher and local historian in County Mayo, Ireland, shared with me his knowledge of life, customs and language of late nineteenth century Ireland. Any historical inaccuracies are to be laid at my feet, not his.

My sister, Maureen Higgins, for her insightful comments and suggestions.

My excellent editor, Gerald William Shaw, author of "The Complete Guide to Trust and Estate Management" for his invaluable input.

To those who read my manuscript and offered suggestions and encouragement: Yusiana Basuki, Diana and Elvira Chiritescu, Joseph Doyle, Edwina Ferony, and Caroline Maher.

Give me your tired, your poor,

Your huddled masses yearning to breathe

   free,

The wretched refuse of your teeming
   shore,

Send these, the homeless, tempest-tossed

   to me:

I lift my lamp beside the golden door.

Emma Lazarus

Chapter 1

THE VOYAGE

November, 1887

Until now the worst part of the trip across the Atlantic Ocean had been the almost inedible food and the reeking stench of unwashed bodies. But suddenly the skies turned as black as the men's dirty trousers and the sea churned beneath them, tossing the ship from side to side, and intermittently raising the bow and slamming it back onto the foaming waves. The passengers grabbed for buckets as the vomit rose up in their throats, but there were not enough pots available to accommodate the quantity of foul-smelling emissions spewing from the mouths of the seasick immigrants.

Mary Alice fought her way through the jammed ship as far forward as her seventeen-year-old, five-foot-four body could manage, pushing herself past the burly unshaven men and the crying women, many of whom were holding babes to their breasts. She needed air desperately. As she was about to pass a middle-aged lady lying on a cot, the woman grabbed her hand and pulled Mary Alice towards her pleading, between the racking coughs that shook her body, "Help me girl. Please help me."

Mary Alice got down on her knees beside the woman, but recoiled slightly as she observed the red-rimmed eyes and pale, sunken cheeks.

"What can I do fer ye? Shall I be fetching ye some water?" She had seen many sick people in Ireland, but none looked as bad as this woman, except for her mother hours before her death.

"Ah, if ye please, bring up me bag from under the cot and raise me up. Put the bag under me head."

The effort it took the woman to speak produced another coughing spell that sent her body into spasms. Mary Alice pulled a handkerchief from her pocket and placed it on the woman's mouth and she spit out the bloody phlegm clogging her throat. When the choking stopped and the woman regained her breath, Mary Alice tugged the bag out from under the cot, raised the suffering woman to a near sitting position, and gently leaned the frail body up against the satchel. She reached into her pocket and handed the woman the three remaining mint drops her father had pressed into her hand at the dock in Cork City before she boarded the ship to America.

"Maybe these will help ye."

"Yer an angel, ye are, and a pretty one at that, but nothing can help me now but the Almighty. I'll be gone before the ship reaches the harbor."

"Now don't ye be thinkin' like that. I'll fetch the ship's surgeon." Mary Alice stood up ready to get help, but the woman clutched her hand. "He's been here and gone. No hope, says he."

"Well there are more powerful healers than him. We'll pray to the Virgin Mary fer yer recovery." Mary Alice withdrew rosary beads from her pocket and began praying aloud, but the old woman stopped her, and taking the young girl's firm hand in her pale, weak, trembling fingers, thanked her for the kindness she had shown a stranger. "Reach in me pocket, lass. There be an envelope. Take it out."

Mary Alice fumbled in the woman's well-worn jacket and retrieved a small packet and offered it to the woman who refused, saying, "It's fer ye, lass. A small payment fer the kindness ye've shown a dying woman. No, no don't go interrupting me," she gasped. "If ye donna take it, the sea will after they slip me body over the side."

Upon opening the envelope Mary Alice found a wad of dollars and a scrap of paper. The dying woman seemed to sense the girl's unspoken thoughts as to why she was dying alone in the Atlantic Ocean so far from home.

"It's not much money, but it's all I've got, and I don't want it to go to the grave with me. It's fer ye, fer doing me the favor I'm goin' to ask of ye. There's a paper inside the envelope with me brother's name and address. William Peyton. He's expecting me. Could ye visit him in New York City and tell him the pneumonia did me in? I was to live with him, but the Lord had other plans. Will ye do that fer me, lassie?"

Mary Alice assured her she would follow her wishes and asked the woman her name.

"I'm Catherine Peyton, from County Clare," she gasped, as the coughing began again, small coughs this time, and then her eyes closed. "I'm going to sleep now," she mumbled, and Mary Alice gently placed the blanket over her, kissed Catherine's hot, wet forehead, and raced toward the open deck where she thought she might be able to breathe again.

The skies had opened up, and the rain poured down, and her new skirt and tweed jacket were almost soaked through, but she felt no discomfort, only relief. She looked at her sodden clothes and remembered her Aunt May's letter to her from New York a few months earlier.

My darling little Mary Alice,

I'm sending ye some money for yer passage and to buy clothes you'll need for yer journey to America. I've a position waiting fer ye here with me at the Birmingham estate in a town called Tuxedo Park, and I can't wait to see ya. Have a safe trip, and I'll be there when yer ship arrives to take ye to yer new job with me. Write me the date of yer ships docking in New York.

Yer loving Aunt May.

It was over a week since Mary Alice boarded the ship and left Ireland from the port of Cork, and she knew this misery would be behind her shortly and she would disembark this death ship and step into the sunlight of New York on to streets paved with gold. She consoled herself with the thought that Aunt May would be waiting for her at the dock, enfold her in her arms, and take her to the new job that would provide enough wages to send her father the money he needed to pay his Irish landlord, money that would prevent him from being evicted from the tenant farm on which he had labored for more than twenty years.

But now her stomach growled from hunger, and she remembered her mother's words a month before she died: "Sit down, Mary Alice. Leave the pots till later. Eat yer bacon and cabbage and the potatoes before they're cold. Ye've worked hard all day, and if the men haven't enough brains to come fer dinner on time, it doesn't mean you have to starve till the cows come home."

But she could tolerate the hunger. After all, if the Lord Jesus fasted for forty days and nights in the desert, she knew she could get by quite well on the meager provisions doled out by the ship's galley.

Now on deck she felt revived by the sea air. She had not succumbed to the seasickness plaguing the other passengers. She had been raised by the sea in County Galway, where her father propped her up in the back of his currach when he rowed out on the choppy bay to catch mackerel and cod fish to supplement the vegetables he grew, and the cheese, butter and milk supplied by their one cow whose life span was rapidly coming to an end. She had been chosen to go to America as her two brothers were needed on the farm for the heavy work of planting and reaping, seeing after the few remaining sheep, and keeping up the house and barn. And it was easier for an Irish girl to find work than for an Irishman in the new world. Her sixteen-year-old sister, Norah, remained in Ireland to take over the household chores Mary Alice assumed when their Mother died two years previously.

Mary Alice opened the dying woman's envelope and counted out fifty dollars. A fortune. Then she looked at the scrap of paper and William Peyton's address under the name of a law firm on Broadway, wherever that might be. But Aunt May would know, and her first duty would be to visit Mr. Peyton and deliver the sad news of his sister's death. She prayed he would not break down before her, or even worse, think his sister had given her more money and she had pocketed the rest of it. But she would give him the fifty dollars, as it was rightfully his. She carefully placed the money and the slip of paper deep into the pocket of her skirt.

While she calculated how long she would have to work to accumulate enough money for the purchase of a new cow, a tall, hulk of a man clipped her shoulder as a gust of wind propelled him past her, almost causing her to lose her grip on the railing. As the man lay prone on the deck, Mary Alice lashed out at him. "Haven't ye got yer sea legs yet? Ye almost threw me into the drink, ye hooligan!"

The young man tried mightily to contain his embarrassment at falling down, his anger at the young woman witnessing it, and his disbelief at her disdainful attitude. This Irishman was accustomed to adulation from everyone in his home town who appreciated his uncommonly good looks and his above average intelligence. How dare this brash little being speak to him that way, when bumping into her was a mere accident caused by the rolling of the ship. He quickly got to his feet and confronted her, and though still angry at the girl, but mindful of the good manners his mother had so diligently instilled in him, he apologized.

"I beg your pardon, lass. Are you all right?"

"That I am, but it's no thanks to yerself." She straightened her jacket and placed her hands on her hips. "And where might ye be comin' from?"

He suppressed his initial reaction to tell the little snip it was no business of hers. But his heart softened at the sight of her rain-soaked hair and wet boots. "I'm Matthew Clarke from Claremorris, County Mayo, where my father's the local schoolmaster."

"And I am Mary Alice O'Laughaire from Galway, where my father's a farmer. And why have ye left Ireland?"

"A year after my mother died my father took a new wife. She resented my presence in the house, so to keep the peace I decided to seek my fortune in America. I'll be working with my cousin in Pennsylvania. He farms and breeds horses. His business is growing and he needs more help."

"So you're going to work on a farm?"

"Yes, but not for long. I intend to better myself once I get my bearings. And what would be taking you to America?"

He smiled down at her, and she marveled at his white, evenly spaced teeth, recalling that most of the young men she knew in Ireland were missing several teeth by the time they reached this stranger's age, either due to brawling, or lack of medical care.

She pushed her sodden hair over her forehead and looked directly into Matthew's eyes, partially covered by a shock of fair hair, and confessed, "I too have a position awaiting me." She lowered her eyes and slowly continued. "I'm to be a scullery maid in the kitchen of a rich Protestant family in Tuxedo Park."

"You'll be living in a park?"

The pitying look on his face annoyed her. "Of course I won't be living in a park. What do ye take me fer, a tinker? Tuxedo Park is the name of a very fine town, or maybe it's a village, just a stone's throw north of New York City, I'm told. Out in the countryside."

"Well, I never heard of it."

7

"There are probably thousands of places ye've never heard of, even if yer father's a teacher."

He contained his annoyance and continued. "And by what good fortune did you manage to gain this position?"

"Me Aunt May's worked fer the owners, the Birminghams, fer the past ten years as their cook, and she recommended me. But I won't be peeling potatoes and washing dirty dishes fer the likes of some rich Protestants fer long. I will raise meself up. I'll learn the ways of this new country and start me own business in the city of New York, I will."

"And what kind of business do you have in mind?"

"Why, maybe a little pub, after me Aunt May teaches me to cook the foods these Americans eat."

"It won't be easy for a woman to open such an establishment in New York. They're frequented by men, and men want to be in the company of men. Mary Alice, you know that in Ireland women aren't even allowed in a pub."

"Aye, but men like to eat, and this is America, and it's the women who know how to cook. Since I was fifteen I worked in Galway City on the weekends, cooking in an inn and the men were very pleased with me food. So it's me goal to have me own place to do what I'm good at."

"You might consider something more appropriate for a young woman."

"And what might that be, Mr. Clarke?"

"Well," Matthew thought for a moment. "You could be a sales girl in a ladies garment shop."

She raised her eyebrows in surprise. "Ye think I'd be content fitting fat rich ladies with corsets and lying to them that the dress they picked out flattered them when it really belonged on a girl half their age and weight? No, Matthew Clarke. I will own restaurants. I'll cook food fit for royalty and the customers will come, no matter that I happen to be a woman. Just ye wait and see. It's determined, I am. And no one can take me dream away."

"I hope you're right, Mary Alice. But be prepared for a long, rocky road."

"It may be rocky, but by God, it won't be long."

Matthew admired the spunk of this Irish country girl, but could not help thinking her life would be harder than she now imagined, and so probably would his. He removed the woolen scarf from under his jacket and gently placed it over Mary Alice's soggy hair and folded it back over her shoulders.

"Wouldn't want the pneumonia to get you, now would we?"

She blushed, thanked him for the scarf, and covered her embarrassment by telling him of the sick woman on the cot below and promising to visit her brother and tell him of his sister's fate.

"You're a kind girl, you are. And I know giving the man that information won't be easy. But you're strong, and you'll find the right words when you meet him."

She felt uncomfortable by his compliments, and quickly turned the conversation away from herself.

9

"So tell me, have ye left any brothers or sisters at home?"

"No. I'm the only child of Sean Clarke. But who knows? That might change. That new wife of his may have other ideas."

"I'm glad me Da hasn't remarried. At least my brothers will get to keep the farm instead of some money grabbing local widow."

"We can't run our parents' lives, Mary Alice. It's enough trouble running our own."

"Well, yer father has a good job teaching, and he'll have a pension to retire on. Ye don't know what it's like fer me two brothers. All they have to look forward to is making a living by farming the rocky soil for the rest of their lives. That's if Da has any sense in his head and doesn't give it all away by marrying again. Yer father's lucky he hasn't spent his life digging in the soil."

" My mother's people were from the O'Brien clan, descended from Brian Boru…"

"The great high king of Ireland?" she said. Matthew had finally managed to impress the girl.

"One and the same. My family had a great deal of wealth and property until the Brits ran them off their estate in County Meath. They settled in the west, in Mayo, and the men, who were all scholars, took up teaching the local children."

Mary Alice frowned. "It must have been very hard fer them to leave their home for the unknown land in Mayo. Parting from me family for the boat in Cork was more like a wake than a sailing. Me Da looked at me like he'd never lay eyes on me again, and having to leave Ireland put a pain in me chest. It was all I could do not to start blubbering. Me sister, Norah, sobbed and sobbed, and I had to shake her back to her senses and tell her she was doing Da no good acting that way. She's a year younger than meself, and fer sure all her tears were more fer the extra work that would fall on her than the loss of me presence in the house."

The rain had tapered off slightly, and they remained on the deck. Mary Alice continued. "But it was me duty to leave. Someone had to earn the money to keep the farm going. And there's money to be made in America, not in Ireland."

"Well, it looks like we're both in the same boat," Matthew laughed, "physically and monetarily."

"Ye do have a way with the words, Matthew Clarke. Why didn't ye become a teacher yerself?"

"Don't have the patience for it. But I'll make my mark, and not by farming. I'll find something better. If you work hard enough in America, anything's possible. But look, you're shivering. Let's get below."

When they reached the shelter of the hatchway, Matthew stopped and retrieved a pencil and some paper from his shirt pocket. "Now tell me where I can write you."

"Write me?"

"Of course. We don't want to lose track of one another in our new country, now do we?" He smiled down at his bedraggled shipmate.

She took the pencil from his hand and carefully wrote: 'Mary Alice O'Laughaire, c/o Mrs. Birmingham, Tuxedo Park, New York,' and gave it to Matthew. He then handed her a slip of paper on which he'd written 'Matthew Clarke, c/o Liam Clarke's Farm, Johnstown, Pennsylvania.'

"Now you promise you will send me a letter as soon as you're settled?" he said.

"That I will. And will ye write me back?"

"You can be certain of that. And we'll meet again in New York. It's not that far from Johnstown and we Irish must stay in touch. I especially want to know how you do at the Birminghams."

As they were about to descend the staircase, he impulsively took her face in his hands and gently touched his lips to her cheek and said, "Take good care of yourself, Mary Alice. We'll meet again in New York."

Her heart beat erratically as they parted. She had allowed no man to touch her in Ireland, and now found herself entranced by a stranger. She eagerly anticipated exchanging letters with this bold Irishman with the face and body of an ancient Celtic warrior.

Once below, her elation turned to sorrow as she passed Catherine Peyton's empty cot, and she searched in vain for Matthew to comfort her. But her next glimpse of Matthew would be his flashing smile as he waved goodbye to her above the crowd the following day as they disembarked the ship in New York Harbor, each to go their separate ways.

Chapter 2

THE GREAT BLIZZARD

December, 1887-1888

The night before the boat docked in New York, Mary Alice washed her hair in the small basin by her cot, and sponged her entire body with the last piece of soap left in her toilet kit. She rubbed her teeth and gums with salt and rinsed her mouth with the little water that remained. She desperately wanted to look presentable for her Aunt May, who she remembered always appeared so neat and tidy. She would not want to disappoint or shame her by having a niece who looked like an unkempt country bumpkin.

In the morning, she tied back her shiny auburn hair with a white ribbon and put on the new blue dress she had carefully kept clean to wear on her arrival in New York. Mary Alice's cheeks were rosy from the fresh sea air, and her green eyes sparkled with excitement at the thought of starting her new life. The gang plank opened and she and her fellow passengers made their way off the ship and into the immigration room. Mary Alice searched the throng of people waiting for their friends and relatives, and spotted May at the back of the hall. She noticed her aunt's brilliant red hair that she had so admired was now streaked with grey, and though she had just celebrated her fortieth birthday, she appeared ten years older. May, her mother's sister, was the first of the family with enough courage

13

to leave home for the New World in hope of supporting her Irish family. She had dutifully sent back enough money to keep them afloat for the last ten years, and financed the ship's passage for Mary Alice, who would then contribute to the flow of money back to Ireland to sustain the farm in Galway.

In the processing room, Mary Alice forced herself to hold her tongue while undergoing the indignities of a medical examination as a doctor tested her heart, made her cough, searched her hair for lice with a fine tooth comb, and asked numerous personal questions. Then the officials infuriated her by their inability to spell her name correctly. She kept telling one authoritative young man her name was O'Laoghaire. But she left the Castle Garden immigration center with papers and a new name, Mary Alice O'Leary. Oh well, she thought, it's close enough, since I'll probably be married before too long and be given a new name. And since that's the way it will be, I might as well change me first name to what me mother wanted to call me but for the priest's objection that it was not a saint's name. From now on I will be known as 'Nancy O'Leary.'

She pushed her way through the crowd to her aunt's side and they embraced, laughing and crying until May held her niece at arm's length and nodded approval.

"Well, haven't ye grown into a fine looking woman since I last saw ye ten years ago as a mere child. Ye could be a bit taller, but yer hair's a lovely shade and yer eyes are as green as the meadows of Galway."

Nancy smiled at her aunt, who was often oblivious to how her brutal honesty sometimes verged on cruelty.

"Well, I'll probably not be getting any taller, but I'll make up fer me lack of height by using me wits."

"Aye, I'm sure ye will. After all, yer an O'Laoghaire, and besides givin' us beauty, the good Lord saw fit to give us brains. Now tell me, did ye have a good crossing?" May asked as she led her niece towards the exit.

Nancy thought of Matthew Clarke and Catherine Peyton and replied, "Yes and no."

"Well, come on, tell me about it," said May.

"I will, but first, let me tell ye what they did to me here. The Americans at immigration, they've gone and changed me name. They could not spell O'Laoghaire, so me papers now read O'L-E-A-R-Y. Can ye imagine that?"

May smiled knowingly at her niece. "It happens all the time, darlin'. The Irish come over here with their Gaelic names and they end up being spelled the English way. But it's still pronounced the same. So don't give it two thoughts. It's not the name ye have, but what ye make of the name."

Mary Alice thought a moment about her aunt's comment and replied, "Tis true. But if they can change me last name, I can change me first. Do ye remember how me Mom wanted to call me Nancy? She told me often enough. But Father Egan wouldn't allow it and refused to baptize me, so Mom named me Mary Alice after her sisters, you and Aunt Alice. So from now on I'm to be called Nancy. Nancy O'Leary. What do ye think of that?"

May showed no surprise at her niece's declaration. Even at ten years of age she showed independence and spoke her own mind.

15

"So, Nancy it will be," smiled May. "Now, come meet Patrick, the Birmingham's driver, and he'll take us to the train and we'll be off to Tuxedo Park. The old troll allowed Patrick to bring me here as I haven't been to Manhattan since I got off the boat ten years ago, and she feared I'd never make it back to the house on me own to cook her bloody dinner."

Nancy suddenly remembered her errand and said, "Aunt May, can we make a stop at Broadway first?" She explained Catherine Peyton's dying wish on the ship and the mission the woman had entrusted to her.

"Of course. We couldn't deny a dying woman her last wish. Patrick will know how to get us there."

They found Patrick standing by the curb. The handsome young Irishman, donned in a black suit and peaked cap, said, "Welcome to New York, Mary Alice," and bowed slightly and tipped his hat.

"Thank ye, Patrick. But please call me Nancy."

May told Patrick they had a stop to make, and asked if he knew how to get them to Broadway.

"That I do," he responded, and led them towards an oncoming bus being pulled by a giant black steed.

Nancy handed Patrick the wrinkled paper with William Peyton's address, and after a short, jarring ride over the cobblestone street, Patrick rang the bell in the bus signaling the driver to stop and the horse came to a halt before a brick building in lower Manhattan.

"Here we are, lass. Would ye be wanting me to go in with ya?"

"No, but thank ya. And I'll try not to be keeping ye waiting too long."

She opened the door bearing a sign reading Geary & Peyton, Attorneys-at-Law, and entered the waiting room. Leather chairs surrounded a long low table in the center of the room. Paintings of important-looking old men adorned the walls, and a sideboard held newspapers and magazines stacked in neat piles. Nancy thought Mr. Peyton must be a very successful lawyer to afford such a grand office.

Within seconds of her closing the door, a young man appeared from one of the private offices and introduced himself.

"Hello. I'm William Peyton. Can I help you?"

Nancy had expected a grey-haired, slightly stooped gentleman, and was surprised by the tall, slender, distinguished looking young man before her. He wore glasses, and she noticed that the small scar on his forehead did not detract from his even, pleasant features.

"I'm Nancy O'Leary." She curtsied slightly and he bid her to sit down.

"What can I do for you, Miss O'Leary?"

"What I have to say is not an easy thing fer me to do, Mr. Peyton."

"Now, just relax. All my clients have problems and find them very difficult to talk about. But I'm here to help. So just tell me what I can do for you."

"Well, it's nothing ye can do fer me. It's I who have the sorry task of bringin' ye bad news."

William Peyton took the chair next to Nancy and wondered what this young girl could be talking about.

"And what bad news would that be?"

Nancy described meeting his sister Catherine on the boat and told him her last wish before she died was that Nancy contact him.

"Yer sister had an easy death. It was the pneumonia. She made her peace with God, and we prayed together."

So far the man had taken the news quite well, and that relieved Nancy. It was difficult enough to deliver such sad tidings, but to have to deal with a distraught man might have been too much on her first day in America. Then she pulled the envelope from her pocket and lay the money on the table.

"This is rightfully yours, even if yer sister said I should keep it. There was no need fer Catherine to pay me for a simple act of mercy."

William Peyton's eyes grew moist as he listened to Nancy's recitation, and he picked up the money and counted it. "Fifty American dollars. She even thought to change the Irish pounds to our currency. Catherine was always a very organized woman. This must be what was left of her inheritance after my father died. He was born in County Clare, but then moved us to Dublin where he worked in a textile factory." He paused, then continued on as if talking to himself. "Over the years he was put in charge of the business. He was a frugal man and saw that his children were well taken care of. I took my share and headed for America and law school. Catherine had a young man, so she remained in Dublin, but after years of his postponing marriage, she finally decided to join me here."

He ran his hand across his eyes and through his hair. "Poor Catherine did not have a very happy life. But I thank you for taking care of my sister during her last hours. She wanted you to have the money, so yours it shall be." He then took her hand and gently placed the bills in her palm, and said, "Take it."

Nancy just stared at him. He frowned in silent question at her reluctance to accept the money, until she found her tongue and protested.

"But it's so much. It wouldn't be right fer me to take it."

"My sister was a good judge of character. You needn't have told me about the money. I would never have known. You're an honest girl."

"Well, of course I am!" Nancy replied.

"Forgive me, but I've become somewhat disillusioned after practicing law in New York. You hear so many lies, and are privy to such evil doings. It's refreshing to witness such honesty."

Nancy froze in silence. His generosity was such as she had never known. She slowly wrapped her fingers around the bills.

"Thank ye, sir," she said softly. "But I must be goin' now. Me aunt is waiting outside. And I thank ye and may God bless ye."

He smiled and closed her hand around the bills. "Now, put the money in a safe place."

Nancy smiled and tucked it deep into her pocket.

"I wish you good luck in America. Where will you be staying?"

"I'm to work for a family named Birmingham in a place called Tuxedo Park."

"Well, you'll have your hands full with the lady of that house. Old man Birmingham made a fortune in banking, and when he died his widow retained a colleague of mine to settle the estate, and he told me Mrs. Birmingham was a royal pain in the butt throughout the whole proceeding."

The look of alarm on Nancy's face made William Peyton immediately regret his statement.

"Her two sons are off at university in London, so it's just Mrs. Birmingham you'll have to deal with. And a smart Irish lass like you can handle that old biddy. Just never disagree with her and all will be well."

"Thank you, Mr. Peyton. I'll be keepin' out of her way." She smiled, but her eyes were wary.

"And here," he said. "Take my card. Contact me if you ever need anything."

Nancy left and Bill slumped over his desk. That plucky little Nancy had somehow brought a bit of brightness to his day, despite her breaking the bad news of his sister's death.

Patrick helped the ladies onto a bus that would leave them at the train station. The horses clip-clopped up Broadway, creating almost unbearable noise from the metal wheels rolling on the cobblestone street, crowded with carriages and trucks. Nancy gaped out the window at the chaotic scene; vehicles of all sorts, men in long overcoats and high hats and women who lifted their skirts to avoid the horse dung. Then May began a litany of the rules she must follow at her new place of employment.

"Now listen good to me, Nancy. You eat only what yer given at meals, and never snatch leftovers, no matter that no one else touched them. These people don't eat very much. I guess they've never gone hungry, and they leave a lot of food on the platters. But don't ye dare touch it. Mrs. Birmingham has us chop what's left over for her beloved dogs, that spend their lives running after hares and foxes while her friends chase after them on horses.

"Ye work from seven in the morning until seven at night, unless they're having dinner guests. Then you keep at it till the work is done. And they insist ye take a bath every Friday night, whether ye need it or not, so don't slip up. The mistress has spies all over the house who'll turn ye in, and then she'll turn ye out on the street to fend fer yerself. And ye have a half day off on Tuesday, and Sunday to go to church, but ye must be back by three o'clock because they have dinner at five.

"It's all right to talk to Patrick when yer alone, but ye can't in front of the Madam unless it's about yer duties. She's a real stickler fer proper behavior and ye do best by keeping quiet when she's about. The most important rule is we're the servants and we don't intrude on the family. Never speak unless yer spoken to. Never give any opinion and don't draw attention to yerself. We're supposed to be like mice. They know we're there, but if we don't squeak they can pretend we don't exist, until they want something. Then ye must fetch whatever they wish as quickly as yer legs can carry ya. And no matter how ye may be provoked, hold yer tongue and remember these people pay us the money we need and that's our reason for being here. And ye do not talk to their guests unless they speak to you first. Just give a little curtsey to let them know ye understand how important they are. Hummph!"

While May stopped to catch her breath, Nancy silently absorbed the description of her future life, and it did not sit well with her. She realized the only way out of this servitude would be to learn the ways of the entitled class in America as well as she could and as quickly as possible. She must work on losing her Irish expressions and learn to speak as Mr. Payton, using the English language properly.

A couple of hours later they disembarked the train and walked the quarter mile to the Birmingham estate. The size and magnificence of the mansion so startled Nancy, she could not contain her thoughts and blurted out, "Jesus, Mary and Joseph! It's bigger than the grand houses in Dublin."

"Now don't you go blaspheming, young lady. It's just a house, and remember that. Get yer things from Patrick and I'll take you to yer room."

May led Nancy to the servants' entrance and down to the basement, where Nancy's euphoria turned to dismay as she surveyed the six-by-nine-foot space that was her new home. A narrow bed lined one wall, a small dresser and chair the other, and a porcelain chamber pot stood beneath a small table that held a water pitcher, a wash bowl, and a single glass. There were no windows, and she noticed the door had no latch. How could she be happy here, she thought, remembering her bedroom in Galway with the large window opening above the rose bushes and overlooking the sea in the distance. This room resembled a cell she had seen in a newspaper where the English incarcerated their Irish prisoners. Well, she thought, I have my work cut out fer me, and the sooner I learn enough the sooner I can escape and get on with things, fer I don't think I can survive very long in this maid's dungeon in the mistress's mansion.

The next morning May began instructing Nancy in kitchen procedures. As she was the new girl, Nancy was delegated the most onerous chores; scrubbing the burnt remains off roasting pans, washing and drying dishes, cleaning the grease off the sinks and swabbing the kitchen floor, seeing to the garbage, and peeling pound after pound of potatoes. But the most distasteful chore was cleaning the guests' chamber pots. She tried not to breathe, but the odor still turned her stomach and left her gagging.

At the end of her first week in the scullery, Nancy's hands were red and painful. Blisters developed on her fingers from contact with the scalding hot water in the sink. A kind-hearted maid from Donegal slipped her a cup of cooking oil and warned her to hide it in her room and apply it every night to her raw, cracked fingers. It helped a bit, but by the end of the next day her hands were again red and sore.

One evening, after several weeks in Tuxedo Park, when her work was completed, she sat on her small bed with her feet tucked under her legs, and mustered up the courage to write Matthew.

Dear Mr. Clarke:

Do ye remember me? We met on the boat to New York a while back. I hope ye don't think me too bold writing ye, but I did promise to and so I do.

By now ye're probably settled in Pennsylvania, as I am in Tuxedo Park, New York, working for Protestants who allow me the privilege of going to Mass on Sundays, but that's about all I get from them except fer me small salary, which I send half of to me family in Galway.

They work me very hard. I'm learning their ways, but I miss the old country and me family. The people in America have so much money and such grand lives. I promised meself I will someday make me fortune here. I sneak into the library at night and snatch books to read on me time off. I've read a few plays by that old Englishman, Shakespeare. Such goings on he writes about. I don't understand everything he says, but some of it is sinful. Women pretend they are men and lovers kill themselves. It's easy to see Mr. Shakespeare wasn't an Irishman.

Well, tis late and I am weary and I've gone on too long about meself. I wonder how ye are doing and would be happy to hear how yer life is going, if ye have the time to write me. May the Lord take good care of ye.

Sincerely, Mary Alice O'Laoghaire

Her exhaustion led her to make a disastrous mistake that would change her life profoundly. She'd forgotten Mary Alice O'Laoghaire did not exist in the Birmingham household. There she was known as Nancy O'Leary.

When Matthew's cousin, Liam, handed him the letter, he excused himself, went to his room and ripped open the envelope. At last, he thought, and quickly read through it, then slowly read it again, and immediately wrote back to the lass he had met that rainy day on the ship to America.

Dear Miss O'Laoghaire,

It was with great pleasure that I received your letter and learned you are well, though sadly overworked, as we all are in this land of opportunity. The fortunate part is we are being paid for our labors, eat well, and do not have to fear the British banging down our door in the middle of the night and hauling us out of our beds. We have much to be grateful for.

Mr. Shakespeare is indeed not easy to understand. But he was brilliant, despite the land of his origin. If you wish to learn about our new country, may I suggest you read works by Mark Twain, Nathaniel Hawthorne and Herman Melville. And the newspapers, if you can come across them. May dad's favorite saying is "Knowledge is Power," and I believe it to be true. I have begun studying the sciences and will complete my education. I don't intend to do menial labor all my life.

My cousin, Liam, has a lovely family and there are so many Irish in America that I am not lonely, except when I think of you and our time on the boat. Please write to me again, soon. God bless you.

Sincerely, Matthew Clarke

After a few months of service, during which Nancy had scrupulously obeyed her Aunt May's directives on proper behavior, Mrs. Birmingham became aware of Nancy's abilities and promoted her to serving girl, catering to her guests. Nancy had not expected her life to be easy in America. She willingly worked hard, but she had not anticipated having to fend off the advances of male guests who frequently pinched her behind as she removed their salad plates, while Mrs. Birmingham and the other guests laughed at Nancy's embarrassment. She was sorely tempted to slap their sassy faces, but controlled her temper and focused on her goal. She listened carefully to the speech patterns of the New Yorkers, and practiced proper English every evening before bed.

Whenever possible, she carefully watched May cook, and learned how to prepare the dishes the elite favored: Curried lamb, lobster bisque, cheese soufflé, chicken in wine sauce and the strange fruits and vegetables uncommon in Ireland, such as asparagus, zucchini and artichokes.

"Now look here, Nancy," said May one day as she prepared breakfast. "This is a melon. It's a fruit ye always serve raw. Just cut it up as I'm doing. One day I was feeling out of sorts and slept in, and the new girls made breakfast. They cut the melon up and boiled it and served it to Mrs. Birmingham like stewed apples. She fired the poor lass who brought it to her right on the spot. And she, just off the boat, had never laid eyes on a melon before. The poor thing came crying to me saying, 'but in Ireland we boil everything.' So let that be a lesson to ya."

Nancy's dislike of Mrs. Birmingham grew with every story she heard about the woman's cruelty to her staff. The English mistress of the house showed only disdain for her Irish servants, and made no pretense of her feelings. Nancy's impatience to be out of Tuxedo Park increased each day.

So she carefully studied her Aunt May creating elaborate desserts covered with fresh berries and meringues, and learned how to churn ice cream, assemble Peach Melba, decorate chocolate cakes with icing to resemble flowers, and bake fancy fruit tarts and pies, and committed all the recipes to memory.

She ended her days completely exhausted, and after finishing her English grammar lesson, said her prayers, and fell into a deep sleep. Occasionally dreams of Matthew wakened her and she felt deeply disappointed that he had not responded to her letter. But she would wait. He must be very busy.

Upon arising at six-thirty she washed, dressed and went to the kitchen for breakfast before beginning her chores. This morning she sat drinking her tea by the window, mesmerized by the blanket of white covering the back lawn and the snow falling on the pine trees beyond.

"Ya look as though ye've never seen snow before," May remarked.

"Well, not in mid-March, and not as heavy as this, I haven't. It doesn't snow often at home, if ya remember."

May thought she detected a snide tone in her niece's voice, but attributed it to fatigue. Nancy and all the servants worked very hard and it sometimes led to bad dispositions.

"Fer sure, it'll be a blizzard before it's over, and we'll be housebound for weeks if me instincts are right. They have Patrick out shoveling the driveway for two hours now, but as soon as he clears a path, it's full up again with snow and he has to start all over."

"That's not fair," observed Nancy.

"Fair or not, we do as we're told."

Nancy offered to bring him some hot tea.

"That's a good girl," said May, and poured out a cup. "Here, take this to the lad before he freezes to death. Grab a coat and some boots from the mud room. The man's likely to come down with the pneumonia, being out so long in this weather."

Nancy carried the cup, covered by a saucer, towards Patrick, whose black overcoat and cap were now white with snow. She found it difficult to negotiate the slippery path, but arrived by his side with most of the tea still in the cup.

He smiled appreciatively through his shivering lips as he sipped the hot brew and felt the welcome warmth spread through his body.

"It was kind of ya to bring me the tea. But go back to the house. There's no sense in gettin' yerself all covered with snow fer the likes of me."

"I could not believe you've been out here all these hours alone. Why is Mrs. Birmingham so cruel?"

"Well, I heard that she tried to get out today to see how her dogs were doing and slipped and twisted her ankle. That's when all hell broke loose and she ordered all of us out here to shovel. Ye know how she loves those animals."

"More than she loves human beings, that's fer sure," said Nancy. "May God help the old biddy. I can't wait to get away from her and those worthless creatures she invites to her dinner table."

"Now, now. Don't let it get ya down. She does give us a salary, and I think she's lonely since her husband died."

"To hell with her!" Nancy muttered under her breath. She brushed the snow from her face and turned up her coat collar.

"You'd best be gettin' back now, lass, out of this bitter cold before ye catch yer death."

Again, Nancy did as she was told and trudged back up the path to the house, trying to shake off the snow that had begun to freeze into clumps on her brows and eyelashes.

"Good girl," May complimented her as Nancy returned with the empty cup. "Now get yerself dry and start peeling the potatoes and carrots. The guests from last night are still here and by the looks of it outside, the trains won't be running to Manhattan and we'll be stuck with them for Lord knows how long. So we have our work cut out for us and need plenty of food."

"It's not right to keep Patrick in the cold so long. Can't the mistress send someone else out there?"

"In another hour it will be the gardener's turn and we'll sit Patrick down here before the stove to warm up. Now you get to the vegetables. And tomorrow while the guests are in the dining room fer breakfast, you'll have to do up their rooms, make the beds, clean the chamber pots, and see that everything's neat and tidy."

Nancy cringed and almost gagged at the thought of emptying the guests' bodily wastes and washing the containers, but said nothing to May. She realized she must move up her departure date and be rid of Tuxedo Park sooner than she anticipated.

Nancy took the paring knife and spread old newspapers on the counter near the sink and began peeling the ten pounds of potatoes and five pounds of carrots, and thought of Mrs. Birmingham resting snugly under down coverlets in her luxurious four-poster bed and tried to suppress the anger that constricted her chest. Why do some people have so little concern for the well-being of those they feel are not their equals, she pondered. And they have the nerve to call themselves Christians as they parade into their Protestant churches every Sunday in their finest attire, drop a dollar bill in the basket and bask in their generosity and godliness.

Nancy tried to shake off her anger as she realized she too was exhibiting un-Christian feelings, and resolved to curb the disgust she felt at the actions of God's other children. She was also upset at Matthew Clarke. Months ago she had written to the address in Pennsylvania he had given her but had heard nothing from him. He had seemed so sincere, she was thoroughly confused by his sudden silence. Fear griped her as she thought something might have happened to him. An accident, an illness. Oh, please God, let Matthew be alive and well, she prayed. She would be patient, and eventually he would write, she was certain.

The next day she asked May if any letters had arrived for her.

"Only the ones I gave ya from yer father that he put in the same envelopes with his letters to me." Nancy had become so accustomed to her new name, it did not occur to her that Matthew knew her as Mary Alice O'Laoghaire.

Nancy was unaware that Mrs. Birmingham's maid brought all the morning mail directly to her mistress while she breakfasted in bed. After the fourth letter from Pennsylvania arrived addressed to Mary Alice O'Laoghaire, Mrs. Birmingham lost all patience.

"Why do I keep receiving these annoying letters?" She barked at the servant girl. "We have no one here by that name. Don't even bother to bring me another if it arrives. Just throw it out." And as Mrs.

Birmingham had done in the past, she tossed Matthew Clarke's letter into the wastebasket next to her bed and proceeded to sip her coffee and devour the eggs Benedict prepared so skillfully by Nancy's Aunt May.

That evening Nancy collapsed on her bed after an especially arduous work day, more tired than she'd ever been before, and quickly drifted off to sleep, only to be awakened an hour later by a knock on her door. May quickly entered the room and whispered, "Nancy, I'm sorry, but the snow's kept falling and the mistress fears the roof might collapse from the weight of it all, and wants you to go up there and shovel it down to the ground."

"What? I'm to get up on the roof?" Nancy's eyes widened in astonishment.

"I know, darlin', I know. But the mistress says you're young and fleet of foot and the men are busy with the driveways and seeing to the horses, and she wants you to do it now, because the snow is still falling. The worst they've ever seen around these parts. Did I not tell ya it would be a blizzard? Now be a good girl and do as she says or you'll put a black mark on all of us."

Nancy could barely control her anger, but quickly dressed and followed May up the stairs where she was outfitted with boots, gloves, coat, and an orange rubber hat they called a sou'wester. May carried up a shovel and when they reached the attic tried to open the trapdoor to the roof, but it would not budge.

"Ye'll have to go from the outside," May sighed. "And we must get Patrick to haul out a ladder."

31

The snow continued to fall as Patrick stabilized the ladder against the house, arguing that he should take over the task, but Nancy refused his offer. "It's me the mistress wants to risk my life, not you."

Nancy stuck the shovel inside the belt of her dress, and slowly ascended the ladder as Patrick held it anchored in the snow. She reached the top of the flat roof and immediately fell on her face when her feet slid over the icy crust beneath the newly fallen snow.

"Are ye okay?" Patrick called up to her.

"I think so," she replied, picking herself up and removing the shovel from her belt. The fall had driven the handle into her hip and she felt acute pain, but she called to Patrick, "I'll be all right. Just let me get this over with as fast as I can. You won't leave me up here alone, will you, Patrick?"

"No, lass, I'll stay here to see ya down safely."

Nancy began quickly throwing one shovelful of snow after another off the roof. Her arms began to ache, then her shoulders and back. She worked quickly, thinking the faster she progressed the sooner the agony would be over, but it seemed an endless chore.

After about half an hour she had removed most of the snow, but the ice beneath it caused her to slip and slide and fall on her backside so often, her body rebelled and she knew she could go no further. She felt she had done a credible enough job, and called to Patrick to help her climb down the ladder. He told her to descend slowly and he would keep her safe.

Her body shook from the cold and her arms throbbed with pain. Carefully, she put one foot after another on the steps of the ladder, which was now covered with snow. Half-way down her numb fingers lost their grip on the railing and she tumbled backwards, her hat flying off, and she cried out, "Oh, no, dear God!" but Patrick caught her in his arms before she hit the ground, and as they fell onto the snow he raised his leg and pushed the falling wooden ladder away before it could slam into their bodies. He wiped the snow from her face, wrapped his scarf over her head, and gently lifted her up and carried Nancy back to the house.

They sat before the kitchen fireplace and May brought them hot tea laced with brandy that she had pilfered from the Birmingham's liquor cabinet.

"Are ye all right, lass?" Patrick inquired as he massaged Nancy's icy cold hands and feet.

"I will be, once I get away from here. And I will do that as soon as I am able. And I will never forget the cruelties that were done to me, and will never allow anyone else to repeat them. And if you are as smart as I think, Patrick, you'll leave too. They're almost as bad as the bloody English. No, they don't fire bullets at us. They just kill us more slowly, sapping the life's blood from our veins. I'm finished with this life of service and I'm leaving here as soon as I can."

Patrick and May looked at Nancy with concern, and told her she just needed a good night's rest and not to make any hasty decisions.

"None of my decisions are ever made hastily. They're mostly made for me by other people. But that will not happen anymore. Now I'm going to bed. Thank you, Patrick, for saving my life."

Patrick held her hands, and May turned her head. She knew Patrick was smitten with her niece, and May remembered the young suitor in Ireland she had dismissed too quickly, only to find him haunting her dreams, and unable to forget what might have been. She hoped Nancy and Patrick would find a better future than she.

"Please don't leave," Patrick pleaded. "I'll miss ye too much."

Nancy gazed into his anxious dark eyes and realized how much she would miss this 'black' Irishman.

"Then come to New York with me. We'll both find work."

"Yer a stronger woman than I am a man, Nancy. But my soul holds you close to me heart. Maybe someday ..."

"I'll let you know when I'm settled. Then it's up to you." She gently disengaged her hands from his and smiled saying, "Thank you again for saving me, but I must get some sleep." She left the kitchen and made her way down to her room. She quickly undressed and got into bed, shivering, not so much from the cold, as from the look in Patrick's eyes when he revealed how he felt about her.

At nine the next morning, Nancy grudgingly began cleaning the guest rooms. Making beds proved quick and simple, as did hanging up the garments strewn over chairs, folding nightclothes and placing the guests' unmentionables neatly in bureau drawers and lining up shoes and slippers on the closet floors. What self-indulgent slobs these people are, she thought. Why, they can't even put their underwear out of sight! Then she tackled the disgusting task of emptying chamber pots. She proceeded as quickly as possible, barely able to keep down her own breakfast. Why can't they clean up their own messes like the rest of us? Do they have no pride at all? Or is it they have too much pride to engage in such mundane tasks only fit for their servants? Then she went to her room in the basement and scrubbed her hands with lye soap until she felt rid of all traces of human waste.

While the guests amused themselves playing cards in the parlor, Nancy took the heirloom silverware from the mahogany cabinet in the dining room and began setting the table for lunch. May interrupted her.

"Nancy, the mistress asked that ye go up to her room. She has something to talk to you about." May's brow wrinkled with concern. "I don't know what she wants, but it'll be fer the best if ye don't keep her waiting."

Nancy turned, ascended the circular staircase, knocked on Mrs. Birmingham's bedroom door and heard the command, "Enter."

The lady of the house, perched in a velvet boudoir chair, her arms folded beneath her amble bosom, came right to the point.

"Mrs. Morgan's diamond bracelet has been stolen. You were the only one in her room this morning. If you do not return her property immediately, I will notify the police and you will be put in prison."

It took Nancy a few moments to absorb the fact that she was being accused of theft, but she remained calm.

"I did not see, or take Mrs. Morgan's bracelet. I do not steal. I made her bed and cleaned her chamber pot."

"Now come, Nancy, admit your sin and return the bracelet and I will forget the whole shoddy event. Everyone's tempted at some time in their lives. You must understand how very embarrassing this is for me. Mrs. Morgan is a good friend, and a guest in my house. Do you realize how this makes me look in her eyes? To have her think I have thieving servants? Why, all New York would know about it

35

within a week and none of my friends would ever set foot in my house again." Mrs. Birmingham stood now, and moved menacingly towards Nancy. "Now, for the last time, I'm ordering you to return the bracelet or you will face the consequences and they will be harsh. I promise you that!"

Now Nancy could no longer contain her anger.

"I did not steal any jewelry. And if you don't believe me, you can go to …"

The knock on the door prevented Nancy from finishing her sentence which would ensure her immediate dismissal, or worse, imprisonment.

"Enter," pronounced Mrs. Birmingham, and Mrs. Morgan barged in smiling. "Guess what, my dear. I'm such a silly goose. I put my bracelet in the pocket of my robe last night, and some sweet maid hung it up for me. When I made a thorough search just now when I was dummy during our bridge game, there it was!"

The woman dangled the bracelet on her pinky for all to see and apologized to Mrs. Birmingham for causing such a commotion.

"I'm delighted," said Mrs. Birmingham. "Nancy, you may leave now."

Nancy thought Mrs. Morgan certainly was a dummy, and not only at the bridge table. She turned quickly and left her employer's bedroom and returned to the dining room where May had finished setting the table.

"What did the mistress want?" May asked.

"To put me in jail for stealing Mrs. Morgan's diamond bracelet. But that foolish woman came in and announced she'd found it in her bathrobe pocket, just before I lost my temper. So, it's out of here I am as soon as possible."

"Oh, me poor Nancy. Yer goin' through a rough time now, but ye must hang on. The Lord has a way of smoothing things over."

"I can't wait until the Lord sees fit to look kindly upon me. I must take my life into my own hands. And that I will."

Over the last few months, Patrick and Nancy had grown closer. They spent some of their Tuesday afternoons off together, and on spring days Nancy would prepare picnic lunches for them and they lazed on a blanket in a meadow under the warm sun, revealing their hopes and desires for the future. One day Patrick tentatively took her hand; the next week he put his arm around her shoulder; he finally summoned up enough courage to kiss her cheek and tell her how much she meant to him. She was pleased, but it did not diminish her resolve to leave Tuxedo Park, with or without him.

Chapter 3

THE END OF THE BEGINNING

May, 1888

After six months at Tuxedo Park, Nancy had accumulated enough money and knowledge to break free of Mrs. Birmingham and told her astonished aunt that the following Friday she would leave for New York City to pursue a career in the restaurant business.

"Have ye lost yer mind? Do ye have any idea how those people down there feel about us? There are signs all over shops needing help that read, 'No Irish Need Apply.' And that's meant fer the men! Who do ye think will give ye any better job than ye have here? Ye foolhardy girl! Ye've a job here that hundreds of girls would give their eye teeth fer and yer ready to throw it all away. Throw away yer livelihood."

"Oh, Aunt May, I'm not throwing away my livelihood. I'm beginning my own life."

May was left with the unpleasant task of telling Mrs. Birmingham that Nancy had contracted a chest ailment and must leave for Manhattan for treatment.

"Just contact the agency in New York and have them send up a permanent replacement," the mistress ordered.

May felt relief at not being questioned further, but also dismay at how Mrs. Birmingham cared so little about the people whose labor enabled her to live such a luxurious, care-free life, and she worried over the fate that awaited poor Nancy, venturing into the unknown big city.

But Nancy had no fear, and was not venturing into completely unknown territory. On her Sundays off she met other young Irish servant girls at church, and after mass they talked and became friends, and Nancy eventually obtained all the information she needed. Bridget, who worked for neighbors of the Birmingham's, was fairly content with her lot in life, as she had a beau who worked nearby. She offered to contact her uncle, Mr. Lally, a policeman who lived in lower Manhattan, and he would find Nancy a position and a place to live. Her relatives were part of the tight-knit Irish community which helped newly arrived immigrants get started in New York.

Nancy packed her two dresses, one skirt, two shirtwaists, undergarments, toiletries and her Bible and rosary into the small leather bag she had brought from Ireland, slammed the door of her room at seven that morning, and had her last breakfast in the kitchen. May looked solemnly at her niece as she placed a plate of ham, eggs, scones and canned peaches before a surprised Nancy. She handed her a huge cup of tea, with sugar and cream.

"And where did you get all this? I'm used to toast and black tea for breakfast."

"God forgive me. It's from the mistress's private stock, but to hell with her. Yer going to have a proper meal before your long trek. And here." May gave her a paper bag filled with meat sandwiches, apples, and her fresh-baked cookies. "You'll be needing something to eat on yer journey."

Nancy faked a sneeze so May would not notice the tears brimming in her eyes, and uttered a low 'thank you.' She finished her meal and regained her composure and told May how grateful she was for all her aunt had done, and promised when she became settled in New York she would send for her this time, and free her from this life of drudgery.

Ah, May thought, she's pipe-dreaming again, but she wished Nancy luck and that God go with her, and made her swear she would send a letter once a week so May would not be fretting over her circumstances. They gave each other one last hug, and the tears flowed freely.

"Don't worry, Aunt May. I'll not leave you here for long." And with that Nancy threw on her jacket and picked up her tattered bag and left to meet Patrick. Mrs. Birmingham had granted him permission to take Nancy to the train, preferably as soon as possible.

Patrick and Nancy walked to the train station. He told Nancy they had a ten-minute wait, if the train was running on schedule.

"I'll not go back to that house if it takes all day for the train to arrive."

As they waited, Patrick took her hand in his and said, "Nancy, ye must be careful in New York. An unmarried young lass like yerself, with no one to protect ye. I'm afraid fer ya. Men could try to take advantage of ya."

"I'm not afraid. And if any man dares, he'll be the sorrier for it."

"Ye do know how fond I've become of ye, Nancy, now don't ya? And how me heart is full of admiration fer yer courage to set out by yerself in the big city of New York? But it's so worried I am that harm might come to ya."

Nancy smiled. "Didn't I ask you to come with me? You weren't so concerned about my fate when you turned down the idea."

"Well, I've done some thinking about that. Me fear of not having ye here everyday is greater than me fear of starting out in a new place. I've saved some money, and if I had a chance at a job in New York, I'd gladly follow ya."

Nancy's feelings for Patrick were more deep friendship than love, but his words touched her deeply.

"I'm sure our Irish people in New York can find you a position, as they will me."

"Then if ye'll give me a bit of hope that ye might consider me humble self with thoughts of matrimony, it's to New York I will be going."

His clumsy proposal left Nancy speechless. And when the handsome black Irishman politely asked permission to kiss her goodbye, she nodded affirmatively, expecting a peck on the cheek. But she underestimated Patrick's ardor. He took her in his arms and gently, then passionately kissed her, arousing yearnings she had not felt before. She released herself from his arms and gravely told him, "We must keep the Holy Ghost between us. It's a dangerous thing we've done."

Nancy now realized why those hapless unmarried young girls were sent by their mortified parents to Magdalen houses in Dublin where

41

they would deliver their babies, who were then given away for adoption. She once scorned those wayward young girls, but now understood the power lust had over mere mortals and chastised herself for the pride she felt in her chasteness. She remembered all the many cold nights her mother, the local midwife, woke her and her sister Norah to help deliver a neighborhood woman's baby. Nancy knew how babies were born. She also knew by observing the animals on her farm how babies were conceived. But only now did she fully comprehend the reason why the act of procreation proved so desirable to both humans and animals. Desire felt good. She knew she must keep a fierce check on her emotions so as not to slide down the same slippery path to destruction as those pregnant girls who found themselves confined in Magdalen houses in Dublin.

She gave Patrick her address in Manhattan and said, "Write to me. When I'm settled in, if you still want me to be your bride, I might not be opposed to the idea."

Patrick was elated, and tried to take her in his arms, but she moved away. The approaching train whistle shrieked and she grabbed her things and said "Goodbye, Patrick. Write me." She then dashed for the train and boarded the half-empty car. She took a seat by a window that afforded her a last glance of Patrick gazing forlornly at her as the train pulled away.

She stared at the rolling hills behind the evergreen trees and said goodbye to Tuxedo Park. A great burden had been lifted, and the only sadness she felt was not knowing when she would see her beloved Aunt May again. She felt a deep friendship for Patrick, but the memory of Matthew Clarke still remained. He had never answered her letter. How quickly the man had forgotten her once he reached Pennsylvania. But Patrick cared for her. And though he might not provide the blissful state she had expected marriage to be, it would be quite tolerable. He was kind, hard-working, and a good Catholic. She suddenly felt very tired and drifted into a fitful sleep, awakening only when the train jolted to a stop at Grand Central Station in Manhattan.

She stepped off the train and stood mesmerized by the noise of the horses, carriages and wagons rolling down the street, and the chattering of the crowds going this way and that, everyone seeming to be in a great hurry. Many men wore work clothes and carried lunch pails, but an equal number sported white starched shirts and dark suits and hats, even though the heat of the July sun was almost unbearable. She opened the two top buttons of her dress, took off her gloves, and fanned herself with her hat. Remembering the coolness of the Irish summers, she registered amazement at the fashionably dressed women, obviously wearing tight corsets beneath their dresses. They looked as cool as swans, swimming in a pond, she thought, and it gave her some hope that one day she would become accustomed to this tropical summer climate.

A man of about fifty years of age approached her and asked if she might be Nancy O'Leary. The girls haven't failed me, she thought, as she shook Brian Lally's hand and thanked him for rescuing her from the surrounding chaos.

"Come with me, girl. The Missus is waiting for you with a good dinner on the stove and we'll get you settled in. We'll just hop on the bus here and be home in no time." She pulled up her skirt and followed Mr. Lally up the few steps into the crowded car, but before they could find seats the horses started off and she flew backwards and grabbed the arm of an older woman, her satchel grazing the woman's neck.

"Watch what you're doing, missy. You almost knocked my head off!"

Nancy apologized but the woman huffed and muttered about the disrespect of the younger generation. Brian Lally sat Nancy down and calmed her, told her not to let the old lady worry her, and the horses pulled the bouncing bus over the rough cobblestone road till they reached their destination. But Nancy was distressed at the bad impression she had made on nice Mr. Lally on her first bus ride.

"We're here, lass. This is where we get off. Now give me that satchel and watch the stairs." He must think I'm as clumsy as an ox, she thought. I'll have to be more careful.

He took Nancy's elbow and ushered her through the crowds to a nearby tenement and led her up to his third-floor apartment where she received a warm welcome and a plate of beef stew from Mrs. Lally.

"Now set yerself down and have yer dinner and we'll get acquainted. I'm told ye know yer way about a kitchen and don't shy away from hard work." Nancy nodded, but could not get a word in as Mrs. Lally continued her monologue.

"Himself has gotten ye a position at Charlie Murphy's Tavern, just a good stretch of the legs from here. Yer to be his assistant; washing glasses, sweeping up, serving the customers, and all the other odds and ends. He's a widower with no wife to help out. But he's a good man and will pay ye a fair wage. Himself will take ye there tomorrow morning and get ye started. Yer room is to the left there, and the bathroom is down the hall. We're very lucky. We only have to share it with two other families."

Mrs. Lally stopped speaking and took a closer look at Nancy. "Ye can't be wearing that heavy dress in the heat of the summer. Do ye have some cotton dresses?"

Nancy hid her embarrassment and just replied, "No."

The woman took Nancy into her bedroom and opened the closet, looked the girl up and down, then pulled out two cotton dresses and held them up to Nancy's shoulders. "These might do. Take off yer clothes and we'll see what's needed."

"Take off my clothes?" Nancy hadn't been in her underwear in front of anyone since she was six years old.

"Hurry up. I have things to do." Then Mrs. Lally began undoing the buttons on the girl's dress as she continued talking and Nancy froze. "Come now. I'm a seamstress. I work for the best dressmaker in these parts and we'll fix ye up proper in no time. Now, step out of the dress."

Nancy, thoroughly mortified, let the garment slide down around her feet. Her shift was paper thin from years of washings and dotted with patches where she had stitched up torn spots. She felt practically naked, and the shame on Nancy's face softened the seamstress. "Don't be embarrassed girl. This is the way we all came over to America. This is why we came. You'll never have to worry about having proper dresses and bloomers again."

Tears welled up in Nancy's eyes and Mrs. Lally took her in her arms. "Shush, shush, lass, there, there. I'll have ye looking like a queen before we're through."

"Please don't judge me too harshly by my simpering. It's just that so much has happened to me in such a short time, I've lost my bearings. I'm really a strong person but ..."

"Now stop it! You're a fine figure of a woman, and smart to boot, I'm told." She took a measuring tape out of a bureau drawer and circled it around Nancy's chest, waist and hips, then gave her a robe and told her she would have the dresses altered by morning, and Nancy should go to bed now as she must be exhausted from her long day. Nancy murmured a thank you as the woman pulled down the bedspread and pointed her towards it.

"I'll wake ye at seven," she said, and left Nancy alone in the small room. But at least it had a window, which looked out over an alley where young boys were tossing a ball and whooping and hollering. Tomorrow she would have new clothes, a new job and a new start, she thought. And now I must find a way to get Patrick and Aunt May out of that Birmingham house. Then she drifted off to sleep.

The next morning Brian Lally appeared at breakfast looking very professional in his policeman's uniform, and after a plate of ham and eggs, he took Nancy to meet Charlie Murphy. Mrs. Lally proved as good as her word, and Nancy felt quite the lady in her newly altered pink cotton frock.

The size of the tavern surprised Nancy. It was at least three times as big as the typical pub in Ireland. Three smaller rooms lined the main area, which was dominated by a twenty-foot-long gleaming mahogany bar. Brass spittoons were placed strategically among the high leather-covered stools, and a mirror ran the length of the wall behind the bar. Shelves of bottles of every size, color and description were reflected in the mirror, and an upright piano stood against the back wall.

"Hello, Charlie," Brian Lally greeted his friend. "And how are you this beautiful day?"

"I'm grand. Just grand, Brian. Now will you introduce me to the lovely young lady at yer side?"

Mr. Lally turned to Nancy and said, "This is yer new boss, Charlie Murphy. And a fine man he is. Charlie, this is Nancy O'Leary, yer new assistant."

Nancy smiled and gave a small curtsey. "I'm pleased to meet you, Mr. Murphy. What a wonderful establishment you have here."

"Welcome to New York, Nancy. And aren't you a fine looking lass. What county are ye from?"

Nancy smiled, taking the compliment with her usual graciousness, having been reminded many times before of how the good Lord had blessed her, and shook the man's hand, expressing her gratitude at the opportunity to work for him, and said she was from Galway.

"Ah, then we're neighbors. I'm from County Clare."

After a bit more chit chat, Brian Lally announced he must be off to work keeping the streets of New York safe for its good citizens, and wished Nancy good luck in her new job.

As she scanned the tavern, Nancy noticed her work would not be easy. On close inspection she decided the place had probably not had a good cleaning in months, and as she mentally took note of the sawdust covered floors, the cobwebs in the corners, the tarnished brass foot rail, the streaked drinking glasses behind the bar and the moldy smell of dirty bar cloths, she suddenly realized Mr. Murphy had been speaking to her. The affable, nearly bald man, with a slight paunch above the apron that covered his trousers, looked quizzically at his new employee. Could she be hard of hearing, he wondered?

"Forgive me, sir, but I was thinking of my new job and where to begin. May I ask you to please repeat what I was so rude as not to hear?"

Mr. Murphy was impressed by her honesty and good manners, as well as her pulchritude. He twirled up his dark red moustache and said, "The tavern needs a good cleaning, but you can do that in stages, when there are no customers. To begin with you could wash the glasses and serve drinks to the patrons. Some of them come in a small group and sit in the reserved room off the bar. They talk business, ya know, and like their privacy. Just keep a record of how much they owe and give me their bills, and never ask those customers for money. I'll handle that. I keep track of the drinks the customers at the bar order, so ye need not worry yerself about that."

Nancy was puzzled by this distinction between customers who were asked to pay at the bar and those in the room who were not, but it would take months for her to discover the mystery behind that inequity.

Her working hours would be from eleven in the morning until eight at night. But she'd have to stay until ten o'clock on Friday and Saturday when the tavern was at its busiest. She had Tuesdays off, and worked Sunday from twelve to five. He would pay her minimal salary until she proved herself.

"What shall I do first today?"

He said he would fetch her an apron to cover her pretty dress, and she could begin washing the glasses, pointing to the smeared stack behind the bar.

"I don't have the time to clean them meself." He hesitated a moment, then confessed, "God forgive me fer lying, but the truth is, I can't abide washing those things. I shouldn't have said that. My tongue wags faster than a hungry dog's tail. It's not so bad cleaning them in the kitchen with a sink filled with soap, but sometimes I get backed up with the customers and just rinse them. So, you see why I need you, lass."

"Maybe more glasses are needed." Nancy immediately regretted her impudence, but Mr. Murphy laughed, and admitted she was probably right. This young thing had a head on her shoulders, and guts to boot, he realized. It was ten o'clock and the bar was empty, and she suggested she start by sweeping the floor of sawdust.

"Oh, no, lass," he objected. "All taverns have sawdust. It soaks up the phlegm the patrons spit on the floor and prevents them from sliding on the mucous and breaking their necks."

"A clean floor would make the men think twice before spitting and maybe a wealthier clientele would begin to frequent your tavern, like the politicians, businessmen and lawyers who work nearby."

While Mr. Murphy scratched his balding head and considered her proposition, she asked where the kitchen might be.

Upon entering the large, almost empty room, she was appalled. It would take her two full days to clean the filth off the stove, sink, windows and floors. But no matter, she thought, this was the beginning of her new life, and she would be appreciative of her opportunity and not grumble at a little dirty work. Lord knows, she was quite accustomed to it.

After examining the area, she found the stove worked, and there were two burners on top for frying and boiling. The ice box appeared large enough to hold a week's worth of food, and a square table in the corner would provide her with a work area.

"Mr. Murphy, is this where you cook the food?" Nancy surprised the man with her question.

"We don't serve food. This is a bar, and the profits come from the sale of alcohol. The stove is used just for making coffee and tea."

"But if you feed people they will drink more, and not fall on their faces plastered from your whiskey and beer and have to be escorted out the door with a wad of bills still left in their pockets."

Mr. Murphy tugged at his moustache, mulled over her statement, and realized the girl made sense. Food was cheap, but who would prepare the food?

"I am a good cook. I've learned from masters in a mansion in Tuxedo Park."

Charlie Murphy listened as the enthusiastic young woman recited her list of culinary specialties, and realized the possibilities of her proposal. If she proved half as good a cook as she claimed, he could double his profits in liquor and create a restaurant at the same time. And this young immigrant hadn't even mentioned salary as yet.

"Well, Nancy, I'll try out your idea for a month and see how it works. Mind ye, now, this is only a test. One month. If me profits increase, we'll talk more about continuing yer cooking."

"I'll not be disappointing you, Mr. Murphy. We'll have the customers eating out of your hands, so to speak, and drinking up your spirits until you won't be able to tie the strings on your purse it will be so full of money. But you must provide me with the funds in advance to purchase meats and vegetables, and plates, silverware and pots."

Charlie reached into his pocket and counted out thirty dollars, and said if she were as good as she professed to be, the money would cover a week's worth of food and the kitchen supplies, and she could keep whatever was left over for her efforts.

"You won't be sorry for giving me the chance, sir. But if my efforts prove favorable to you, we will need to renegotiate my weekly salary."

"Aye, we will. But I'm puzzled. Ye don't talk like a lass just off the boat. Did ye go to university?"

"No, sir. I've taught myself to speak proper English."

What a shrewd young lass I've found, Charlie Murphy smiled to himself. And if she makes me as much money as she expects to, I can afford to pay her a bit more.

"Well, I'd best be getting started." She picked up a large tray leaning against the wall and collected the glasses from the bar. She piled them carefully in the sink she had filled with hot, soapy water and left them to soak while she swept up the sawdust. Nancy sang softly to herself as she went about her work, delighted by how easy it had been to convince Mr. Murphy to begin her restaurant career.

Chapter 4

THE FLOOD

November 1887-1889

Matthew Clarke received a grand welcome from his cousin, Liam, on his arrival in Pennsylvania in November of 1887. Maeve, Liam's wife, made him feel quite at home, plying him with good food and making plans to introduce him to the eligible Irish girls in Johnstown. But Matthew had no interest in pursuing woman. He could not forget Mary Alice and reread her letter every evening after regaling Liam's two small boys with tales of Ireland, as they sat spellbound at his feet imagining the leprechauns, ghosts and banshees that roamed the old country.

Matthew had promised to write his father and keep him apprised of his progress, and after two weeks with Liam he felt sure enough of himself to fulfill this obligation.

Dear Da,

Cousin Liam has done quite well for himself in America and has become a wealthy man. He built a grand house in Johnstown. I work from six in the morning till three o'clock learning to break horses and train them. It's hard work, but Liam pays me well. I've found a retired teacher outside of town and am studying chemistry and biology with him every day from four o'clock until suppertime. My instructor, Mr. Grunwald, is from Germany. He's very kind and does not charge me very much for his services and thinks I have an aptitude for science. He gives me great encouragement to further my studies, as you always have, so I'm taking the advice of you both. I'll not be riding horses all my life.

I miss you very much, but somehow feel at home in this new country. Not only because Pennsylvania resembles Ireland, but because there are so many Irishmen here. Liam and Maeve have taken me under their wing and are very good to me. Every Sunday after Mass, Maeve serves up a roast, potatoes and vegetables, and a pie or cake. After that, Liam and I nap for an hour or so until the Irish neighbors arrive with drums, tin whistles and fiddles, and the singing and dancing goes on until dark. Then it's to bed and another work week begins.

Well, it's time now for sleep. I hope all is well with you. Goodnight now, Da. God bless you.

Your loving son, Matthew.

Life progressed busily for Matthew for a year and a half, working and studying with Mr. Grunwald. But at night, alone in his room, his mind turned to Mary Alice. He had written her four letters since he received hers months ago, and still had not heard from her. Could he have been so bad a judge of character? Had she met a man in Tuxedo Park and totally dismissed him? Well, there are plenty of blooms on the rose bushes just waiting to be plucked, Mary Alice. And from now on, you'll be receiving no more letters from me, and I'm blocking you out of my mind once and for all.

On May 31, 1889, Mr. Grunwald was explaining the Periodic Table of the Elements when the first screams reached them through the open windows of the teacher's house which was situated high on a hill overlooking Johnstown. The human cries were quickly quieted by the thunderous sound of crashing brick and roaring water. Matthew followed his teacher to the window, but they could not locate the town. It was covered by an ocean of water obliterating what was once a center of manufacturing, surrounded by tidy homes and farms of hard-working citizens. Stunned by the sight of seventy-foot-high water rushing over the city, they gaped in silence and wondered if this could be the promised apocalypse.

They watched in horror as houses, bridges, steel mills and livestock were swept away by the raging torrent. Mr. Grunwald shouted, "Ach, the dam, the dam!"

"What are you talking about?" yelled Matthew.

"The dam must have broken. The dam under the lake. I have heard people say they were worried about it. The fishermen talked about how they saw weak spots, that it looked frail. The water from the lake must have broken through and collapsed the dam."

"Well, what are we going to do? My cousin and his family..." Matthew's voice trailed off, realizing the enormity of the catastrophe he was witnessing.

The two men stood silently by the window, immobilized by the destruction confronting them from their safe perch above the city. Matthew scanned the valley on the outskirts of town until he located the site of Liam's house and found it had disappeared. A river of water flowed over what had once been his cousin's house, stables and farmland, carrying with it furniture, rooftops and uprooted trees. And bodies. Human bodies, sucked down into the churning water, only to resurface yards away. Bodies with outstretched arms, buckled legs, hair streaked out behind them like Halloween witches' wigs. But the worst sight was the small dead children, being bounced up and down by the pull of the water. Pink and smooth, their clothes ripped from their bodies, they resembled newborn calves and piglets rather than human beings.

"I have to get to my cousin's," Matthew roared and he rushed to the door, but Mr. Grunwald grasped his arm and gently told him there was nothing he could do now. There was no way to reach the city. They would wait. There would be much they could do later to help, but now all they could do was be patient and pray. Matthew slumped in a chair, his face in his hands, as he knew the truth of Mr. Grunwald's statement. Liam, his wife and children were most likely dead. Matthew's chest constricted so tightly that for a moment he thought he was near death himself. His breathing was labored and the pounding in his head echoed the fury of the raging water.

His teacher walked slowly across the room and retrieved a bottle of brandy from a small cabinet and poured two drinks. His hands trembled as he handed Matthew a glass and began speaking slowly, his eyes moist with tears.

"We must remain calm, Matthew. This event is beyond our control. I am as heartsick as you. I have many friends in Johnstown. People who took care of me when I arrived from Hamburg years ago. Good people who didn't care that I was Jewish. Good people who accepted me, let me teach their children, invited me into their homes, did not make fun of my accent. I drink to them, and to all the innocent souls who were taken from us today."

Matthew emptied his glass in one swallow and almost choked from its potency. His familiarity with alcohol had been limited to an occasional glass of beer. But slowly he experienced its impact, and a calmness settled upon him, and the pain in his chest subsided.

Mr. Grunwald said they must wait until the water receded before he and Matthew could attempt to help those still alive. He refilled their brandy glasses and the men sipped their drinks, paced around the living room, and stared intermittently out the window at the carnage that once was Johnstown.

"The telegraph must have gone down. It may take days for help to arrive. It's impossible to walk to Johnstown. There will be five feet of mud there when the water is finally absorbed into the earth. We'll spend our time on your studies, and you will sleep here. We will see what the conditions are like tomorrow."

"How can you expect me to concentrate on science when I've just lost my family?" Matthew had passed the shock stage of bereavement and progressed to anger.

"Because you will need to know certain things in order to help people. I will teach you the basics of anatomy. Show you how to put a splint on a broken bone. How to dress wounds. You are not ready to study now, so we will put together the materials we will need to help the survivors."

Matthew listened intently. "You sound like a doctor."

"I studied medicine in Hamburg for three years until my money ran out. Then I came here and could only find employment as a science teacher. But I have kept up with the medical field. Unfortunately, I do not have the necessary equipment or supplies. But we will do the best with what we have. Come, let us gather what we can to help the wounded."

Matthew's respect for the man increased with each sentence he uttered. Mr. Grunwald beckoned him towards the bedroom, then opened dresser drawers and closets and pulled out sheets, blankets and towels. He handed Matthew a scissor and instructed him in how to cut cloth into proper-size bandages.

"Come, follow me." He then led Matthew to the back of the house. Bright sun shone through the large windows that surrounded the room, filled with healthy green plants and flowering shrubs. "We must resort to herbal remedies, as all I have is peroxide. This tree is the white willow. Its bark alleviates pain and brings down fever. We will make poultices that promote wound healing from this echinacea, that comfrey, and the chamomile there in the corner. The valerian in the blue pot is a sedative to ease those in an agitated, or potentially fatal state. And we will prepare some ginger and make an extract of the yarrow plant to also help fever."

"Where did you learn all this?"

"In Germany. We had to make do with what little we had."

Matthew's awe of the man's knowledge left him speechless, and he followed Mr. Grunwald's directions as they cut leaves, barks and plants, smashed them with a pestle in the mortar, and wrapped the healing herbs in small pouches.

"Now we will go outside and collect dead tree branches and shape them into splints."

After an hour of work they had as many pieces of wood as they could carry, and Dr. Grunwald suggested they have dinner before packing up their supplies. In the kitchen, Matthew put up a pot of coffee while his mentor fried sliced potatoes and sausages and placed a bowl of apples on the table.

"Ach, I almost forgot. We will need plenty of clean water. Go to the well and pump as much as you can into the barrels from the shed and put one on the wagon. Hurry, before the well becomes contaminated. Then feed the horse and give him water. We will need him."

Matthew rushed out to fulfill his orders and Mr. Grunwald stirred the potatoes. "Mein Gott," he whispered to himself. The survivors will need food and shelter. They will have no place to go. What will become of them?

The waters had not subsided enough for them to begin their rescue mission, so for the next two days Matthew studied rudimentary anatomy. On the third day, when it seemed they might be able to reach the town, they hitched the horse up to the wagon loaded with water and medical supplies and slowly approached Johnstown. They passed hundreds of dead bodies encased in muck, and several people wandering aimlessly about, wet, dirty and disoriented. One man stumbled against their wagon and Matthew jumped down and grabbed him under the armpits just before he fell.

"He's got a gash on his head and his lower arm is bent," he shouted up to Mr. Grunwald, who then instructed Matthew to apply a poultice of chamomile and echinacea to the man's head, tie a string around the bandage, and apply a splint to his arm, carefully and slowly. Matthey lay the man down by the wagon and rummaged through the medications as Mr. Grunwald nodded silently, and a slight smile came to his lips. This young man has potential, he thought.

After treating the man's wounds, Matthew lifted him onto the wagon and the horse slowly continued on. When Matthew had tended to two other bleeding men and one limping young woman, they returned to the house. There was no space in the wagon for more patients. They brought the wounded into the main room, laid them on the floor and covered them with blankets.

"Water, water, please," the man with the head wound whimpered. Matthew quickly fetched a cup and held it to the man's lips. When his thirst had been quenched, he touched Matthew's hand with his fingers extending from his splinted arm and with tears in his eyes spoke words Matthew would never forget. "God has given you a gift, lad. Don't ever lose it."

The next day, after checking their patients, feeding them and tending to their wounds, the two men went out again to search for survivors. But the muck was so thick the wagon could not proceed very far. They passed bodies buried under two feet of mud, arms and legs protruding out of the mire. They picked up two other men, Matthew treated their wounds, and brought them back to the house. Now they had six patients to care for and feed.

Mr.Grunwald warned Matthew an outbreak of typhoid fever was very possible because the cesspools had been destroyed, and the decaying bodies that lay beneath the mud would contaminate the water. He ordered him to pump as much water as he could from the well immediately. They would need all they could get. While Matthew pumped water, Mr. Grunwald fed the patients rice and beans, the fruits from his orchard, and herbal teas. Then he checked their wounds, replaced bandages, and gave them all the encouragement he could.

Matthew tried to convince Mr. Grunwald to go out and search for more victims.

"We can do no more. The corpses under the mud are a health menace to anyone who approaches the area. The State must provide doctors who are experienced in epidemic caused by infection. We will care for our patients and wait until it is safe again to go outside. We must boil water from now on before we drink it. The city is destroyed. Thousands of lives have been lost. But you saved the lives of six human beings. That is a great tribute to you, Matthew. You should attend medical school and become a doctor, as you have all the attributes necessary for such a calling. You will fulfill the dream I never achieved."

Matthew felt great pride in his teacher's accolades, but admitted, "I don't have the means to pay. I now have no job, no place to live, no family."

Mr. Grunwald interrupted him. "You have me, my boy, and I have friends. You will study with me for six more months. Then I will send you to New York City to continue your medical education with a friend of mine from Germany, Doctor Weitz. He will see to all your needs. You will be his assistant. He will train you, let you live in his house, and he will pay you a small stipend. It is settled. Now, go down to the cellar and bring up a ham and some jars of vegetables the good ladies of the community give me every year, and I will make the bread."

Matthew's mind raced, trying to sort out the plans for his future. He would study medicine while Mr. Grunwald baked bread? The incongruity of the situation brought a burst of laughter from him and elicited a stern look from his teacher.

"Do you find something I said amusing?"

"Just that," he hesitated and tried to stop laughing. "Just that you, a brilliant man, will train me, a young know-nothing, to be a doctor, while you stand there like a woman baking bread. It just does not seem right."

"So you think it is a shameful thing for a man to bake bread?"

"No, no, that's not what I meant."

"I should hope not. Because if you did I have seriously overestimated you, Matthew. No work is beneath any human being. And it would not harm you to learn another skill. It may be necessary someday. Come over here and start kneading the dough. We have mouths to feed."

Matthew sheepishly began working side by side with Mr. Grunwald, disgusted by the arrogance he had displayed towards this kindly man, and vowed to subdue the feelings of superiority instilled in him by the townspeople of his home in Ireland.

"Now we let the dough rise, and you go to the cellar. Do you remember what I told you to bring up?"

"Yes, sir. Ham and jars of vegetables."

Days later, when they felt it safe to travel, Matthew and Mr. Grunwald approached Johnstown. They saw that help had arrived. Over fifty tents stood at the end of the city, occupied by doctors, volunteers and board of health workers, and many homeless people. But dismayed by the stench of decaying bodies and the threat of typhoid fever, the teacher decided their best course would be to return home, keep themselves healthy, and care for their patients.

Weeks later a military crew reached Mr. Grunwald's house and transported his patients, now in good health, to other quarters supplied by the State. Then Matthew's studies resumed in earnest; not only science, but cooking, and after a few months he could put a decent meal on the table, bread and all, besides being able to locate and name, in Latin and English, almost every bone, muscle, nerve and organ in the human body. He also learned to milk the one cow in the barn, and to churn butter and make cheese. Four piglets had been born, and he tended them. Mr. Grunwald decided Matthew was ready to experience an anatomy lesson first hand. The time had come to slaughter the old sow.

Matthew's nervous system reached a state of high anxiety as he watched his teacher smash a large hammer on the pig's head. The sow died immediately.

"See? She felt no pain. Only shock. We must be kind to our animals."

With the pig laid out on the hay in the barn, Mr. Grunwald put on old leather gloves and took a large carving knife from his bag. With one quick movement he sliced off the head, and blood gushed from the pig onto the hay. Matthew felt vomit coming up his throat, but managed to suppress it.

"Help me, young man. She's heavy." He gave Matthew some rope, they tied the feet together, then threw the rope over a beam and hauled the animal up to drain.

"It won't take long for the blood to come out. There are many parts of a pig's head that are edible, so bring it here to me. Pickled pigs ears and feet are a favorite in Germany. 'Waste not, want not' is a very true old saying."

Matthew watched the procedures carefully, and wondered if he could ever swallow pork again.

Mr. Grunwald hoisted the pig down and picked up his knife, sliced open its belly, and pulled the carcass apart. "Now look here. There's the liver, kidneys, heart and lungs. This is the stomach, digestive track and colon. Feel them. They are attached by cartilage and muscle. Here, take the knife and carefully cut them out."

"Me?" Matthew recoiled in horror.

"Yes, you. It's just like preparing a chicken. And I've shown you how to do that."

"But the chicken was dead!"

"Matthew, what is wrong with you? Is not the pig dead, too?"

"Yes, but it was alive just a few minutes ago."

"Come, show me some spunk, young man. The animal can't hurt you."

Matthew proceeded to remove the organs while being lectured on their function and placement, and his knowledge of human anatomy would be enhanced from this exercise.

"Now it will be smoked and there will be ham, bacon and sausage. Food for quite a while. I'm proud of you. See how the universe works together? We gave the sow a long and good life, and now she provides us with the sustenance we need. We took care of her, she takes care of us. Quid pro quo."

After six months of intensive lessons, Mr. Grunwald decided the time had come for Matthew to venture on to New York. His cousin Liam and his family, along with many others, had never been found. As Johnstown cleared out the flood debris, the bodies of most of the thousands who died had deteriorated so badly by the time they were excavated from the mud, they could not be identified. Matthew accepted he would not find his future in Johnstown, and must move on. But Mr. Grunwald had become more than a teacher to him, and he uncharacteristically broke into tears at the train station.

"Come with me, Mr. Grunwald," he pleaded.

"Your future is ahead of you. Mine is behind me. You go and do what I could not achieve. Now get on the train and make me proud of you, Mein Sohn."

Chapter 5

THE ENTREPRENEUR

Spring, 1890

Nancy's innovations to Charlie Murphy's tavern proved highly successful. Word of the excellent food now served at Murphy's spread quickly among the businessmen in the area, and attracted a large lunch and dinner crowd. Mr. Murphy replaced the sign before his establishment with a new one with gold lettering emblazoned on dark wood reading, "Murphy's Bar & Grille." He raised Nancy's salary and along with the tips she received from the well-fed diners, she managed to put away a good bit of money. She spent very little on herself, and she paid nominal rent to the Lallys. She sent enough money to her father in Ireland, and deposited whatever she had left in the bank and happily calculated the interest her money earned every month. Occasionally she would purchase fabric and pay Mrs. Lally to make her a dress. She did splurge on a new hat, feeling she must look presentable at Mass on Sundays.

She and Patrick had been corresponding weekly, he telling her how much he missed her, and she detailing the changes she suggested Mr. Murphy make to the bar and how, when he put them into practice, his business had increased. But Nancy's position did not fulfill all her needs. Her days were occupied, but at night, alone in her room, she was lonely. The Lallys were wonderful to her, treating her as their own daughter, but something was missing. So when Patrick wrote that he had saved a tidy sum, and again proposed they marry, she considered it carefully.

She had been in America over two years, and just celebrated her twentieth birthday. Most girls her age were married, but she felt no attraction for the men she met at the restaurant who were obviously interested in her. She thought that by combining her money with Patrick's, they would be able to afford their own apartment and also fulfill her dream of opening her own small restaurant. Though she cared very much for Patrick, she was not in love with him, but she had given up all hope of seeing Matthew Clarke again. And after all, she thought, in Ireland many weddings were arranged by a marriage broker who brought strangers together, and over time love developed between them and they led happy lives. And Patrick, a good, upstanding, Catholic man, would make a good father.

She made her decision and spoke to Mr. Lally about his obtaining a job for Patrick. She told him they were to be married, and after a brief period, they would leave for a home of their own. The affable policeman showered congratulations on Nancy, and promised by the next evening he would secure a position for her husband-to-be.

That evening Nancy took up her pen.

Dear Patrick,

It is with happiness and pride that I accept your gracious proposal of marriage. Mr. Lally will see that you have a job awaiting you on your arrival in Manhattan. We will be wed the day you arrive, and we will live with them until we find new lodgings. You will like the Lallys and feel comfortable in their presence. I eagerly await your letter telling me when we should meet your train at Grand Central railroad station. I will make arrangements at the church to have the banns posted so we can be married that day. We could not live together unless we were married, you understand. Please tell Aunt May that I will bring her to New York soon. I have wonderful plans for all of us, as I will tell you on your arrival.

From your bride-to-be, Nancy.

Patrick's heart jumped with pleasure on reading Nancy's letter, and he immediately gave the mandatory two weeks' notice of his leaving to Mrs. Birmingham.

"Well, good luck to you," she sneered. "I hope you will enjoy digging ditches. Leave your uniforms with the laundress. That will be all."

Patrick went to his room to reread Nancy's letter and noticed her language had become Americanized. No more ye, yer, tis, or meself. I must lose my Irish ways, he thought. She's made such a success of herself, I don't want to sound like a dumb greenhorn when I meet her friends and embarrass the lass. There I go again, he thought. I must remember that in America they are called girls.

He sat with May in the kitchen and told her the news. She too, was ready to leave Tuxedo Park, and asked Patrick to arrange it as soon as possible. She would miss the lad, as she did Nancy, but she took heart in knowing they would all be together again soon.

Nancy and Mr. Lally met Patrick's train at Grand Central and the men hit if off quite well, talking about Ireland and laughing at their mutual problems assimilating into this new country.

"Your young lady has arranged everything, and as soon as we get you settled at home we'll head for St. Bridget's Church. Well, look at yer hair and yer eyes. You're black Irish fer sure! Must have some Spanish blood in ye. But yer a fine looking specimen of a man, ye are."

They hopped on the trolley and Nancy noticed how different Patrick looked without his sharp chauffeur's uniform. The clothes he wore were shabby, and though he had been in America for ten years, he still looked like an Irishman just off the boat. But she would fix that by getting him some proper attire.

Patrick looked at Nancy, with her silky auburn hair piled high on her head, and noticed her trim, but curvaceous figure. The lass has filled out a bit, he thought, and he considered himself a very lucky man to be marrying this smart, ambitious, beautiful young woman.

The ceremony at St. Bridget's took only fifteen minutes, as they did not have a nuptial mass, and Mr. Murphy and the Lallys were the only others in attendance. Nancy had purchased wedding rings; a wide gold band with a Celtic cross for Patrick, and a plain band for herself.

After they vowed their "I wills" and the priest pronounced them husband and wife, they returned to the Lally's apartment for an elegant dinner, complete with cheap champagne and expensive Irish whiskey. After dinner, Mr. Lally stood up, raised his glass to the newlyweds, and proposed a toast.

"May ye live as long as ye want, and never want as long as ye live."

Not to be outdone, Mrs. Lally raised her glass and said:

"May there be a generation of yer children on the children of yer children."

Mr. Murphy told the bride and groom he regretted his wife had not lived long enough to be part of this glorious day, and wished them a long and good life together.

After dinner, and copious amounts of wine and spirits, Patrick stood, a little unsteadily, and thanked his hosts for their kindness. Nancy took her tipsy husband's arm and announced it was time for bed as her new groom had been through a long day and needed his rest, for tomorrow he began his new job.

Nancy had anticipated her wedding night with an equal amount of happiness and trepidation. But she need not have feared her first carnal experience, for as soon as they entered their room Patrick flopped on the bed and passed out. She took off his shoes, threw a blanket over him, put on her nightgown, and carefully edged her way under the covers to the small space her sprawled-out husband allotted her.

Well, she thought, with a combination of disappointment and relief, what a wedding night this turned out to be. Himself will be suffering mightily tomorrow for his excesses tonight. Then it occurred to her he had not held her hand, or kissed her, or said one loving word since she first saw him at the train station. She supposed he was too tired or shy. But he would get over that, she assured herself.

The next morning Patrick's head throbbed and his stomach felt queasy as Nancy, already dressed, poked and prodded him, warning he could not be late his first day on the job. He reluctantly rose and headed for the bathroom, which he reached just in time to avoid the mortification of evacuating the contents of his churning stomach in the hallway.

Mrs. Lally had breakfast waiting for them, but the most Patrick could ingest was some toast and tea. Mr. Lally, looking fit and handsome in his police uniform, was ready to transport Patrick to the hole in the ground where he would labor, helping to build the new city underground train system.

"We'd best be getting on so ye won't be late the first day on the job. Mayor Van Wyck threw out the first shovel of dirt just last week, so yer getting in on the ground flow, so to speak," Officer Lally laughed. "I'll take you over to Bleeker Street where they're starting to lower the main sewer and I'll put you in the safe hands of the foreman, Tom Healy, a good friend of mine. Just do whatever he asks of ya, and all will be fine."

Mrs. Lally handed Patrick a small pail covered with a cloth containing bread, cheese and fruit for his lunch. Nancy bid him goodbye and good luck. She noticed he wore the same clothes he had been married in the day before, and saw she had her work cut out for her. She must talk to Mrs. Lally about where to purchase some work clothes and a Sunday suit for her husband, but now she must get herself to her job at the restaurant.

That evening Patrick arrived home exhausted, his face and hands covered with grime. Nancy demanded he change his dirty, stinking clothes immediately and go clean himself up in the bathroom. She had unpacked his bag and handed him a clean shirt and pants, and brushed the gunk off his shoes.

He returned from the bathroom looking quite improved, and lay down on the bed. "I don't think I can do this kind of work, Nancy, shoveling and lifting heavy material all day. Me legs barely carried me home."

"You've just gotten a bit soft from living at the Birmingham's. Your strength will come back in a few weeks. Mrs. Lally has supper almost ready, but I must go back to the restaurant in time for the dinner crowd." She handed him a bottle of liniment. "Rub this on your legs and you'll be a new man in no time."

"It's not a new man I'm looking to be. I want to feel like the man I was before they almost killed me today." Within minutes he was fast asleep and Nancy left for work.

Charlie Murphy, after observing the amazing efficiency of his new assistant, allowed Nancy to adjust her working hours to suit both their needs, and she never disappointed him. The food was ready when needed, and the bar cleaned, even if she came in some mornings at six and left for her own errands at different times during the day. He was well pleased with their arrangement.

Nancy arrived at work the third day after her wedding and the place was almost empty. One man sat reading a newspaper in the corner, and three young men who worked night shifts were having a beer at the bar before going home to bed. Nancy had the food ready for lunch and it only needed heating up. But she felt frustrated by Patrick's lack of stamina and wondered if he might be right, that he was not cut out for heavy manual labor. She sat on the piano bench in the rear of the room and ran her fingers silently over the keys, remembering the lessons her mother had forced her to take from an old maid who lived nearby. Without thinking, she tentatively played the melody to "Athlone." Then, lost in the moment, put her feet to the pedals and her left hand gently touched the accompanying chords.

When she finished the piece, the three young men at the bar burst into applause. She turned to them, startled by their reaction, and apologized for interrupting their conversation. Mr. Murphy gazed with admiration at Nancy as he handed a bar towel to one customer, who could not control the tears streaming down his face.

"Give us another round," he told Mr. Murphy. "Can ye play it again and sing the words fer us, lass?" One of the men requested.

"Go ahead, Nancy," Mr. Murphy encouraged her. And she sang the song in a clear soprano voice:

"Oh! I want to go back to that tumble-down shack,

Where the wild roses bloom round the door,

Just to pillow my head in the old trundle bed,

Just to see my old mother once more."

She stopped singing when she noticed the overly sentimental effect the words had on the men, and immediately began a light-hearted, humorous Irish ditty. The men tapped their feet in time with the music, and at the conclusion they applauded again, with broad smiles on their faces.

She got up from the piano, took a slight bow, and reminded them she must get to the kitchen or there would be no lunch today.

The wheels in Mr. Murphy's brain were spinning. The girl could sing and play piano! What a great draw that would be. He'd have her perform after dinner and the customers would linger on, ordering more drinks. He vowed to speak to her about it that evening, but the bar was so busy it slipped his mind.

Nancy arrived home that night to find Patrick, once again, sprawled out on the bed in his dirty clothes, snoring. Well, I'll not take his shoes off tonight, she thought. I'll wake him in an hour to clean up for dinner.

In the kitchen, Mrs. Lally's fried chicken sizzled on the stove as her husband burst in the door grinning from ear to ear.

"Well, if it isn't you I was hoping to see. Nancy, you've made quite a reputation fer yerself, young lady."

"I've done nothing wrong," Nancy said.

"Just the opposite. It seems an old friend of mine, Joe Hannigan, was having his coffee and reading the newspaper at Murphy's Bar one morning and heard you perform. Hannigan owns a restaurant and dance hall further uptown, and found out you lived with us. He stopped in at the precinct and asked me to convey a message to you. He'd like ye to come work for him in the evenings, singing and playing the piano, and he'll pay you double what Murphy's giving you now. And ye won't have to cook. What do ye think of that?"

The astonishment on Nancy's face prodded him to continue.

"Oh, it's a very reputable restaurant. Rich married couples have dinner there, then stay for drinks and some dancing. There's a small band that plays, but Hannigan doesn't have a singer and your voice and good looks impressed him."

Her frown kept him talking.

"It's a very high-class establishment, and just think, double the money."

She was thinking, very hard. More money would enable her to open her own restaurant that much sooner, and the idea of singing and playing the piano seemed very enticing. Still, she felt a loyalty to Mr. Murphy for giving her a start in America. Her emotions were in turmoil.

"You have to grab an opportunity when it presents itself. And lass, forgive me for saying this, but I have deep doubts that your bridegroom will be working on the train tracks much longer. I've been told he's not carrying his weight. The foreman is disappointed in his performance and is thinking of letting him go."

"But Patrick has been working only a few days. Won't they give a man a chance in this country?"

"There are fifty men lined up waiting for his job. He only got it because of me. I can recommend men, but I can't do the work for them. It breaks me heart to tell you, but he's not cut out for it. And this is your golden chance. Don't let it slip through yer fingers."

"Thank you, Mr. Lally. I'll sleep on it."

But she could not sleep. Doubts about changing jobs troubled her. Her father always said, "Better the devil ye know than the one ye don't." But Mr. Murphy was more angel than devil. And Patrick would soon be out of a job, and for how long she could not estimate. She counted on his salary to raise them up, and in a few days he would be unemployed. She tossed and turned on the tiny bit of bed left to her by her snoring husband. Three days had passed since their wedding and their marriage had not been consummated. Looking at

Patrick, she lost her eagerness for being introduced to the joys of the marriage bed. Perhaps her desire would return when he more resembled the man who rescued her from the roof in the blizzard of 1888 at the Birmingham's.

Upon arriving at work the next morning, there were no customers at the bar. She placed herself on a stool before Mr. Murphy, who was engaged in paperwork.

"May I speak to you, sir?"

"There is no one I'd rather speak to than you, my little song bird. Did ye see the customers crying their eyes out when ye sang 'Athlone?' Why did ye never tell me ya had such talents?"

"This is very hard for me to say, but some other gentleman here has, as you say, noticed my talents, and offered me a job. He wants me to sing and play piano at his club."

"The son-of-a ...forgive me, God and you. I never speak that way. But that vulture has no right to try and steal me employees. He enjoys a fine business of his own. But he's from Northern Ireland, ya know. What should I expect? I think he was one of those English they transported to take over our country. And, so what did he offer you?"

Her lips trembled as Nancy uttered, "Double my salary. But the thought of leaving here would never have occurred to me until I learned last night that my husband will be losing his job. I must think of him, and the family we hope to have some day. And I must make more money to get our own apartment. I don't want to leave here. You've been very good to a poor immigrant and my heart breaks when I think you might find me ungrateful, which I am not. It

75

is just as I said. My husband and I find ourselves in a difficult position."

Mr. Murphy poured Nancy a glass of ginger ale as he pondered the dilemma. He thought hard and fast and came to a decision.

"Nancy, I don't want to lose you. Everything ye've done here has increased me business three-fold. I have a proposal to make. Stay here with me, and I'll make ye a partner. Not a full partner, mind ya. But I will give you twenty percent of the profits, net of course, and I'll get you a girl to help in the kitchen and you'll continue to sing and your money problems will be solved. You'll still get the same salary and all yer tips. Does that sound fair to ya, lass?"

It took only a moment for Nancy to grasp the enormous financial possibilities his proposal presented. Overwhelmed by his generosity, and the idea of being part owner of an already successful business, she put her hand out to Mr. Murphy, and beamed with gratitude. "We have a deal. Thank you so much, sir. But may I be so bold as to make a suggestion?"

"Get on with it."

"Instead of hiring a girl to help me in the kitchen, would you consider taking on my Aunt May? She taught me everything I know about cooking and would not disappoint you. She's served the Birminghams for ten years, and they're quite pleased with her."

"Then bring your aunt down and I'll welcome her with open arms." Mr. Murphy had no idea how true that statement would prove to be.

They shook hands. "That makes it official," he said. "We don't have to spit in our palms before closing a deal as they do in the old country, do we?"

"No. That's a very unsanitary custom. But we must have a written agreement, to protect your interests," she said.

That afternoon at the bar Nancy made an extra apple pie to take home to the Lallys to celebrate her good fortune. Patrick was waiting for her, and looking very glum.

"They let me go today, lass. I'm sorry to let ye down. Don't think too badly of me, please."

"Well, you'll find something else." Nancy was not surprised. "Let me tell you my news."

Patrick listened to the deal his wife and Mr. Murphy entered into with a mixture of pride and envy. His wife was a success and he was a failure.

Officer Lally arrived home, once again with good news for the young couple. "Patrick, there's a night watchman's job open at the Triangle Shirt Waist Factory, and it can be yours if ye want it. What do ye say, lad?"

Patrick's heart sank. He could not very well turn down a job with Nancy standing there smiling at his good fortune. But working alone all night seemed a fate close to death. He would then have to sleep most of the day and never see his bride.

"It will just be temporary until I can get ye something else. But they'll be no heavy lifting, and you can read the newspapers when ye're not making yer rounds," Officer Lally encouraged Patrick.

Nancy asked if the job was dangerous, and Mr. Lally assured her it was not. The owner needed someone to check out the lighting, look for water leaks, have the furnace going when the girls came to work in the morning, and handle routine maintenance problems. And as there was no money left in the building at night, as any burglar worthy of his craft would be aware of, Patrick need not fear any physical harm.

"Well," said Patrick, "Tis true I need a job and will take whatever I can get, and I thank ye fer yer help."

Nancy took his hand and smiled up at her husband. "You won't be a night watchman for long. Something else will turn up."

The touch of her hand reminded him he had not yet even kissed his new wife. He mightily yearned for her since their marriage, and now that he had escaped the heat and filth of the train tunnel he would fulfill his husbandly duties with great delight as soon as possible.

That evening Nancy wrote Aunt May and told her to give notice to Mrs. Birmingham and prepare to come live with her in New York. The next day she began searching for an apartment with two bedrooms. She walked as if on air. She now had her own business, a husband, her Aunt May, and soon her own home. America is a wonderful country, she thought.

Nancy searched through her papers and finally located the business card: William Peyton, Attorney-at-Law. And a week later she and Mr. Murphy went to his office on Broadway. Bill Peyton was amazed that this self-assured, beautiful, smartly dressed young woman sitting across the desk from him was the same little Irish girl he'd met two years ago, bringing him news of his sister's death on the boat from Ireland.

He had thought of her on occasion and wondered what had become of her, fearing she labored in a factory, or still worked as a maid in Tuxedo Park. But no. Here she was with this cheerful Irishman who was giving her a twenty-percent interest in his bar.

As a lawyer, he was naturally suspicious of the circumstances that led Mr. Murphy to engage in such a business dealing with this pretty young woman. Could they be in some kind of intimate relationship? Was his initial admiration of Nancy's character misplaced? He could not contain his curiosity and needed to know what prompted Mr. Murphy's largess. So he asked, "And what shall the contract list as Miss O'Leary's responsibilities in return for her interest in your business, Mr. Murphy?"

"Well, cooking the lunches and dinners, and serving the food and drinks, and singing and piano playing after dinner, and the running of the restaurant, and," Charlie Murphy scratched his balding head, thinking. "I don't know everything she does, but she's increased me business over forty percent since she spruced up the place and talked me into serving food, and I don't want her to quit."

Bill's spirits rose as his worst fears were put to rest, and he proceeded drawing up the contract, asking questions and offering suggestions. When he finished typing the agreement, he asked for the exact spelling of their names, above which they would sign.

"Charles J. Murphy."

"Nancy O'Leary Devlin."

Bill Peyton stopped writing, took off his glasses, and looked at Nancy. "Devlin?"

"Yes, Mr. Peyton," smiled Nancy. "I've become a married woman. I am now Mrs. Patrick Devlin."

The lawyer's heart sank, and he experienced a strange sense of disappointment and loss. "Well, let me offer you my congratulations. You've certainly achieved quite a bit since I first saw you the day of your arrival in New York."

Nancy thought she detected a note of disapproval in his voice and responded, "I've worked very hard and made new friends who've helped me find my way in America. I met my husband at the Birmingham's in Tuxedo Park, and as you told me, the mistress of the house was harsh, but I persevered, learned the ways of the rich, and used that knowledge to advance myself. I listened to the rich women talk, and taught myself to speak like them. Mr. Murphy took some of my suggestions, and his business prospered. And I intend to continue advancing, just as you have, Mr. Peyton, in this country that offers such great opportunities to everyone."

The lawyer smiled at Nancy, and finished the contract, which both parties read, agreed to, and signed.

"Now, how much do we owe you for your services?" Nancy asked, standing and opening her purse.

Bill took off his glasses and smiled. "A free dinner at your restaurant, and a couple of Irish whiskeys."

Mr. Murphy clasped Bill's hand, told him he would be welcome anytime, and hoped his visit would be sooner rather than later. As Mr. Murphy left the law office, Nancy lingered behind and spoke to Bill.

"You've become my friend. And I thank you for letting me keep your sister's fifty dollars which got me started, and for all you did for me today. You are a good man, Mr. Peyton."

"And you are an exceptional woman, Nancy. I'm sorry you went and got married before giving me a chance at winning your affections."

She blushed, and inwardly felt the same regrets. Bill Peyton was a man of parts, and she could easily have been seduced by his charms. But she had too quickly betrothed herself to Patrick, oblivious to the possibilities that might present themselves. She had no knowledge of her worth, and offered herself to the first bidder. How many other women, she thought, had fallen into the same trap of underestimating themselves and grasping at the first proposal they received. What made women so anxious and insecure that they had to settle for less for fear of ending up alone. Being alone now seemed more enticing to Nancy than being married to Patrick.

She left the office and joined Mr. Murphy in the sunlight beaming down on Broadway. Her eyes twinkled up at her new partner, and she said, "Mr. Murphy, I'm worth a twenty-percent partnership. But I would have settled for ten."

That evening in bed Nancy reread the contract which made her part owner of a tavern in New York City. She could not believe her good fortune, and studied the signatures attesting she actually owned a piece of the establishment. "Nancy O'Leary Devlin." Now doesn't that sound nice! Then she lurched straight up in bed. But my name is Mary Alice O'Laoghaire! That's what I wrote on the paper Matthew gave me on the ship. Dear God! No wonder I never received a letter from him. Mrs. Birmingham would not have recognized my name.

What a fool I am. She fell back on the pillow, her arms around her chest. Well, it's too late now. My name is Mrs. Patrick Devlin!

Chapter 6

THE MEDICAL STUDENT

1890-1891

Matthew arrived at Dr. Weitz's house in New York in late November of 1890, bursting with anticipation at the prospect of learning medicine, yet acutely aware of his lack of credentials. But his natural self-confidence returned when he looked back at his accomplishments in Johnstown over the past two years and remembered Mr. Grunwald's parting words: "Make me proud of you, Mein Sohn."

A dark-haired young woman answered his knock and opened the door. She ushered Matthew into Dr. Weitz's office just off the foyer. The short man looked to be in his early sixties, with graying hair and large, dark eyes. He stood up from his desk and extended his hand. "You must be Mr. Matthew Clarke."

"That I am, sir. I am delighted to meet you, and you have my heartfelt gratitude for giving me this opportunity."

They shook hands and Dr. Weitz introduced him to Rachel, his daughter, who had remained standing by the door.

"Come in my dear. Meet the newest member of our medical practice, Mr. Matthew Clarke."

The girl smiled shyly and nodded her head. "Welcome to our home. While you talk with Father I will bring you tea, then I will show you to your room. Dinner will be in one hour."

Matthew muttered, "Thank you," as she turned and left, quite taken by her beauty and regal bearing.

"So, you studied with my good friend, Mr. Grunwald. You are a very lucky man to have been tutored by someone of his stature."

"For sure I know that. He is a rare man indeed. His knowledge is outstanding and his character is first-rate."

"And he is Jewish, as am I."

"And I am Irish," replied Matthew, a bit bewildered.

"Did it not bother you that he was a Jew?"

Matthew scowled, his brow furrowed. "And why would that bother me?"

"You are a Catholic, and your faith teaches that the Jews killed Christ."

"My Irish priests taught me that we are all God's children. The basic tenet of Catholicism is to love God above all and your neighbor as yourself."

Matthew stood up. He was angry. "Catholics believe it was the divine plan to have Jesus crucified. If He chose the Jews to fulfill the prophesy, well that was God's decision. Maybe that is why you are called the Chosen People. I think I had better go, Dr. Weitz."

"Sit down, Matthew, and forgive me for testing you."

"Testing me?"

"Many people in America dislike the Jews. They call us Yids and Hebes. In Europe the Jews were discriminated against, suffered persecution and hatred by many Christians. Of course, not all felt that way. Some became good friends and neighbors. Some even went so far as to inter-marry. But we still feel the wounds, as you Irish do against the British for taking over your country."

"We'll get our country back from the English; it's just a matter of time. Our men in all the counties have banded together, and even here in New York they're planning ...."

"Stop! Do not tell me any more. Talk like that is dangerous. Do what you will, but keep it to yourself."

Dr. Weitz became silent as Rachel knocked, then opened the door carrying a tea tray, and placed it on a table before the sofa.

"Thank you, my dear," said Dr. Weitz. Rachel poured the tea, and left the room.

"Well, Doctor, have I passed your test?" Matthew asked.

The doctor picked up his cup and leaned towards Matthew. "Yes, my friend. You have received an A. From now on you are not only my protégé, but a member of my family. Please forgive an old man his wariness of strangers."

The door opened and Rachel said, "Father, come immediately. A patient has arrived, a young boy bleeding from a knife wound to his arm."

Dr. Weitz rose and said, "Come, Matthew. Your training begins."

They entered the examining room off the hallway and found a distraught mother clutching a slightly built boy of about sixteen, pressing a bloody towel on his forearm.

"And what has happened to you, young man?" The doctor asked the frightened boy.

The mother answered for her son in a heavy Italian accent. "It's a those Irish hooligans again. They stopped my Roberto on his way home from school and wanted money. He didn't have any, so they stabbed him. They were drunk!"

The woman began sobbing and Rachel put her hand on the woman's shoulder and assured her Dr. Weitz would take good care of her boy, and led her to a bench in the hallway.

Rachel returned and prepared a tray of sterile instruments, bandages and a needle and surgical thread while Dr. Weitz examined the wound. The boy lay on the table moaning in pain.

"Look, Matthew, the knife cut into some flesh, but luckily did not reach any tendons or ligaments. Rachel, the antiseptic and the anesthesia, please." Then he spoke to the boy. "Roberto, I am going to put you to sleep for a few minutes so you will feel no pain when I stitch your arm. Matthew, watch. I put a few drops of chloroform on this cloth and hold it on his nose and mouth for a few seconds. Then we must work quickly. The effect will wear off in ten minutes. But give a patient too much chloroform, and it is very dangerous. Now watch me carefully, for you will be doing the sewing next time."

Rachel handed the threaded needle to her father and the doctor quickly and deftly attached the cleaved skin with five stitches. And after he knotted each one, Rachel snipped the black threads. In five minutes the procedure was finished and Rachel applied a bandage to the groggy boy's arm.

"Well, Matthew, what do you think? Can you do this?"

"My mother taught me to sew my torn britches, but this is a different matter altogether."

"Not so different, really. Skin is just thinner than cloth, so you have to treat it more delicately. You will learn. Can you put the boy's arm in a sling?"

"That I can do," said Matthew.

Rachel brought the boy's mother into the room and instructed her to keep the bandage dry, not let Roberto move his arm unnecessarily, and gave her an appointment for the following week. The woman expressed her gratitude effusively, saying Dr. Weitz was a miracle worker, handed Rachel five dollars, and led her son out of the doctor's house.

"You don't tell the patients how much they owe you?" Matthew questioned.

Dr. Weitz shrugged his shoulders. "They pay what they can. And she must be able to afford five dollars. Some cannot. It all evens out."

Rachel bid the men to come into the dining room. The table had been set with a centerpiece of fresh fruit between two silver candlesticks. She lit the tapers and placed a glass of red wine before each plate, then brought in a platter of roast chicken, surrounded by carrots, potatoes, boiled onions and green beans.

Dr. Weitz bowed his head and said a prayer of thanks for the blessings God had showered upon them, then raised his wine glass and said, "Le'Chayim." Turning to Matthew he translated: "That means 'to life' in Yiddish."

Matthew replied, "Go raibh maith agaibh. That means 'thank you' in Gaelic. And 'slainte.' That means 'to your health'."

They all laughed at the strange sounding words, and toasted each other's similarities and differences and enjoyed their dinner.

That evening Rachel led Matthew to his room on the second floor and he put down his suitcase, and turning too quickly, brushed her arm.

"Excuse me. I've had a long day and it's left me clumsy," Matthew said.

"You have done no harm," she smiled, and as she turned down the covers of his bed, he objected. "You don't have to do that for me. You are not a servant. You're the mistress of the household."

"Oh, it is no trouble," and she walked towards the door.

"May I ask you something?" She stopped, smiled, and nodded.

"Rachel, you were so magnificent today working on that boy. Are you in training to be a doctor, too?"

She laughed, and replied that women were only encouraged to enter the medical profession as nurses. "And besides, I am left-handed."

"What does that have to do with anything?"

"Only about ten percent of people in the world are left-handed. And a left-handed doctor could be a problem in an operating room. All the equipment would have to be laid out differently, and there is a danger of nurses putting the instruments in the wrong hand of the doctor, and some think left-handed doctors might operate on the wrong side of the patient. And also, the doctor might want to stand on the opposite side of the patient than a right-handed doctor would, and that could cause confusion."

"That's ridiculous. I saw how you conducted yourself today. You would make a wonderful surgeon."

"Thank you, Matthew. But I do not have a choice, really. Medical schools are very particular about whom they accept, and I am a woman, and a foreigner, so I suppose I will remain a nurse, and I will say goodnight, Matthew. Breakfast will be at seven-thirty. Do you want anything else?"

Yes, he thought, I want to tell you how wonderful you are, despite being left-handed. But he settled for asking, "Tell me, do patients come in all day? Or only by appointment?"

"We have both. Your days will be busy, but your evenings will usually be free unless there is an emergency."

"And are your evenings free?" He blurted out the words before thinking of the implications of his question.

A slight blush rose on her cheeks. "I usually spend my nights reading medical books. When we have no patients on the weekends I go to the park, or sit by the river and watch the boats sail by and the gulls fly over. The sight and sound of the water relaxes me after all the sorrow and pain I see here all week."

"I understand, and as I am new to this city, maybe some weekend you can take me to the river to experience the peace you find there."

He immediately wondered if he had gone too far, too quickly, and regretted his impulsiveness.

"I will ask Father, and if he approves, we will go together and enjoy the tranquility of the East River. Now I must leave and prepare the kitchen for breakfast. Goodnight," she smiled up at him, and left the room.

Matthew began to sweat. What the hell have I done, he thought? The first night in this man's home and I exhibit the traits of a scoundrel. For sure he will throw me out tomorrow and I wouldn't think the less of him for it. But Rachel had touched his heart and his brain had reacted without considering the consequences of his actions. What was wrong with him, he asked himself. She was Jewish, and he Catholic. He had no future with Rachel.

He spent a fitful night and decided the best course of action would be to confess his conversation with Rachel to Dr. Weitz, first thing in the morning.

At breakfast it became apparent Rachel had not revealed the events of the previous night to her father. Dr. Weitz was enjoying his smoked salmon and brown bread, and Matthew his scrambled eggs and toast, as Rachel refilled their coffee cups. Dr. Weitz was in a good mood, and while he ate, began a dissertation on the food preferences in America and Europe. "I hear in Ireland and England they eat herring for breakfast, but in Germany we have, ah, we have…." The doctor stopped speaking and began gasping for breath.

"Father, what is wrong?" Rachel cried.

Matthew rose quickly and began slapping the doctor's back, but the man had stopped breathing and held his hand to his throat. Rachel panicked and began crying. "Papa, what can I do?"

Matthew pulled Dr. Weitz up from his chair and lay him belly down across the table. He put his fingers inside the man's mouth to open his airways, and continued to pound the doctor's back. Within ten seconds, just as Dr. Weitz's complexion began to turn ashen, the doctor spewed out the salmon bone that had become lodged in his throat, and slowly began breathing again. Matthew lifted him from the table, and gently sat the doctor in his chair and told Rachel to bring her father some water. Slowly the color returned to Dr. Weitz's face, and he was able to speak, but very slowly.

"You saved my life, Matthew. I will now lie down for a while and thank God for sending you here. You must tell me later how you learned to do what you did to save me."

Matthew told the man it was only instinct that prompted his actions.

"Matthew, your instincts are a gift from God," Dr. Weitz replied in a raspy voice. "And you are destined for a great career in medicine. But now I must rest. Rachel, walk me to my bedroom, please."

After Rachel had settled her father in, she returned to Matthew. She rushed toward him, flinging her arms around his neck, murmuring, "Thank you, thank you, thank you." He quickly held her at arm's length and told her his actions were reflexive, and not to give him too much credit.

"God was in the room with us," he said.

"But it was you who removed the fish bone from my father's throat, and I will never forget what you did today." She turned quickly and left, leaving Matthew elated that he had saved the doctor's life, but concerned about the strong feelings Rachel apparently had towards him.

Later that day, Dr. Weitz had recovered and returned to his office, and with Matthew, treated patients with various maladies, ranging from a woman apparently dying from a tumor, to a man with a gunshot wound to his leg. He had been hauled in by an obviously inebriated comrade. While preparing the man for surgery, Matthew quietly asked the doctor why the man had not been taken to the hospital.

"We will talk later," he said. Rachel led the drunken companion to the bench in the hallway, but as she turned back to the examination room, the man grabbed her, threw her across his lap, and began groping her. Hearing her screams, Matthew rushed out and saw Rachel desperately trying to extricate herself from the drunken man's grip. Matthew tore her away from him and brought her back to the operating room. When she assured him she had not been harmed, he returned to the waiting room, pulled the drunk up by his coat collars, and barked, "If you ever touch that woman again, you will be a dead man." Then he tossed him to the floor where he lay in a stupor.

Dr. Weitz left his bleeding patient when he heard Rachel's cries and witnessed Matthew's actions in defense of his daughter's honor and well-being. Dr. Weitz had taken Matthew into his house; now he took him into a deep place in his heart. The men returned to the patient and found Rachel, poised as ever, holding the instrument tray out to her father.

"The man is so drunk, I doubt you will need chloroform, but it is ready if he starts thrashing about," she stated.

Matthew stared in amazement as father and daughter calmly went about preparing the man for treatment, as though the assault on Rachel had never occurred. And after examining the patient, Dr. Weitz informed Matthew it was only a flesh wound. There was very little bleeding, so the bullet had not hit an artery. If it had, the man would probably be dead by now. No anesthesia proved necessary, as the patient had ingested plenty during the day at a local tavern. Dr. Weitz removed the bullet, all the while instructing Matthew in the intricacies of surgery and anatomy.

"Please put three stitches in his leg, Matthew."

Matthew froze as Rachel handed him the threaded needle. "I don't think I'm ready, Doctor."

"Yes, you are. Just imagine this man is your father and you are the only person who can save him, and you will do a fine job."

Rachel took pity on Matthew and suggested she would close the wound. That was all he needed to restore his confidence and straighten his spine. He would not have her consider him a weakling. He took the needle and closed the wound and she rewarded him with a smile of approval.

"Good job, Matthew," Dr. Weitz said. "Now get that other drunk in here to rid us of this human garbage."

The doctor washed his hands as his assistant did as he was bidden. Matthew threw some cold water on the semi-conscious man's face, and told him to take the patient home. The friend staggered into the examining room, picked up the patient, and left the office without a word. Matthew's disbelief registered on his face and he could not control his anger.

"He said not a word. He did not pay you. He did not even thank you. What kind of men are they?"

"Pieces of dreck!"

Matthew did not understand. "Dreck?"

"I'm sorry, my friend. But sometimes under stress I resort to Yiddish. Dreck means shit. But the Hippocratic Oath I swore to does not allow me to pick and choose whom I will treat. Rachel, please bring us some tea. Then the three of us will talk."

Matthew and the doctor sat silently until Rachel arrived and poured the tea. Her father asked her to sit with them, as he gave Matthew a lesson in survival in lower Manhattan.

"Now, this is serious, Matthew. And you must contain your anger or we will all be put in jeopardy. You asked me what kind of men our last patient and his friend were. I will tell you bluntly. They are evil men. And I am sorry to inform you, Matthew, they are Irish. They are members of a vicious gang of young hoodlums that has terrorized this area for years. One of their members probably stabbed that young boy we treated this morning. You asked why the man with the bullet wound did not go to a hospital? His friend probably feared they would be arrested. But they probably would have been quickly set free. They are called the Short-Tail Gang, and among their other evil deeds, they rob liquor stores, and feel entitled to free drinks in saloons, but should the owner ask for payment, they shoot him."

Matthew's temper came to the fore. He stood up demanding, "Why are they not arrested and put in jail?"

"Matthew, take a deep breath and calm down. The gang owns the area, and the police are rightly afraid of them. They are animals, and have shot many Irish policemen, so you cannot blame the cops for looking the other way. These hoodlums go to court and the judge sentences them to only a few days in jail. The police fear retaliation on themselves and their families. Many gang members have been arrested for being drunk and disorderly, and then let out of prison in a few hours. That is why I did not ask for payment for my services. It is like it was for us Jews in Germany. One must do what is necessary to survive and protect one's family. Do you now understand how important it is for you to let go of your anger and accept what is a fact of life in New York at the present time?"

Matthew tried to contain his fury. His own people, the Irish, had become terrorists in America, and there did not seem to be anything he could do about it but feel terrible shame at the atrocities his countrymen were committing.

"I'm sorry, Doctor, that some of my own have brought such disgrace to the Irish. I apologize for all the good, God-fearing people of Ireland and America. And I promise to protect you and Rachel from that gang if I have to kill every last one of them myself."

"You will kill no one, my friend. We each have our purpose in life, and God put you here to save lives. Do not anger your maker. It is the task of others to deal with the gang. Now let us go to bed to be restored and prepared for whatever tomorrow may bring."

For the next two months Matthew learned how to practice medicine at Dr. Weitz's side, and studied chemistry, biology and anatomy in the evenings. On late Saturday afternoons, before the Short-Tail Gang went on the prowl, he and Rachel, with Dr. Weitz's permission, spent an hour by themselves talking and laughing, as they threw bread crumbs to the diving gulls at the East River.

Rachel's twentieth birthday was approaching and Dr. Weitz decided a celebration was in order. He would take Matthew and his daughter to a nearby restaurant everyone at the hospital was raving about. They said the food was excellent, and at certain times a piano player and singer entertained; a place called Murphy's Bar & Grille.

Chapter 7

A HOME OF HER OWN

1891

Now that Nancy was assured of a steady income from her partnership with Mr. Murphy, and with Patrick's salary as a night watchman, she began searching the lower East Side for an apartment on cold mid-December days, trudging through the slush of the latest snow storm. But she would not complain after suffering through the scorching summer heat in New York.

She eventually found a nice two-bedroom apartment on the second floor of a tenement not far from her place of business, which had its own private bathroom. She was elated. She then scoured second-hand furniture stores and purchased necessary items, but bought brand new linens, dishes and kitchen ware. She found some fabric and Mrs. Lally sewed up curtains for her; not lace, but she knew that luxury would be hers in the not too distant future.

The furniture was delivered the week before Christmas, and Nancy decorated her new home with red candles and boughs of evergreen, and had Patrick buy a small, live fir tree, which she draped with cranberry garlands and silver bows.

Moving day at the Lallys caused emotion to run high, ranging from joy to sorrow, and laughter to tears. Nancy and Patrick Devlin expressed their deep appreciation for all their friends had done for

97

them, and promised they would remain close forever. Nancy invited them to dinner at her new home on Christmas Day, and they accepted with delight.

Mrs. Lally joked to her husband that he could anticipate a better meal than she had ever set before him, and as the couple were leaving she whispered into Nancy's ear, "Didn't I tell ye, me girl, ye'd never have to worry about having worn out under things again?"

"And, I make you a promise," said Nancy. "You will never be in need of anything for as long as I live."

A few days before Christmas, Patrick and Nancy finally consummated their marriage. Patrick arrived home at six in the morning after imbibing whiskey all night at the factory. He found his wife sleeping soundly, her long hair strewn across the pillow and the blanket at her waist, revealing the slow rise and fall of her ample breasts under her thin cotton gown. He quickly undressed and silently slid into bed beside her and began caressing the still figure. He put his arm under her head and gently pulled her towards him. She awoke, roused by passion, but the act was completed just as she began to feel the first joys of womanhood. Patrick lay back on his pillow feeling quite satisfied and proud of himself, unaware he had left his bride frustrated and confused. After kissing her goodnight, and vowing his eternal love, he promptly fell asleep.

Nancy lay quietly beside him. So this is what it is all about, she thought. This is the process by which babies are born and men find such great happiness. All she felt was a terrible void, and an unfulfilled yearning. She decided to discuss their interlude with Patrick the next day.

At six the following morning she lay with her eyes closed, feigning sleep, as Patrick once again slid under the covers, naked. He began stroking her and she turned towards him and kissed him longingly. He, delighted by her ardor, began to repeat his performance of the previous morning, but she gently touched his chest and suggested he might prolong the act so she could also find satisfaction.

Patrick, mystified by her statement, retreated and asked her to explain.

"Well, I do like this, but I would wish it to last a bit longer until I feel as you do."

"I'm sorry, Nancy, but as yesterday was me first experience, you'll have to forgive me lack of knowledge. I'll try to do better the next time."

But the next time would never occur. Patrick's mortification at his bride's outspokenness prevented him from trying again. In the following days Nancy made attempts to arouse him, but he pleaded exhaustion, his pride so deeply hurt he feared another premature failure.

Two days before Christmas Aunt May arrived in Manhattan, thrilled to be back with Nancy and Patrick and free of servitude to Mrs. Birmingham in Tuxedo Park.

"So what did the mistress of the mansion say when you gave your notice?" Nancy asked.

"The old biddy told me to be sure the new cook knew all my recipes, and that if her dear departed husband were here he would call me a turn-coat. That's the English in her, ye understand. Not a word of thanks or encouragement did she give me. I'm glad to be out of there. But I fixed her. I left some ingredients out of all me recipes."

"Good for you. We'll be eating high on the hog while she's choking on her dinner. But you're home now with us and we have Christmas to celebrate with the Lallys, and we must serve up the best dinner we've ever made."

"That we will, Nancy. Just lead me to the kitchen."

Patrick's job left him lonely and depressed. For years he had been accustomed to seeing and talking to people all day, and now he found himself spending hours alone at night, and sleeping all day while Nancy worked. He wondered if he would ever see sunlight again. To ease his loneliness on the long nights, he began stopping at a liquor store every day for a bottle of whiskey, which he sipped all night after completing his rounds.

The state of his marriage left him doubting his manliness. His job was unfulfilling, and the days and nights he spent alone began to wear on him. I might as well have become a priest as me Mother wished, he thought, feeling very sorry for himself. As his duties took up very little time, and reading had never interested him, once he flipped through the newspaper and the boredom set in, whiskey became his nightly companion.

Christmas morning arrived and Patrick panicked, realizing he had forgotten to purchase a gift for Nancy. His good standing with his wife left much to be desired, and he could not face further humiliation by having nothing under the tree for his bride. But all the stores were closed for the holiday. In a flash of brilliance he remembered something from long ago that would serve as quite an acceptable gift from a loving husband. While Nancy and May were busy in the kitchen, he sneaked into the bedroom and rummaged through his belongings until he located the object of his search. He wrapped it in a clean handkerchief and found some ribbon Nancy used to tie her gifts, and with great relief, put the parcel in his pocket and went to the dining room to sample May's Christmas punch.

The Lallys arrived at two o'clock, and the aroma of the beef roast and cinnamon punch filled the apartment with holiday cheer, and everyone embraced. Patrick poured cups of punch, surreptitiously doctoring his own from the flask he now carried daily.

"Welcome, welcome, my friends, to our new home. And Merry Christmas to ye all," he shouted. Nancy's face registered her disapproval. She and May had attended Mass that morning, but Patrick would not accompany them, using the excuse that he was too exhausted from his night's work. Nancy noticed he always found some reason lately for not going to church, and reminded herself to discuss this with him. But Christmas day was a cause for celebration, and she would keep quiet until the proper moment presented itself.

After dinner, and a glorious fruit-studded cake with hard sauce, Nancy began distributing presents. She opened the Lally's package first and her eyes widened at the sight of the Waterford cut crystal vase.

"This is so beautiful, but it is too much."

"I brought it over from Ireland and I've enjoyed it fer many years, and as the Lord decided we were not to be blessed with children to hand it down to, I want to see you enjoy it while I'm still alive," smiled Mrs. Lally.

Anne Higgins Petz

Nancy placed it in the center of the table and repeatedly thanked her friends for their generosity.

Then she handed them her gift, done up with bows and ribbons, and apologized how insignificant it appeared compared to the vase. But Mrs. Lally expressed delight with the lace antimacassars, and said they were just what she needed to perk up her living room chairs.

Nancy gave Patrick a bright green sweater. "To keep you warm during the cold nights making rounds in the factory. And to wear at the parade on St. Patrick's Day."

Patrick fumbled in his pocket and withdrew his gift for Nancy. And with, "Happy Christmas to me bride," he gave her the clumsily wrapped parcel.

After opening the handkerchief, Nancy stood stock still, staring at a large gold cross and chain.

"I was given that by me father when I was just a babe. I thought you might like to have it."

"Thank you, Patrick. It's beautiful." On examining it more closely, she found the back inscribed with indecipherable Gaelic words. She would ask Patrick later what they meant, but dinner was on the table.

At six o'clock Mr. Lally stood and said, "We've had a lovely time, but must be leaving now." Nancy fetched their coats from the bedroom, and they said goodbye to their hosts. Patrick helped himself to more punch, again secretly lacing it with whiskey, and slumped down on the sofa.

"Patrick, what does the inscription on the cross read?" Nancy asked.

"I don't know. I never learned Gaelic. It's most likely a prayer. They probably made thousands of them in Ireland years ago. Just like the Waterford vase from the Lallys."

May finished cleaning the dishes and brought a pot of tea into the living room, but Patrick declined and stumbled off to bed.

"Patrick drinks too much, and he embarrasses me in front of our friends. Did you see how he staggered a bit, then slurred his words as the Lallys left? What am I to do with him?" Nancy asked May.

"Ye might mention it some time when he's sober. Like tomorrow. I'll make him a nice meal when he gets home from work in the morning and things will be fine."

"If he doesn't go to the bar first. Anyway, food won't solve our problems," Nancy lamented. "If it would I'd stuff him like a pig."

A few days after Christmas, instead of going home after his shift, Patrick stopped at Murphy's Bar for beer, eggs and bacon. Two men arrived and went into one of the small rooms off the main bar area. Craving human companionship, Patrick took his drink and followed them, asking if they were open to some conversation. The two men exchanged wary glances, then nodded for Patrick to join them. They were discussing Ireland, and the sorry condition their country found itself in, ruled by the bloody British who inflicted their harsh tyranny on the Irish. Patrick's patriotism rose, and in a fury, he agreed with the men that something must be done. After an hour of talking, and many more beers for Patrick, the men decided him suitable to attend one of their meetings.

Callahan, a large man with a thick black moustache, told Patrick to meet them back there two days hence, at seven in the morning, and instructed him to tell no one about their business. Patrick readily

103

agreed and with his chest puffed up with newfound importance, he left for home and bed.

"This man could be of great use to our cause," Callahan said, sipping his coffee. "I've gotten the inside dope on him from Murphy. He's got enough love for Ireland, and plenty of hate for the Brits, and seems to need a great deal of approval. If we give it to him he'll be putty in our hands. But he's not a fool, so we must be careful. He does drink too much. Someone will have to keep an eye on him. That's the wife over there," Callahan said pointing to Nancy as she arrived for work. "She's the brains in the family. We must have him take a vow to tell her nothing of our business. We'll put him through his paces and see how he holds up."

The other man nodded in agreement and they left the tavern, happy to have a new recruit in their organization.

A few mornings later, Nancy served him coffee when Patrick returned home from work, and it was apparent he had stopped for some beers. After he devoured the ham and eggs, she felt ready to ask again about the cross. She had brought the subject up twice before, but he always found an excuse to avoid the subject.

"Tell me, Patrick, how long have you had that cross you gave me?

"Are we back on that again?" he snarled.

She held her temper and waited for his response.

Eventually he spoke. "I suppose I never told you I was adopted at birth by the Devlins of Dublin."

"You certainly did not tell me," said Nancy.

"They rescued me from a Magdalen House. Those places that used to be just fer prostitutes, to let 'em earn a living doing laundry. Then unwed mothers were sent there by their shamed parents to have their babies and then give them up fer adoption. But me adoptive parents told me early on and I never thought much about it. Da and Ma were the best parents a lad could have, and I grew up a happy boy. They gave me the cross on me eighteenth birthday and told me that when they adopted me the head mistress gave it to them. I don't know who it's from, probably me real mother, but I never gave it much thought. Til this Christmas. Then I gave it to you."

Emotion overcame Nancy, and she took her husband's hands and told him how very sorry she was he never knew his birth parents.

"I have no lack of love for me adopted parents, and no resentment towards the woman who bore me." He was becoming annoyed. "Can we just forget it? I'm tired. Will ye let me go to bed?"

"Of course. I'll see you tomorrow morning."

"Oh, I'll be a bit late. I have things to do after work." He would be meeting with Mr. Callahan, as he was eager to find out the business the large man had alluded to when last they spoke.

Nancy examined the cross more closely, staring at the tiny Gaelic letters. What could it mean? She would look into this further, but for now she had a more pressing problem on her mind. For the past week she had not felt well. She tired easily, and had very little appetite. She prayed mightily that her symptoms resulted from too many hours at work, and the relentlessly cold, snowy winter, but deep inside she knew her path in life was about to take an unwanted detour and there was nothing she could do to change its direction.

Promptly at seven the following morning, Patrick arrived at Charlie Murphy's Bar, slipped into the side room, and settled himself before Mr. Callahan and his friend, Tom Aherne. Callahan had ordered

Patrick breakfast and a beer so they would waste no time getting down to business. As Patrick devoured his bacon and eggs, he learned the business entailed raising money in America for a group of underground patriots in Ireland to obtain the guns and ammunition needed to fight off the Brits.

It was common knowledge among the Irish in New York City that the freedom fighters in Ireland depended upon them for money to advance their cause, but actually meeting men brave enough to engage in this risky business left Patrick's heart pumping with pride. Of course, he told Callahan, he would do anything to help the cause. But first Patrick would be required to swear a pledge of his loyalty before the other members of their group, and he readily agreed.

Things were looking up for Patrick, and for the first time in his life he felt important. The pride of being accepted into such a prominent group of men brought a twinkle to his eyes, and he left the bar with his shoulders straightened and a purposeful look on his face, wanting desperately to brag of his new endeavor to Nancy. For now, however, he would remain quiet. But someday she would learn her husband was much more than a lowly night watchman.

Aunt May left the kitchen just in time to see Patrick strutting jauntily out the bar door and wondered what brought this new air of self-confidence to the man.

Mr. Murphy gave May a cheery smile from behind the bar, and asked that she keep him company for a bit before resuming her kitchen chores.

"And how are you today, my pretty lass?"

A pink flush appeared on May's face. She had been told by Nancy she seemed ten years younger since escaping the stress of working for Mrs. Birmingham, and after discovering how henna dye could miraculously restore her graying hair to its original reddish hue.

"I'm quite well, Mr. Murphy. And you?"

"I would feel a lot better if ye'd stop calling me Mr. Murphy and use me given names, Charles. Or Charlie, as I'm known to me friends."

May decided she would call him Charles. "It suits you better; more aristocratic." Now it was Mr. Murphy's turn to blush, if he could have, but he took the compliment graciously and told May, "From now on to you I will be Charles."

He asked about Nancy, observing how she seemed a bit off her stride lately, but noting that her piano playing and singing had brought in quite a number of new customers. May confided that Nancy and Patrick's marriage seemed a bit rocky at the moment, but she had confidence their differences would be resolved in time. And she would resist her impulse to voice her opinions, and let them solve their problems by themselves.

Charles Murphy mentioned there was a dance at the Knights of Columbus hall next week, and asked if May would accompany him. "We work so hard. Don't we deserve a night out on the town?"

"I haven't danced since I left Ireland," May observed, glowing. "And I'd love to try it again, fer sure. But now it's time for me to start cooking, Charles."

Patrick attended Mr. Callahan's meeting in a small apartment, not far from his own. Seven men stared stonily at him while he swore his allegiance on the Bible, learned the secret passwords, and was taught the fellowship's handshake. They then all clasped his hand and accepted him into the New York City division of the friends of the Irish Republican Brotherhood. His duties in the organization would eventually be revealed, and he must be ready to carry out orders when directed. The men stood and toasted, "Here's to Charles Stewart Parnell and the Land League!"

Patrick accepted all the conditions of his initiation, and left the meeting room feeling like a true son of Erin, ready to defend the old country at all cost. He now had a purpose in life, and had found people who would appreciate his talents and efforts. Nancy might be the queen of Murphy's Bar, but he was a warrior in Callahan's army.

Chapter 8

THE ENCOUNTER

January 1892

Neither the Lallys nor May could decipher the words on the cross, so Nancy brought it to Mr. Murphy. But he also was of no use, as when he was a lad in school the British had forbidden the teaching of Ireland's native tongue, and English was spoken except for a few isolated areas in the West.

Mr. Murphy put two glasses of beer and a cup of tea on a tray and bid Nancy take them to the customers at the table by the windows. The tray almost slipped out of her trembling hands as she looked upon Matthew Clarke. Jesus, Mary and Joseph, she whispered. After all these years the teacher's son is back. And with a woman. Probably his wife. Dear God, give me strength. And, please God, make my hands stop shaking. I can't let him see me this way. I am Nancy O'Leary. I have my pride. I must remember that and show him I have done very well without him.

She lingered by the bar, slowly rearranging the beers and tea cup on the tray waiting for her heart to stop racing and her breathing to return to normal. When she felt ready, she walked smartly to the table and lay down the drinks before Matthew and his friends.

Matthew perfunctorily said, "Thank you," then bolted upright in his chair. "It's you!"

"And so it is. And I suppose you are the Matthew Clarke whom I thought must have drowned in the Johnstown flood some years ago," she replied.

"Yes …, no …," he stammered. "I did not die. But many others did. But I'm forgetting my manners. Dr. Weitz, this is Mary Alice O'Laoghaire. Mary Alice, this is Rachel, Dr. Weitz's daughter. Mary Alice and I traveled over on the same boat from Ireland a few years ago."

Dr. Weitz asked if she had time to sit with them for a bit, as the bar did not seem too busy.

"That I will, if you'll just give me a minute to fetch a cup of tea."

When she returned, now fully composed, she explained she was, thanks to the ignorance of the men at immigrations on how to spell her Gaelic name, now known as Nancy O'Leary.

"Well," said Dr. Weitz, "this really is a special occasion. My daughter's birthday, and the reunion of old friends. Let me toast you all. Le'Chayim." Without thinking, Matthew responded "Thank you" in Gaelic.

"Do you speak Gaelic?" Nancy asked Matthew.

"Just enough to please my father. Do you remember I told you he was a school teacher?"

"I remember quite a bit of what you told me."

Rachel looked from Matthew to Nancy, and her chest began to tighten as she observed they had been more than just strangers on a ship.

"So, do you now live in New York?" Nancy inquired.

Matthew responded affirmatively, and told her briefly of his time with Mr. Grunwald, and his now being trained by Dr. Weitz.

"So, you're to be a doctor?" she asked with obvious admiration.

"Yes, and I see you've gotten out of Tuxedo Park to a better job."

"It's not just a job I have here. I'm part owner of this bar." Now it was Matthew's turn to be impressed, and he praised her ingenuity and hard work.

"Speaking of which, I must get back to my duties. But could I ask a favor of you, Mr. Clarke?"

"Anything," he replied.

Nancy took the cross from her pocket and asked if Matthew could translate the Gaelic inscription. He carefully examined the back and front of the cross.

"The words are engraved in very small letters," he said, as he held it up close to his eyes. "Yes, I think I can read it, but it seems very odd and does not make much sense to me."

"Matthew, get on with it please," she urged. "What does it say?" Nancy took a pencil and bill pad from her pocket and wrote the words as he spoke.

"God bless you, my son, Patrick. Dig behind gravestone…"

"Go on!" Nancy pressed him.

"Give me a minute, will you? I'm trying my best."

"Well try harder."

Matthew gave her a warning glance and proceeded to figure out the remaining words. "I think it reads, 'Dig behind gravestone of Ellen Flynn, Knock Churchyard, County Mayo'."

"What do you make of it, Matthew?" asked Nancy.

He thought for a moment, then ventured a guess.

"Something of value must be buried behind a tombstone in Ireland, and it belongs to the owner of the cross, who apparently is named Patrick."

"Thank you, Matthew," Nancy said as she took the cross from Matthew's hands. "And in honor of Rachel's birthday, dinner tonight will be on the house. I recommend the leg of lamb, and not just because I cooked it myself. But now I must get back to work."

As she stood to leave, Dr. Weitz and Rachel expressed their happiness at meeting her. Nancy thanked Matthew for the information he had given her, and the look on Matthew's face as Nancy strode briskly back to the kitchen forced Rachel to accept that this woman exerted more power over Matthew than she, and the time had arrived for her to face the reality that the problems between her and Matthew were insurmountable. It was not only religion that would keep them apart. He was in love with another woman.

The interaction between the three young people had not escaped Dr. Weitz's attention, and he inwardly breathed a deep sigh of relief. He had watched the growing affection between Matthew and his daughter with some concern, but he wisely kept out of it, knowing life seemed to have a way of working things out. He had come to love Matthew as a son, but was reluctant to face the difficulties entailed with his becoming a son-in-law. Now he must see to it that

Rachel worked fewer hours, and introduce her to eligible young Jewish men. It was time for his daughter to marry and provide him with grandchildren.

After they finished dinner, Nancy brought a small cake to their table, and instructed Rachel to make a secret wish and blow out the candle. Rachel closed her eyes for a moment and prayed that Matthew would lose his affection for Nancy. But even if her wish were fulfilled, she knew a Jewish woman could find no future with a Catholic man.

The next afternoon, Matthew left Dr. Weitz's office on the pretext of having his hair cut at the local barber shop, and made his way swiftly to Murphy's Bar. He waited until Nancy finished serving drinks to a nearby table, and then approached her.

"I must talk to you. Can we go outside for a few minutes?"

She glanced at the few patrons in the room and said, "Yes. This is a good time."

They stood together on the sidewalk, Nancy looking sternly up at the tall fair-haired man. "Well, what is it you want to say?"

"Why did you never answer my letters?"

"Because I never received any letters from you. I wrote you once, and you did not reply."

Matthew looked confused. "But I sent them to the Tuxedo Park address you gave me. Four letters I wrote. The postal service never returned them. How could that be, Mary Alice?"

It had become clear to her a while back. She told him how her name had been changed at immigration, but with all her work and

113

exhaustion she'd forgotten about it and the name she handed Matthew on the boat. Once in New York she realized her mistake and that Mrs. Birmingham would not recognize the name Mary Alice O'Laoghaire, and probably threw out his letters. By then it was too late.

"Well, please don't think badly of me. Nancy, as I'll now call you. I did not forget you. And now that we've found each other again, would you have dinner with me? And would you attend a dance with me?"

Tears of anger and frustration filled her eyes.

"What is it Nancy?"

She bitterly spit out the words, "I'm married."

"But you can't be!"

"I thought you were dead, or had forgotten about me. And there's something else." She hesitated, hung her head, and barely audibly whispered, "I'm with child."

He groaned, then slammed his hand against the building and silently cursed man and God. "Well, I suppose that settles things. But are you certain? Are you positive? Have you been to a doctor?"

"Not yet, but I am fairly sure," she answered.

Regaining his composure, and remembering his profession, he ordered her to see Dr. Weitz the following day.

"How far on do you think you are?"

"Exactly two months."

"How can you be so sure?"

"There was only one occasion."

"Ah, so you don't love him, do you?" Matthew sighed.

"No," she confessed, and regretted the tendency to bluntness she had never been able to overcome.

"God forgive me, but I'm glad of that. Now let me see that you're taken care of."

Mr. Murphy interrupted them by beckoning Nancy from the front door of the tavern to come in and attend to her duties. Matthew handed her Dr. Weitz's card and told her to be at his office at three o'clock the next day, turned, and walked dejectedly back to his office.

Dr. Weitz examined Nancy privately, asked a few questions, and then confirmed she would bear a child in seven months. She felt none of the elation typical of a mother-to-be; only sadness that this child would bind her forever to Patrick.

Matthew saw to it that he was not present when she visited Dr. Weitz. He sat in a nearby park and tried to find a solution to the impossible problem he faced, but could come up with no answer.

Nancy walked slowly back to the bar, her emotions in turmoil. She had been wrong about both Matthew and Patrick; Matthew did care for her, and Patrick had proved quite lacking as a husband. She had prided herself on her ability to recognize worth and character in those she encountered, but in the most important decision of her life, her instincts had failed her. Must she remain forever tied to Patrick? Or could she somehow find a way to release herself from this drunken, fallen-away Catholic, who in two minutes had fathered her child and unalterably changed the course of her life.

In the kitchen, May was busy cutting onions and carrots for the evening's beef stew. Her now red hair was on top of her head, and beneath her apron she wore a new lime green dress that accentuated her still girlish figure. Nancy had been so involved with her own life she had not noticed that May had become quite a fashionable woman.

The sight of her niece alarmed her. "What is it, Nancy? You look awful. Are you sick?"

"I'm heartsick is what I am. In seven months I will be having a baby."

May thought that wonderful news, and took Nancy's hands and began spouting off all the items they must buy, and where the crib should be placed, and how happy Patrick must be with the news.

"He doesn't know yet. I've just come from the doctor. I had to be certain before I told him. What am I going to do, Aunt May? What about my job? I've worked so hard to make the tavern a success, and now I'll have to leave and give up all I've accomplished. And Lord knows we need the money I make here. Yes, I am heartsick."

May thought quickly. "Well, you could work until your sixth month at least, then we would hire a temporary waitress, and two months after the baby is born you could return to the tavern."

"One month!" Nancy interrupted her, beaming with new-found optimism.

May agreed, and continued. May would work at the tavern mornings and lunch, then come home and take care of the child while Nancy handled dinner and the music hour. The plan sounded plausible, and Nancy felt a great relief that at least one problem had been solved.

But she kept her most important problem to herself: Matthew Clarke.

Matthew worked harder and put in longer hours than ever before, and Dr. Weitz's impression of the young man's talents and dedication prompted him to consult his colleagues on the procedures to enroll his protégé in medical school. He inquired about the entrance examination and knew Matthew could easily pass the test, despite his lack of formal education, and with the help of the doctor's influential friends, Matthew was accepted to Bellevue Medical College, not far from Dr. Weitz's home.

Matthew was elated, but shook his head sadly. "I haven't the money for tuition," he anguished.

"My boy, I have discussed that problem with certain friends, and they agreed to provide you with a loan, with a low interest rate, to be paid back after you begin your own practice."

"But they don't even know me."

"Ah, but they know me, and trust my judgment. And you will continue to live here and help me when necessary. And I will hear no more from you on the matter. It has been decided."

Matthew sat across the desk from Dr. Weitz, with his elbows on the table, and rested his chin in the palms of his hands. "I have no words to express my gratitude," he spoke slowly. "I have done nothing to deserve what you have done for me."

"You have done nothing to deserve this?" The doctor interrupted him. "Have you forgotten you saved me from choking to death on that salmon bone? And how many lives you saved in Johnstown in the flood? Or how you risked your life while protecting Rachel from

117

that drunken gang member in my waiting room? That man could easily have stabbed you, but you showed no hesitation in rescuing my daughter. You have been a faithful assistant to me in my practice, and you are a good person. Are those not enough reasons for me to help a brilliant young man join the ranks of the medical profession?"

"But, Rachel…"

Dr. Weitz cut Matthew off saying, "Do you not think I have eyes in my head? You and Rachel were not meant to be. She will meet some nice Jewish boy and marry. But you and Nancy? I do not know what will become of you two."

"She's married," Matthew confessed.

"Then I feel very sorry for you. In time, work will ease your loss. For now, you must concentrate on perfecting your skills. Most importantly, your surgical skills. After observing you these months I feel that should be your area of specialty. And Bellevue Hospital will provide you with many opportunities to become proficient in the art of cutting and sewing."

Dr. Weitz went to a cabinet behind his desk, took out two glasses and a bottle of red wine. As he poured, he told Matthew, "Life does not always turn out as we wish, but God has a plan for every one of us. We must trust in His judgment. Le'Chayim."

"Go raibh maith agaibh."

Matthew received top grades on the entrance examinations at Bellevue Medical College, and shortly thereafter began the grueling schedule of all day classes, studying at home every night, and assisting Dr. Weitz on weekends when needed. He saw very little of

Rachel. Their encounters were limited to dinner, at which there was very little conversation between them. Matthew noticed some young men appearing at the house on weekends to escort Rachel, to where he knew not. But her mournful eyes, whenever she looked his way, left him with pangs of guilt. He had unwittingly led her to believe they might have a future together.

Matthew stopped at Murphy's Bar & Grille weekly to speak with Nancy, inquiring after her health and updating her on his progress at Bellevue. His longing for her made it necessary to at least look upon her and hear her voice occasionally.

At first she resented seeing him, because after he left she would spend days bemoaning her fate. But she soon came to look forward to his visits, and if he missed a week she became downhearted and longed for the sight of his smiling eyes as he went on with enthusiasm about cutting open the human body. She tried following his conversation, but her eyes moved from his taut body to his flaxen hair and angular features. She thought him the most perfect creature God had ever created.

Chapter 9

THE MISSION

February 1892

Nancy woke Patrick on Sunday morning after she and May returned from Mass, and told him she had several things of importance to discuss.

"Can I at least have me coffee first?"

She brought him a cup and he sat up in bed, his dark hair matted and the bags under his eyes becoming more pronounced each month. Oh why, she thought, did I marry this poor excuse for a man.

"Well, get on with it," he said.

She told him briefly of meeting Matthew Clarke at Murphy's Bar and his translating the words on the cross.

"Dig behind a grave? Now what would that mean?" He asked.

"I've given it a lot of thought and came to the conclusion that your natural father must have put the cross around your neck before you were adopted. And that he might have hidden something of value for you behind the grave of Ellen Flynn, who was probably related to you."

"Something of value, ye say?" She now had his attention.

"It must be if your father went to the trouble of having the cross inscribed in tiny Gaelic letters. Should the cross fall into the wrong hands, the message would not be easily deciphered."

"Ah, it's probably just a letter apologizing fer giving me up."

"He could have given a letter to the nuns for your new parents to hand you when you were grown. The man thought this out carefully. I think he wanted to give you some sort of legacy."

"I'll think about it. Now, what's the next thing yer going to tell me?"

"I'm having a baby."

"A baby! Now that's grand, it is. I'm to be a father. Ye've given me the best of news, me darlin'. Ah, yes. Now ye can leave Murphy's Bar and be home where I can catch a glimpse of ye more than thirty minutes a day. This is lovely news." The man beamed with delight.

"But I plan to work as long as I can. My singing brings in more customers every week and then I earn more money from my twenty percent of the profits. And with a baby on the way, we'll need as much money as I can make."

"Is money the only thing that matters to ye?"

"Well, it has to matter to one of us, and I don't see you out searching for a better paying job. I came to America to raise myself up and that I will do, whether it suits you or not."

Patrick thought for a moment. He did not bring enough money into the household as befitted a husband with a child on the way and that shamed him. Maybe the cross did hold the key to a small inheritance.

"I want to meet this Dr. Clarke who read the cross and talk to him meself," he demanded.

"I'll tell him your highness requests his presence immediately," she retorted.

Their tempers were rising to a dangerous height, and as Nancy stood up to leave the room, Patrick remembered to ask when the baby would arrive.

"Seven months from now," she said, and slammed the door behind her.

She tried to calm the rage within her; the anger at the manner in which Patrick blithely dismissed her carefully thought out analysis of the enigma of the cross, and then his self-centered reaction to their becoming parents. He had not even asked about her physical condition; his major concern seemed to be that having a child would leave her more time to wait on him.

He is a selfish man, she thought. And yes, I will have him meet Matthew and put him face to face with a real man of substance, not a whimpering, lazy drunkard like himself. And she would be certain to attend this meeting of the prince and the frog, and enjoy seeing dull Patrick squirm in the presence of genius.

That night, as she lay under the comforter, she examined her conscience and asked God to forgive her sins, and grant her the grace to accept the fate she had freely chosen. Her union with Patrick made before a priest in the sacrament of marriage could not be dissolved. By lusting after another man, she had broken a commandment. God, please help me, she begged, to be a better wife and free me of this passion for Matthew that holds me so tightly in its grip. Sleep did not come easily, and she awoke tired and anxious. She must go to church on Saturday and confess her sins.

Eight men were sitting around a long, narrow table as Patrick entered the room. Mr. Callahan called the meeting to order. The men recited the secret oath in unison, and then Callahan spoke.

"The men in the West of Ireland are ready. All they need is money and arms. Thanks to the faithful sons of Erin in New York, a great deal of money has been collected. Once it's delivered to our Irish brothers, they will obtain guns and ammunition from our French comrades. Now what we need is a volunteer to escort the money to Ireland. The trip back and forth will take almost three weeks, if all goes as expected. And the volunteer must leave New York in two weeks hence. Is there anyone here with enough strength to take on this mission?"

The men looked down at the table, their hands clenched before them. Most of them had families to provide for and their jobs did not allow for a sudden three-week vacation.

"Speak up. Is there no one among ye who can meet the challenge?"

Patrick realized the cross provided him with a legitimate reason to return to Ireland, and spontaneously stood up, sending his chair tumbling backward in his haste, and announced he would proudly transport the money to his native land.

Mr. Callahan stared him in the eye and asked if he were certain he was up to the assignment.

"As long as ye give me the proper instructions and the money for the boat passage, I'm yer man."

"But you cannot tell anyone, not even yer wife. Do you agree to that?" asked Callahan.

"I rule the roost in my house, and I'll tell her I'm visiting me mother."

"And what about your job?"

"I'll tell them me mother's gravely ill, and I must see her one more time. And if they won't grant me leave, I'll quit."

The tips of Callahan's black moustache turned up as he smiled at Patrick, and told the men to stand and applaud Mr. Patrick Devlin for his devotion to the cause and his courage to take on this risky task.

Patrick basked in the approval from his new-found friends, and never felt as proud of himself as he did at that moment. Callahan opened a bottle of whiskey and the men, with drinks in hand, toasted their new comrade with cheers.

"Here's to you, Patrick," said one. "God bless you," cried another. "You're a true Irishman," toasted Callahan.

Then Callahan got down to business and told Patrick, "You will board a ship for Ireland two weeks from today. You'll be met at the port in Cork by one of our men. You will wear an orange bandana around your neck, provided by me, so our contract will recognize you. The bandana will be in the pocket of a jacket, also provided by me. But before you do anything, wait until the man asks you a question. If you do not give the correct answer, I suggest you run for your life. Otherwise, accompany the man to a safe house and hand over the jacket. The money's been sewn into the jacket lining.

Another coat will be given you to wear back home. Do you have any questions?"

Patrick's bravado began to leave him, and he waited to hear the question and answer, knowing his life might depend upon his remembering them exactly. But Callahan said he would give Patrick the code, with the bandana and the jacket, at the bar at lunch on the day of his departure. Patrick was thanked again by all, and Callahan adjourned the meeting.

Nancy stopped at Dr. Weitz's home and slipped a note under the door addressed to Matthew.

Dear Matthew,

I do not wish to inconvenience you, but would it be possible for you to come to the bar tomorrow morning about seven before you go to class? My husband would like to discuss your Gaelic translation of the cross. The meeting would not take long, and I would appreciate if you could bring this mystery to a close. Thank you. Nancy.

At seven the next morning Nancy, Patrick and Matthew arrived at the bar and took a table in the corner. Aunt May was behind the bar preparing for the day's customers. Nancy gripped her hands on her lap and unconsciously twisted her wedding band. Her nerves were frayed, and she prayed Patrick would not make too big a fool of himself, or that he would notice the feelings existing between her and Matthew.

"So, ye met me wife on the boat from Ireland, did ye? Ye have to admit, she's a beauty, she is. I told her when she left Tuxedo Park to be careful of the men in New York, that they'd all be after her."

"Mr. Devlin, I assumed you wanted to discuss the cross," said Matthew.

"Aye, that I do, and call me Patrick. Nancy, tell the doctor...."

"I am not a doctor yet Patrick, only a student. Call me Matthew."

"Well, that's just a matter of time," said Patrick. "Nancy, explain to Matthew yer idea of what the message means and see if he agrees."

Matthew felt uncomfortable with Patrick, the father of the child Nancy carried, and wished to be out the door and free of him. But his curiosity overcame his revulsion. He must learn more about the man who had married Nancy.

Nancy told Matthew that she only lately became aware that Patrick had been adopted from a Magdalen House in Dublin, and surmised his actual father gave the cross to the nuns running the home to give to the adoptive parents to present to Patrick when he came of age.

Patrick was impatient. "So Nancy tells me ye think there might be something valuable buried behind a tombstone?"

"There very well could be. But there might be several Ellen Flynn's buried in Knock Church Yard. It's a common name in Mayo."

Patrick, who was from Dublin and unfamiliar with the west of Ireland, asked how long the journey from Cork Harbor to Knock would take. Nancy was stunned. Did the man actually plan to leave her here pregnant, and go hopping over to Ireland for a month? But she kept quiet and listened.

"Can you ride a horse?" Matthew asked him.

"Of course I can. Can't every Irishman?"

Matthew held his temper and estimated the trip to be a bit over a hundred and fifty miles. "Depending on how many hours you ride a day, and the stamina of your horse, and the weather, of course. It could probably take a few days. Now tell me how you propose to dig around graves and not be noticed and thrown in jail. You know Knock Church is where the miracle occurred."

"Of course I know that. The Virgin and some saints appeared to the villagers."

"And you know pilgrims come from all over to see the shrine?"

"So?" questioned Patrick.

"The graveyard is right next to the church. Aren't you afraid you'll be noticed?"

Patrick pulled on his ear lobe and thought a moment. "I'll dig at night!" he announced.

Matthew began to find perverse enjoyment in the conversation. "And you think a man wandering through the cemetery at night carrying a lamp will go unnoticed?"

Little beads of sweat appeared on Patrick's brow. This man created more problems than he solved, he thought, so I'll let the good doctor figure it out fer me.

"So, Matthew, how would ye go about it?"

"I would go in broad daylight, maybe on a Sunday after Mass when the parishioners are visiting the graves of their dearly departed. I would carry a bouquet of flowers, and walk slowly through the cemetery until I found a tombstone engraved 'Ellen Flynn,' then place the flowers behind the stone, kneel, and remove the small spade I carried in my pocket. I would assume a position of grief, and with one arm around the tombstone, dig into the earth. If anyone caught me, I would manage to shed a few tears and confess my Aunt Ellen's superstitious nature, and how she feared flowers appearing before her grave would attract evil spirits and they would never let her rest in peace. You know the Irish, Patrick. They would find that explanation quite plausible and give you their blessing.

"If I found nothing buried there, I would plant a few flowers and find the next Ellen Flynn. If I were caught again, I would say that in my haste to pay tribute to my beloved relative, I misread the date of her death, and planted the flowers at a stranger's grave. But I doubt anyone would have the time or inclination to question me. They would consider me an eccentric, grief-ridden man and pray that God would grant me peace and restore my sanity. When I discovered my quest, I would quickly put it in my coat pocket, cover the hole with dirt, and get the hell out of there."

"Brilliant, Matthew, perfectly brilliant," said Nancy.

Patrick reluctantly admitted to himself that she was right, but still resented her enthusiasm in praising Matthew's powers of deduction. He tried to find a flaw in the doctor's plan, but nothing came to mind.

"Well, I'll think it over, but I thank ye fer yer advice."

As Matthew stood up to leave, two men suddenly burst into the tavern and approached Aunt May at the bar. They were obviously inebriated after a long night of revelry, and demanded a bottle of whiskey. May produced it and said "That will be two dollars, please."

"There will be no dollars, lady," growled the tall, burly man. "Don't ye know who we are?"

Aunt May innocently replied, "It's the same price for everyone. We don't give credit."

After watching the encounter, Matthew moved towards her. "May, let the men have the whiskey."

But Patrick, enraged by their attempt at thievery, rushed towards them and yelled, "Get the bloody hell out of here!"

The tall man backed away from Patrick and picked up a bar stool, and as May ducked down, he flung it over the bar and smashed half the mirror, showering shards of glass down upon May, now cowering on the floor.

Matthew grabbed Patrick's arm and shoved him back into his chair, and authoritatively ordered the hoodlums to take the whiskey and leave. "Take the bottle and get out! I know who you are."

The short man spoke up. "At least there's one smart Irishman in this joint," and the pair took the bottle and stumbled out the door.

Matthew ran behind the bar and helped the whimpering May up to a seated position. Her hair and face were covered with bits of glass, many of which had become embedded in her skin.

"Nancy, get me a clean cloth and some hot water," he ordered. Then Matthew dabbed at the drops of blood dripping down May's face. He called for Patrick to give him a hand, and they carried the moaning woman to a chair.

"May, May, you'll be all right," Patrick comforted her. "There, there, I'll get ye some water."

"I need my instruments to remove the glass from her face," Matthew said, and Nancy offered to go to Dr. Weitz's house and retrieve his medical bag.

"Good girl," Matthew smiled up at her while treating May's wounds. Mr. Murphy arrived as Nancy rushed out the door, took in the destruction of his bar and May's condition, and ran to her side.

"What's happened here?"

"The Short-Tail Gang," Matthew spat out.

Patrick went to the door and yelled back, "I'm getting Officer Lally."

Charlie Murphy dropped to his knees before May, took her hand, and held it to his face.

"Oh, darlin', darlin', what have they done to you? I'll kill every last one of those low-life bastards! Now the good doctor here will fix ye up, May, don't despair. Doctor, can I give her a wee bit of sherry?"

"Better make it a brandy. There's a lot of glass to be removed."

Nancy returned with Matthew's instrument bag within fifteen minutes, and the doctor tweezed the numerous shards of glass out of May's face and arms, applied an antiseptic, and bandaged the wounds, leaving her covered with small white squares resembling postage stamps.

Patrick barged into the tavern, Officer Lally at his side, and with outstretched arms cried, "Look at what they've done! Ye must arrest 'em and put 'em in prison where they belong."

Officer Lally was well aware of the Gang's history, and its ability to avoid being incarcerated by instilling terror, not only in the citizens, but in the police and judges as well. But they committed this crime on his own people who Officer Lally knew and loved, good God-fearing people who had never harmed anyone. If he could be assured of his friends' cooperation, he would vigorously pursue the criminals and try to put an end to their wanton lawlessness.

He asked if all present would agree to identify the criminals at the police station and then testify in court. He warned them that it might provoke others in the Gang to seek revenge, and they must consider their response carefully. In the anger of the moment, all the witnesses agreed to fight the Gang and bring them to justice. The officer praised their bravery, and instructed them to appear at the station house the next day to look at photographs of suspects and identify the two Irish thugs who perpetrated this crime on their own people. He assured his friends that if they were brave enough to stand up to the Gang, he would use all his powers to bring them down.

Charles Murphy remained at May's side, comforting her. "Are ye in much pain, darlin'?"

"Charles, the only pain is to me pride having you see me this way, lookin' like a patch work quilt."

He laughed, and said, "May, no matter what, yer always beautiful in my eyes. And to prove it, I'm going to jump the gun, as they say here in America, and ask you something I planned to do next month." Still down on his knees before May, he took her hands in his and said, "Would you do a worthless Irishman the great honor of becoming his wife?"

"Charles, yer never to call yerself worthless." And then with tears in her eyes she responded, "If ye can ask fer me hand, in the condition you find me in now, you are a prince among men, and I humbly accept yer proposal with love and gratitude, and I will be the best wife any man ever had."

Charles kissed her hand and stood up, calling everyone to attention. "I have an announcement to make. Miss May O'Connor has just this minute agreed to be me bride."

Everyone clapped and offered congratulations. Nancy, stunned by the news, wondered what would become of their plan to take turns watching her new baby. May would move into Mr. Murphy's house, leaving Nancy alone with her child. But she quickly chastised herself for being so self-centered, and rejoiced in her aunt's happiness.

May noticed the look of concern cross Nancy's face and called her to come sit beside her. "Don't you worry, Nancy. I remember our arrangement. And after I marry Charles, it's just a good stretch of the legs from his place to yours, and our plans about the baby haven't changed. Ye didn't think I'd let ya down after all ye've done fer me now, did you? After all, tis you who found me a husband."

Nancy put her arms gently around her aunt and whispered, "Thank you. I love you more than you will ever know."

At the police station the following day, the witnesses appeared to examine photographs of possible suspects. All were able to identify the two men from the many pictures they were shown. A complaint was filed, and Officer Lally obtained a warrant for their arrest. He suggested that Charles Murphy put new locks on the door and only allow known customers into the tavern, as other gang members might very likely attempt to extract retribution. They were accustomed to getting away with their crimes. He instructed his friends to individually write down the sequence of events and have all their stories match so the defense attorney could not trip them up. He would ask the district attorney to begin the trial as soon as possible.

On the way back to the Bar, noticing that Patrick was engaged in conversation with Officer Lally, Matthew took Nancy aside and warned her to be vigilant.

"The Short-Tail Gang members would kill their own mothers to save their hides. So tomorrow morning I am bringing you a small pistol to keep in your pocket in case of an emergency."

"But I've never fired a gun before, and if I did try I'd probably shoot myself instead of the intruder."

"I'll give you a quick lesson on how to use it tomorrow. It's really very easy, and I'd feel much better knowing you can protect yourself." He reached for her hand and smiled down at his little Irish colleen, her auburn hair disheveled after running to retrieve his medical bag and her dress splattered with her Aunt's blood, and said "I won't have you taken from me by a drunken murderer."

It slowly dawned on Patrick that his mission was to begin in a few weeks and he might not be in New York for the trial. But he rationalized there were enough witnesses to testify and his absence would not affect the case. He contacted his employer at the Triangle Shirt Waist Factory, requesting three weeks leave, which was promptly denied, and was told he would be fired if he did not show up for work. Well, he thought, there are lots of jobs to be had, and he would find a new one when he returned from Ireland. Mr. Callahan would certainly obtain a position for him after he successfully completed his assignment.

That evening Nancy received a letter from her sister, Norah, in Ireland.

Dear Mary Alice,

It's a bad state I'm in. Da's to marry the widow Finnegan. You remember her. The husband Joseph farmed two miles up the road. He passed on last year and the landlord is repossessing the farm. Da has taken up with the dead man's wife, Bernadette. She's a nasty piece of work when out of Da's view, and no matter how hard I try to be nice, the woman can't seem to stomach me. Fer sure she's out to find a husband, and to tell the truth, she's not hard to look at, and has wrapped dad around her little finger. Please rescue me. Da thinks I'm daft when I tell him Bernadette is just after someone to put a roof over her head and food on the table. Can ye help me? I know Bernadette will find a way to put me out. Herself is determined to be mistress of the household and makes it very clear she doesn't need the likes of me about.

Can I come to America and stay with you? I'll work at anything to pay fer me keep. But I do need ye to send me passage money. I pray ye can post it to me at the earliest, as I must get away before I lose my temper and haul off at the nasty biddy.

The brothers are in good health and Bernadette puts on a good face fer them. I guess because they tend the farm, she'll accept them, but she doesn't take kindly to the idea of two women in the kitchen.

Please help me, Mary Alice. God Bless. Your loving sister, Norah.

The next day Nancy withdrew money from her bank account and sent Norah her passage, telling her after she booked the first ship available, to write her immediately and she would meet her at Ellis Island and bring her to safety at her home in New York.

At six o'clock that evening, Bill Peyton, Nancy's lawyer, arrived at the Bar. Nancy spied him standing at the doorway and approached him.

"Well," she said smiling, "It's about time you showed up. Mr. Murphy and I have been waiting to repay you for drawing up our contract. Follow me."

Bill grinned at the assertive co-owner as she led him to a table near the piano. "I've been very busy, Nancy, or I would have been here weeks ago."

"Well, sit yourself down and I'll bring you the Irish whisky you ordered last we met. And," she said gently, "it is good to see you again."

She returned with his drink and sat down beside him. "Now, what's been keeping you so busy that you couldn't find time to visit us?"

"Oh, contracts, loan agreements, wills, and all sorts of boring legal matters I won't bother you with." Bill glanced around the restaurant and complimented her on the décor and the gleaming floors and sparkling windows and mirrors.

"Mr. Murphy knew what he was doing when he made you a partner. I stopped in here a year ago and the place was so dismal I never came back."

"Well, now I hope to see you every week. And after you taste my cooking, I have no doubt you'll become a regular customer."

Suddenly Patrick emerged from Callahan's side room where he had been fortifying himself with whisky and beer, and spied his wife sitting next to an attractive man, nattily dressed in an expensive suit and silk tie. He proceeded to their table and pulled up a chair.

"So, Nancy, are ye going to introduce me to yer friend here?"

She tried to hide her annoyance and anxiety at the state of her husband, who obviously had imbibed too many drinks, and pleasantly said, "Patrick, this is Mr. William Peyton, Esquire, the lawyer who drew up my contract with Mr. Murphy. Bill, this is Patrick Devlin, my husband."

Bill offered his hand to Patrick, who ignored the gesture, and instead took a swig of his drink.

"So," Patrick said to Nancy, "Mr. Peyton's a lawyer, now is he. Ye certainly have made yerself a lot of fancy friends, doctors and lawyers, and maybe ye have some politicians and bankers ye haven't told me about, eh?"

Bill Peyton stood up and apologized for having to leave, but just remembered he had an appointment with a client.

"Goodbye, Mr. Devlin. It was very interesting meeting you. Nancy, tell Mr. Murphy I'll be back for dinner next week." And with that he left the restaurant, avoiding an inevitable scene with Nancy's drunken husband.

Nancy pushed her chair out from the table, gave Patrick a scathing stare, and returned to the kitchen, thoroughly disgusted by his behavior and the insinuation he made about her character to Bill

Peyton. Though she had never loved Patrick, she once respected and liked him. Now she felt nothing for him but loathing.

Chapter 10

THE CONFESSION

March, 1892

True to his word, Matthew arrived at the bar the next morning at eight and found Nancy alone, setting up the coffee and tea urns. She locked the door behind him and nervously led him back to the kitchen. Matthew reached into his jacket and handed Nancy a small packet of herbs.

"This will help your nausea," he said, and then retrieved a small pocket gun and held it out to her. She recoiled in fear.

"I can't take it. It might go off by mistake and kill someone."

He reassured her and showed Nancy how to put the bullets in the chamber and use the safety catch. Matthew told her she must know how to protect herself and her friends should the Short-Tail Gang attack again. He patiently taught her how to work the trigger, then how to aim the gun and shoot. She took the pistol and repeated his instructions until she felt comfortable enough with her ability to use the weapon properly.

An insistent knock on the door startled them. Matthew put three more bullets in Nancy's hand, she dropped them into her skirt pocket, and they left the kitchen to see who had interrupted their pistol lesson.

Nancy unlocked the door and in strode Patrick. He had just left his night watchman's job and was ready for his beers and breakfast. Patrick looked from Nancy to Matthew, and the tension between them was palpable, until Matthew greeted him heartily and congratulated him on his upcoming fatherhood.

"Dr. Weitz asked me to bring Nancy some ginger root powder to help relieve her morning sickness. Now Nancy, be sure you take a half teaspoon when you feel nausea coming on, but not more often than every four hours. Now I must get to the hospital. Good to see you again, Patrick. Take care of the little woman." And Matthew left them, hating himself for his obsequious behavior, hating to have to leave Nancy, but most of all, hating the intolerable situation in which he found himself.

While Nancy poured Patrick a beer, he looked carefully at her and slowly said, "I see you've taken Officer Lally's advice."

"About what, Patrick?"

"Keeping the door locked."

Nancy's heart skipped a beat at the hidden implication behind his comment.

"I thought it prudent to follow his suggestion."

"Aye, so it is. And wasn't it gentlemanly of the good doctor to personally deliver your medicine from the old kike?"

"Don't you ever refer to Dr. Weitz that way again. He's a good man. And Matthew did not go out of his way. He just stopped off here on his way up to Bellevue Hospital."

Nancy felt she must change the subject quickly, as Patrick's suspicions of her and Matthew were making her acutely uncomfortable.

"Have you thought any more about the cross?"

"Oh, yes," he said, with a noticeable improvement in his mood. "And I've been meanin' to tell ya what I've decided. In two weeks or so I'll set sail for the old country and follow the good doctor's advice and find out fer meself what's buried behind that grave."

Nancy, stunned by his announcement, sputtered, "You'll leave me while I'm with child?"

"Well, do ye think it better I go after the birth and leave ye alone with a babe to tend? And aren't ye the one who's been tantalizing me with this legacy business?"

Her first reaction was relief at the thought of being rid of him for a while, but then she reminded him of the impending Short-Tail Gang trial.

"They don't need me there. The lawyers have you, May, and the good doctor to testify. Anyway, I'll probably be back before the trial starts. Ye know how slow the courts are."

"But they do need you. You were the one who rushed at the men and then went to fetch the police. And would you please stop calling him the 'good doctor.' His name is Matthew."

"Aye, that it is. But he's almost a doctor, and I suppose he's good, but now I'd like another beer and some eggs and bacon, if it's not too much trouble fer ya."

Nancy poured the drink and turned on her heel and headed for the kitchen, her stomach in turmoil, knowing Patrick suspected her feelings for the 'good doctor.' It would be best for everyone if he went off to Ireland and left her alone until she could sort things out. This attraction between her and Matthew had to be terminated, not because of Patrick, but for the sake of her immortal soul. She must go to confession and obtain the strength she needed to overcome her concupiscence and return to the state of grace.

Patrick ate his breakfast, and silently drank two more beers as Nancy prepared lunch in the kitchen. As he left for home and his bed, he called out sarcastically to his wife, "Now don't ye go forgetting to lock the door behind me."

Nancy felt for the Derringer and the bullets in her skirt pocket to assure they were hidden under her apron. She briefly thought of the great satisfaction she would gain by using it on Patrick, but quickly asked God's forgiveness and bolted the door behind him.

On Saturday Nancy gathered up her courage and entered St. Bridget's Church in lower Manhattan. In the dim candlelight she made out three old women sitting in the pews, their veiled heads bent over rosary beads. She entered the dark confessional booth and knelt, and within seconds the priest slid open the black curtain that separated them. She could just make out the profile of a man, but could not distinguish his features.

"Bless me Father, for I have sinned. It has been four weeks since my last confession."

"Go on, my child," said the priest.

"I lusted after a man who is not my husband."

"You must not see this man again. He is an occasion of sin for you."

She pleaded, "But I cannot help but see him. He comes to my place of business. But I swear I will overcome my feelings."

"Then I will give you absolution, but you can never be alone with this man. For your penance say a rosary to the Virgin Mary, and recite a perfect Act of Contrition." He made the sign of the cross and said, "Go and sin no more."

"Thank you, Father."

The priest closed the dark curtain between them and Nancy left the confessional booth to kneel in a pew and begin her prayers, thanking God for his forgiveness. She did not notice Father Gannon quietly open the door of the confessional and silently search the pews for the wanton woman to whom he had just given absolution for her sins. His eyes finally fell on Nancy, whom he had noticed often at Sunday Mass with the Lallys, friends of his for some years now. He then quickly stepped back into the booth and gently closed the door.

Nancy left the church with a happy heart and a jaunty step, the weight of her sins having been lifted from her, and strong in her resolution to conquer her feelings for Matthew and sin no more. She knew she would never stop loving the man, but she could learn to control her emotions and stay in God's good graces.

She returned to Murphy's Bar by six o'clock, in time to finish the dinner service and begin entertaining the customers. Now, free from the burden of her sins, she sang with renewed exuberance, and the customers clapped and cheered and she stood up and acknowledged their acclaim. Demands of "more" and "give us another one" rang out from the delighted crowd.

She nodded, smiled and returned to the piano bench. The room fell silent as she played the opening chords, and began singing, "Wearing of the Green."

"Oh! Paddy dear, and did you hear the news that's goin' round. The Shamrock is forbid by law, to grow on Irish ground! Saint Patrick's day no more we'll keep, his color can't be seen, For there's a bloody law agin' the Wearing of the Green."

Callahan and his men in the side room, upon hearing the tune, strode into the bar and listened respectfully to Nancy's silver tones as she finished the song's plaintive closing:

"They're hanging men and women there, for Wearing o' the Green."

The Irish patrons rose to their feet and rewarded Nancy with thunderous applause.

When the bar was crowded, Mr. Murphy felt it unnecessary to lock the door, as the craven Short-Tail Gang only attacked when bars were empty. The door opened and in walked Patrick, refreshed after sleeping all day, and with a few hours remaining to imbibe some spirits before his shift began. Callahan and Ahern, themselves jubilant due to many whiskeys and the nostalgic music, spied their new comrade and welcomed him, patting him on the back and calling for Mr. Murphy to give Mr. Patrick Devlin, a true Irishman, a double whiskey.

Nancy took in the scene as Callahan and his cohorts stood in a semi-circle with their arms around Patrick's shoulders. The events of late began to fall into place. The private room where the patrons did not pay for drinks; Patrick's new-found sense of self-importance; his overindulgence in alcohol; and his sudden decision to visit Ireland. Nancy knew quite well about the New York Irish underground movement to help the motherland free itself from British rule. She had been asked many times to contribute money to the cause, and had on occasion slipped a few dollars to Mrs. Lally for that purpose.

But to know her husband was so personally involved with the cause frightened her, not for Patrick's sake, but for her own and that of her unborn child. The Protestants in New York did not look with favor upon the Irish cause, and would construe these actions as another reason to demean and socially attack Irish immigrants.

Callahan bid Nancy to play "God Save Ireland," the unofficial Irish national anthem. She saw no way out as the men roared their approval. She played, and the men sang with feverish gusto.

"God save Ireland! Save the heroes; God save Ireland said they all. Whether on the scaffold high or the battlefield we die, Oh, what matter when for Erin dear we fall!"

Nancy watched as the men cheered and clapped for the cause of Ireland's freedom, and she felt a chill in her bones as she returned to the kitchen, after smiling and nodding thank you to the raucous bunch of Irishmen.

She asked May to bring Patrick back to the kitchen, as she must speak to him. Patrick, annoyed at Nancy intruding on his moment of glory, barged into the kitchen asking, "What is it ye be wanting now?"

"I'm worried about what you're getting into. We're Americans now, but you're acting like a Fenian, and they died out twenty years ago. Are you trying to get yourself killed? And me in the bargain?"

"The Fenians were trying to free Ireland from the Brits, and I'll never stop trying till I breathe me last breath. But ye, an American as ye say, seem to have forgotten the old country. But I haven't. And don't be butting yer American nose in my Irish business. Now I'm going to have another whiskey with me friends, and then I'll be off to work, and I ask ye not to bother me again tonight." And with that he left Nancy in the kitchen to wonder what had become of the charming young man who loved her so during the blizzard of 1888 in Tuxedo Park.

At home that night May took Nancy's hand, sat her down on the sofa beside her, and revealed with girlish glee that she and Charles Murphy had set their wedding date for a month hence.

"I'm so happy for you, Aunt May. This is wonderful news. What have you planned?"

"We'll have a nuptial Mass at eleven o'clock, then a private party at the Bar at twelve with drinks and lunch for all our friends, and be finished by three. Then the Bar will reopen for business. What do ye think?"

"It's perfect." Nancy hugged her aunt with unrestrained happiness. And now that her sister Norah would be arriving from Ireland soon and living with Nancy, May would not have to take care of the baby. Their lives were falling into place, and the future looked bright and shiny.

"Now Norah and I will cook the meal so you'll have nothing to do but enjoy your wedding day. We'll bake a ham, and for such a momentous occasion, I'll roast a fillet of beef, and make a large bowl of colcannon …"

145

May interrupted her. "Colcannon. Why I haven't eaten that since I left Ireland; the chopped cabbage and mashed potatoes and scallions. Ye have me mouth watering. Why don't we serve that at the Bar?"

"We've become too Americanized. We'll put it on the menu right after your wedding. And we must have some smoked salmon on brown bread for luck. In New York the Jews call it lox, but we'll Irish it up with some chopped onions on top. And I'll make soda breads with raisins, and a beautiful wedding cake. And we'll have a champagne toast and flowers on the tables …"

"You'll be doing too much," May interrupted again.

"Nothing I do for you is too much. You're the one who brought me here."

May took her niece's hand and asked if she would consent to be her matron of honor.

"Consent?" Nancy exclaimed. "If you asked anyone else I'd be crestfallen."

"Charles will be asking Officer Lally to be his best man. I hope that won't put Patrick's nose out of joint."

"Patrick won't even be here. Don't give it another thought. I must tell you the truth, Aunt May, though I know you care very much for my husband, he's not the man he used to be."

May agreed he had changed since leaving the Birmingham house, and admitted she felt sorry for Nancy's plight, being married to a man who drank too much, had no ambition, and had become too cozy with the Callahan group, which could only cause them all trouble. She went on to tell Nancy that Patrick had insulted her friends, the Italian couple who ran the bakery down the block.

"Mrs. Feroni is my friend, and a very nice lady, and she works very hard. I've invited them to the wedding, and it's just as well Patrick won't be there. Mrs. Feroni told me to try and keep Patrick away from her shop. He goes in and squeezes all the rolls and breads, then buys a cookie and tells her she charges too much and they're stale. He makes fun of her heritage. He calls her an EYE-talian, instead of IT-alian, and mocks her accent, and she feels very hurt. I don't know what to do. Patrick is not the same person I knew in Tuxedo Park and it breaks me heart. I don't know what's gotten into the man."

This revelation of Patrick's prejudice upset Nancy. Only a few years ago their part of New York City was all Irish, but had now become more homogeneous. Germans, Italians and Jews had moved into the neighborhood and all strove for upward mobility. They had different accents, customs, religions, food and dress, and many harbored resentment against one another. The American melting pot had reached a boiling point. Young Italians fought the Irish kids, German boys fought the Jews, and the police were kept busy trying to maintain peace in the community.

"What you've told me of Patrick's behavior to the Feronis disgusts me, and I'll speak to him about it when he returns. But for now, let's concentrate on your wedding, and teaching Norah the in's and out's of the restaurant business."

Thinking of Norah, Nancy asked her aunt. "Do you think it would be possible to invite Bill Peyton to your wedding? He's the lawyer who drew up my partnership with your future husband."

"You me darling, can invite anyone ye wish. After all, you made it all possible."

May had invited thirty guests to the wedding, including Dr. Weitz and his daughter, Rachel, Matthew Clarke, Mrs. Lally's employer, the dressmaker, Mr. Callahan and Mr. Ahern, some of the regular customers at the Bar, and the priest who would marry them, Father Gannon. Nancy did not know Father Gannon was the priest she had confessed to, and later peeked out the confessional to identify the lustful sinner. But it would eventually become apparent, and create a dramatic change in her life.

Chapter 11

THE SISTER

April, 1892

On a bright and balmy spring day in late April, Nancy and May met Norah when she left Ellis Island, the new immigration center, which had just opened that January. They exchanged tears and hugs and kisses. May had last seen the twenty-year-old Norah when her niece was only a child, and was delighted that the scrawny little girl had developed into a trim, lovely young woman with dark brown wavy hair flowing down her back.

On the trip to Nancy's house, Norah filled them in on all the news from home, going into great detail about her soon-to-be stepmother, Bernadette.

"Oh, I'm so glad to be free of that two-faced harridan. Fer sure, she's only after Da to support her now that her husband's dead. You'd think Da could see through her conniving ways, but no, she compliments him left and right and he swallows it like a cat lapping up milk. It's disgusting."

May and Nancy smiled secretly at each other and let Norah vent her anger at being displaced as mistress of the household. Nancy remarked that Bernadette might prove to be a blessing in disguise, because now Norah could begin a new life in America, the land of golden opportunity, and she could follow any path she chose. And, of course, there were many more available young men in New York than in Galway. The word 'men' caught Norah's attention, and she noted how she'd love to go to some dances, and did Nancy know any young men she could meet?

At the apartment, out of earshot of Norah, May whispered to Nancy. "She's a darlin', but I fear we're going to have our hands full with that one. She's after a man, she is." Nancy laughed and agreed, but felt between the two of them they could keep her in line.

Norah expressed amazement and delight at Nancy's apartment and complimented her on the tasteful furniture, lovely curtains, gleaming silver candlesticks, and Mrs. Lally's Waterford vase.

"And look at such a beautifully set table," she gushed. "Are ye expecting company?"

"No," replied Nancy. "It's for our dinner."

"You go to all this fancy fuss just for us?"

Nancy looked at her sister sternly. "We're not living on a farm in Galway anymore. We're in New York. We've moved up in the world. Now you will have to share a room with Aunt May for a few weeks until she's married to Mr. Murphy, my partner in the Bar, and moves into his place."

"I'd share a bedroom with the devil himself to be away from Bernadette," she blurted out. "Oh, begging yer pardon, Aunt May. I meant no offense. But Nancy, you own a pub?" Norah's eyes widened with admiration for her sister.

At that point Patrick emerged from his bedroom, dressed for work and ready to eat. Nancy introduced her husband to her sister, and

Patrick's eyes lit up and a bit of his old charm emerged as he clasped Norah's hand and welcomed her to his home.

"Well, yer a fine looking lass, and I know you'll be happy here in America. There are more Irish in New York than in Galway, so you'll have no trouble meeting people of yer own kind."

Norah thanked him effusively. She could see he had once been a handsome man, with his dark hair and eyes and well-formed features. She knew he was seven or eight years older than her sister, but he looked twice that. Like some of her father's friends in Ireland, it was obvious he was a heavy drinker and his fondness for alcohol had taken its toll. His once sharp features were now pudgy and swollen, and his jacket buttons were stretched to the breaking point over his bulging beer belly.

Nancy warmed up the beef stew May had made that morning and placed the tureen on the table with the biscuits she had baked. Then she poured coffee for everyone, and they sat down to dinner. May made the sign of the cross and they all bowed their heads as she prayed: "Bless us, Oh Lord, for these Thy gifts which we are about to receive, from Thy bounty, through Christ our Lord, Amen."

Patrick dug into his stew and biscuits with the fervor of a prisoner eating his last meal before his execution, while the ladies delicately savored their dinner.

"I have some bad news to tell ye, May. I've got to go to Ireland to see me dying mother and I won't be here fer yer wedding."

Nancy almost choked on her stew as she heard Patrick's bold-face lie slip so glibly from his lips.

"Oh, we'll miss yer presence," said May. "But I understand yer mother must come first."

Mr. Murphy agreed to Nancy's suggestion that Norah would work at the Bar while Nancy awaited the birth of her child. So the next morning she began instructing her sister in her duties; cleaning the floor, washing glasses and dishes, setting tables, and scrubbing the kitchen. Norah had expected a more glamorous job, such as a salesgirl in a clothing emporium, but she did not complain and learned quickly. At noon she peeked out of the kitchen and watched Nancy take orders from the well-dressed business men gradually filling up the dining room. My, she thought, they do look rich; the pickings are good here in New York City. She couldn't wait for the day when Nancy would permit her to serve the gentlemen their lunches and exhibit her charms to the unmarried ones.

After a week of drudge work, Nancy allowed Norah to help prepare the food, starting with peeling the mounds of vegetables consumed every day. Norah wedged open the kitchen door to glimpse the lunchtime crowd as she worked on a heap of turnips. With one eye looking into the restaurant, she chopped the rock hard turnips, and the knife slipped.

Nancy ran to the kitchen when she heard the scream. Blood was pouring from a large gash on Norah's index finder and her face was ghostly white. Nancy grabbed a clean towel, wrapped it around the wound and covered it with chipped ice and another towel.

"Come with me," she commanded Norah, and helped her outside to the trolley stop. She held the shaking girl around the waist and reassured Norah everything would be okay. They boarded the trolley and within five minutes were knocking on Dr. Weitz's door. Rachel led them into the examination room and said she would summon Matthew, as her father was unavailable.

Norah's trembling had not abated, nor had the color returned to her face. Nancy feared her sister might be going into shock. Matthew appeared with Rachel and immediately began removing the towels from his patient's hand as he asked Nancy what had happened.

Norah spoke up. "It's me own fault. Me mind wandered as I chopped the turnips and I sliced into me finger."

Nancy introduced her sister to Matthew, who smiled at the girl and welcomed her to New York. Norah was mesmerized and could not take her eyes from Matthew's face. She had never seen a more handsome man, with his brilliant blue eyes and shock of golden hair.

Matthew cleaned the wound and said it required a few stitches and that might hurt a bit.

"If you can guarantee me you'll keep your hand absolutely still, I won't have to give you chloroform to ease the pain. But it will go easier for you if I put you out for a few minutes."

"I won't move a muscle, Dr. Clarke. I don't need any pain killers. Do what ye will."

Nancy could not believe what she had just heard her sniveling sister tell Matthew. The girl seemed to have miraculously regained her composure.

Matthew sutured the wound and Rachel cut the thread after he tied the stitches.

Norah thought she would rather die than appear weak before this god of a man, so gritted her teeth and uttered not a sound nor moved the slightest bit as Matthew put four stitches in her finger. Beads of sweat appeared on Norah's forehead, but she remained perfectly still. Matthew bandaged the wound and she smiled with delight as he told her how much he admired her.

"I've sewn up a lot of cuts, Norah, but I've never had a patient as brave as you've been today. Come back in a week and I'll remove the stitches. Don't let the dressing get wet. And move that finger as little as possible. And no more peeling turnips for a while."

Norah thanked Matthew profusely, and told him what a wonderful doctor he was, and she would follow his directions and be a good patient. Then Rachel ushered Norah out to the waiting area, sat her down, and went over the doctor's instructions.

Nancy and Matthew, now gratefully alone, exchanged a secret smile. She said May would be inviting him to her wedding, and unfortunately Patrick would not be in attendance. His smile grew larger.

"You couldn't have given me better news."

"But I must go now," said Nancy. "I'll bring Norah back in a week."

Once on the sidewalk, Norah could not contain her excitement, and bombarded her sister with questions.

"Is Dr. Clarke married?"

"No."

"Does he have a sweetheart?"

Nancy hesitated before saying, "Not that I know of."

"Oh, that's splendid. And Aunt May told me he'll be at her wedding. Then I'll have my chance. Nancy, he's the most wonderful man I've ever met. Do you think he liked me?" Her total infatuation with Matthew began to annoy Nancy.

'I suppose he liked you as well as any of his other patients."

"Oh, I'm going to be more to him than a patient. I've got my cap set for Dr. Clarke. And don't be surprised if one day soon people will be calling me Mrs. Clarke. I usually get what I want when I put me mind to something. And I really do want him."

"Now don't go making a fool of yourself and disgrace us all," said Nancy. "He's an educated man, far above your station in life."

Norah smiled. "Don't worry. He'll never know what happened to him."

Nancy's chest tightened and her head began to throb. Her sister and Matthew? The very thought of them together sickened her, and the love she had for Norah had been replaced by fear and animosity bordering on hatred.

When Nancy left Ireland over four years previously, the sisters had been very close, but even then Norah exhibited a willfulness that brought her whatever she set out to obtain. She had a way about her that Nancy found difficult to pin down, but her ability to manipulate people, which had amused Nancy in the past, now filled her with dread. Nancy surely could not tell her sister that Matthew belonged to her; she was married! But she must think of something to prevent Norah from using her charms on Matthew. Although he loved Nancy, he was vulnerable and lonely, and men in that position were susceptible to the wiles of determined females.

Nancy remained silent on the trolley ride back to work, listening to Norah prattle on about her new prince charming. Once back at

Murphy's Bar, Norah announced that since she could no longer prepare food with her injured finger, maybe she could take dinner orders from the customers.

Nancy quickly agreed to the idea. Maybe her sister would take a liking to some other young man and forget Matthew. But deep in her heart Nancy knew that was a pipe dream. Norah wanted Matthew.

That evening Patrick stopped into the bar before work and told Nancy he had booked passage on a ship bound for Ireland in a few days. He asked that she pack his bag, press his suit and a few shirts, and anything she felt a man would need for a three-week journey, and to please give him some traveling money from her savings.

As Nancy's thoughts still dwelt on Norah and Matthew, she calmly agreed to his requests.

"Now, that's the way a good wife should treat her husband. If ye acted so nice more often we'd get along much better."

She gave him a wan smile and as she drew him a beer, she thought, oh, Patrick, if you only knew how little desire I have to get along better with you. Oh, please God, let the ship be destroyed in a storm and set me free of this miserable man. Then she caught herself. Oh, God, what have I just wished for? Forgive me, Lord, she prayed. And Nancy knew she must go to confession again this week to be forgiven her evil thoughts so she could receive communion at Aunt May's nuptial mass. As Nancy prayed for absolution, Patrick took his beer and disappeared into the side room where Callahan held court. Ahern handed him tickets for a ship leaving New York in ten days, and an envelope of cash for his use in Ireland, and showed him a well-worn jacket.

"The money to be transferred will be sewn into the lining of this jacket. Don't ever take the coat off, except when you're sleeping. Then hide it under your mattress. You lose the jacket and the whole mission is doomed," Callahan warned him.

"I understand. Now what is the password?"

"Listen carefully," said Callahan. "A man will approach you and he'll ask, 'Do you know Brian Boru?' And you will respond, 'Sure, the old man who worked the farm next to my father's.' Do you understand that?"

Patrick looked puzzled, but he repeated the sentence back to Callahan. Then he said, "Are ye referring to the old high king of Ireland?"

"Indeed I am. Brian Boru who defeated the Danes at Clontarf in 1014," replied Callahan.

"Then why …why should I say he was my father's neighbor?"

"Use yer head, man!" Callahan wondered if he had overestimated Patrick, and explained only Patrick would reply that Brian Boru was a farmer. "It's the code! That way the contact could be sure he found the right man."

"Oh, now I understand."

"Then yer all ready. Nothing more fer you to do except pick up this jacket here at one o'clock on the day of your sailing. We'll have lunch here before you leave for the dock. I won't see you again before that. I'm taking a little trip to Boston. Can I count on you?"

"As God is my judge, and Ireland is me country, ye have nothing to fear. I'll do ye proud, Mr. Callahan."

"You'll notice, if you look at the tickets, you have an extra week in Ireland to do what you will. Visit your relatives and friends. That's a bonus I'm giving you for taking on the assignment."

Patrick enthusiastically shook Callahan's hand and thanked him. He said he hadn't seen his mother in over ten years, and yearned for the sight of her, as the Lord only knew how many years she had left before she went to her eternal reward. He thought now he would have ample time and money to get back and forth from the Knock cemetery, and as he hadn't kept in touch with his mother, for all he knew she could by now be resting peacefully in a grave in Dublin.

"Now leave us to discuss other business, and remember Ireland is counting on you," said Callahan as he dismissed Patrick and turned his attention to Ahern. Patrick left the room with a buoyancy in his step and without speaking to Nancy, left the Bar and made his way to the liquor store to purchase the six bottles of whiskey he would pack in his suitcase to accompany him on the boat to Ireland.

An early spring was in full bloom a week later. The trees sprouted pale green leaves, and flower boxes hanging from the windows of the tenements overflowed with geraniums, pansies and petunias, brightening up the grim gray and dirty red-brick buildings. Nancy and her sister walked slowly down Second Avenue to the doctor's office to have Norah's stitches removed, and the closer they came to Matthew's office, the more Norah's mood improved.

For the past week Norah handed out menus to customers, and explaining, without being asked, how she sliced her finger chopping turnips. The diners appreciated this pretty young woman's charm, but Nancy noticed her sister spent more time taking orders than was necessary and warned her, "You are not behaving professionally. You are here to work, not search for a husband."

"I'm not searching for a husband. I was just being friendly. Matthew Clarke will be me husband."

Nancy realized her mistake. She fought the urge to slap the girl's face and send her back to Ireland on the next boat. But after all, isn't that what she wanted Norah to do? Meet some other young man and have her forget Matthew?

"I'm sorry, Norah," she said. "Yes, continue being friendly with the customers. You're doing a good job. Just don't be too forward. But I don't want to see any flirting, or any tiny bit of over familiarity with the doctor today. No batting your eyelashes at him and telling him how wonderful he is. You will learn to behave like a lady and not bring shame upon me, or I will fire you and throw you out of my house and let you fend for yourself. Remember, I am part owner of Murphy's Bar and what I say goes."

Norah thought she would obey her sister for now, but she knew that at Aunt May's wedding she would do as she pleased. It was her one chance to get Matthew's attention and she would not let the opportunity slip by.

After Matthew removed the stitches, and pronounced Norah healed, she offered a demure "Thank you, Doctor," and the woman returned to the Bar.

The day had arrived for Patrick to leave for Ireland. Nancy had his bags packed, and they sat talking and drinking coffee at the dining room table.

"How will you get from Cork Harbor up to Knock?" Nancy asked.

"I'll find out how long it takes, and then pay some farmer for the use of a horse, and maybe a cart, then deliver it back to him before I board the ship home." He sipped his coffee and smiled.

"Thank ye fer packing me bag," Patrick said.

"I put in some apples and brown bread should they not feed you enough."

"Ah, thank ye. And when I get back things will be better between us. I'll be home at night and ..."

She interrupted him. "What about your job at the Triangle Shirt Waist Factory?"

Patrick stared at his coffee cup, and confessed he had been fired.

Nancy's mouth fell open. "You told me they gave you three weeks off!"

"Only on the condition that I get them a man to replace me, temporarily, and fer the life of me I couldn't find any one foolhardy enough to work at that stinkin' job. But Mr. Callahan will find me employment when I get back."

"Oh he will, will he? I wouldn't count on that. Mr. Callahan only helps people who help him." Nancy could envision Patrick out of work, sleeping all day, then arriving at the Bar for free liquor and food.

"But I do help him, and he appreciates it."

"And what is it you do for him?"

Patrick looked down and mumbled, "I can't tell anyone, not even you."

"It's a dangerous thing you've gotten yourself into."

Patrick lost his temper. "Will ye stop nagging me, woman! I'll see who I please, and go where I please." He went to the bedroom and crammed the bottles of whiskey he'd bought the night before into his suitcase. "Now I'm off to catch the boat. I'll see ye in three weeks." Then he picked up his bag and abruptly left the apartment.

He had lunch with Callahan in the private room at Murphy's Bar and was given the heavy tweed jacket, stuffed with money. Then Ahern accompanied him to the pier.

Nancy rested her chin in her hands and slowly shook her head. What have I done, Lord, she thought, to be burdened so: a man I love but can't have; a lazy husband addicted to the drink; a sister trying to steal Matthew from me; and me with a baby on the way. What do You have in store for me next?

Norah came out of her room upon hearing Patrick's loud voice and asked what was wrong.

"Patrick's gone off to the boat. He'll be back in about three weeks."

"Oh," said Norah. "Well, now that we're alone, let's talk about Aunt May's wedding. Ye see, I don't have a proper dress to wear, and would be forever in yer debt if ye could lend me some money to buy something suitable fer the party."

"You can wear one of my dresses," Nancy replied, not bothering to hide her disinterest.

"But then all yer friends will know I'm wearing a hand-me-down. And what would they be thinking of you, letting yer sister appear at such a grand occasion in a frock they'd seen you wearin'? You don't want to be bringing shame on yerself now, do ye?"

Nancy thought her sister might have a point, and advanced her fifteen dollars, emphasizing it would be taken out of her first month's salary. Norah hugged her sister and picked up her purse. "I'll be running to the dress shop down the block and pick up something that will make ye proud of me," and she darted out the door before Nancy thought to tell Norah to take her business to the seamstress, Mrs. Lally.

Nancy sat sipping her coffee, going over what had just happened. How easily she manipulated me, she thought. And I fell right into her trap. How did she do it? Ah, she appealed to my pride and I took the bait. She's a clever one, she is. And she never asked me to go with her. The Lord only knows what she'll bring home. I have to be more careful in my dealings with her in the future. But now Nancy had to get to work and prepare for the dinner hour.

Ahern and Patrick made their way to the pier. The hot sun beat down upon them and Patrick perspired profusely. His shirt stuck to his wet back under the heavy tweed jacket. But he dared not remove it for fear of some young hooligan snatching it from under his arm. He remembered Mr. Callahan's instructions to wear it at all times. So he'd suffer now and be rewarded for his discomfort when he returned to New York to a hero's welcome.

They reached the pier in good time for the five p.m. departure and Ahern left Patrick, who boarded the ship and went to his cabin. It was small, but enough for his needs. He lay on the small cot. The heat of the day and the excitement of his mission had exhausted him, and he promptly fell asleep.

He awoke hours later in the pitch black cabin and lit the oil lamp on the small table next to the bed. He looked at his pocket watch, and found it was almost midnight. He had missed the dinner hour. He searched his bag for Nancy's bread and apples, and after eating wondered what he would do with himself until breakfast, as he was now fully awake.

Craving company, he went up on deck and approached three men singing old Irish songs under a full moon, which cast a bright yellow shadow over the placid Atlantic Ocean. He joined in the singing and soon one man drew a bottle of whiskey from his pocket and passed it around. Each man took a long slug and toasted the old sod they would soon set foot upon. After an hour passed and the bottle was empty, they said their good nights and left Patrick alone on deck, still wide awake and once again lonely. He picked up a discarded issue of The New York Times newspaper, went back to his cabin, opened a bottle of whiskey and read the newspaper and drank until it was time for breakfast.

Norah darted in and out of five shops until she found the perfect dress for the wedding. She thought to herself, if this frock doesn't weaken Dr. Clarke's knees, nothing will. She also purchased white leather-buttoned ankle boots, and a vial of perfume, guaranteed by the saleslady to bewitch any man not yet in his coffin.

After work that evening, Nancy asked to see Norah's new dress. Her sister went to her room and returned holding the garment up to her body.

"Isn't it lovely?" Norah beamed with delight.

Nancy felt relieved at the sight of it. The dress seemed perfectly demure and acceptable. The emerald green silk flowed almost to the floor. The fitted jacket had long sleeves and tiny fabric covered buttons which reached the neck, and was edged with white lace. She reluctantly admitted it seemed quite appropriate, and thought ruefully to herself that there was nothing as lovely in her closet.

"And look at me boots," Norah boasted. "See how the color matches the trim on the jacket?"

"Yes, I see. Now it's late and I must get some sleep."

"And what will ye be wearing to the wedding?" Norah asked.

"I haven't given it any thought yet."

"Well, ye can't even see yet that you're with child. Sure all yer old dresses must still fit ye."

The phrase 'old dresses' brought Nancy to her senses, and anger to her eyes. "Maybe I too will pick up a new frock. After all, I am Aunt May's matron of honor. Goodnight."

In her bedroom Nancy was furious with herself at allowing Norah to once again get under her skin. The girl does have a cleverness about her, Nancy thought, as she threw on her nightgown and slipped under the covers, exhausted. Here I am, trying to save money to buy a house and move uptown, and I've let her manipulate me into spending money on a new dress I don't need. I wish I'd never brought her over from Ireland. I'm beginning to hate her and want to be rid of her. I must get her married before she drives me stark raving mad. And it won't be to Matthew Clarke! I'll ask the Lallys and Mr. Murphy if they know of some young man willing to woo her and get her out of my house. And I will not buy a new dress!

The following Saturday afternoon Nancy went once again to St. Bridget's Church to beg God to forgive her sins. She prayed in the almost empty church until a man came out of the confessional box, then steeled herself to the task before her. She opened the door and knelt quietly until the priest slid open the curtain between them. The darkness helped Nancy bare her soul.

"Forgive me, Father, for I have sinned. It's been two weeks since my last confession."

"Go on, my child," said the anonymous voice.

"Father, I have sinned in my thoughts. I wished for my husband's death and I had very bad thoughts about my sister."

After a short pause the priest asked, "And why do you wish your husband dead?"

"He's an alcoholic, and mean, and I've lost all my love for him. But I'm sorry for thinking such evil thoughts."

"And your sister?"

"Well, she just seems to try and irritate me and it brings out the worst in me."

The priest recognized the voice as the woman who confessed her feelings for another man, and knew it was Nancy O'Leary kneeling to his left.

"You've committed a grievous sin wishing for the death of your husband. Have you any other sins to confess?"

"I have seen a man in private that at my last confession I promised not to do. But we committed no sin." Nancy's hands began trembling and she gripped her rosary beads and fought the rising urge to flee the darkness and the shadowy figure about to pass sentence on her.

"This man is an occasion of sin for you. There must be no further contact between you."

Nancy remembered hearing the same words from a priest at her last confession. Even though innocent of any actual wrongdoing, she would be punished.

"I will try my best to avoid him."

"My child, you must do more than try. You must see to it for the sake of your immortal soul."

"Yes, Father." The words automatically came from her lips from years of obedience to the pronouncements of men in robes inside dark churches.

"Then I will give you absolution. Say an Act of Contrition and a rosary to the Blessed Virgin and go and sin no more."

After the priest made the sign of the cross, Nancy quickly left the church intending to say her rosary at home. The cool late afternoon breeze restored her equilibrium, but she was still in a dilemma. There seemed no way for her to avoid Matthew, even if she wanted to. So she would dwell on that problem later, and for now enjoy her freedom from the confessional box.

Chapter 12

THE WEDDING

May, 1892

The day before May's wedding, the women cooked the food for the reception and stored it in the ice box at the Bar. That evening at eight o'clock, they hung a "CLOSED" sign on the door, and with Charles Murphy's help, tables were arranged and covered with white linen cloths, candles, and small vases of pink roses and lilies of the valley. Mr. Murphy set up the bar with champagne glasses and tumblers, clean ash trays, and bottles of his best Irish whiskey. The champagne was cooling in the kitchen. Mrs. Feroni, the bakery owner, insisted on making the wedding cake, and would deliver it after the ceremony. When the preparations were completed, they all went home for a good night's rest.

The next morning the sun shone brightly in a cloudless sky. A perfect day for a wedding, thought Nancy, as she rose at seven o'clock, put on a pot of coffee and made toast and scrambled eggs. But after ten-thirty today, May would no longer live with her and she would miss her aunt terribly. On the bright side, she would spend hours today with Matthew, despite the priest's disapproval. However, Norah would be intruding, doing God only knows what to attract his attention. Again, on the bright side, Patrick would not be there to upset everyone, especially dear Mrs. Feroni.

May and Norah rushed into the kitchen, interrupting Nancy's daydreaming.

"What do I smell burning?" said May.

Absorbed in her thoughts, Nancy had burned the toast and the coffee had percolated over the pot. May quickly wiped up the spill.

"Nancy, you're so nervous you'd think this was your wedding day. Now set yerself down and let me see to things."

"I'm going to miss you so much, Aunt May."

May kissed the top of her head and reminded her they would be together every day at the Bar, and when her confinement began, May would stop in to see her each morning before work. Nancy's equanimity returned, and after breakfast, they went to their rooms to dress for church.

Just before leaving the apartment, May clasped Nancy in her arms, her eyes moist with love for her niece. It was through Nancy's bravery, strength and hard work that she had been rescued from a lifetime of misery in the Birmingham kitchen, and been introduced to Mr. Charles Murphy, today to become her husband.

"What do ye think of me dress?" Norah interrupted their sentimental moment.

"You look fine," said May. "But it's time to go." May kissed Nancy on both cheeks and thanked her for being the best niece any aunt could hope for. "If I had ever been blessed with my own daughter, I couldn't have done better than you."

Norah tapped the toe of her new white boot, impatiently waiting for the maudlin scene before her to end, then grabbed her purse and opened the door saying, "We'd best be going now or Aunt May will miss her own wedding."

The Lally's were waiting at the curb to escort the future Mrs. Murphy the few blocks to the church. Mrs. Lally admired May's dress, telling her, "Don't ye look grand! What a lovely outfit."

And May did look marvelous in her off-white gown with its dark blue sash around her still girlish waist. She carried a bouquet of blue bells and lilies, and with her red hair pinned up she looked ten years younger than her actual forty-five years.

Once in the church, Mr. Lally led the ladies to the first pew and the nuptial mass began. Nancy mentally thanked Father Gannon for giving her absolution so she could join the line of worshipers and receive communion, as her sins had been forgiven.

Then Charles Murphy and May O'Connor stood before the priest and each reverently responded, "I will," and were then pronounced man and wife.

As they left the church, Matthew walked by Nancy's side and told her how lovely she looked, and admired her pale blue gown. "You look like an angel," he whispered.

Nancy tried valiantly to disguise her joy, but if anyone looked her way they could not help but notice the radiance on her face. "Thank you, Matthew. I have missed your visits to the Bar."

"They've been working me day and night at the hospital. I'm taking advanced courses to become certified in two years instead of three, and all I do is study and assist at surgery. You'll never know the pains I must take every day to keep my mind on my work," he smiled.

Nancy's heart beat faster, and for a moment she thought she might faint, but quickly regained her composure as Norah appeared at Matthew's side and fluttered her eyelashes at him, while thanking him for repairing her injured finger.

"It's as good as new, thanks to you, Dr. Clarke. I don't know what would have become of me if it weren't fer you. I could have bled to death."

"No, you wouldn't have. Your sister handled the situation perfectly, and stopped the bleeding. And she brought you to me in good time to prevent any problems. So don't thank me, Norah, thank Nancy."

The petulant look on Norah's face relieved Nancy. Maybe now her sister would give up hope of seducing Matthew and Nancy could breathe freely again.

After a short walk under the warm spring sun, the gaily clad group entered the Bar and was welcomed with loud applause from the guests. Mr. Lally, dressed in the kilt he wore every St. Patrick's Day when he marched in the parade up Fifth Avenue, picked up his bagpipes and began playing a rousing Irish tune. Mr. Murphy and Matthew poured drinks for all, and Father Gannon put down his whiskey and lifted up his champagne glass, and toasted the newlyweds:

"May the good Lord shine His light on May and Charles and grant them a long life of happiness and prosperity."

Norah asked Nancy to play, "Believe Me If All Those Endearing Young Charms," for the wedding couple, and as Nancy began the first notes, Norah urged the newlyweds to dance. Within moments she requested the guests to join in and soon the Bar came alive with music, dancing and laughter. Norah took Matthew's hand and drew him to the floor and they danced to the slow, haunting melody. Matthew could find no way to gracefully avoid Norah's advances. He glanced at Nancy at the piano, and she did not look pleased. Norah smiled up at Matthew and gazed into his eyes, her body a bit too close to his, and began complimenting him on his attire, his skill on the dance floor, and his great surgical abilities. Suddenly the music stopped. Nancy played only the first verse of the song, then took Norah from Matthew's arms and instructed her to bring the food from the kitchen and lay it out on the buffet table.

Norah hid her anger and did as she was told, but she was furious with her sister and would tell her so when they were in private.

Callahan and Ahern had come prepared, bringing a fiddle and tin whistle, and when Officer Lally put down his bagpipes to take a breather, they began playing a jig and several women took to the floor. With their arms rigidly at their sides, they clicked their heels and toes in a lively Irish step-dance, to the delight of the guests.

Matthew stood beside Nancy and they clapped their hands in time to the music. The guests helped themselves to drinks, and enjoyed the entertainment. Dr. Weitz, caught up in the festivities, told Matthew that at Jewish weddings the guests danced the Hora, and Nancy requested he and Rachel give them a demonstration.

At that moment the door opened and a man entered the restaurant. Matthew took Nancy by one hand, and Dr. Weitz by the other, and pulled them towards the door.

"Mr. Grunwald! What are you doing here? It's so good to see you!" Matthew cried.

Dr. Weitz explained. "I wanted to give you a surprise, Matthew, and I see I have succeeded. Mr. Grunwald is in New York to pay us a visit and have a little vacation. He didn't know what time he would be arriving, so I left a note on my door with directions and told him to meet us here." Looking at Nancy, the doctor said, "I hope you do not object to my taking the liberty of inviting my old friend."

Nancy had heard much from Matthew of Mr. Grunwald from Johnstown, and answered she could not have been more pleased to meet the gentleman who pointed Matthew towards the practice of medicine.

Matthew hugged his mentor and told him repeatedly how glad he was to see him, and led him to the bar. "What will you have? Champagne or Irish whiskey?"

"The whiskey," he said. "It reminds me of the brandies we shared in Johnstown. Now introduce me please to these beautiful young women," he requested, referring to Rachel and Norah.

Father Gannon stood at the end of the bar drinking whiskey and observing the scene. What in God's name, he wondered, are all these Jews doing at a Catholic wedding?

Bill Peyton, Nancy's lawyer, also observed the scene, but it wasn't the presence of Jews that attracted his attention, but the two lovely girls with Nancy.

Norah had filled the buffet table with roasts, salads, smoked salmon and vegetables, and the guests began helping themselves and taking seats around the festive tables.

Mrs. Feroni, with the help of her husband, carried the large, three-tiered, beautifully decorated wedding cake to a table by the buffet.

About an hour later, after the guests were well-fed and happy, Callahan and Ahern took up their instruments again and the music and dancing resumed. Nancy's keen eye scanned the room to be sure everything was in order, and noticed Norah had neglected to place a knife and serving utensil beside the wedding cake. She went to the kitchen and opened a drawer where the cutlery was stored.

As she wore no apron today, beneath which to hide the gun Matthew had given her, that morning she placed it behind the utensils. How foolish of me, she realized. Norah, if her mind had been more on her work and less on Matthew, might have found the gun while looking for the cake knife. She wrapped a dish towel around the pistol and reminded herself to slip it in her purse before leaving the party that afternoon. She brought the cake server and knife to Mrs. Feroni, and returned to the kitchen, safe in the fact that Matthew's attention was now directed toward Dr. Weitz and Mr. Grunwald, and Norah's plan of attack had been temporarily thwarted. Nancy sat in the kitchen and relaxed. She thought of how far she had come in a few short years from a naïve, young country girl, to a smart partner in a prosperous business, with many new friends around her. And she took pride in the wedding she had given her aunt: the beautifully set tables, the music, and the excellent food were in sharp contrast to weddings of other Irish immigrants in 1892 in New York who placed pitchers of beer and a plate of sandwiches on the table.

Nancy bowed her head and prayed, thanking God for all he had given her, and for helping her pull herself up from her lowly beginnings. But Nancy aimed even higher. She felt there was more for her to achieve, for herself and her baby, who now began stirring within her.

The music had begun again. The sound of Officer Lally's bagpipes blared into the kitchen, and as Nancy stood up to join the festivities, Father Gannon walked into the kitchen.

"Oh, hello, Father. Are you enjoying the party?"

"Yes, I am." He held a glass of whiskey in his hand and asked Nancy how she felt.

"Oh, I'm quite well. And you?"

He smiled. "I could be better, and in a bit I will probably feel much better."

Nancy noticed he was slurring his words. He had obviously consumed too much whiskey.

"Would you like a cup of coffee, Father?"

"No," he replied. "That's not what I'd like. But what would you like?"

Nancy began to feel strangely ill at ease in the presence of this drunken man of God, and made her way towards the door.

"Now where do you think you're going?" the priest asked as he blocked her way.

"I have to preside over cutting the wedding cake."

"Ah, so you do believe in weddings, and the sanctity of marriage?" The priest moved closer to her, his eyes full of longing, and Nancy became frightened.

"Of course I do!"

As he approached her she retreated, but he kept inching towards her until her back hit the wall. He threw his drink glass to the floor and pressed his body against her. Then he put his hands over her breasts and fondled them, while clumsily searching for her lips. She felt the bulge under his cassock rubbing against her and smelled the sickening odor of rotting teeth and whiskey emanating from his mouth.

Though Nancy was terrified, she instinctively raised her arms, and with a great deal of effort, shoved the heavy-set priest off her. Gasping for breath, she shouted, "Keep away from me!"

But Father Gannon had other ideas. Now in the clutches of desire, he had lost all power of reasoning. He came at her again, with one hand on her breast and the other between her legs. "I know you like this. You've told me so. And I'll give you what you need." He pushed himself into her until her back hit the cutlery drawer.

Nancy's heart raced, and repulsed by Father Gannon's actions, once again she shoved him away, filled with righteous anger. The priest staggered backwards, giving Nancy just enough time to retrieve the gun from the drawer before he regained his balance and made his way towards her again. While the bagpipes blared from the restaurant, she reached into the cabinet, withdrew the gun and fired a shot. The bullet hit the approaching priest, and he fell to the floor.

Oh, God, I've killed him, she thought, and ran to the kitchen door. She stood there a moment, trying to regain her senses, then called out to Matthew. He quickly entered the kitchen and found the priest lying on the floor, a pool of blood by his leg.

Nancy rushed into Matthew's arms sobbing, and gasping for breath, and told him what had happened.

"I should let the bastard bleed to death," Matthew roared, as the bagpipes kept the sound of his voice from reaching the wedding guests. Then he leaned over the priest, pulled up his the man's cassock, and tore open the leg of his trousers from where the blood was seeping, and found the man had suffered only a flesh wound. It was the fall that had left him unconscious.

"Get me some kind of liquor," he told Nancy.

She went to the pantry and took out the brandy she used for desserts, and handed him the bottle.

Matthew poured the antiseptic over the wound and bandaged it with a clean kitchen towel. Then he threw a glass of cold water on the priest's face, and gradually the man regained consciousness.

"Get up, you filthy pervert! And if I ever see your sorry face again, by God, mine will be the last face you'll ever see!"

The priest tried to stand, but could not raise himself from the floor. Matthew pulled him up and threw him against the wall, and the priest's Roman collar flew off his neck and landed in a garbage pail. How fitting, thought Matthew.

"Nancy, bring Officer Lally in here. Tell him the priest slipped on some water from the ice box and cut his leg on the broken whiskey glass. But wait. Look at you. Oh, my poor Nancy. Your hair's all undone, and your eyes are red from crying. I'll get Lally. You fix yourself up. Pretend your tears are for concern over the priest's accident."

He then took Nancy in his arms, and as she clung to him the kitchen door opened slightly and Norah, after witnessing their intimacy, retreated. Ah, so that's what all her fussing's been about, Norah thought. Nancy's sweet on Dr. Matthew herself! All she had to do was tell me and I'd not of gone after him. Oh, but how could she, her being married and with Patrick's child! If it is Patrick's child. But of course it is. Nancy would never betray her wedding vows. Oh, me poor sister. She's gotten herself into a fine kettle of fish. So I'll let the Doctor off the hook and Nancy will be happy and I'll throw me line to other fish in the sea. And with that she placed herself at Bill Peyton's side and began fluttering her long, dark eyelashes at the man who would become her next object of desire.

After Nancy calmed her nerves, and rearranged her hair, Matthew felt it safe to fetch Officer Lally to take the priest back to his rectory. Father Gannon sat on the floor by the stove, his face pale and his eyes closed. Nancy returned the gun to its hiding place, and poured herself a cup of tea, still shaken by being alone in the presence of her attacker. But Matthew returned in a flash with the police officer, who escorted the drunken priest out of the kitchen.

When they were alone again, Matthew and Nancy sat in adjoining chairs, their hands entwined, her head resting on his shoulder.

"It's my own fault," she said.

"Don't be ridiculous, Nancy. You did nothing wrong."

"I went to confession and told Father Gannon of my feelings for you, not by your name, of course, and asked for absolution. I think somehow he found out who I was and felt I was a wanton woman."

"Don't talk like that. He probably took a look out of the confessional to see who you were. It was his fault. He's a priest, and bound by the secrecy of the confessional box."

"Well, it's not like he told anyone of what I confessed. He just used the information for his own pleasure. How could a man of God do such a thing? Does he confess his sins to another priest? Does he receive absolution, or do they just have a good laugh over it. Would he dare confess to another priest who would chastise him and forever know what a vile man Gannon is? Do you think the Bishop would be informed? Oh, no, of course not. The sanctity of the confessional would not allow that. But I must confess that as a married woman I cared for another man, and that gives Gannon permission to assault me? There is something very wrong here. I confessed my sin to a man of God, asking to be forgiven, but instead he took it upon himself to punish me by abusing me.

"But I won't have to worry about being betrayed by a priest in the future. No man will ever again know my sins. I will confess directly to God, and only to God."

"What are you saying, Nancy? You can't give up the church because of the sins of one drunken priest."

Nancy stared at Matthew with a determination he had never seen before in any human being.

"Oh yes I can. And I will. From now on I will not attend Mass, I will not go to confession, and I will receive communion by myself, by praying over a sliver of bread before I rest it on my tongue. I will not submit myself to the perversity of sick men, living under the illusion that they have the only direct link to God; that we must go through them to reach the Lord. I can do that alone!"

Matthew understood that Nancy had undergone a terribly traumatic experience, not only physically, but emotionally and spiritually, and he would not push the matter any further today. She needed time to put things in perspective, and when she could see more clearly, she would return to the faith. She told him they should go back to the party, and he took her in his arms and gently kissed her.

Officer Lally had explained to the guests that the priest accidentally slipped on water from the ice box, and they all commiserated with the good priest's misfortune. Matthew, trying to restore some festivity to the occasion, urged Dr. Weitz and Rachel to perform a Jewish dance, and they agreed to do the hora.

"I don't know the music," Nancy said.

"We do not need music," said Dr. Weitz. "We will make our own."

Rachel, her father, and Mr. Grunwald joined hands and sang, "La, la, la la, la la la," and more la las, as they formed a semi-circle and swung around, turning this way and that, until they had most of the guests on the floor imitating their movements, while the others clapped in rhythm to their steps.

The rapid dance left Norah very warm, and she removed her jacket, exposing quite a bit of flesh. Bill Peyton found his blood pressure rising as he gazed at the ample amount of cleavage visible above her low-cut dress. After the dance, he sat with Norah and quenched his thirst with a beer, while she demurely sipped lemonade. She continued her plan of attack by flattering him outrageously, smiling coyly up at him, and innocently touching his hand during their conversation on the pretext of making a point.

As the guests began to depart, they dropped envelopes on the bar; their cash gifts for the bride and groom. And by then Norah had achieved her objective, and Bill Peyton found himself quite smitten with the charming little Irish colleen. As he took his leave, he requested she attend a dance with him the following week, and she accepted with effusive pleasure.

Dr. Weitz, Rachel, and Mr. Grunwald were leaving, and Matthew felt obliged to join them. He would rather have remained with Nancy, but told her he would stop by the next day to check on her. He worried more about her emotional well-being, as her body was strong and resilient.

"Don't stew over Gannon. If I see him anywhere near you, I'll take care of him." He drew her into the kitchen for one last, long embrace.

"Thank you, Matthew. Thank you, my love," she whispered.

Nancy and Norah returned alone to the apartment, leaving Aunt May to go to her new home with Charles Murphy.

"Now sit yerself down. I'll make us a pot of tea, and we can have a nice chat," said Norah.

What's on the girl's mind now, Nancy wondered. The last thing she needed was to hear her sister natter on about her infatuation with Matthew. Nancy wanted to fling herself into bed and have sleep erase the memory of Father Gannon's hands on her body.

While the tea brewed, Norah came right to the point. "Why didn't you tell me how ye felt about Matthew? I never would have set me cap fer him if I knew."

Her words came as such a shock to Nancy all she could say was, "What?"

"I happened to be going to the kitchen for something and I saw ye in Matthew's arms. You'd think ye could confide in me, yer own sister. But I don't blame you, having to live with that Patrick, a poor excuse fer a husband. He could drive a woman to the drink, he could, the way he behaves."

Nancy, so taken aback by her sister's nonjudgmental attitude, blurted out, "You don't understand. I loved Matthew from the first moment I met him on the boat from Ireland years ago."

She told Norah the story of the promised letters that never arrived, and Mrs. Birmingham's part in the deception, and how she lost faith in Matthew, and then in despair, settled for Patrick Devlin.

Norah expressed extreme sympathy for her sister's plight, and after serving her tea, took Nancy's hands in hers and told her to be strong.

"God has a way of righting wrongs, and ye must be patient. You'll deliver a baby in four months, and the wee one will distract yer thoughts from Matthew."

"And what about your thoughts of Matthew?" Nancy asked.

"Oh, once I knew you wanted him I went after Bill Peyton, and in a few hours had him eatin' out of me hand. Ya know his real name was PAYTON, with an A, but at immigration they misspelled it, just like they did ours. But we're going dancing on Saturday. I've got him on me hook, and next week I'll reel him in."

The sisters laughed, and Nancy felt a great sense of relief. Her secret could now be shared, and a great burden had been lifted from her. The two had become sisters once again.

Chapter 13

PATRICK IN IRELAND

May, 1892

The Atlantic Ocean flowed calmly as Patrick stood on the deck staring at the stars flickering in the black sky. Now, at two in the morning, he still could not sleep. His job at the factory kept him up all night and he found himself unable to reset his internal clock, so he continued to drink all night and sleep all day, missing many meals aboard ship. He did manage to get to breakfast on time most days, and occasionally arose in time for dinner. But most of his waking hours were spent in an alcoholic haze, wandering about the ship, searching for company. The heavy tweed jacket, stuffed with money, weighed him down during the day, and it was a great relief when he shoved it under his cot before bed. The voyage proved to be almost as boring as his job, and he anxiously awaited its conclusion.

The boat's arrival at Cork Harbor was scheduled for seven that morning and it could not come too soon for Patrick. In only five hours he would complete his mission and be off to the Knock churchyard to begin the quest for his legacy. He hoped he would find more than a heartfelt apology from the man who had left him a bastard, in the true meaning of the word. He expected to find at least a few pounds buried behind Ellen Flynn's grave to compensate for his father's sin. And, as he mulled these matters over, he opened the last bottle of whiskey and sipped till the black sky turned grey and gradually pink, as the sun began to break on the horizon.

As he was finishing off the whiskey, the ship began to come alive. Gulls flew in the distance, and he could make out the shoreline of Ireland. The crewmen on deck hustled about, and Patrick went below to pack up his things and be one of the first to leave the ship when she docked.

Giddy with anticipation at his adventure, and by the bottle of whiskey he just finished, Patrick returned to the deck and gazed longingly at the homeland he left so many years before. Though he was an American now, Ireland remained in his soul.

After docking and dropping anchor, the crew lowered the gangplank with a loud clang, and Patrick was one of the first passengers to disembark. His legs were like rubber as he reached the dock, and the mass of people following jostled him and he stumbled and landed on one knee. Pain shot up his leg as he pulled himself to his feet. He limped away from the rushing throng behind him, and leaned against a pole, rubbing his injured leg.

After most of the passengers had departed the dock and Patrick's contact had not yet arrived, hunger pangs, his throbbing knee, and the whiskey contributed to his disorientation as he scanned the area searching for Callahan's contact person.

At last, a scruffy looking man sidled up to him and asked, "Do you know Brian Boru?"

"Of course I know Brian Boru," Patrick answered. "Doesn't every Irishman?"

The man quickly turned and hurried off towards Cork City as Patrick regained his senses and cried, "Wait! It's me!"

He tried to follow the man, but his knee hurt so badly he could only manage a slow limp, and soon the fellow vanished from sight.

Fear gripped Patrick. He had not given the contact the correct password. He began to sweat profusely and reached into his pocket for his handkerchief and pulled out the orange bandana.

"Sweet Jesus," he muttered. "I even forgot to put on the damn scarf."

He had failed his mission. What should he do now, he wondered? His mind swirled with thoughts of hiding out in Ireland for the rest of his life, but he couldn't do that as his wife was with child. Then he thought of ending his life completely by jumping into the Lee River. He felt his never learning how to swim might now be an advantage, but he really did not want to die. The only saving grace he could cling to was that he hadn't lost the jacket with the money. His addled brain entertained the fantasy that Mr. Callahan might forgive him; maybe even give him another chance to make the delivery.

Well, he wouldn't stew over that now. He'd go to Knock and complete his personal mission. But first he must have something to eat and find a horse. Now that his knee was injured, he must have a cart as well, for the long trip to Mayo. It was many years since he last rode, and besides his knee injury, he was physically out of shape. Embarrassing though it might be for a man of his young age, but knowing the mercurial Irish weather, the cart must have a top, or he would be soaked to the skin on the first day of his journey.

Patrick made his way through the winding, narrow streets of Cork, teeming with morning shoppers and men on their way to work. He stopped in a pub and inquired where to get the necessary transportation to Knock. The publican gave him directions to a local livery stable where he could rent a horse and cart, and after his bacon and eggs, Patrick set out on the short walk north to the outskirts of Cork Harbor. Not far from the massive tower of Shandon Church, he found his destination.

The owner harnessed up a horse, put some hay and a covered pail of water in the cart, and told Patrick he must pay in advance, and return the animal within a week. Then he gave him directions for the shortest route to Knock, and recommended an inn where he could stay the first night of his journey. After paying the man, Patrick took the reins, shouted, "giddy-up," and off he went.

His body ached all over, but especially his butt from bouncing on the hard seat of the cart for two days, but he would be at Knock churchyard the next afternoon, and the thought of being so close to solving the mystery of the cross cheered him on. He hoped Nancy's premonition of a legacy would prove true, and he had not undergone all this torture for a letter of apology from a stranger.

The next morning he awoke in good spirits, full of anticipation and purpose. He had taken good care of his horse, as without him Patrick knew he would be in dire straits. The animal cantered on the rocky roads, galloped on the straight-aways, and trotted past sheep grazing on meadows, and finally brought Patrick to Claremorris, a short distance from his destination. His impatience tempted him to proceed, but his stomach and thirst won out and he stopped at a pub for lunch.

Two hours later, after ingesting many pints of Guinness stout, and chatting up the customers with tales of the great success he had made of himself in America, he felt ready to proceed; then he remembered he must procure flowers and a trowel. He told the barkeep he was visiting his mother's grave, and the man accommodated him by going out the back door to his wife's garden and returning with a bunch of early blooming daffodils and a small spade.

Patrick thanked him, paid for the trowel, and began the last hour of his trek.

He tied up his horse to a post before the Knock cemetery, which lay behind a small, stone church on a country road in County Mayo. He shoved the spade in his belt and carrying the flowers, walked gingerly around the graves, searching for a tombstone engraved 'Ellen Flynn.'

It was mid-afternoon, with no mourners about. A stroke of luck, he thought. But then his luck turned, as black clouds from the Atlantic Ocean suddenly loomed overhead and large drops of rain began to fall.

The rain now came down in earnest, but he continued his search, slipping and sliding on the now soaked ground. He peered at the names on the gravestones, barely visible through the torrent of water slashing against them.

Then he found her! Ellen Flynn. He followed the procedure outlined by Matthew Clarke, and got down on his good knee behind the grave and began digging in the soil. After turning up several spades of earth, the trowel made a sharp, clinking noise, metal against metal. Patrick dug with the ferocity of a man possessed until he finally unearthed a small tin box. He dragged it out with his fingers, shoved it in his pocket, pressed the daffodils into the upturned soil, and sloshed through the muddied graveyard as fast as his injured knee would allow. He unhitched his horse, jumped up on the cart, and rode like a banshee till he found Reilly's Pub.

He trembled like a man down with influenza, but only partly because of his cold, rain-soaked body. It was his intense curiosity that drove him, and the anticipation of what the box held and how it might change his entire life.

He entered Reilly's Pub and asked the barkeep for a pint of Guinness and a double whiskey. He picked up his drinks and limped to a small table in the farthest part of the room. He gulped down half the whiskey and sat back, trying to calm himself. He pulled the orange bandana from his pocket and wiped off the rain dripping from his hair and face, then cleaned the mud from his hands. As there were no other customers in the pub, he felt it safe to open the tin box.

As he removed it from his pocket and placed it on the table, his hands shook. He slowly lifted the lid, and found an envelope with the word 'Patrick,' written in black ink. His heart sank. Ah, the letter of apology from the man who couldn't keep his pants buttoned, he thought.

After a long swig of his stout, he removed the envelope. Beneath it lay a small black silk purse. Unable to curb his curiosity, he laid the envelope on the table and opened the purse, but not before looking around the pub to be sure he was not being observed.

His eyes bulged as he dropped the object from the purse into his hand. Could this be real, he thought, as he stared at a ring, a large glittering diamond, surround by what seemed to be five brilliant emeralds. He was stunned by the beauty of the jewelry, and its obvious worth, and immediately returned it to the purse.

Maybe the letter would explain this, he thought, and carefully opened the envelope.

To my dear son, Patrick,

By the time you read this, I will most likely be dead. I will never know you, but you will always live in my heart. The love your mother and I had for each other brought you life. I only hope you can forgive us for not being able to keep you with us. When you read this, I pray you will have the maturity to understand human frailties and not think too badly of us. Your adoptive parents were instructed to present the cross to you on your eighteenth birthday.

In this box is my gift to you, a ring your grandmother, my mother, inherited from her family. You come from a long line of proud Irishmen, once a very wealthy clan until the invaders took our land and drove us to the barren West of Ireland. But your grandmother kept this ring as a legacy for her grandchildren, and you, above all, deserve it most. It is worth quite a bit of money, so if you choose to sell it, spend the income wisely; for your own education, or raising a family. Please go on to university. Knowledge is power! My profession was teaching. Your mother was a nurse.

The saddest day of my life was when I had the cross engraved and gave it to the nuns to present to your adoptive parents. I wish you a happy life, my son. And may God bless you always. Your loving father.

Patrick folded the letter and gently replaced it in the yellowed envelope. I guess me parents did love me after all, he thought, as he pressed his fingers on the black silk purse. He had no idea of the worth of the ring, but knew he had become a rich man. His birth father's guilt had provided him with funds it would have taken him a lifetime, if ever, to accumulate.

He put the letter in his pocket with the ring and took a seat at the bar. He had come this far, and was so close, he couldn't leave Ireland without finding out the truth. The bartender, a man appearing to be in his early sixties, asked if Patrick would like another drink.

"A pint of Guinness, please." There were no other patrons in the pub, so Patrick felt it a good time to begin his search.

"Here ye go," said the bartender.

"Would you be Mr. Reilly?"

"That I am. Call me Seamus. And where are ye from?"

"Dublin, originally. Now New York City. I'm here for a week on business."

The bartender, lonely for company, began talking, and commented on the rainy weather they'd experienced for a month now, and how many farmers would lose their crops to the flooding. Patrick pretended sympathy, and shook his head sadly.

When Seamus stopped for a breath, Patrick thought he might as well take a chance, and asked if there was a school nearby.

"Oh, fer sure there is. Right down the road. Why now would ye be interested in that?"

"A friend in New York knew I was going to Knock, and asked that I give his regards to his old friend, a teacher, but fer the life of me I can't remember the man's name."

"Well, there's only one school here, and one teacher. So it must be Sean Clarke yer friend was referring to."

"Aye! That's it indeed. Sean Clarke," Patrick lied, and thought he might as well try and get more information.

"Now it's all coming back. Me friend said it was a shame what happened to poor Ellen Flynn. I think he said she was the teacher's lady friend."

"That she was. I remember the lass. She was a nurse, and sweet as could be. A beautiful girl. Dark hair and eyes. Black Irish, ye know. It must be about thirty years ago when Ellen went to visit relatives in Dublin, and she was brought back in a coffin. T'was the influenza that did her in. Poor Sean Clarke. Broke the boy's heart, it did. But he was a young lad then, and as they say, time heals all wounds. Sean married six or seven years later. He had a son who went off to America, like yerself. Sean comes in fer a pint every week. Told me last how well his boy is doing in America. Studying to be a doctor, he is. Sean's so proud of him, the man beams from ear to ear at the mention of the boy's name."

Patrick had quietly digested Seamus' information, and innocently asked, "And what name would that be?"

"His son? Why he's Matthew Clarke."

Patrick asked for a double whiskey, and attempted to sort out what he had just heard. His mother was Ellen Flynn. His father was Sean Clarke. Matthew Clarke was his half-brother, and he, Patrick, was a bastard.

Seamus took out his pocket watch. "Tis almost half past three and school will be dismissed soon. If ye want to talk to Sean, just go up the road, past the church, and a half kilometer to the left you'll find the school. He'll be on his way home."

Patrick gulped down his drink, thanked the bartender and left the pub. He got in his cart and followed the directions he had received. The rain had stopped and the sun shined on the glistening blades of grass as Patrick reined in his horse a few yards from the school, and waited for the teacher to emerge.

The door opened and the children rushed out of the single room schoolhouse, delighting in their freedom after seven hours of laboring over books and sums. Ten minutes later a man left the school, locked the door, and mounted his horse. Patrick observed that Sean Clarke was the spitting image of Matthew, and as his horse passed Patrick on the road, Sean Clarke smiled, and waved a hello to the man he did not know was his son.

Patrick tipped his cap as his father's horse galloped by, and with moist eyes whispered, "Goodbye, Da."

Chapter 14

THE TRIAL

Late May, 1892

On Mr. Grunwald's last night in New York before returning to Johnstown, Rachel prepared a special dinner. She brought a succulent roast turkey to the table, and set it between piping hot dishes of aromatic sage stuffing, boiled potatoes and buttered green beans. She filled the wine glasses, then lit the candles.

"Let me make a prayer," said Dr. Weitz. "Dear God, please shower your blessings on all at this table, and grant Isaac Grunwald a safe return to Pennsylvania. Thank you for our food and please look kindly upon us."

"Now, which one of you surgeons would like to carve up the turkey?" Rachel asked.

Matthew suggested Mr. Grunwald should have the honor, and then regaled the group with the gory details of how his mentor introduced him to anatomy by having Matthew disembowel a pig in Johnstown. Rachel wriggled her nose and told Matthew that was not proper dinner table conversation, and they all laughed. The tension between Rachel and Matthew had dissipated now that she had a new beau, a man Dr. Weitz hoped would soon ask for her hand.

Mr. Grunwald adroitly carved the bird and Matthew became melancholy at the realization his friend would be leaving in the morning.

"Why don't you stay in New York? We could find you a job as a medical assistant. Why, you know more than most doctors."

"No, I must go back," said Mr. Grunwald. "There's an old saying: 'Those who can, do; those who can't, teach.' And I have a new student who seems almost as promising as you once were. And when he is sufficiently prepared, I will send him also to my friend, Dr. Weitz here, and hope he, too, will make me proud. Oh, by the way, Matthew. Johnstown seems back to normal. But as you know, many bodies were never found. I had a plaque engraved with your cousin's name, and those of his family, and placed it in the Catholic cemetery of the church they attended. A small token of my esteem for you and your beloved relatives."

"That was very kind of you. I am ashamed it hadn't occurred to me to do so. I'm still haunted by their deaths. And it breaks my heart they are gone and I could do nothing to help them. I ask God why I was saved and they had to die? They were such good people. Mr. Grunwald, I still have nightmares about the flood and how terribly the children must have died, their lungs filling up with water and mud, and their parents' terror as they watched their children swept away by the waters."

"Stop it, Matthew. That will pass. Now you look up and the skies are dark with black clouds. But some day soon the heavens will become blue again, and when you raise your eyes the clouds will have turned to white, and the sun will shine upon you. Just be patient, mein Sohn."

193

"Thank you, sir. You are right." Matthew raised his glass and said Le'Chayim, and the others repeated his toast. When Dr. Weitz apologized for not being able to offer the unpronounceable Gaelic response, a bit of levity returned to the previously solemn table.

Officer Lally entered Murphy's Bar & Grille early one morning and found Nancy and Charlie Murphy alone, engaged in conversation over a sheaf of papers at a table in the far corner. He took a seat next to them and began talking.

"The trial date for the Short-Tail Gang boys has been set fer next week. You'll all be receiving subpoenas to testify, so ye may want to talk to a lawyer to prepare yerselves fer the ordeal, along with May and Dr. Matthew. The Gang's lawyer is a shrewd one, he is. He's gotten many of the members off scot-free, and others only sentenced to a few days, or a week at most. All of ye have copies of yer signed statements, so go over them. The prosecutor will call ye down to the courthouse for a pre-trial meeting and explain the procedures."

"Will you be there too, Officer Lally?" Nancy asked.

"Aye, I must be. Yer husband brought me to the scene of the crime. I'd have him read his statement again, too."

Nancy paused, then admitted Patrick was in Ireland and would not be home in time for the trial.

"Why in God's name did he leave now? Didn't I tell him the trial would be coming up this month?"

"Yes, you did," said Nancy. "Patrick said his mother was dying and he wanted to see her one last time."

Officer Lally did not hide his anger, an emotion he rarely displayed. "The man's missed May's wedding, and now he'll miss the trial of those bums who almost killed her. What kind of man is he?"

Nancy lowered her head and did not answer. She knew all too well the kind of man her husband had become, and acutely felt the shame of being Mrs. Patrick Devlin.

"Now calm down, Lally," Charles Murphy ordered. "The rest of us will be there to testify, and we're probably better off without him. The Lord only knows, he might show up in court drunk, and how would that help our cause?" He quickly turned to Nancy. "Forgive me, lass, I meant no disrespect."

"Well, then yer right. He'd do us no good getting on the stand with a snout full. But I must be getting back on patrol," said Lally, and left Nancy and Mr. Murphy to return to their work.

Looking over the papers before him, Mr. Murphy said, "Nancy, we've done much better than I expected these past three months. Yer share of the profits, if they keep up like this, will make you a rich woman. But you'll be in confinement soon, and without your entertaining the customers, I expect the profits will drop off."

Nancy mulled over his encouraging, then discouraging assessment of the business, and had a thought. "Mr. Murphy, Norah can't play the piano, but she does have a lovely voice. What would you think of her filling in for me and singing a cappella?"

He looked quizzically at his partner, and asked, "Is that an Italian song?"

Nancy laughed, and explained it meant singing without any musical accompaniment.

195

"Well, if ye think she's good enough, it won't hurt to try her out now, would it? And if she does well, we'll hire a piano player. That would be good for you, too. The patrons could get a better look at my beautiful partner while ye have them crying in their beer."

When Nancy broached the subject with her sister that evening, Norah skipped around the living room with delight.

"I'm going to be a singer. A star, like you."

"Well, your star won't be shining very long if your voice doesn't bring a twinkle to the customers' eyes. Now give me a demonstration of your talents that I bragged about to Mr. Murphy today. Sing me something, as you would with no piano to cover up any mistakes."

Norah sang a currently popular song, quite well, but Nancy said the customers preferred Irish songs, and asked that she include those in her performances. Norah then belted out an old Irish rebel song, and Nancy approved.

"You've done well. And you won't have to sing a capella for very long. Mr. Murphy and I have decided to hire a piano player to accompany you. But you must have five or six songs ready every night. And space a little time between them. Go to the kitchen and wait five minutes so the customers can order another drink before you reappear."

"Oh, I see now why yer such a good businesswoman. Aren't you the clever one. I'll go now and write me a list of songs and practice them in the bedroom while you rest. You look tired. Is the wee one moving about?"

"He's been kicking me all day, and has left me weary."

"Ah, so ye've decided it's to be a boy?"

"A girl would have better manners than to treat her mother so harshly," Nancy said with a smile. Then she remembered the trial, and gave Norah a reason to smile.

"I need you to visit Bill Peyton." Her sister's eyes widened with pleasure and she gave Nancy her full attention.

"Tell him we need his help. Ask him if he could meet with us to prepare for the trial next week. Mr. Callahan is on a trip somewhere, so the side room is vacant. Ask Bill to come for dinner as soon as possible."

Norah began primping before the mirror, and displeased with her appearance, said she would go right away to his office, but must first change her dress.

Nancy hid her amusement. "I didn't mean you must go immediately. Look out the window. The sky is black and I hear thunder. It will be pouring down rain in a few minutes, and you'll be drenched if you leave now."

"Don't worry. I'll throw a wrap on me back and a scarf on me head and all will be well. Maybe I won't change me dress."

And with that Norah rushed out the door, calling to Nancy, "I'll be back soon."

Norah hopped off the trolley not far from Bill Peyton's law office, and landed in a puddle of water. Her boots were soaked, and her scarf was plastered against her dripping wet hair. Oh, what a sight I am, she thought. Seeing me looking like a bedraggled cat will undo all the effort I've put into landing him, she bemoaned. Well, it's too late to turn back, and I was foolish to start out, but now that I'm here I'll be going in.

She opened the door to Bill's law firm and found him facing her, apparently about to leave. But he sat her down, removed her wet outer garments, and without speaking a word, led her into his private office. He brought her a towel to wrap around her head, and took a coat from the closet and draped it over her shoulders.

"Now, what are you doing out in this kind of weather?" were his first words to Norah.

"Nancy needs yer help with preparing for the trial of the Short-Tail Gang."

"I'd be happy to do that. Now let me get you a glass of sherry to warm you up."

"I never drink liquor, but if ye have some hot tea I wouldn't refuse it."

Bill put a kettle on the smoldering stove in the corner, and took out two cups and saucers from the cabinet.

"It's good to see you again," he said, smiling warmly.

"Well, I would have liked ye to see me again looking less like a wet hen."

He laughed. "You never look anything but beautiful in my eyes."

"Do ye mean it?" Norah gazed adoringly at him.

"Would I say something I didn't mean? Don't you know me better than that by now?"

A silent moment passed before the two drew closer together, and their lips almost touched, but they were startled apart by the hissing of the tea kettle.

"Ignore it," said Bill, and they exchanged their first, but by no means their last, kiss, and they kept kissing until the sound of the kettle irritated Norah so much she got up and turned off the stove in frustration, then returned to Bill's side and they continued where they had left off.

Matthew, along with Rachel and Dr. Weitz, accompanied Mr. Grunwald to Grand Central Station to catch the train back to Pennsylvania. Matthew's spirits were particularly low, not knowing if he would ever see his friend again. Mr. Grunwald had aged over the past few years; his shoulders stooped, his gait was halting, his hair had thinned out, and his beard was now totally white. As they disembarked the trolley at Forty-Second Street, they caught the attention of two young Negro boys, loafing before the terminal.

"Hey, look at the Yids," one shouted, pointing to the skull caps the men wore. Then they ran to a nearby vender's cart, grabbed some vegetables, and threw them at Mr. Grunwald and Dr. Weitz.

"Go back where you came from," one called out as he hit his mark, and juice from the tomato dripped down Mr. Grunwald's face, turning his beard a pale shade of pink.

Matthew erupted in a fury of anger and he rushed towards the young men. He grabbed them by their necks and lifted them off their feet. As they gasped for air he shouted, "You little bastards. How dare you. I should beat the hell out of you right here!"

Dr. Weitz pulled at Matthew's arm, begging him to regain control. A crowd had begun to gather around them and he feared the arrival of the police.

"Stop, stop. This will only bring you trouble. Let them down."

Matthew took a deep breath, threw the two teenagers to the pavement, and they quickly scrambled away into the hidden recesses of the city's dark alleys.

"Thank you for coming to our aid, Matthew," said Mr. Grunwald. "But this is nothing new to us. It is the same as in Europe. Like they say in America, we, all of us, are in the same boat. The poor black people were brought from Africa to America as slaves. We, the Jews, were made to leave Europe for fear of our lives. The English took over Ireland. And during the potato famine I heard the starving died with green lips after eating grass, the only thing left to them. You see why there is so much hatred in the world? The powerful trample on the weak. Then the weak take out their anger on others. But we Jews, ach, we will never be forgiven by Christians for killing their savior."

Matthew was livid. "That's not what they won't forgive you for. What they won't forgive is that you're smarter than they are. You work harder than they do. You achieve more than then do."

Dr. Weitz put his hand on Matthew's shoulder. "And who, my friend, are 'they'?"

Matthew did not have an answer.

"Ach," Mr. Grunwald said. "Those you call 'they' are the uneducated, the other minorities, the prejudiced. But there are more people like you, good people, than there are 'theys.' There will always be more of you. Do you not understand? Some day the Jews, the Irish, the Negroes, the Germans and Italians will become the majority, and the 'theys' of today will become the minority. It is just a matter of time, mein Sohn."

Matthew sadly watched the train pull out of the station and wondered if he would ever see his mentor, his beloved friend, Mr. Grunwald, again. He and Dr. Weitz silently boarded the trolley for home.

The witnesses were all present in Callahan's private room at the tavern. When they finished dinner, Nancy called the meeting to order. It was time to get down to business.

"Bill, as we don't know the ins and outs of the rules of law in our new country, we need your guidance to get through this ordeal. Officer Lally told us the prosecutor would meet with us and tell us what to expect, but as you're a lawyer, and one of us, we need your advice."

"To begin with, tell me exactly what happened," he said to Nancy.

When she had finished the story of that dreadful day when the Gang smashed the bar mirror with a stool and left poor May studded with glass shards, Bill shook his head.

"These people are out of control, and have to be stopped. I have an idea, but first let me impress upon all of you to tell the total truth, just as you saw the events unravel that day. It might present a problem that Patrick isn't here to testify. He did make a rush at the two gang members and he was the one who fetched the police. But, we'll get along without him."

Nancy thought how she could get along without Patrick quite handily for the rest of her life.

"Mr. Murphy, round up all your bills for property they destroyed. And calculate the amount of income you lost from having to close the restaurant for repairs to be done. May, do you have receipts for your medical bills?"

"Dr. Clarke did not charge me anything."

Bill smiled. "Good for you, Matthew. But when you testify, don't play down May's injuries."

"You can see some scars close to her hairline," Matthew said, lifting May's hair and pointing to them.

"Good. Oh, forgive me, May," Bill apologized. "That was the lawyer in me talking."

Bill became serious and said, "As you are no doubt aware, this Gang's been around for years terrorizing the neighborhood. And the prosecutor and judge are just as afraid of them as are the citizens, so we can't expect too much from them. We have to rely on the jury. But they're afraid of repercussions from the Gang, too.

"I told you before I had an idea. This is it: I'm submitting a motion to the court which would allow me to act as amicus curiae. That means 'friend of the court' in Latin. Specifically, if my motion is granted, I will be able to speak to the judge about the case, but the purpose is really to speak to the jury. I will represent the views of the people who, though not directly involved in this particular case, will be affected by its outcome. That's the key part. They will be affected by its outcome.

"And all the people of this area will be affected by the jury's decision, whatever the verdict: Should the Gang members get off with a few weeks in jail, the message will be that the Gang has the permission of the people to continue their lawlessness with impunity. Should the judge hand them a tough sentence, save five to ten years, which would not be cruel or unusual punishment considering they could have killed May, the message will be that the people and the court will no longer tolerate their illegal behavior."

The women clapped and the men stomped their feet as Bill Peyton finished his explanation of amicus curiae.

Charles Murphy scratched his balding head thoughtfully. "You certainly sound like ye know what yer talking about, but I have one question. What does 'impunity' mean?"

"Ah," said Bill. "That means exemption from punishment. And that's how the Gang feels it can operate. And so far it's proven to be the case. They can get away with anything. Even murder. Now, all I have to do is get the court to approve my motion."

The men raised their glasses to Bill Peyton, the woman lifted their tea cups, and all wished the lawyer good luck in his endeavor and said they would pray for his success.

The next day their meeting with the prosecutor was short and perfunctory. He had their statements and would proceed to charge the Gang with destruction of property.

Matthew interrupted the prosecutor. "What about theft? The bottle of whiskey."

"But you told them to take the bottle, did you not?"

"Yes, but only to get them out of the bar before they caused more harm. And what about the injuries to Mrs. May Murphy?"

"Her injuries were unintentional. Did she incur any medical bills relating to the incident?"

"No. I treated her at no cost," replied Matthew.

"Well, then, we'll have to leave the charge at destruction of property."

Matthew glared at the prosecutor. "I see. So that's the way it will be."

The prosecutor ignored Matthew's insinuation, and concluded the meeting by advising them to tell the whole truth in court, and not to elaborate on their answers on the witness stand.

"A simple yes or no will be sufficient. Please arrive at court on time. Now you may leave."

As they left the man's office, Mr. Murphy's face had turned red with anger. "So they won't be punished for hurting me May," he growled. "And they call that justice?"

"Simmer down, Charles," said May. "Remember we have that smart Mr. Peyton on our side, with his, what does he call it? Friend of the court! He'll see us through."

Matthew took Nancy's arm as they navigated the twisting streets of lower Manhattan, now teeming with lunch time businessmen, jostling past them on the narrow sidewalks. They were pushed against each other, but felt no resentment towards the arrogant pedestrians. They were enjoying the closeness forced upon them, and Matthew whispered in Nancy's ear, "I can't stand being away from you anymore. I must see you alone."

"We'll go to the restaurant for lunch. When everyone's eating, come back to the kitchen."

"Are you okay?" asked Matthew. "Have you gotten over that business with the priest?" They stood in the far end of the kitchen where they could not be observed.

"Oh, yes. The thought of him still disgusts me, but it doesn't give me nightmares any longer."

"Good. So I'll see you at Mass on Sunday."

"I've gotten over him, but not what he represents. As I said, I'll no longer go to church. I'll worship God alone."

Matthew's spirits dropped. "Nancy, you can't lose your soul because of one man."

She stared up at Matthew, her eyes wide with disbelief. "Now surely our Lord would not punish me for ignoring the rules made by ungodly men! I've been reading a lot of history lately, and learned many of the Popes were just as lecherous as Father Gannon. You don't think God expects me to abide by decisions set down by a bunch of sinners, do you? I will follow His word, not theirs. And He will forgive me my sins, for I am only human, not divine."

On the day of the trial the courtroom overflowed with people from the lower East Side; patrons of Murphy's Bar & Grille and all their friends, plus neighbors who in one way or another had been victims of the Short-Tail Gang, or knew someone affected by their violence.

Nancy, May and her husband Charles, Matthew, Officer Lally and Bill Peyton sat in the front row. The prosecutor sat at a small table before the judge, and the attorney for the defense at another table with the two accused Gang members. The chatter in the courtroom silenced as the bailiff cried, "All rise," and the judge, a frail man in his sixties, slowly entered the room and assumed his position on the bench.

The proceedings began, and the prosecutor briefly outlined the charge against the defendants, and then took his seat. The defense attorney stood and pleaded the whole situation was a misunderstanding. One of his clients had been celebrating his dear old mother's fiftieth birthday, and had raised the bar stool in a salute to her. Then his friend slapped him on the back, congratulating his mother's longevity, and the stool flew out of his hands. It hit the mirror behind the bar, shattering the glass, through no intent on his part, or malice aforethought.

Uproarious laughter erupted from the courtroom spectators, and the judge banged his gavel on the table and shouted, "Order. Order in the court!"

The prosecutors then called the witnesses, asked each one or two questions, and dismissed them. The defense attorney did not cross-examine any of them, and within a half hour the attorneys finished their brief closing arguments. The case would now go to the jury. Matthew sat rigid, astounded at how the prosecutor acquiesced to the defense attorney.

"This trial is a sham," he whispered to Bill Peyton. "We're done for. We might as well be in Ireland before an English judge, for all the justice we'll see done here today."

"Hold on, now," Bill calmed him. "The judge has granted my motion. I get to speak next. Cross your fingers, or better yet, say a prayer."

Bill rose and approached the bench. "Thank you, your Honor, for granting my motion to appear as amicus curiae, a friend of the court.

"I am here today speaking for those in the community who, though not involved in this specific trial, will be affected by its outcome. The defendants," he said, pointing to the two young men dressed in suits and ties, sitting next to their lawyer and smirking confidently, "are members of what is called the Short-Tail Gang, who have menaced the good citizens of this neighborhood for many years."

"I object," shouted the defense lawyer. "There is no evidence to suggest these young men are part of that so-called Gang."

"Sustained," said the judge.

"Excuse me, your Honor. But these men's latest blatant criminal act involved these people here," he pointed to the first row. "Upstanding members of the community. The defendants entered Mr. Charles Murphy's Bar & Grille and demanded a quart of whiskey, and when asked for payment, they refused, threw a stool at the mirror behind the bar, and rained shards of glass down upon this woman." He pointed to May, and asked her to lift the hair from her face.

"The scars on this woman's face and neck will remain permanently, as will the trauma these men inflicted upon her. Had a piece of glass hit the carotid artery in her neck, she could very well have bled to death. This man," he pointed to Matthew, "is a doctor. He saves lives. If he had not been there and told the defendants to take the whiskey bottle and leave the premises, and instead fought them as was his first inclination, they could very well have killed him with the knife found concealed in that one's pocket." He pointed to the shorter defendant. "Dr. Clarke's death would have affected the community by future lives being lost that his expertise could have saved.

"This man," he pointed to Mr. Murphy, "owns the bar. He was not present at the time. But the bills arrived for all the damage the defendants inflicted on his property. So he did not lose his life, but he could very well have lost his livelihood, and that would affect his employees.

"The entire neighborhood is aware of the terror inflicted by a small group of people who hold its citizens in a grip of fear. But their reign of terror must come to an end. And it can! How? By sending more policemen to patrol Delancy Street and rooting out this evil group; by having our juries summon up the courage to convict the guilty parties; by having our judges subject those convicted to harsher sentences befitting their crimes, and not let them off with a slap on the wrist and two weeks in jail where they'll spend their time laughing with their fellow criminals and plotting their next caper.

"And the first step in taking our community back for the law-abiding citizens rests with this jury's decision. And the second step lies with you, your Honor, to send a powerful message to all those who endanger our citizens by putting all the perpetrators behind bars where they belong, for the longest period of time the law allows. Thank you, your Honor."

As Bill Peyton returned to his seat, the audience burst into cheers and clapping, and once again the judge banged his gavel. The crowd quieted down and the judge ordered the jurors to leave and deliberate on the fate of the defendants.

"Court is adjourned," the judge announced, and he left the bench for his chambers.

It did not take the jury long to bring back a verdict of guilty. The judge sentenced the men to seven years in jail, a victory for the neighborhood, and a personal triumph for Bill Peyton.

The next day a newspaper headline read:

LAWYER'S IMPASSIONED PLEA SIGNALS END OF SHORT-TAIL GANG

The publicity brought Bill many new clients, eager for the services of a brilliant, honest lawyer. Politicians began courting him, taking him to lunches and dinners at their private clubs, and suggesting Bill should think about running for public office. The attention flattered Bill, but did not go to his head. After some more time had passed, he would consider his options; but for now his law practice would remain paramount in his life.

Norah would have been more annoyed at his increased work load and frequent social engagements, if she had not been concentrating on her major interest at the moment , which was practicing songs for her debut at the restaurant once Nancy's confinement began the following month. She was going to become a star!

Chapter 15

THE RETURN OF PATRICK

June, 1892

Nancy made some changes to her apartment during Patrick's absence. She bought a new single bed and moved Norah's bed into her own room. The marriage bed and Patrick's belongings were put in Norah's old bedroom. In the future her husband would no longer be sleeping by Nancy's side.

Her pregnancy was beginning to become apparent. Soon she would have to leave her job and spend the next several months at home. The thought of being alone all day and night depressed her. What would she do? There were only so many booties, caps and blankets she could knit before she went stark raving mad, she thought. Of course, she would continue doing some cooking for the restaurant; fruit desserts, cakes and meat pies that Aunt May would pick up and deliver to the tavern. But that would still leave her with a great deal of free time; too much time for her mind to contemplate the agony of childbirth and fret over the health of her yet unborn child.

She would read, of course. Reading had become her favorite activity over the past few years. But not all day and night. She glanced at two books by the Bronte sisters on the table by her new bed, and suddenly a plan began to evolve.

All her life she'd been praised for her writing ability; first in school, and then by everyone who received her letters. She'd often been told she had a gift for words. And now she had the time to try her hand at the craft of writing. She would start out slowly with a short story, not a massive undertaking of a novel like the talented Bronte girls wrote. But how would she know if she had any real aptitude for the creative art of holding a reader's attention, or would she just be making a fool of herself?

Then everything fell into place. Writing would give her the opportunity to see Matthew. She would have him critique her work. Oh, she would try her best, but had no grandiose visions of herself becoming a successful author. Her reward would not be fame and fortune; it would be precious time spent in Matthew's presence. And no one could accuse a woman with a bulging belly of any impropriety when her doctor visited to humor her in her latest fancy by reviewing her efforts.

She looked carefully at herself in the bedroom mirror. Her hair still shown, the auburn streaked with glints of gold; her long dark eyelashes accentuated the green of her eyes; her lips and cheeks were still pink, and her ivory skin flawless. She was quite pleased with her appearance until she looked lower at her growing waistline and the protuberance beneath it.

Oh well, she thought, my child is worth the loss of my figure, and it will return to normal once my baby is born. I'll just have to make Matthew concentrate on looking at me from the waist up. She then took some writing paper and a pencil from her small desk, and searched for an idea with which to begin her writing career.

It rained on and off for the three days it took Patrick to travel from Knock to Cork Harbor. But his emotions fluctuated so much he hardly noticed his wet clothes and aching knee. The muddy dirt roads slowed his horse and forced him to make frequent stops at pubs and inns to refresh himself and the animal. As he finally neared Cork, he pulled up before a pub, and after eating and drinking stout, bought six bottles of whiskey for the ship.

He was not sorry to leave Ireland, but was afraid of returning to America to deal with Mr. Callahan's wrath when he must confess the failure of his mission. The diamond ring, now his, elated him, but the letter from his father, Sean Clarke, left him uneasy. He would show the letter to no one, not even Nancy, nor tell anyone that he and Matthew Clarke shared the same father. He'd heard of these kind of things happening many times before while he lived in Ireland, so let the past be dead and buried, he thought. But he would show the ring to Nancy, and anticipated the look of respect he would see on her face. He now had more money than she had squirreled away in her bank account over the past years, and that made him feel very happy.

After returning the horse to the livery stable on the day of the ship's departure, he waited for boarding time in a pub, rereading his father's letter and taking quick glances at the ring. And the more spirits he consumed, the better his spirit became.

He boarded the ship in plenty of time, went below and lay down on a cot, still wearing the damp jacket. At least I have the money to return to Callahan, he thought, as he shivered from the cold. He got up, opened his suitcase, tore off the hated jacket, and put on the heavy green sweater Nancy had given him for Christmas. He had worn that filthy jacket every day for over three weeks now, as Callahan instructed, but was damned if he would wear it any longer. He shoved it under his cot and fell asleep.

The ship arrived in New York over a week later, and Patrick arrived at his apartment unshaven and unkempt. Nancy took one look at the vagabond and recoiled, demanding that he head for the bathroom at once and "wash yourself so you're fit to be in the company of human beings." She threw him some clean clothes and withdrew in disgust.

He did as she said, and reappeared looking more like the man who left weeks ago.

"Here's yer cross back, me love," said Patrick, and returned the gift he had given her for Christmas. She looked it over and found it had not been damaged, and slipped it in her pocket.

"So, how did the trip go?" Nancy asked, not really caring.

Patrick, pumped up with pride, told her to close her eyes and he'd show her how the trip went.

She was in no mood for games, and made no bones about it. "Say what you have to say!"

"Okay, me love," he said, and took the ring from his pocket. "Now, what do ye think of this?"

Nancy was dazzled by the magnificent ring, and was at a loss for words. "Was there a letter?" she managed to ask.

"No. And I dug it up behind the grave, just as the good doctor told me to do. I guess people will think I'm a rich man now."

"You are not going to show that to anyone. Are you asking for trouble?"

"No, me lass. I'm going to the pawn broker tomorrow and see what I can get fer it."

She stared incredulously at the man. "Patrick, that ring's antique value is probably double its diamond and emerald value."

"So where do I go to sell it?"

Nancy thought a moment, and suggested they go to Cartier or Tiffany and have it appraised. "You must see where you can get the most money for it."

"There ye go again. Always thinking of money."

She tried to suppress her rage, and steely asked, "And how much salary are you contributing to the household, now that you have no job? Oh, I forgot. Mr. Callahan will see that you become gainfully employed again. Am I right?"

Patrick turned away from Nancy. "No," he said. "I think I'll ask Lally or Murphy if they know of anything."

Nancy became more upset. "Mr. Lally has done enough for you. Go out and find a job for yourself. And where will you keep the ring so you don't lose it?"

Patrick walked towards their bedroom saying, "In me dresser drawer."

"Oh, your things are in Norah's old room. The child's been kicking a lot and I need a bed of my own."

Patrick gave her a sneer. "So, ye've kicked me out of the marriage bed, have ya?"

"Only temporarily," Nancy lied.

He looked at her enlarged abdomen and told her he agreed. It would only be until the babe was born.

"Now, do ye have anything to eat fer a man returning home from a long journey?"

Nancy insisted she accompany Patrick to the jewelry stores to find out the worth of the ring. After two antique gem dealers assessed its value at many thousands of dollars, she led him to her bank to open a safe deposit box.

"We can't take the chance of losing it, or someone stealing it," she wisely advised, and Patrick agreed.

Nancy rented the box in both their names, and the bank official gave them each a key. Then Nancy, in a generous mood, told Patrick to come to the Bar for lunch. His hunger overcame his prudence, and he gladly accepted. But once inside, he noticed the door to Mr. Callahan's private room was open. As he passed by, Callahan shouted, "Devlin, get in here!"

Nancy looked questioningly at her husband, and Patrick shook his head, indicating all was well. But he did not believe that as he entered Callahan's domain.

"So, my friend, did all go as was planned in Ireland?" he smiled at Patrick, who began trembling.

"Well, not exactly, Mr. Callahan. I got a little mixed up with the code, and the contact ran off."

Callahan quickly stood up. "So the exchange was not made?"

"No, sir. But I still have the money."

Callahan held his temper and asked for the jacket with the cash.

"It's in my apartment, sir. I never took it off until today."

"Then get it immediately and bring it here to me," he commanded.

Patrick ran from the bar like a whip had struck his back. At his apartment, he picked up the coat, and hurried back to the Bar, sweat pouring down his face from the summer heat and the fear flowing through him.

He handed the smelly jacket to Callahan and said, trying to redeem himself, "You'll see all the money is still there. I never took the coat off, as ye told me."

Ahern gave Callahan a knife. He slit open the seams and pulled the money from the lining. His nose twitched from the stench of mold, and he gave Patrick a withering look as he drew out the bills, clumped together in a sodden mass.

Trying to regain some stature, Patrick defensively told Callahan he had risked pneumonia wearing that damp jacket for all those weeks, day and night. "And why didn't ye wrap the bills in something waterproof? I did what I could, and I'm sorry it didn't work out. I'd be willing to try again if that's what ye want."

"That is not what I want. You're through. You're a failure, to your country, and as a man. Get out! And I don't want to see your face in this tavern again!"

"But me wife is part owner!"

"It's no matter to me. This is my office and yer not welcome here anymore. And if I ever see you here, I'll rip you apart. Now get out of my sight," he roared.

Patrick left in a rage. It was all Callahan's fault, he thought. First he confused me when he gave me the code, saying that thing about Brian Boru at the battle of Clontarf. Then he hadn't wrapped up the money securely. But the money would dry out eventually. The insults were bad enough, he felt, but banning him from his wife's Bar was too much to swallow. He would make Callahan pay for this, he promised himself, one way or another.

After Patrick left Callahan spoke to his men.

"The man failed his assignment. He made a fool of us before our Irish comrades. He knows too much about our operations. He's a drunk and cannot be trusted. You heard them read his affidavit in court. He gave up the Short-Tail Gang at the trial over a bottle of whiskey and some scratches on Mr. Murphy's wife. I say he'd give us up without a second thought if it were to his benefit. He must be eliminated. Does anyone want to speak his piece?"

Ahern agreed with everything Callahan just said, but did offer one suggestion.

"Banning Devlin from his own wife's Bar will cause trouble. I know you spoke in anger, but I think it would be more prudent to let him think he's still one of us. That way he'll keep the code of silence until the deed is done."

Callahan thought for a moment, then admitted he acted too hastily. Ahern was right. "After we vote, one of you go to his apartment and bring him back here. Tell him all is forgiven and he's invited to lunch. Now we'll take the vote."

He handed out slips of paper to the seven men. "Write yea or nay and put your ballot in this glass."

217

Callahan counted the votes and announced: "Yea eight; nay zero. The vote is unanimous. I will take the necessary steps. But we must wait and pick the right time."

Patrick had not been in his apartment for more than fifteen minutes when Ahern knocked on the door. He told Patrick that Callahan wanted to apologize for his actions; he spoke too quickly, and understood Patrick had done his best, and sometimes missions fail, and all was forgiven, and he wanted him to come have lunch with him and the men.

"That I will. And I'm glad he came to his senses," Patrick replied. "And because of the mission I lost my job, so maybe Mr. Callahan can find me a position."

Ahern marveled at the man's gall in the face of failure and disgrace, and smiled to himself. Yes, Callahan will find you a position: Flat on your back five feet under in a cemetery. Then the men walked back to the restaurant under the warm June sunshine.

A few days later, Matthew stopped for dinner at Murphy's Bar, and Nancy joined him at a table near the kitchen.

"So what did Patrick discover on his ghoulish quest in the Knock graveyard?" Matthew asked.

Nancy described the diamond and emerald ring, and something jogged Matthew's memory. The description of the ring reminded him of something he had seen as a child. But then, he thought, memories were often distorted by the passage of time.

"So you now have a rich husband," he said.

"Rich or no rich, he's not the husband I want." She looked longingly at Matthew. "Anyway, I had him put it in the bank before the man started bragging about it to anyone who would listen and then be knocked on the head and have it stolen from him. I'll decide what to do with it later."

"You're a wise woman, my love."

Chapter 16

THE BEGINNING OF THE END

July-September 1892

Matthew finished his classes and left Bellevue Hospital at five o'clock, physically exhausted and mentally depleted. He had spent the entire day standing, performing autopsies on cadavers under the watchful eye of the chief of surgery, and looked forward to settling into one of the big leather chairs in Dr. Weitz's living room, his feet up on a hassock, and sharing a glass of wine with his benefactor.

Rachel greeted him with the news, "Father has been called out on a consultation, but you should sit down and rest." She brought him a glass of wine and handed him his mail. "Dinner will be ready in one hour."

He casually leafed through the envelopes until he noticed a Pennsylvania postmark, and quickly opened Mr. Grunwald's letter, delighted to hear from his old mentor.

Matthew, Mein Sohn,

I trust you are in good health and proceeding well with your studies. Except for some old age arthritis, I cannot complain. But there are ill winds blowing that I want you to be aware of. Save your money. A crisis will soon be upon us, if I am correct. I have witnessed the signs in Europe and now I see them here in America. In

Pennsylvania, coal, iron and steel prices have dropped. The bureau of railroads has stopped growing, and many companies have discontinued paying dividends to their shareholders.

The agricultural prosperity we are so accustomed to here in America has been devastated by storms and droughts. Cotton and wheat prices have fallen. I am certainly not an expert in the science of economics, but I would urge you to consult with people in New York who are more knowledgeable than I. Ask if they see what I see. And, please write to me when you find time.

Your friend, Isaac Grunwald

Callahan bided his time enforcing the vote to eliminate Patrick Devlin, and found him the most demeaning job available; janitor at St. Patrick's School. He began work at four in the afternoon after the children had left, and worked until nine, cleaning the bathrooms, sweeping the floors, and emptying trash. Once again, he worked alone, except for his companion in his pocket, a pint of whiskey. But now that he was once again employed, he hoped Nancy would stop harassing him.

Most days he remained home until two o'clock, but Nancy stayed in her bedroom writing, and he saw no more of her than before. He would have lunch at Murphy's Bar& Grille, drink for a few hours, then go to the job he hated, and his resentment towards Nancy grew and his drinking increased.

Matthew stopped at Bill Peyton's office the next day, showed him Mr. Grunwald's letter, and asked his opinion. The lawyer had heard rumblings among his colleagues of a possible depression, but hadn't put much stock in it, thinking them fear mongers, until now, as he read Mr. Grunwald's warning. The rumors fell into place, coinciding with the news of the drop in steel, iron and coal prices.

"Hard time will not affect us much," Bill told his friend. "Lawyers and doctors will always be in demand. It's the workers who'll be laid off, and the small businesses that will suffer."

"I must tell Nancy about this," Matthew said, and got up to leave.

"Depression or not, men will always find money for drink, so I wouldn't worry too much about the Bar. But you should warn her anyway; tell her to salt away some cash just in case."

"I'll do that, Bill. Now I must be off. Thank you for your help."

The following day after finishing up at the hospital, Matthew stopped at Nancy's apartment. Patrick and Norah were at work. They would have two hours alone. He hugged her and told her how beautiful she looked, and she laughed.

"It's nice of you to be such a gentleman, but haven't you noticed I'm bursting out of my dress?"

"Every woman with child is beautiful. But especially you. Now I have something important to speak to you about." He showed her Mr. Grunwald's letter and told her of his discussion with Bill Peyton. She listened carefully, asked some questions, and mulled over the catastrophic event that would most likely occur by the beginning of the New Year, if the men's predications proved correct.

She thanked Matthew for his advice, and changed the subject to the short story she had just finished writing.

"Please read these few pages and tell me if I should continue scribbling or go back to knitting, and I'll make us a cup of tea."

Matthew read the tale of a young Irish girl whose widowed father was about to remarry. The woman wanted desperately to get his daughter out of the house and did every nasty thing she could think of to encourage the girl to leave. But when the father was present, she was all sweetness to the young girl, and appeared to be a loving, kind, future stepmother. By a clever ruse, the girl managed to manipulate the woman into revealing her true character, unaware the girl's father was within earshot. The jig was up, and the father called off the marriage.

Nancy brought the tea tray to the table as he put down her manuscript.

"Well?" Nancy asked.

"Keep the pen in your hand and throw away the knitting needles. And am I right in assuming your story is based on Norah and your father?"

"Basically. But I made up all the details. And I made the woman probably much worse than anything Norah told me of her."

"It's really very good, Nancy. Would you mind if I borrowed it to show a friend of mine?"

"Go right ahead. Just don't tell him who wrote it. I'd be mortified if he laughed at it."

"We have a few of those new-fangled machines at the hospital. Typewriters they're called. Let me take the story and have it typed up for you."

"Oh, no. It's not nearly good enough for that much trouble."

"I think it is," said Matthew. "Are you saying you don't trust my judgment?"

Nancy became flustered. "Of course I trust your judgment. It's just that, well, it's the first story I wrote, and ..."

"And it won't be your last."

Matthew put the pages in his case. "Now please pour me some tea, my lady."

The next day at the hospital Matthew approached a secretary he knew and asked for a favor.

"I would be most appreciative if you could find time to type four copies of this little story one of my patients wrote."

"I'd be happy to help you, Dr. Clarke," the young woman smiled up at him. All the ladies at the hospital were enamored to some extent by Matthew, but Eileen's heart palpated at his mere presence.

"Thank you, Eileen. And I intend to compensate you for the work."

"Oh, no, doctor. It would be my pleasure to type this for you. I'll have it finished tomorrow. I could drop it off at your house tomorrow night."

"That would be too much to ask. I'll stop by in a few days and pick up the copies and thank you so much for your help, Eileen." Matthew had become accustomed to the fawning females at his workplace, and though flattered, their attentions made him acutely uncomfortable. Later that week, he picked up the typed copies, and thanked her for her efforts by presenting Eileen with a large box of chocolates. Once back in his office, he mailed the stories to four magazines, knowing at least one would publish it and anticipated the delight on Nancy's face when she saw her story printed in a national publication.

After Matthew left, all Nancy could think about was the impending recession. This was the first she'd heard of any financial crisis, so apparently most of her neighbors were unaware of the problem. She sat sipping tea for the next hour, analyzing the situation, and forming a plan. When Patrick arrived home, she had his dinner waiting, and two sheets of paper filled with numbers, dates, and lists of things to be done. Nancy knew Patrick very well, so she had carefully laid out the approach she would take in presenting him with her idea.

When Patrick had been well fed, and in a fairly good mood, Nancy poured him a small whiskey and said she had come up with a wonderful plan.

He looked askance at his clever wife, and wondered what could be in store for him now.

"How was the job today?"

"As miserable as ever."

"Well, I've been thinking a lot lately, as I don't have much else to do, and it breaks my heart that a man such as yourself has been reduced to work at such a menial job; a janitor, cleaning toilets and washing floors all night. You're much too smart to settle for that."

Her compliment drew him up and he gave her his complete attention. "And what do ye have in mind I do?"

"You know Bill Peyton and Norah have become close, and it wouldn't surprise me if he asked for her hand. Well, he is a very smart lawyer, and he mentioned the country might be experiencing some financial problems come next year. So the idea occurred to me that we should buy a tavern and open our own business. You would run the bar."

"But if the country's going into a slump, we'd have no customers," he lamented.

"Oh, Patrick, men always find money for drink. But we'll open a different kind of tavern. We'll offer free lunch and dinner."

"Free! How do ye expect to make money giving away food?"

"Patrick. Food is cheap. And I'll make it myself, so there would be no labor costs. And we'd give them simple food, not like the fancy menu I have at Murphy's Bar & Grille. I'd make some corned beef and cabbage and boiled potatoes one day, a few pot roasts with sauerkraut and noodles the next. And that would bring in a slew of customers. They'd spend all their money on beer and whiskey, which is where the real profits are, and think they were getting a bargain."

His interest had been aroused. "But where do we get the money to buy a tavern?"

"Why from selling the ring. It's not making us any income sitting in a box in the bank. And now's the time to act. Yesterday I passed two taverns on Second Avenue while I was shopping. They each had 'for sale' signs on the door. We could bargain down their asking price, and have a place of our own for very little money."

"Well, if they're so anxious to sell, they're not making any money. We'd be buying a pig in a poke.

Nancy became more animated and explained that was the beauty of her plan. Free lunches! All the local merchants and laborers would be lined up waiting for the tavern to open.

Patrick scratched his head. "As I see it, some of those big ditch diggers and the unemployed men would fill their plates up again and again and order one beer."

"No, Patrick. After they order a drink, you will give them a food ticket which they'll present to me, so I'll know they are eligible for lunch. I will plate the food, a reasonable amount, one to a customer. And no second helpings will be given."

"And while yer dishing up the food, who is it that will be taking care of the new babe?"

"Why, Norah, of course. She's not due at Mr. Murphy's till seven o'clock for dinner. Aunt May can handle the lunch customers and cook the dinners before Norah gets to work."

Nancy stood up and spread her arms as far as they would reach. "I can see it now. A big, gold lettered sign over the door reading, 'Devlin's Tavern'. And you, the proprietor, standing behind the bar in a clean white shirt, wearing a vest and a fancy tie, serving drinks to the customers and chatting them up. Why, with your personality you'd made the perfect bartender. Of course, you could not drink during working hours, but customers would come in just for the craik, as they say in the old country; just for the entertainment your conversation would provide them."

Patrick was enthralled by the idea, and imagined himself in the setting Nancy had so cleverly evoked.

"And with your own establishment, you'll become a respected member of the community, a businessman. And you'd become rich. Doesn't the thought of it fill you with pride?"

And it did. Patrick's chest puffed up and his heart was near bursting at the idea of no longer working alone, but being in the company of men who respected him, as the proprietor of a going concern. Oh, me Nancy is one clever woman, he thought, and when she suggested they sell the ring, he quickly agreed. He was smart enough to realize the money from the ring would have made him a rich man. But the money would not have brought him the stature in the community which he so craved.

Bright and early the next morning, Patrick and Nancy retrieved the ring from the bank and brought it to the antique dealer who had offered the highest price. With the heirloom sold, they immediately deposited the check in the bank and went off to purchase themselves a tavern.

At the first establishment they entered with a 'for sale' sign on the door, the owner seemed very eager to talk business. As Patrick chatted with the proprietor, Nancy toured the facility and quickly decided it would not do.

The second tavern had possibilities, but it needed a lot of work. But its location was perfect. The underground train was being built nearby, and it was at a very busy crossroad. The owner named his price, and Nancy shook her head, indicating it was too high. Patrick stood by silently and let his wife do the negotiating.

"It would cost us a fortune to fix this place up. You've run it into the ground. It needs new floors, new paint, the kitchen is almost unusable, and there's no mirror behind the bar," she said.

The owner tried to put on a good face and said he would lower his asking price a few thousand dollars. But Nancy raised her eyebrows, indicating if there was to be a deal, he must go much lower. It was apparent the man was extremely anxious to sell, and he again lowered the price, but not enough for Nancy, as she knew she could get better.

"If I offered you all cash, what would be your bottom-line price?"

The man's greed glimmered in his eyes, and he lowered the price by so much Nancy shook the man's hand and said they had a deal. She would have her lawyer contact him and draw up the sales agreement.

Once outside, Patrick looked at his wife with respect. "Yer a shrewd barginer, ye are. And I'm proud to have ye fer me wife. I promise ya, in the future, I'll do better, and maybe someday you'll be proud of me."

Nancy smiled at her husband, but all she felt was pity for the man who could never live up to her expectations, and pity for herself for marrying him in the first place.

The heat of July in New York had taken its toll on Nancy, and she clung to Patrick's arm and asked him to get her to their apartment as quickly as he could. She felt weak and very tired. Patrick hailed a horse and carriage and helped his wife into the shaded, somewhat cooler vehicle, and they returned home. After climbing the stairs, Nancy went to her bedroom exhausted, but not before telling Patrick to see Bill Peyton immediately and have the necessary papers drawn up, declaring them the new owners of the tavern.

As she promised, Aunt May visited Nancy every morning before work, while her niece stayed home awaiting the birth of her child. May brought all the gossip from the neighborhood and Murphy's Bar, and picked up the food Nancy had prepared and tried to raise her niece's spirits. But the oppressive August heat enervated Nancy. She did not sleep well. The weight of the baby in her womb felt like a watermelon hanging from her waist, and prevented her from turning on the bed to find a comfortable position. The lack of sleep caused her to feel drowsy all day, and she told Matthew to stop visiting her.

Bill Peyton drew up the sales agreement and after all the parties signed the papers, Bill notarized them, Nancy produced the cash, and Patrick and Nancy became the new owners of Devlin's Tavern. She instructed Patrick on the renovations that were to be made, and he followed her orders. He quit his job as school janitor and devoted all his time to their new enterprise. He began drinking less and working more, and became infinitely happier, and eagerly awaited the birth of his child. Devlin's Tavern was developing into a showplace compared to the other bars in the area. It was elegant, clean, and an equal of Murphy's Bar & Grille, all due to Nancy's keen eye and good taste.

The grand opening was scheduled for late August. Nancy would not attend. She could barely walk. Her uterus had expanded so much she felt it might explode at any moment. So she spent her time in the bedroom, writing her stories, and in the kitchen, making cakes and pies for Murphy's Bar. She desperately wanted the baby to be born and the waiting preyed on her mind. She wanted to feel good again, regain her strength, be over her fear of childbirth, and experience the joy of delivering a healthy child.

Patrick ordered a sign reading "Devlin's Tavern," in raised gold letters on a green background, and had it hung above the entryway. His tavern was far enough from Mr. Murphy's place so Patrick could not be accused of stealing his friend's regular customers. But the location was good, and there would be no lack of thirsty men to fill up the barstools.

Patrick told Nancy, "Let's not serve food right away. We'll wait a few months after the baby is born and ye feel well enough to be doling out the free meals."

"I think you're right, Patrick. I'll need time to recover. And I want to spend some time with my new baby before I let Norah take over his care."

So far the rumored economic downfall in the country had not elicited must publicity, so Patrick felt he still had time to establish a good customer base. But all was in readiness, with a sparkling kitchen installed in the back room.

After paying for the tavern, and depositing the remaining money from the sale of the ring into Nancy's growing bank account, that nest egg, combined with his new station in life as a businessman, changed Patrick. The return of his self-esteem seemed to flow over into all his actions. He became more solicitous of Nancy, and would give her back rubs at night to alleviate the soreness caused by the heavy burden of the baby. He would brew a pot of tea for her and sit and discuss their new business and make plans for the child she was carrying. One day he brought home a small cradle and placed it beside Nancy's bed saying, "No child of ours will be laid on a blanket in a dresser drawer as I was."

Nancy was heartened by the change in Patrick. He came home sober every evening, and no longer carried a pint of whiskey in his pocket. The charm and caring that had endeared her to him in Tuxedo Park was once again apparent, and she remembered why she had accepted his marriage proposal, and experienced pangs of guilt over her feelings for Matthew. But she could not change that now. Patrick's new attitude had occurred too late. She felt kindly towards her husband, but her love belonged to Matthew, and she took out her rosary and asked God to rid her of this emotional adultery, because she herself could not.

On September seventh, Nancy awakened at four in the morning with a nagging pain in her back. She lay still, waiting for it to subside, and tried to sleep. But the pain returned at regular intervals and with greater intensity.

She called to Norah, sleeping soundly in the bed across the room. After several cries, Norah awoke and came to her side.

"I think it's time," groaned Nancy. And Norah, having been rehearsed in the procedures to be taken, dressed quickly and retrieved the packed bag from the closet, then woke Patrick for the trip to Bellevue Hospital.

The pains in Nancy's back were becoming more frequent, and radiated towards her abdomen. She tried to raise herself from the bed, but her efforts only intensified the grip of the cramps. She fell back on the pillow, and felt warm water gushing from her and soaking the bedclothes.

Norah returned to the room with Patrick, who was pulling up his suspenders, and they rushed to Nancy's side and tried to lift her from the bed. But she froze, as the insistent band of pain encircled her abdomen like a vise.

"I can't move," she whispered.

"Come now, lass. We must get ya to the hospital," Patrick coaxed his wife. "Yer a strong girl. Now, just try and put yer feet on the floor. Norah and I will raise up yer back."

Nancy tried to do as they bid her, but the slightest movement left her exhausted. She gasped for air between the spasms of pain racking her body, then lay back in resignation to a power greater than hers.

Patrick stood by helplessly, not knowing what to do, so Norah took control.

"Go fetch Dr. Matthew. Right away," she ordered Patrick. "Tell him to get himself here as we can't move Nancy. Go now!"

Patrick ran through the quiet, moonlit streets and banged on Dr. Weitz's door. Eventually Rachel appeared in her bathrobe, and Patrick, by now in a state of high anxiety, with sweat pouring down his face, told the young woman to wake Matthew, as his wife's baby was ready to be born and she could not be moved.

Matthew appeared shortly, carrying his medical bag, and the two men rushed back to Nancy's apartment. Her cramps had been occurring more frequently, Norah told Matthew, and Nancy had been in extreme agony.

"Boil water for my instruments, and bring me lots of clean towels," Matthew softly instructed Norah as he went to her sister's side. "Now, why did you have to go do this in the middle of the night?" he smiled at Nancy, as his fingers gently palpated her abdomen.

Nancy mumbled, "I'm sorry," and closed her eyes in shame, as she knew Matthew would deliver her baby, and after seeing her private parts in such disgusting circumstances, he would not longer love her.

Matthew requested Patrick leave the room. "I don't want to have to tend to you if you faint. And a father should not be a witness to his child's birth." Then he asked Norah if she were up to assisting him.

"Oh, fer sure. In me village in Ireland I helped me mother bring many a newborn into the world. There wasn't a doctor to be found when the time came. Just tell me what to do, and I'll be here fer ya."

"Good girl, Norah." Matthew uttered a sigh of relief that Patrick had gone and Norah was by his side. He looked at Nancy, suffering extreme distress, and he was determined to forget his love for her and concentrate on delivering a woman's child.

He instructed Norah to bring pillows or rolled up blankets, and place them under Nancy's knees, so he would have a clear view of the vaginal opening. After Norah adjusted Nancy's legs in the proper position, brought the pot of boiling water and placed the instruments into it, she put a cold cloth on her sister's forehead and gently spoke encouraging words.

"Hold me hand when ye feel a pain, and ye can squeeze it as hard as ya want. Don't worry. Before long this will all be over and you'll have a beautiful baby. Just remember that and it will help with the pain. And think, if this is so bad, why would women go on and have more babies? They do because they forget this pain. You'll be so happy with the wee one, fer sure you'll want more."

After Matthew examined Nancy, he knew he was in for trouble. The baby's bottom could be seen, instead of the head, which indicated a breech birth. There was no way he could extract the baby without making an incision between the vagina and the anus.

"Nancy," he said. "I can't give you anything for the pain. But you're in such pain now, you really won't feel what I'm about to do. But the baby is in the wrong position. I have to take it out with an instrument. I want you to take deep, slow breaths. And within a few minutes it will all be over. Can you do that for me?"

"I can do anything for you," she admitted in her semi-conscious state.

Matthew carefully sliced into her flesh and performed an episiotomy to enlarge the vaginal opening. Nancy clung to Norah's hand and moaned from the pain. Then she let out a horrific scream as Matthew carefully extracted the baby, cut the umbilical cord, and packed a towel into Nancy to stem the flow of blood. He then put in several sutures to close the incision, and after pushing out the afterbirth, inserted clean towels between her legs.

He handed the baby to Norah, who cleaned out its throat and nasal passages, washed the blood from the infant's body, and after wrapping the newborn in clean towels, placed the crying baby gently into his mother's arms saying, "Nancy, you have a son."

Nancy held her child and gazed into Matthew's eyes and said, "Thank you. Without you I would have died with the child still inside me." Then she closed her eyes and fell into a deep sleep.

Norah removed the infant from Nancy's arms and placed him in the cradle and brought Patrick into the room to meet his new son. Matthew washed his hands and congratulated the new father.

"It's no wonder Nancy had such a hard time. Your son's a big boy. Must be almost nine pounds."

Then he turned to Norah. "You did a wonderful job. Next time I deliver a baby, I'll call you to assist."

"Oh, go on with ya," she said, blushing with delight. "But I might need you first to take care of me fingers. She nearly broke them all, she squeezed me so hard."

Matthew examined her hand and wrapped it in a cold, wet towel. "It should be fine in a day or two. You're a strong girl."

He was about to leave as Patrick said, "I can't thank ye enough fer saving me wife's life and giving me a son. Can I get ya a drink after all ye've been through?"

"No, thank you. I must get to the hospital, but I'll be back tonight to check on Nancy." He took Norah aside and made sure she knew how to teach Nancy to feed the baby, and Norah said she would, just as she had done with other new mothers in Ireland.

Then Matthew proceeded home. He would not attend classes today. His heart was too heavy after having delivered Patrick's baby. Nancy's child should have been his.

That evening he went back to visit Nancy. She looked shyly up at Matthew, and then dropped her eyes. He instinctively understood her embarrassment.

"Nancy, now listen to me. I'm a doctor. What I did for you this morning is part of my job. I love you no less for what I saw. And you were a perfect patient. You went through the ordeal better than any other woman whose baby I delivered. You should be proud of yourself. You handled your pain and anguish with dignity. I've had women curse, scream, and damn their husbands during delivery. You were magnificent."

Nancy looked deliberately into his eyes and said, "How can you still feel the same about me after spreading my legs and pulling a child from me? How disgusting it must have been for you."

"Oh, you silly, innocent little fool Don't you know the difference between a doctor and a lover?" He kissed her cheek. "Now open your legs and the doctor in me will see how you're recovering."

Nancy gingerly moved her legs, and Matthew removed the towel and pronounced her well on the road to recovery. "I'll remove the stitches in a few days," he said.

"Stitches?" she cried.

"See? You didn't even know I put them in. Trust me, my love. I told you there would be no pain." He raised her up, held her in his arms, and kissed her gently.

"Matthew, you saved my life. You saved my son's life. But can you save our lives?"

"Be patient, darling. The Lord accomplishes what we mortals never can. Have faith. We were meant to be together. Maybe not here, but definitely in the afterlife."

"I don't want to wait until the afterlife. I want you now."

"Well, I've been thinking about that. I could speak with a priest and find out if an annulment would be possible. You were very young when you married Patrick, and weren't aware he was an alcoholic. You only had sexual relations with him once. The church might consider that grounds for annulment."

Nancy cared little for the rules of the Catholic Church after being molested by Father Gannon, and would feel no compunction obtaining a civil divorce. But Matthew's deep Catholic faith remained strong and his allegiance to the Church had not diminished.

"Oh, Matthew, could it be possible? Please look into it right way. Tomorrow?"

He took her hands in his and assured her it would be his top priority.

Nancy did not sleep well that night. Her mind raced making plans for her new life as Mrs. Matthew Clarke. She brushed aside what Patrick's reaction would be to losing her and baby Sean. He'll just have to accept it, she thought. He'd brought it all on himself.

Chapter 17

THE BAPTISM

October, 1892

The oppressive summer heat had been replaced by crisp autumn air, and the trees turned into a kaleidoscope of crimson, orange, yellow and bronze. People walked more briskly through the streets. The city smelled better without the garbage rotting in pails on the sidewalks, and the rats were less visible now that their main source of sustenance had dried up.

The time had come for Nancy's son to be baptized, but the name of the child caused some dissention between his parents. Two days after the boy was born, while Nancy was still weak and tired, her husband burst in to her bedroom, waving a newspaper.

"Will ye look at this! Corbett beat the great John L!"

"What are you talking about?" Nancy asked him, totally disinterested in his announcement.

"Boxing! Jim Corbett knocked out John L. Sullivan for the heavyweight championship down in New Orleans. They went twenty-one rounds. And ye know when it happened?"

Nancy feigned interest, but she couldn't have cared less about men beating each other senseless before screaming spectators.

"So when did this momentous event occur?"

Patrick slapped the newspaper against his leg. "On the very day our boy was born! September 7. We'll name the boy John, after Mr. Sullivan, we will."

Nancy could not quite understand. "Wouldn't it make more sense to name him after the winner?"

"No, no. The Great John L. was the best boxer in the world. But it had to end sometime. And it did; on our boy's birth date! So, we'll honor him and call the boy John."

"I don't like that. But I will call him Sean."

"But … I want to call him John," he pleaded.

"Sean means John, in Gaelic. It will be Sean. After my father."

Patrick was confused. "Your father's name is Sean?"

"I told you that years ago. Have you forgotten your own father-in-law's name?"

Patrick's brain was spinning. SEAN! His father, her father, and now my son? I guess it was meant to be, he thought. And I can't tempt fate and bring bad luck upon the boy. "Sean it will be," he consented, still feeling the coincidence could be the work of impish Irish spirits.

Then the couple pondered who to appoint as godfather: Mr. Murphy, or Officer Lally. Both men had been very good to them, but they were too old to assume the responsibility of raising Sean should something happen to Nancy and Patrick. Nancy decided the godparents would be Norah and Bill Peyton. They were young enough and would surely marry in the near future.

"Then I'll make the arrangements with Father Gannon," said Patrick.

"Father Gannon is not to be involved. I'm having his assistant, Father Connolly, perform the ceremony, so you can speak to him about it."

Patrick was again confused. "But..."

"There will be no buts about it. It's to be Father Connolly."

Her husband knew when not to press a point with his wife. When Nancy set her mind to something, there was no changing it.

That having been settled, Patrick went to see Father Connolly to arrange a date for the christening, while Nancy lifted her son to her breast and fed the hungry child.

On a balmy October afternoon, Bill Peyton picked up Norah and the two strolled over to the East River for a picnic lunch. She laid a blanket under a tree, and opened her basket of sandwiches and fruit, and poured iced tea from a covered pitcher into their glasses. The sky was a brilliant blue, dotted with fluffy white clouds, which changed shape as they were tossed about by the wind.

"Norah, when I was a child," said Bill, "I used to look up at clouds like these and see faces, and animals, and all sorts of things. What do you see?"

"I see life passing by, very quickly. See that large cloud to the left?" She pointed to a billowing white piece of fluff, changing its shape by the second. "Now it's here, and then, if you turn away for a moment, it's gone."

"That's a very interesting view of life, my dear. Look," he gestured to another cloud. "When one formation changes, another appears. I see life as constantly changing, with one beautiful shape replacing another. See there," he pointed to a round, bracelet-shaped cloud. "What do you see?"

"A donut," she replied.

Bill laughed. "Ah, but I see something else." Then he reached into his pocket and produced an engagement ring. "I see a circle, a pledge of love. Now, before it is taken away by the breeze, answer me. Will you marry me?"

For the first time in her life, Norah was speechless. She expected Bill to propose at some point, but not today, and not when her mouth was full of chicken salad. She grabbed her iced tea, took a large gulp, and said, "Yes, oh yes." Then she threw her arms around his neck and they embraced.

Bill gently placed the diamond ring on her finger, and with their hands entwined, they looked up at the sky to find Norah's donut cloud had not lost its shape. It had grown larger and more prominent.

The christening was to take place on Saturday. Nancy could not abide the fact that the mother of the child was not allowed to attend the ceremony.

"What is wrong with the Catholic Church?" She asked Aunt May. "They consider the child's own mother not pure enough to witness her son's baptism?"

"Oh, Nancy, it's an old tradition. Tis silly, I admit, but that's the way it's done. And you'll be busy cooking for the party, and before ye know it, we'll all be back at Devlin's Tavern for lunch."

And Aunt May was right. Nancy had regained her strength and was as energetic as ever. On Saturday morning she arrived early at

Devlin's and roasted a loin of beef and two chickens, mashed up a pot of potatoes, sautéed mushroom and onions, and fixed the carrots and peas. Mrs. Feroni, once again, had offered to provide the cake.

With her work finished, Nancy sat and sipped a cup of tea and awaited the return of her son, now free from the threat of ending up in limbo should God suddenly take him from her. She looked over the tavern with pride, and had to give Patrick credit. During the last few months he had worked tirelessly renovating their new establishment, and now it sparkled with gleaming mirrors and shone with polished tables and a new wooden floor. She heard the door open and sounds of laughter filled the tavern as Patrick ushered their friends in. Nancy rushed to Norah, who held the newly baptized Sean, and asked how the ceremony had gone.

"The little darling did ye proud. Not a sound came out of him when Father Gannon poured the holy water on him."

Nancy's head jerked up. "Father Gannon?"

"Yes. Father Connolly was to do it, but he fell ill. T'was a lovely ceremony, it was."

Matthew's usually laughing eyes were stern as he strode towards Nancy, who instructed Norah to see to Sean while she checked the kitchen. "Matthew, will you come help me lift the roasts from the oven?"

He followed her to the kitchen. She was livid. "How could you allow Father Gannon to perform the baptism?"

"What could I do? The other priest was sick. It wasn't my place to call it off. But then Patrick invited Gannon back here for lunch ..."

"He did what? I'm sorry I gave you back that pistol. I might need it again today!"

"Calm down, my love. And you won't need a gun anymore. This could be the beginning of the end of the Short-Tail Gang, and I've taken care of Gannon. I took the priest aside and told him if he dared set foot in here again he would never again set foot outside. The man turned white, and scurried back to the rectory, like the filthy vermin he is."

Nancy regained her composure, and thanked Matthew. "I could kiss you for that, but someone might barge in. Oh, I love you so dearly."

"And you, my darling, look absolutely beautiful. No one would know it was only a month ago that Sean was born. You look so trim and fit."

She blushed, remembering him delivering her baby.

His eyes were laughing. "Will you ever stop thinking about that?"

She gently brushed a stray lock of flaxen hair from his brow, and said, "So, it's not only my body you know intimately, but also my very thoughts."

Matthew turned serious. "I have some news for you. I spoke to a monsignor I met at the hospital and we discussed annulments. I mentioned your case, anonymously, of course, and he feels there are sufficient merits to initiate the process and thinks the church will probably grant it."

"Matthew, that's wonderful! What do I do to begin this?"

He took an envelope from his pocket. "Here are the papers you must fill out and mail to the archdiocese. Then they'll contact you for an interview."

"That seems easy enough." She threw her arms around Matthew's neck. "Thank you, darling. Thank you, thank you. You've made me so happy!"

They had just disengaged themselves when the door opened and Norah entered carrying Sean. "Come quickly. The toasts are beginning."

Patrick, behind the bar, looked quite presentable in his new suit and tie, as he poured drinks for the assembly.

"Ah, Nancy," he said. "Yer just in time."

They all held up their glasses and the godfather, Bill Peyton, said a few words wishing the Lord's blessings upon Sean and everyone drank to the child's health and long life.

Officer Lally looked at Patrick's glass. "What's that yer drinking?" he asked.

"It's what I'm not drinking that counts. Now that I have a wee son, I've decided to put down the drink. From now on, it's soda water for me. I can't be drinking up all me profits now, can I?"

"Good fer you, Patrick. Now I have a bit of news. After twenty years on the force, I've decided to retire. I've risked my life every day for long enough, and don't want to push me luck. I'm getting out while I'm still alive."

The group congratulated both men and Nancy stood silently, stunned by their decisions. Patrick would stop drinking! She never thought that day would come. And there would be no Officer Lally to turn to in times of trouble. Norah was getting married, Devlin's Tavern would officially open tomorrow, a depression would hit the country in a few months, and she had the new responsibility of raising a son. During the four years she had been in America, her world had changed dramatically.

She watched as Patrick took Mr. and Mrs. Feroni aside. She was within earshot, and heard her husband abjectly apologize for his behavior towards the Italian bakery owners, and asked if they could find it in their hearts to forgive a foolish Irish immigrant. Mr. Feroni shook his hand, and said all was forgiven, and they would be good friends from there on.

Would wonders never cease, thought Nancy. Had the birth of his son made a new man of Patrick? Of course not. It was his new status in the community by being the owner of a tavern that brought about the change in him, she realized.

"Now it's the new father's turn to toast his friends for all the well wishes they bestowed upon his first born son," said Nancy, and she handed him a glass of ginger ale.

Patrick frowned at her. "Ah, Nancy, but this is an occasion for a real drink. My son was baptized today. It won't hurt to take a nip on this special occasion to thank our friends and family."

Nancy tried to dissuade him, but Patrick poured himself a large glass of whiskey, raised it up, and said, "To me good friends. Thank ye all fer being here with us today. May God's blessings be showered upon ye all and me son, Sean, on this his baptismal day." And then he drank the glass of whiskey that would return him to his former state and the beginning of his undoing.

The grand opening of Devlin's Tavern took place the following day, and proved to be a great success. A constant stream of people arrived, all praising Patrick and his handsomely appointed, sparkling clean establishment. When he closed up that night Patrick rewarded himself with another large whiskey as he counted the profits, and felt quite pleased with how well he had done. And that was achieved without giving away any of Nancy's food. As Patrick locked the door behind him and headed for home, he was a very happy man.

Chapter 18

THE PUNISHMENT

November, 1892

Nancy's days were full; taking care of her child, writing her stories, cooking for Murphy's Bar & Grille, and keeping the accounts for the two taverns. Matthew stopped by every few days on his way home from the hospital to check on Nancy and the health of her newborn. He always came upon the same scene; the baby sleeping serenely in his crib, and Nancy sitting at the dining room table surrounded by piles of paper and sharply pointed pencils working diligently on writing her stories.

"Well, how's my budding author doing?"

"Struggling along. And how are you?"

"I'm tired. It's been a long day." Matthew examined the sleeping infant and reported to Nancy that the boy was thriving and looked well fed."Now, how many more stories have you written?"

"Two more. I'm just starting my fourth, but I've reached a

roadblock. I can't come up with a good ending."

"You will," Matthew assured her, touching her hand. "Inspiration will come eventually. But for now, I'd like to read the others you've written."

"But you haven't given me my first one back yet! Did you like it or hate it? Should I go back to the knitting needles?"

He laughed. "Oh, my silly darling. No more needles, only pencils. And I did like it. I just wanted to leave it for a while and reread it to see if I have any constructive criticism to offer. Not that I'm a literary scholar, but I'd like to look at it again with a fresh eye."

"Whatever you say. You're the doctor," and she handed him the other two six-page manuscripts.

He kissed her forehead. "Must go now. Lots of medical reading to do tonight."

She clasped his hand. "Come back soon, Matthew."

He took her in his arms. "That I will, Nancy. You can be sure I will." His kiss left her breathless, and then he was gone.

Patrick had begun drinking again in earnest since his baby's christening. He spent his sober hours rocking little Sean on his lap and regaling the infant with tales of old Ireland. Though the child understood not a word of what his father said, he stared up at Patrick in rapt attention, listening to the pleasing cadence of the man's Irish brogue.

Patrick looked over at Nancy and once again brought up the subject of buying a horse and carriage. The Devlins had enough money to do so, but Nancy felt no need for that.

"But we look like paupers to our neighbors," Patrick pleaded.

"Walking is good exercise, and we have no reason to try and impress anyone. Are you not the owner of Devlin's Tavern? Is that not prestige enough? And the money will be saved and put to better use."

"Tis all ye think about is bloody money, it is. Money is meant to be spent while yer alive, not thrown in the coffin as they lower ye into yer grave."

"Have you no recollection of the coming recession? A nest egg is what we need to get through the hard times."

Patrick threw up his hands. His parting words were, "Well, keep yer nest full of eggs and hope they're not cracked by the time ye decide to fry them."

She ignored her husband's testiness and reminded herself that Norah's singing at Murphy's Bar kept bringing in customers, so Nancy could remain at home with Sean and write her stories till the depression hit and she would begin cooking free lunches at Devlin's Tavern.

Callahan, Ahern and the other members of the alliance talked quietly in their room at Murphy's Bar & Grille. It had been four months since the vote had been cast on Patrick's fate, and Callahan saw no reason to delay the execution any longer. Patrick's failure to deliver the money to his Irish contacts had caused him extreme embarrassment and his anger at the man grew each day.

"Now that he owns a bar, he'll be shooting off his mouth to the customers, bragging about his affiliation with us and our activities, and probably blaming me for his failure to complete his assignment, just trying to impress his customers. It must be done now," decided Callahan.

One member mentioned that Patrick had cut back on his drinking since he became a father.

"I don't give a tinker's damn about his being a father. He'll go back to the bottle. Once a drunk, always a drunk," Callahan spat out. "Any one of ye notice he doesn't come to meetings anymore? If there's any man here who thinks another vote should be taken, raise yer hand."

Callahan's rhetoric proved persuasive, and the men's hands remained on the table. Callahan's fury at Patrick had increased immeasurably as his contacts in Ireland made no secret of their disgust with the way Callahan had handled the aborted mission. They blamed him for choosing a man incapable of completing the job, and Callahan would not rest until he destroyed Patrick for ruining his reputation. He stood up and stated, "Then I will meet with the proper person and have it arranged."

While Irish thugs evolved into the Short-Tail Gang, a small segment of Italian immigrants were creating their own up-and-coming terrorist organization, with members willing to do anything in return for the almighty dollar. The next day Callahan met with Mr. Petrillo, the leader of the Italian group whom he had dealt with in the past, and requested his help in disposing of Patrick. After hearing Callahan's plan, the man told him the price would be two hundred dollars, in advance. Callahan agreed, and after Mr. Petrillo instructed Callahan to have his man meet with the assassin, Guido, the following night on Mott Street at ten o'clock to work out the details, the conspirators drank to old times over a bottle of Chianti.

Callahan met Ahern the next morning at Murphy's Bar & Grille and repeated Mr. Petrillo's description of the killer, Guido, who Ahern would meet that evening. But except for Guido being eighteen years old, Ahern felt he would look no different from any other Guinea on the lower East Side.

"Tell this Guido guy we want it to look like the Short-Tail Gang killed him. And it should look like a robbery. Have the kid take any money there is in Devlin's pockets. And he should use a knife. Have it done one night this week when Devlin's on his way home after locking up that new tavern of his. Then tell Guido to leave the body in an alley. You'll meet the kid at night to set things up, so it will be easy to disguise yerself. Wear glasses, and pull a hat down over yer face. And take that off! Be Jaysus, anyone could identify it," Callahan gestured to the large gold ring with a prominent black onyx stone on Ahern's finger.

"And don't give him yer name. Yer to call yerself Farley. Mr. Farley. Do you have any questions? Have I forgotten anything?"

Ahern thought a moment, and remembered what Callahan told him months ago. "You wanted the executioner to shed suspicion on the Short-Tail Gang by leaving a special mark. I'll tell Guido what to do."

"Good man," said Callahan. "And one other thing. Tell Guido to burn down Devlin's Tavern." With that, Ahern left to start the wheels of Patrick's hearse in motion.

Later that night, Ahern had no problem recognizing the arrogant young man swaggering towards him as he waited in the shadowy doorway of a locked up grocery store.

"Guido, over here," Ahern called softly. The assassin surveyed the area, looking carefully over his shoulders for any witnesses, and when assured they were alone, asked, "Who are you?"

"I'm Farley." And as Ahern foolishly reached in his pocket for something to wipe the sweat from his face, Guido's knife touched Ahern's chest.

"Stop!" Ahern yelled. "I was just getting out me handkerchief!"

"Then take it out slow. Very slow."

Ahern knew Mr. Petrillo had chosen the right man for the job. Guido's instincts were sharper than the knife still threatening Ahern's aorta. But as Ahern dried his face, Guido relaxed and listened carefully to his assignment. "What time does the guy close the Tavern tonight, and what's his name?"

Ahern gave him the information, and Callahan's special request. Guido smiled menacingly at Ahern, and said, "Boy, you must really have something against this guy."

"It's just business. Only business."

"Okay. Consider it done. I'll meet ya back here at midnight with proof I did the job. Okay?"

Ahern couldn't disguise his surprise at how quickly events were proceeding.

"Ya wanna wait? Or ya wanna get it over with?" Guido was getting impatient.

"Yes. Now is fine. I'll be back here to meet you in two hours," said Ahern, and Guido backed up a few steps, put his knife away, and ambled casually down the street.

Guido made his way to Devlin's Tavern and hid in an alley across the street which offered him a direct view of the tavern doorway. At ten past eleven, a man left the darkened tavern, took keys from his pocket, and locked the door.

As Patrick started down the empty, dark street, Guido checked to make sure there were no people about, then walked towards Patrick. "Mister Devlin?"

Patrick turned to the man and answered, "Aye, I'm Mr. Devlin. What can I do fer ye?"

Once he was assured he had the right man, Guido shoved Patrick into the alley, and pushed him against the brick building.

"What the hell are ye doing? What do ye want!" yelled Patrick, as he instinctively raised his arms and attempted to push the man away. But with lightening speed, Guido withdrew his knife, and plunged it into Patrick's chest.

"Ah, ah. Why?" Patrick gasped.

Guido gave the knife a quick upward thrust, then withdrew it, and Patrick slid down the wall, feeling the sharp, crushing blow to his chest and extreme surprise at what was happening to him. As life ebbed from his body, he asked God to forgive him his sins, and just as the black cloud of death descended upon him, his thoughts were of Nancy and Sean, and he prayed his loved ones would have a safe and happy life without him.

In accordance with his instructions, Guido grabbed the dead man's shock of thick black hair, pulled back his head, and with his knife carved the letters R A T on Patrick's forehead.

He wiped the blood off his knife on Patrick's white shirt, ripped the wedding band off the dead man's finger, and emptied his pockets of money. Guido stuffed the items in his pants pocket, and after carefully checking the street to make sure no one would observe him, he calmly walked back to Devlin's Tavern.

Patrick lay in a pool of blood that had oozed from his chest and dripped down his face. Next to his outstretched hand lay a small slip of paper that had fallen out of Guido's pocket when he pulled out the knife. On it was scrawled, "Mr. Farley, Mott Street, Monday, 10 p.m."

The ever efficient Guido scrambled to the back door of the tavern, smashed a kitchen window, and tossed in the flask he had carried in his back pocket. He lit two packs of matches and threw them deftly over the broken kerosene bottle. The room ignited immediately and Guido vanished back into the night and headed for Mott Street.

Officer Lally had finished his shift and was walking home when he saw smoke coming from inside Devlin's Tavern. He grabbed his nightstick and knocked in the front door window. He put on his gloves and reached in and opened the lock, pulled his scarf over his nose and mouth, and rushed inside. He knew Patrick closed the bar at eleven o'clock, but searched for him anyway. He also knew Patrick was back on the booze, and might have overdone it and passed out. While searching for his friend, he heard a woman scream from the apartment above the tavern and ran next door to the entrance. He raced up the flight of stairs, coughing from the fumes filling his lungs. The woman stood on the landing crying, "My son, my son, he's asleep. Save him, please."

Lally grabbed the sobbing woman around her waist, scrambled down the stairs and laid her on the sidewalk. Then he raced back up to rescue her son. By then the flames had reached the woman's apartment and dense smoke filled the rooms. Lally could barely breathe, but he continued searching for the boy until a burning beam fell on the policeman's neck, and the searing pain forced him to try and escape. His uniform caught fire as he stumbled down the stairs, and his last conscious thoughts were of Mrs. Lally and God.

Ahern was waiting as promised when Guido returned that night two hours later.

"Okay. It's done."

"Did you take his money?"

"Yeah," smirked Guido. "It's my bonus for doin' a job on such short notice. Okay with you?"

Ahern nodded. Guido could keep the cash.

"And I brought you a little keepsake, proof that I did the job." He handed Patrick's wedding ring to Ahern. "I guess the guy was married. Ya might get a few bucks for it at a pawn shop."

"Where did you leave the body?"

"In an alley right near the Tavern. They'll find him in the morning."

"Did you …"

"Yeah," said Guido. "I left the message. In big letters on the guy's forehead, just like ya said."

"And the Tavern?"

"In flames, just like ya wanted." Then Guido vanished into the night.

Nancy was awakened by the sound of fire truck bells and she looked out the living room window. The clanging noise also woke Norah, who said, "What's happening out there?"

"I don't know. But Patrick must be enjoying himself. His coat's not in its usual place, thrown across the sofa."

Nancy opened his bedroom door and found the coverlet still neatly in place. Well, she smiled, I guess that's the end of his promised sobriety, and my annulment will go through without any problem.

"I have a bad feeling," said Norah. "I'll just throw on me coat and go to the Tavern and see if Patrick's all right. He's always home by now."

"Do as you wish. I have a baby to feed. But be careful."

The streets were dark, but Norah kept up a brisk pace and within five minutes she approached the tavern and saw the wagons and the firemen rushing into Devlin's Tavern. As she began to cross the alley, rats scattered across her path. She stopped in her tracks and waited until the rodents retreated. Then she inched her way forward, afraid another filthy beast would appear. She looked cautiously down the alley before going further, and spied a man in a white shirt and green silk tie lying on the ground a few yards from her, and she let out a blood-curdling scream as her world turned black, and a passerby rushed to her side, catching her just before her knees hit the ground.

When she regained consciousness, the police had arrived and surrounded Patrick's body. They pronounced him dead. They lifted the girl up by her arms and carried Norah to the police wagon to take her home.

Norah pleaded with the policeman. "Stop and get Dr. Matthew. My sister will need him now."

Matthew had been working at the desk in Dr. Weitz's office when the doorbell rang. A somber looking cop said, "I've got a problem. I have a girl called Norah in there," he pointed to the police wagon, "And you might want to have a look at her. She fainted, but she's awake now."

"What's happened?" asked Matthew.

"The owner of Devlin's Tavern is dead. Someone stabbed him in the heart and the girl found him in an alley. She wished me to fetch you for her sister."

"Her sister is Mr. Devlin's wife." Matthew rushed into the wagon and Norah grabbed his hand.

"Oh, Matthew, it's a terrible thing that's happened," she uttered between her sobs. "And the worst is what they did to Patrick's face. They cut letters into his forehead with a knife." She began trembling and found it impossible to proceed.

"What letters, Norah?"

But when she could not bear to answer, the policeman stepped in.

"They carved the word RAT onto the poor man's forehead. Now let's get this girl home. She wanted me to take her to you, so you must know where she lives."

"That I do," said Matthew, and as he held Norah's hand, directed the policeman to Nancy's apartment.

They rode the short distance in silence. When Nancy opened the door and saw the three of them, she stood frozen, her eyes wide in anticipation of the bad news she knew would soon be revealed to her.

The policeman ushered Norah to the sofa, while Matthew took Nancy's hands.

"Where is Patrick?" Nancy finally asked, as no one seemed able to speak.

"It's bad, Nancy," said Matthew. "He's gone. He's been murdered. Norah found him in an alley across the street from his Tavern. And they burned that to the ground."

Nancy listened and tried to understand him, but all that resounded in her mind were the words 'murdered' and 'burned.'

"Who killed him?" she finally asked.

"Come, sit down." Matthew led her to the sofa and Norah put her arms around her sister and wept.

"We don't know who did it," said Matthew. "But the police think it might have been the Short-Tail Gang."

"But why would they do that?"

"Probably as revenge for Patrick's affidavit read at the trial of the gang members who wrecked Murphy's Bar. Patrick was the one who brought the police in and his statements were very damaging to the defendants. And then they burned down the Tavern, probably to get back at you and May for testifying."

"But it doesn't make sense. Bill Peyton's the one who swayed the judge and jury." Nancy concentrated on the motive because she could not bear to hear how they had killed Patrick. Maybe later she would ask, but not now. Norah was verging on hysteria and blurted out the details to Nancy. When told about the word carved on her husband's forehead, she put her hands over her ears. "Why? Why would they do that to him?" asked Nancy.

"It's the symbol of an informer, a squealer," said Matthew. He took her hands and said he would give her something to calm her, but Nancy refused. Sean's cries could be heard from the bedroom and Nancy stood and calmly told them she must tend to her baby, then left the room.

While she nursed Sean, Nancy tried to make sense of her life. Patrick was dead, her Tavern had been burned down, and her only income was the twenty-percent interest in Murphy's Bar & Grille. Almost everything she'd worked so hard for had been lost. She had foolishly refused when Patrick urged her to purchase fire insurance on the building when they bought Devlin's Tavern. She had been too frugal and thought it a waste of good money. Could it be true, as Patrick said, that she cared too much about money? That wasn't totally true. She also cared too much about Matthew. But, she felt, she should have been more encouraging of Patrick's efforts to give up the drink. Maybe in the back of her mind she was happy he took to the bottle again as it would ensure her annulment. Oh, forgive me, God, she prayed.

I wasn't like this in Ireland, she thought. What have I become? Now I've even left the Church. Oh, how far I've strayed from my values. This new country has changed me. Everything came to me so easily in America, the land of opportunity. Here there are so many opportunities; not like the hard life we had in Ireland. Here there were so many avenues to explore with no risk of ostracism from ones family, the town's people, or the parish priest, if I took the wrong path. Over the years in New York, greed and self-absorption have replaced my normal ambition. All I needed to do here was use my charm, wit, audacity and take risks, actions that would have made me a laughing-stock in Ireland where they'd quickly put me in my place. I've become too big for my britches, she thought. Pride has been my downfall. In Ireland they sneer at pride. In New York, they celebrate it. Is God trying to teach me a lesson? Put me in my place and remind me that He is the boss and I am the servant?

Norah could not erase the sight of Patrick's mutilated body from her mind, and continued sobbing. Matthew withdrew a packet of valerian from his medical bag and mixed the power in water and ordered her to drink it.

"I can't believe it," said Norah. "Patrick had everything to live for. His new son, a new business, and a good life without the drink, and now he's gone."

Matthew went to the kitchen and put the kettle on for tea and made some toast and eggs, and remembered Mr. Grunwald telling him years ago how knowledge of the culinary arts would come in handy some day. As much as he resented Nancy's husband, he was shocked and sorrowed to see a life taken so violently, so senselessly. Then he remembered Aunt May. She knew Patrick longer than anyone, since they worked together for the Birmingham's. She and her husband, Mr. Murphy, must be told before they heard the news on the street. But it was too late. They were already knocking on the door.

Matthew let them in and Norah ran into her aunt's arms, still weeping.

"It's been quite a shock for Norah," Matthew told them. "She found Patrick." The kettle hissed and Matthew brewed tea, and brought breakfast into the dining room.

The policeman took Matthew aside and told him what needed to be done now. The body had been moved to the morgue, and Nancy would have to identify Patrick before the police released the body to the funeral home. The officer offered to accompany Nancy later that day, and then burial arrangements could be made.

Nancy was at her best when she had things to do and plans to make to keep her mind off her troubles. She went over to her Aunt May and held her, and wiped the tears from the woman's face.

"He wasn't a perfect man," said May, "but no one deserves what he went through."

"You're so right, Aunt May. Now come and we'll say an 'Our Father' and a 'Hail Mary' for Patrick's soul," said Nancy, and they all bowed their heads as she led them in prayer.

Later that morning, Matthew took Nancy to the morgue. Norah told her the word the murderer had carved on Patrick's forehead, but nothing could have prepared her for the shock of actually seeing the letters, RAT, etched into her husband's skin. She gasped and began trembling, and Matthew got her out of there as quickly as possible. Still shaking, she and Matthew stopped at the rectory and spoke with Father Connolly. Nancy requested he conduct the funeral mass and attend the last night of the wake to lead the mourners in the rosary.

The priest agreed, and gently consoled Nancy for her loss.

"It's been a terrible day for all of us, but especially you and Mrs. Lally. The poor woman was beside herself when the police brought me to the house to break the news late last night."

"Oh, Matthew, I've been so wrapped up in myself I forgot to tell Mrs. Lally about Patrick," said Nancy.

The priest looked quizzically at her. "Oh, she knew about Patrick and it grieved her mightily, but she came to see me about visiting her husband, Officer Lally, in the hospital."

Now Matthew and Nancy stared blankly at Father Connelly.

"Oh, forgive me. I thought you knew. Officer Lally was badly burned last night as he tried to save the people in the apartment above your husband's tavern. He managed to bring the woman out alive, and went back up to search for her son. The flames got to him. The firemen took him down while they put out the blaze. A terrible, awful thing. He's in the hospital now, badly burned, but he will live. And the worst part is the seventeen-year-old son Officer Lally tried to save wasn't even at home. He'd snuck out to meet his young friends. God forgive the monsters who did this."

"No, Father, God damn them," said Matthew slamming the palm of his hand on the desk between them. "God damn them to eternal hell!"

"Now, now, my son. You're upset and don't mean what you're saying."

"Oh, but I do. And if God won't damn them our legal system will when they're put behind bars for the rest of their lives."

Nancy sat silently, tears streaming down her face. Officer Lally was the first person she'd met in New York City. He picked her up at the train and took her to live with him and his wife. He arranged for her job at Murphy's Bar & Grille, and started her on a new life. He and his wife had showered kindness upon her and taught her the ways of her new city.

She stood up "Thank you, Father. But I must go to Mrs. Lally."

"I understand. I will make arrangements at the funeral home for your husband. The wake will begin tomorrow afternoon and the funeral three days later. Is there anything special you wish them to do for Mr. Devlin?"

Nancy thought a moment, then requested the casket be covered with a cloth bearing the Celtic cross. "And for the memorial cards, he was born in County Dublin, Ireland."

Mrs. Lally opened her door to Matthew and Nancy and gestured them inside. She's aged ten years thought Nancy, observing the woman's sagging face, and blood-shot, red-rimmed eyes, and took the grieving woman in her arms.

"I just heard about Officer Lally from Father Connelly. I'm so, so, sorry. My heart breaks for him and you and for myself. I love him, too. And I'm sure he will be all right after a time."

"He was to retire from the police force in just five days," she said weakly. "Now he'll be in the hospital for weeks."

Matthew sat the woman down in a chair and without thinking took her hand and checked her pulse. It was slow and irregular.

"Do you have any brandy here, Mrs. Lally?" he asked.

"No, but himself has a bottle of whiskey in the kitchen cabinet. He likes a nip when he gets off duty."

Matthew found the bottle and poured a small glass.

"Here, drink this, Mrs. Lally. It will help you."

She stared at the glass and shook her head. "Ladies never drink hard spirits."

"Oh, but when a lady suffers such a shock as you've been through, it's medicinal. Please. It will help you. And I'll be leaving now for the hospital to check on your husband's condition."

Mrs. Lally mechanically followed Dr. Clarke's orders and wrinkled her nose as she emptied the glass. She looked at Nancy and said, "I heard about Patrick. Tis awful. Now it's a widow ye are. I said three rosaries today, but I don't think the Virgin was listening."

"Oh, she was listening," said Nancy. "Sometimes it just takes us humans a while to hear the answer to our prayers. Now I have a plan. I want you to come stay with me for a while. I'll help you pack a bag and we'll be together during our troubles. I won't leave you here by yourself."

"Whatever ye say, me girl. And don't ye look like a fine lady in yer lovely dress. And didn't I tell ye when we first met that ye'd never have to wear old torn pantaloons ever again?"

Nancy blushed as she noticed Matthew's lips turn up in a knowing smile, remembering the plucky young girl he met on a boat from Ireland.

Matthew learned at the hospital that Officer Lally had been badly burned in the fire. The cartilage surrounding both ears had been destroyed and he suffered extensive burns to his face and hands. The doctors were doing all they could to minimize his injuries. But

Matthew knew the man would be permanently disfigured, no matter how hard the physicians tried to help him.

Patrick Devlin was laid out in a closed coffin at the funeral parlor. A steady stream of people offered condolences to the widow; neighbors, shopkeepers, friends, customers of Devlin's Tavern and Murphy's Bar & Grille, policemen and firemen. Nancy noticed Callahan and Ahern sitting somberly in the back row and read their names on the huge cross of red roses besides Patrick's coffin.

She sat patiently through three afternoon sessions and three nights of the wake, greeting people, accepting their sympathies, and consoling Patrick's friends. Mrs. Feroni had insisted on taking care of Sean while Nancy, May and Norah were at the wake, and brought cakes and casseroles to the house every night for the family and friends after they returned home from their hours of mourning. On the final evening of the wake, Father Gannon appeared in the doorway, apparently ready to lead the rosary. Nancy and Matthew spied him at the same moment and she made a dash for the door, but Matthew reached the priest first, and out of earshot of the mourners asked, "Where's Father Connolly?"

The priest lowered his head. "He's not well."

Nancy stood before the priest with fury in her eyes and whispered, "How dare you show your face here, you filthy pervert!"

The priest moved back as Matthew, his face dark with quiet rage, stepped closer to the man, and Father Gannon turned and quickly withdrew.

Then Nancy strode to the casket, faced the mourners, and announced. "The priest is ill. I will lead the saying of the rosary."

Patrick was buried the next morning. It was raining and a chill wind blew. What else would one expect, Nancy thought. The sun rarely shone at funerals. Father Connolly conducted the service, and if the man had been sick yesterday, today's weather might prove to be the death of him, she thought. As the coffin was lowered into the grave, May cried and Norah sobbed, while Nancy stood stoically, her eyes downcast.

Nancy held her emotions in check before her family and friends, remembering her mother's admonition that a lady conducted herself with grace and decorum in the face of death. All that keening and wailing at funerals in Ireland was just for show, her mother said. A true lady grieves in private, and does not throw herself over a casket to evoke the sympathy of the onlookers. So that night, after the burial, when at last she was alone, Nancy allowed herself to mourn for Patrick. She thought of when she first met him, and how grand he looked in his driver's uniform and cap; how he stood by her as she spent hours shoveling the snow from Mrs. Birmingham's roof, and then caught her as she fell down the ladder; how he gently and nervously let her know of his love for her. Then, after their marriage, how living in New York City changed that sweet man into an insecure, lost alcoholic. And maybe, she thought, it was partly her fault. Did her success intimidate the man? Did she lord it over him and contribute to his loss of self-esteem? But then she remembered the change in him when she became pregnant. He became much more considerate, rubbing her back and brewing her tea, and finally she witnessed his great joy in having a son.

So now she allowed herself to weep for the man she never truly loved, but who had loved her. The man who had been abandoned by his parents, yet took such great pride in his own son, had turned his life around and became, once again, an honorable man.

He did not deserve the fate dealt him, Nancy thought. Patrick had never harmed anyone in his life, except himself. And before she fell into a fitful sleep, she bid farewell to her husband. "Goodbye, poor Patrick. I'm sure you're with the Lord, and I will never let your son forget you. You will be remembered by him. I will speak of you to him. He will never feel abandoned by his parents, as you were."

Ten days after her husband's accident, Mrs. Lally regained her equanimity and told Nancy she would return to her apartment and wait for Officer Lally to be released from the hospital. She would be financially secure with her dressmaking jobs and Mr. Lally's pension. She had been visiting her husband every day and gradually became accustomed to his changed appearance. Her once handsome groom had lost his ears and gained red, striated scars on his cheeks and forehead. But he was alive, and that was the only important thing to Mrs. Lally.

Matthew stopped to see the man every evening after leaving the hospital. Mr. Lally's physical condition had improved, but depression overcame him whenever he passed a mirror. Matthew assured him additional surgery would decrease the size of the scars, but the man's ears upset him the most. Although he could still hear, unfortunately, there seemed to be no surgery to correct that gruesome deformity.

The police continued investigating Patrick's murder. The slip of paper next to the body led them to Mott Street, where they questioned the residents of the area. The word carved into his forehead indicated a revenge killing, but the missing wedding band

and lack of money in his pockets pointed to a robbery. They were confused, but continued to check every available lead.

Matthew was being torn apart by his emotions: His sorrow over Patrick's brutal death, and his guilt over the great elation he felt that now he and Nancy could be together. But he would wait a respectable length of time before asking her to marry him. At least now he could see her openly, without fear of risking her good reputation. So he went back to his work at Bellevue Hospital with renewed dedication, determined to finish his studies, take his final examinations, and set up his own medical practice.

Callahan and Ahern had been drinking in the side room of Murphy's Bar & Grille for hours, and their extreme state of inebriation led them to careless behavior. Their mood was celebratory, and Callahan raised his glass to his friend. "Here's to you, Mr. Farley," he laughed. "I couldn't have done a better job meself!" And he took Patrick Devlin's wedding ring from his pocket and dangled it from his little finger, then placed it before Ahern. "Here, you take it. See if you can get a few bucks for it."

They were so busy toasting and congratulating each other, they paid little attention when May quietly placed fresh drinks on the table. But she noticed the gold ring which resembled Patrick's wedding band, bearing the engraved Celtic cross, and heard Callahan say to Ahern, "Here's to you, Mr. Farley." She silently withdrew, went behind the bar, and whispered in her husband's ear what she had seen and heard.

"Leave now, May, and tell the police exactly what ye told me. Go quickly. Then come back here and act like nothing's happened. Good girl!"

May informed the detectives working on Patrick's case what she had seen, and within an hour two officers showed up at Murphy's Bar & Grille, surprising the drunken men in the side room. They confiscated the ring, now lying on the table before Ahern, and based on what they saw, and had been told, took the men to the police station for questioning.

At the station house, the men were interrogated and pleaded innocent. They swore they had no idea how the ring got on their table, suggesting somebody must have left it there to frame them. Two cops dragged Ahern out of the room and left a seasoned detective alone with Callahan.

"Now," said the detective to Callahan. "It's just you and me." The policeman took out his billy club and to Callahan's complete surprise, rammed it into his stomach. Callahan slumped over the desk, gasping for air. Had it not been for all the liquor he had consumed, Callahan, with his superior strength, could have easily fended off the stick.

"We'll stay here all night till ye tell me the truth about Patrick Devlin." He waited until Callahan regained his breath, then asked how the wedding band came to be in his possession. The man reiterated he knew nothing about it.

The billy club slammed down again, making hard contact with Callahan's arm, and the man cried out in pain as a bone shattered. The cop grabbed the man's shock of red hair and pulled his head backwards. "Will ye make me carve R A T on yer forehead before ye tell me the truth?"

Sweat, mingled with tears, rained down Callahan's face, as intense pain wracked his body. The cop grew impatient, and rammed the stick into the man's groin. The agony became so severe, Callahan could not even scream. He slumped over the table and mumbled, "Okay. No more."

He then told the cop it was Ahern who had arranged Patrick's murder by hiring a man named Guido. He sputtered out the details, still lucid enough to try and exonerate himself.

The cop spilled some water from a glass on the table onto the floor next to Callahan's chair. He then summoned the detective back into the room to take down the confession, saying, "The poor man slipped on the wet floor. I hope he hasn't broken anything."

Callahan looked up at the Irish detective and muttered, "It was for the cause, ye know."

The cop knew what the cause was; the liberation of Ireland. And though he himself was a native of County Mayo, all he cared about now was that Patrick Devlin had been murdered, and Officer Lally had been maimed, and justice would now be served.

Chapter 19

THE DEPRESSION

December 1892-1893

Callahan and Ahern were in jail, awaiting trial for Patrick's murder, and Bill Peyton assured Nancy they would be convicted due to the preponderance of evidence, and they would be sent away for the rest of their lives, along with Guido.

The hot shot, Guido, failed to live up to his reputation as a feared gangster. After the police used some questionable interrogation techniques on him, he broke down and confessed, and implicated Callahan and Ahern. But they all knew better than to bring up Mr. Petrillo's name, which would bring the wrath of God down upon them and their families.

Despite that good news, Christmas would not be a gala occasion, coming so close on the heels of Patrick's death. But people still had to eat, thought Nancy, and her apartment would have to do. She requested that no gifts be exchanged that year.

They all attended Midnight Mass at St. Patrick's. The church glowed with candles, the altar was surrounded by pots of evergreens and red poinsettias, and an organist played as the choir sang carols and hymns. Father Connolly conducted the service. Nancy entertained the perverse thought that Father Gannon probably lay drunk in the rectory, but quickly asked God's forgiveness for her lack of charity. But she could not overcome the horror of the day the priest groped her in the kitchen. This night was the first time she's set foot in a church since then.

Although they were tired the next morning, Nancy, Norah and Aunt May prepared the food for Christmas dinner. Baby Sean lay sleeping in his crib in the bedroom, and the women took turns checking on him while they baked a prime rib roast, two stuffed geese, and platters of vegetables and relishes. Mrs. Feroni brought fancy pastries, and May had baked a traditional Irish Christmas cake the week before, studded with dried fruit and steeped in Irish whiskey. Before dinner the group sat around two large adjoining tables. The men drank whiskey and the women sipped tea.

Officer and Mrs. Lally arrived. The man's face was red and scarred. The bandages had been removed from his now bald head, and all present suppressed a gasp at seeing the sides of the man's head smooth, where once there had been ears. The women averted their eyes when speaking to him, and concentrated on his necktie. But Mr. Lally kept mostly silent during the day, sitting at the table listening to the others talk.

May became nostalgic and remarked how well they had it here in America.

"Yes, we do," Nancy reminisced. "In the old country our parents labored so hard. The men tilled the soil, planted the crops, then harvested them; they saw to the horses, cattle and pigs. The women did all the cooking and cleaning, drew the well water, washed the clothes, milked the cows, churned the butter, baked the bread, fed the chickens, gathered the eggs, and when the chickens grew old, it was the women who cut off their heads, bled them, plucked them, cleaned them and cooked them. But only on special occasions. Here we can have chicken whenever we wish."

Mrs. Feroni closed the fingers on her right hand and gestured in the air. "In Italy, we women must milk the goats, make the cheese, grow the tomatoes, make the gravy and pasta, and do all the other things in the house, while the men," she opened her hand and flung her fingers upward, "they sit and drink coffee and wine all day till they come home and sit down like kings waiting for their dinner!"

Mr. Feroni looked hurt, and said, "But I don't do that here."

Everyone laughed, and Mrs. Feroni took her husband's hand. "No. You a good man. We work together in the bakery."

Dr. Weitz smiled. "I wish we Jews had been allowed such opportunities, hard as they sound. None of us owned land unless we knew people in high places. So we had to resort to commerce and finance, or become shopkeepers. Then they called us shysters, or shylocks, after Shakespeare's character in 'The Merchant of Venice.' I was lucky to have a father who could pay for my medical education."

Matthew said, "We're all in the same boat, so to speak. So let's all thank God that life in America is easier. We still have to work very hard, but at least here our labors are rewarded, and maybe someday we can all get along together in peace. They call the Irish 'Micks,' the Italians 'Guineas,' the Asians 'Chinks,' the Jews 'Kikes,' the colored people 'Niggers' and the Spanish 'Spics.' So, Dr. Weitz, to return to your reference to Shakespeare's, 'What's in a name?' Should we let it bother us?"

Norah added, "There's an old saying, sticks and stones may break my bones, but names will never hurt me."

"Oh, but they do hurt," said Nancy. "They demean us. Calling us Mick's sends a signal that we are inferior to the Limeys."

Everyone laughed out loud, as Nancy blushed with embarrassment.

"See," said Matthew. "We are all guilty. Assimilation is not easy."

Mr. Feroni asked, "Who are the Limeys?"

Matthew smiled. "The Brits made their sailors eat limes to avoid getting scurvy. The Irish call the English Limeys, as some people call the Germans 'Krauts' after the sauerkraut they eat. Limey is not a compliment, just another derogatory term for the prejudice we all must get over to live in America."

Sean's crying interrupted their conversation, and while Nancy tended the baby, the other women began putting the food on the table. When all was ready, everyone bowed his head and said grace, then made quick work of the delicious dinner put before them.

Nancy later went to the piano she had installed in the rear of the living room and played Christmas carols. Dr. Weitz and Rachel joined in, knowing the words to many of the songs after having lived in New York for many years.

Bill Peyton took Norah's hand as they sang, and Matthew sat at the piano next to Nancy. Aunt May, and her husband, Mr. Murphy, sang gazing into each other's eyes. Mr. and Mrs. Feroni sang with angelic voices. And baby Sean slept quietly through it all.

By four o'clock the sky began to darken. The women had cleared the dinner dishes, and Norah and Bill went off to watch the sun set over the Hudson River. The other guests gradually left, leaving Matthew and Nancy alone with Sean.

"I'd best be getting back to the hospital," said Matthew. "Holidays seem to bring out the worst in some people; drunkenness, fights, accidents."

"You're not even going to give me a Christmas kiss?" Nancy pouted.

He drew her into his arms. "You know how much I want you. How long must I wait?"

"Please, be patient with me. Patrick's only been gone less than a month."

Matthew drew her to the sofa and they sat close to one another. He took her face in his hands and told her, "I've waited so long for you, Nancy. I want you to be my wife." He reached into his pocket and placed a diamond ring before her on the table. "Will you do me the honor of marrying me?"

She put her hands in his and answered, "Oh, how I've waited to hear those words. Of course I will marry you, my love."

He slipped the ring on her finger. "I know you can't wear this in public yet, but I want to remember seeing it on your hand on Christmas Day, eighteen ninety-two."

Her heart fluttered and she wondered if one could faint from happiness. "I'll wear it whenever I'm alone, and be waiting very impatiently until I can wear it for the whole world to see."

"And when will that be?"

She furrowed her brow. "Maybe six months would be appropriate."

"That seems like a lifetime," Matthew sighed. "I've loved you since the first day we met on the boat. It hasn't been easy for me all these years alone, then watching you with Patrick when I wanted you for myself."

Tears came to Nancy's eyes and Matthew quickly regained control.

"Forgive me, love, it's just that I think of you all day and want you in my arms all night." He shook his head, sadly. "But I know you're right." He silently calculated, then happily declared, "So, we're to be married in June?"

"Yes, my darling, in June."

Nancy had postponed packing up Patrick's belongings, but now that the New Year had arrived, she resolved to begin this afternoon, unpleasant as the task might be. But first, she would have a cup of tea.

Matthew had shown considerable restraint and consideration of Nancy's status as a new widow, though all they both thought of was now they could be together. Nancy would wait a respectable period of time before the neighbors witnessed their courtship. She would not bring disgrace upon herself or her child, although now that she was a free woman once again, it took all the fortitude and strength she could gather not to fling herself into his bed. So they would marry in June. In the meantime, she could pour out her love to Sean, but Matthew was alone.

A few times a week Matthew came to see Nancy, and they stole some moments alone, but their clandestine meetings only increased their longing for one another. Well, enough daydreaming, Nancy thought. In six months we'll be married. Now I must put Patrick's clothes together and donate them to the poor.

She folded his suits, ties and shirts, collected his old work clothes and shoes, and lay them carefully in cardboard boxes she had brought home from Murphy's Bar & Grille. In a small drawer she found his wedding ring and wallet, which the police had returned to her, but in her state of shock she automatically placed them in his dresser and forgot about it. She would keep those for Sean, she thought. Then she lifted the green sweater she had given him on their first Christmas in their new apartment, and stopped suddenly. Beneath it, hidden at the back of the drawer, was a piece of paper. She unfolded it, and read the letter Patrick had found in the box with the ring, behind his mother's grave in Ireland. Her hands trembled as she returned it to the drawer and decided she would deal with it in the future, when she was calmer.

Matthew wrote his father frequently. But tonight, he had a specific purpose.

Dear Da,

I have the most wonderful news to tell you. On June 20th next, I will be marrying the most wonderful, beautiful Irish lass I could ever hope to call my wife. Nancy O'Leary is from County Galway, and I met her coming over on the boat to America. We lost touch for a while, but God has a way of working things out.

She's a very industrious young woman, and has managed to own twenty percent of a bar and grille, like our pubs, but much fancier, and has begun writing stories. She sings like an angel, plays the piano quite well, and has educated herself to the point you would be proud to call her your daughter-in-law.

I'm almost finished my studies and will be a proper doctor by the time of my wedding. Do you think it would be possible for you to visit New York and be with me on this special day? I'm sending you a bank note, as usual, with some extra added to entice you to book passage for America in mid-June. Nancy's Aunt May and her husband, Charles Murphy, will put you up in their apartment. You'll like Mr. Murphy. He's a prince of a man. Well, it's late, so I'll say goodnight. I must be at the hospital at six in the morning.

Take good care of yourself, and God bless.

Your son, Matthew Clarke

Nancy had written her father, Sean, a similar letter, asking that he attend her wedding, and bring her brothers, whom she sorely missed. She reluctantly mentioned that his new wife, Bernadette, would also be welcome. Nancy could accommodate two of her relatives, and Mrs. Lally offered her spare bedroom for her brothers. Everything had been arranged, and all Nancy wanted now was to look upon her family once again on the day of her wedding. And she dearly wanted her father to meet his new grandchild, his namesake, who would by then be almost ten months old.

In January, Mr. Grunwald's economic prediction came to pass. The country entered a depression that would last for a year and a half. Nancy's idea to offer free lunches to the working men continued to prove profitable. And Norah's nightly singing at the Bar kept the well-to-do customers coming back, though not spending as much as they had in the past. But the sisters remained financially secure through the crisis. Nancy owned twenty-percent of Murphy's Bar & Grille, and saved every spare cent she made to ensure her and baby Sean's security. She did not consider her future husband's earning capabilities. Nancy relied on herself. Whatever Matthew contributed would be a bonus. She was acutely aware of the vagaries of life and was determined never to rely on anyone else.

But for many people the depression took its toll. People were laid off from their jobs, investments were lost, and for those who could find full-time work, their wages were lowered. Pennsylvania had been hit hard, and Matthew received a letter from Mr. Grunwald.

"My dear Matthew,

Things do not go well here. The farmers, they can barely sell their crops for the money it took to plant and reap them. And they cannot obtain credit to tide them over. Many businesses have failed. The young man I tutored left for a better opportunity in California. So, I am remembering the kind offer you made when last I saw you that I could stay in New York with you. Maybe now the time has come for me to leave here. But, please do not feel obligated if your circumstances have changed. I will understand. Please be honest with me, as I have always been with you, Mein Sohn.

God bless you. Your friend, Isaac Grunwald

Matthew wrote his mentor immediately, urging him to come live in New York. Accommodations were not a problem. And Matthew would find him a position at Bellevue Hospital. Matthew felt great joy anticipating Mr. Grunwald coming back into his life, and told him of his impending wedding. "Your letter could not have come at a better time. We will all be together again on this most important day of my life."

Norah arrived home from work one evening after singing at Murphy's Bar & Grille to find Nancy totally absorbed in her work, pouring over ledgers. Norah made a pot of tea and brought it to the table.

"So, are we making money?" she asked.

"Yes, considering the sorry state the country is in. But not as much as we took in last year. I think we'll have to revise our menu at the Bar. The greengrocer and the butcher have almost tripled their costs. But we can cut down by growing our own vegetables in the lot behind the Bar and build a coop to raise our own chickens, if I can talk Mr. Murphy into the idea."

Norah interrupted her. "And whose to do all this work? I hope it's not me yer expecting to dig into the soil and throw feed to a bunch of chickens."

Nancy smiled benevolently at her younger sister. "No, it's not you. Mr. Grunwald will be coming to live here in New York. The man can grow anything from a tiny scallion to a giant cabbage, Matthew's told me. So I think I'll put him to work here before Matthew gets him a job at the hospital. When he has everything in place, we can pay a young lad to work a few hours a week keeping things up for a couple of dollars."

"Fer sure, yer a clever one, ye are, Nancy."

Nancy thought this might be an appropriate time to bring up the subject of her sister's wedding. She took a sip of tea and proceeded. "So, have you and Bill decided on when you'll be married?"

Norah brushed her shiny dark hair from her face, and answered a bit defensively, "Bill hasn't mentioned a date to me yet."

"Can I be blunt with you, Norah, and not have you take offense at what I have to say?"

Norah's eyes widened in apprehension. "Is it something wrong I've done?"

"No, no. It's only that you have to become more Americanized. You are marrying an important, well-educated lawyer. The bigwigs are suggesting he go into politics after he did so well at the trial of the Short-Tail Gang. You must make him proud to have you as his wife. You have to learn to speak like a New Yorker, instead of an Irish girl from the farm. You must make an effort to drop all those ye's, yer's, tis, fer sure, me's, and all the words that mark you as lower class in the eyes of Bill's clients. He would never tell you this, but I will, because I love you and want you to find happiness as his wife, and never cause yourself or him any embarrassment."

"I'm sorry, miss high-and-mighty, that you don't think I'm good enough fer Bill, but he loves me as I am."

Nancy noticed the tears in Norah's eyes, and quickly changed her tactics.

"You're a beautiful woman, and I know Bill loves you. But you hear how I speak now, don't you? It didn't come easily for me. I had to practice. I listened to American women and copied how they spoke. And it didn't take long. And you can do it too."

The shame on her sister's face made Nancy realize how much she had hurt her, and how strong people underestimate the effect they have on those weaker than they.

She abruptly shifted course. "Did I tell you Matthew and I will be married on the twentieth of June?"

Her sister's eyes lit up with happiness, finally, and she kissed Nancy on the cheek. "Good fer … good FOR you. I'm so happy ye …

YOU will have yer …YOUR true love back agin …AGAIN, after all these years.

Nancy hugged her sister after listening to her attempt at proper elocution. She will master the American tongue quickly, she thought. And felt she must reward her sister's efforts. Then an idea occurred.

"Norah, I've written Da to come to America for my wedding and bring our brothers. Would it not be a wonderful event for our father to witness his two daughters married on the same day?"

A wide smile crossed Norah's face. "It would. Indeed it would. Tis …IT'S a splendid idea." Then a shadow crossed her face. "Would his new wife be coming also?"

"I gave Da the option to bring her or leave her home. But don't worry. She'll cause you no trouble with me at your side. She'll be on her best behavior. And if not, I will put her in her place. Now, do you think Bill will agree to have your wedding on June twentieth?"

Norah gave Nancy a sly smile and answered, "Bill will agree to anything I ask."

"Why you devil! You have the poor man wrapped around your little finger. I'm glad you decided not to go after my Matthew."

"Oh, I'd have no chance with him. It's ye …it's YOU he loves."

The next day Norah brought a picnic lunch to Bill Peyton's office. As they ate chicken sandwiches and potato salad, she told her finance that Nancy and Matthew were to be married on June twentieth, and her father would be coming to the ceremony. Norah had not lost her powers of sweet manipulation to achieve her goals.

When you want something, just plant the seed, she felt, and let the other person think it was his own idea.

"My father's never been to America. This will probably be his first and last visit."

"What a shame," said Bill. "Then he won't be here for our wedding."

"Yes, that is too bad. It would make him so happy to see me being wed to such a handsome, prosperous lawyer as yourself."

"Wait a minute," Bill proclaimed, and stood up as though he had just discovered the secrets of the universe. "Why don't we get married on the same day as Nancy? Have a double wedding. Do you think your sister would object? Oh, but more importantly, how would you feel about that?"

Norah smiled to herself, and with great enthusiasm told Bill he was a genius, and she thought his idea brilliant, and she was certain Nancy would be thrilled.

Bill took Norah in his arms. "Then it's settled. We'll be married the twentieth of June, with your father here to witness his two girls walking down the aisle."

Norah held Bill close to her and showed her appreciation with a long, fervent kiss. Eventually, Bill reluctantly disengaged himself from her arms. "We must be careful. You tempt me to go too far."

She ran her fingers gently across the small scar on his forehead. "How did you get this mark?"

"Oh, my scar? Well, when I was a lad my sister, Catherine, you know, the woman Nancy cared for on the boat before she died. Well, she walked me to and from school. And the kids would make fun of me because I wore glasses. They would shout out, 'Here comes four eyes,' and it would drive poor Catherine crazy. She was very protective of me, being my senior by ten years. You know how sisters are."

"That I do," said Norah.

"Well, one day the lads became especially vicious, and began throwing stones at me and laughing. One of the rocks hit my forehead, and that's the origin of the scar." He began laughing. "You should have seen Catherine running after the little ruffian. She caught him and slapped his face, and warned him never again to taunt me. And he didn't." Bill looked into the distance, and cleaned his clouded glasses with his handkerchief. "My sister was a wonderful woman, and I'll never forget your sister, Nancy, was with her during her last hours on earth."

Norah smiled. "I think it's grand for you to have a constant reminder of your sister's love right on the front of your face."

Bill looked lovingly at Norah. "I never thought about it that way."

Nancy arrived at the Bar to talk to Mr. Murphy. "Can I have a few minutes of your time before the lunch crowd comes in?"

He put down the bar rag and said, "I'd be delighted. Now what's on yer mind?"

"Oh, Aunt May," Nancy called to the kitchen. "Can you join us for a few minutes?"

"So it's to be a family conference, is it?"

"I have some ideas that will make us more money," said Nancy. "And I wanted Aunt May's approval, too."

"Well, spit it out girl. This depression's diggin' into our profits."

May pulled out a stool at the bar. "So what's the fuss?"

"Okay," said Nancy, now that the three of them were together. "We have a large yard behind the Bar that could be generating income. All we have to do is plant our own fruits and vegetables and we'll save a lot of money at the greengrocers."

"And how much do we have to pay someone to do all this work?" asked Mr. Murphy.

"Nothing at all. Matthew's friend, Mr. Grunwald, is coming to live in New York and his passion is gardening. He would do all the planting and harvesting for free, he loves it so much."

"And I can preserve and put up the vegetables and fruit we don't use and save them for the winter," said May.

"Does Matthew know yer offering this man's services without payment?" asked Mr. Murphy.

"Oh, yes. I discussed it with him and he thought it would be the ideal way to keep his friend busy until he obtained a position for him at the hospital."

"Well, it sounds like a grand idea to me," smiled Mr. Murphy.

"Another thing," said Nancy. "We have room for a chicken coop in the yard, too. We'd have free eggs all year." She became quite animated. "And we could raise rabbits. They breed so quickly. And we could make hasenpfeffer. The German customers love rabbit stew."

Mr. Murphy took in all Nancy had to say. Her ideas were good, but with chickens and rabbits in the back yard, he couldn't resist chiding her. "Maybe ye'd like a cow or two out there fer free milk."

She wiggled her nose. "No, cows need too much grazing room. But we have that apple tree out back. Why do we buy apples?"

"Because the hooligans steal them all," Mr. Murphy scowled.

"We should pick them as soon as they're ripe and put what we don't use in the cellar with the root vegetables over the winter. And one other thing. We could hire a neighborhood boy for a few dollars and send him over to the Hudson River with a rod and have him catch fresh fish for us. There's a young colored boy, Jim, who moved in near us and I've talked to his mother and he'd be happy to make a few dollars a week helping us. We'd send him to the piers on the East River twice a week to catch crabs. May knows how to make more expensive dishes, like cold crab salad and hot crab cakes that your rich customers would gladly order." Nancy's excitement was contagious, and May clapped her hands.

"Fresh crab here is so expensive, I haven't cooked those dishes since I was a girl in Galway. But I do remember how it's done."

"If we do all these things we can save over half our food costs." Nancy finished her argument and waited for Mr. Murphy's opinion.

The man knew the lass had a brain in her head when he offered her twenty-percent of his business, but now she'd outdone herself.

But Nancy kept talking. "Not only will our eggs be free, but our chickens will when they're old enough. And so will our tomatoes, carrots, onions, turnips, cabbage, strawberries, blackberries, parsley, lettuce, and kale."

"Okay!" said Mr. Murphy. "Start yer farm, me girl. Good thinking."

A few months later, Callahan, Ahern and Guido went on trial for killing Patrick Devlin, and it was Nancy's obligation as the widow to attend the proceedings. As the hearing evolved, she was shocked to learn the real reason for Patrick's trip to Ireland; to deliver money to the Irish rebels. He proved not to be as dense as she'd thought. He had cleverly used Callahan's money to provide him with the means to dig up his inheritance in the Knock graveyard. But his alcoholism proved to be his downfall, and he returned to America without fulfilling his task. Then Callahan became furious, and arranged for Patrick's death and the burning down of his tavern, Ahern told the court.

Aunt May, the main witness in the case, handled herself admirably. She stared relentlessly at the accused men as she recounted seeing Patrick's ring on the tavern table before Callahan and Ahern, and heard Callahan congratulate his cohort, Ahern, and address him as 'Mr. Farley.'

Members of the Short-Tail Gang testified after the prosecutor agreed to absolve them of any involvement, and related how Guido bragged about making fifty dollars for killing an Irishman and torching his tavern.

The prosecutor read the defendants' confessions to the court, and after closing arguments by the lawyers, the jury was sent to deliberate and decide the fate of the three men. It did not take long. One hour later they returned with a guilty verdict. As the judge sentenced the three defendants to life in prison, the spectators were unusually quiet, as they feared the possibility of retribution from Guido's associates, or Callahan's friends. The judge pounded his gavel and the three killers were led from the court room in handcuffs, no longer the big shots they once were, now only disgraced felons, never to be seen again on the streets of New York.

Nancy put her arm around May's waist and told her how magnificently she had performed; stern, resolute, and commanding. Then May broke down and sobbed. "Poor Patrick had just come into his own. He was a good man before he left the Birmingham's. Remember the Blizzard of eighty-eight? How he stayed with you all the while the madam had you shoveling snow off the roof? He made many mistakes, but, I can't believe he's gone forever."

"I do remember," said Nancy gently. "But he's not really gone. He left us Sean." And Nancy also remembered he'd left a letter she found in his dresser drawer; a letter that might change her life forever, and most likely not for the better. She shuddered at what she must eventually do, but would put it off as long as possible.

Callahan's cell broke up, and the members dispersed, leaving the side room in Murphy's Bar & Grille unoccupied, except for the occasional birthday or anniversary party.

The Short-Tail Gang also curtailed its operations. The young hoodlums began to understand and fear the power of the American legal system, and turned to safer means of making money. They obtained gainful employment.

Mr. Petrillo laid low for a while, but in the years to come the Italian mobsters reemerged and became a force to be reckoned with. America's promises of liberty and the pursuit of happiness were taken quite literally by Mr. Petrillo.

Chapter 20

THE REUNION

April-June 1893

Dear Mary Alice, or Nancy, as ye now call yerself,

Yer letter was received with great pleasure. I will be arriving in New York on the sixteenth of June to share in the happiness of my two daughters' wedding day. Yer step-mother will stay in Ireland, as she has a terrible fear of becoming seasick on the voyage. The boys will be busy planting the crops, so they too, will miss this grand occasion.

I look forward to gazing upon me girls' faces again, fer sure. God bless. Your Father, Sean O'Laoghaire.

Nancy's delight that her father would attend the wedding was matched by Norah's upon learning her step-mother would not be accompanying him.

The next day Matthew also received a letter from Ireland.

My dear son, Matthew,

It was with heartfelt delight that I received your letter. Nothing could prevent me from attending your wedding. My ship docks on June the seventeenth, and I'll look for you to meet me as I would be lost in the great city of New York. My chest bursts with pride at your finishing university and officially being a medical doctor when next I see you. From your description of Nancy, I know she will be a great addition to our family, and am very happy you found your mate in life.

Until I see you, may God bless you both. Your loving Father, Sean Clarke.

The letter raised Matthew's spirits. His love for the man reddened his blue eyes, as he had feared he might never again see his father.

Mr. Grunwald sold his little house in Johnstown for a lot less than it would have brought before the depression, but he was happy to have sold it at all. He obtained a bit more money for his furnishings, then packed his bags and arrived in New York in early May. Dr. Weitz insisted his old friend stay with him and Rachel until permanent arrangements could be made. Matthew met his train and enveloped his mentor in a bear hug, and the short man's curly grey hair tickled Matthew's chin. As they made their way to Murphy's Bar & Grille, Mr. Grunwald marveled at the size of the city. "What a place they have built here. And all the carriages and the horses. Ach, you can hardly cross the street without being run down."

"You'll get used to it in very short time." They entered the bar that Saturday morning, and Nancy emerged from the kitchen carrying baby Sean. "Ah, here's my bride-to-be with her bonny son," said Matthew, and the three sat down to chat. Then Mr. Grunwald asked about the job Matthew had promised him.

"I finish medical school in early June. Then I will be a certified medical doctor, and will have more authority than I do now. The chief pharmacist at Bellevue Hospital is a friend. I know he will find something for you, especially with your background in medicine. But in the meantime, Nancy has arranged for something to keep you busy. Tell him, darling."

Nancy outlined her plans for the vegetable garden and chicken coops in the backyard, and Mr. Grunwald's eyes lit up.

"Oh, that I would enjoy. I have been missing my garden in Johnstown already. It would give me great pleasure to have dirt on my hands again."

Nancy laughed. "That is so refreshing. Most people come to New York to be rid of the soil. Come, sit at a table and I'll bring you some breakfast."

Mr.Grunwald patted Matthew's shoulder after Nancy left and said, "God has been good to you, my boy. Your Nancy has beauty, charm, and good common sense. Now, you treat her well!"

"That I will." Then Matthew told him the saga of his relationship with Nancy, the missed opportunities, her life with Patrick, and the arrival of her baby. During Matthew's recitation, Mr. Grunwald periodically shook his head from side to side in sorrow.

"But now you are happy," the old man said. "God performs miracles when He is ready, not always when we think He should. Did I not tell you last we met that the dark clouds would once again become white in a blue sky?"

After breakfast, Mr. Grunwald asked to see the backyard. Once outside he picked up a handful of dirt and nodded approvingly. "I will obtain the necessary tools and get started today. The last frost has passed, so I cannot waste any time getting the seeds in. And with all the horses on the street, we will not find it necessary to buy fertilizer."

Nancy hired Joe Jefferson, the colored boy who lived nearby, to obtain the fish and crabs. The fourteen-year-old thought the few dollars a week he'd be paid by Nancy to be a fortune. And he enjoyed sitting on the piers after school let out, attaching the shiny sinker on a hook and dangling it from his rod in the shallow waters near the pilings. The glittering object attracted the crabs, and at the precise moment Joe would swoop his long-handled net over the crabs and scoop them up. After a few hours his two pails would be full, and he'd start back to Murphy's Bar & Grille, proud of his accomplishments.

One afternoon four young neighborhood thugs, bored and looking for trouble, approached Joe as he set off for the Bar. The biggest one, a sixteen-year old Eastern European boy, said, "What ya got in those pails, nigger?"

Joe walked faster, his heart pounding. "Just some crabs," he said.

"What are ya gonna do with them?" one boy asked.

"Eat them," said Joe, as his fear level approached terror.

The four boys laughed. "You niggers eat those filthy things?" one boy said as he pulled a crab out of the pail and his pals surrounded Joe.

"Then here, let me see ya eat one." And he pushed the quivering crab into Joe's face while another boy pulled Joe's head back. Joe screamed as the crab attacked his face, the claws drawing blood from his lips and cheeks. Joe tried to free himself, but now the other boys held him fast, pinning his arms behind his back.

"You like that one? Tastes good? Have another." Now they held two crabs on his face, snapping their claws on Joe's forehead. Blood streamed down over his eyes and Joe continued screaming and trying to wrestle himself from the kids' arms. A passing policeman observed the scene and shouted at the boys, who threw Joe to the ground, laughed, and ran off. "Enjoy your dinner, nigger," one yelled back.

The policeman picked Joe up, who was now shaking and bleeding profusely.

"I think ye need a doctor, boy," said the cop. "Come with me."

"I have to get my crabs," Joe said. And he quickly picked up his pails as the officer ushered him across the street.

Joe told his rescuer he must deliver them to Murphy's Bar & Grille, and then he'd see a doctor. The cop dabbed at the blood on Joe's face with his handkerchief. "I guess yer not as bad off as ye look. Come on. I'll walk you to Murphy's place."

Nancy was sitting at the bar talking to Officer Lally, trying to avoid looking at the bare areas on the sides of his face where once the man had ears, when the cop strode in with Joe, holding the pails of crabs.

"Mother of God!" Nancy exclaimed. "What's happened to you, Joe?"

The cop explained. "Some hooligans had their fun with the young lad. I think a doctor should take a look at him."

"Dr. Clarke is expected here soon. Come with me, Joe," said Nancy, as she led him to the kitchen. "I'll wash your wounds and put some iodine on your face so it won't get infected. This might hurt a little."

"Okay, Mrs. Devlin. I ain't afraid of pain. I was just afraid they'd steal your crabs."

As Nancy ministered to Joe, the cop sat down next to Officer Lally and explained in detail what had happened. Lally, though now gone from the police force, listened intently, then said, "I'll take the boy back there again tomorrow. One look at me and those hooligans will never bother young Joe again. I'll tell Nancy."

In fifteen minutes Matthew arrived to see Nancy, who had him examine Joe. He found she had done as good a job as he would have cleaning and treating the boy's wounds.

"I'll take him home now and try and explain to Mrs. Jefferson what happened to her son," she said. "If you can wait, I'll be back in less than half an hour."

"I'll be here. Or should I go with you?"

"No, no, Matthew. I'll be all right."

"Don't worry, Mrs. Devlin. It wasn't your fault. And I don't want to lose my job. I can go to a different spot on the pier. If I see those kids again, I'll just run."

Nancy felt such love and compassion for this innocent, hard-working young boy who just happened to be Negro, she had to hold back her tears.

"It wasn't fair, Joe. They are evil kids."

"Most kids are bad until their parents teach 'em how to be good."

"Joe, you're wise beyond your years, and I'm so proud of you. Now I'm taking you home and apologize to your mother."

"You don't need to apologize. You do everything good."

Oh I do, do I? Nancy thought, remembering withholding the letter from Matthew which revealed he and Patrick were half-brothers, and then leaving the Church because of one rogue priest. Oh yes, I do everything good. And now my parsimony caused harm to Joe, and she dreaded his mother's reaction.

Mrs. Jefferson opened her apartment door and gasped at the sight of her son.

"It's not as bad as it looks," Nancy said. "The doctor checked Joe, and he'll be fine. He was attacked by a group of white kids while he was gathering crabs, and they ..."

"I see what they did." She pulled Joe to her and hugged him.

"I'm okay, Mama."

"It was white boys who did this?"

"I'm embarrassed to say yes, Mrs. Jefferson," Nancy said. "And I wouldn't blame you if you decide Joe shouldn't work for me anymore. But if you let Joe continue to work for me, Officer Lally will be on the pier tomorrow to see this never happens again."

"And how can this cop be sure of that?"

"Mama. I'm not afraid of those white kids. I want to keep working for Mrs. Devlin. We need the money."

Nancy assured her that Officer Lally would put the fear of God in those kids, and Joe's mother sadly shook her head.

"It's almost as bad here as we had it in Mississippi. People just hate us no matter how hard we try. Oh, not good people like you, Mrs. Devlin, and your friends. But it's hard. Lord God, it's hard."

Nancy did not know how to reply, so she said the first thing that came to her mind.

"It will get better, Mrs. Jefferson. I know in time it will. Things will change. They don't like us Irish much here, either. They killed my husband. And they were Irish, just like us."

"Oh, Lordie, I forgot. You poor woman."

"Mama. I'm going back to work, okay?" asked Joe.

"Officer Lally will look over him," Nancy said.

Mrs. Jefferson nodded. "If that's what you want, son, you have my blessing. Just be very careful, you hear?"

Two days later, Officer Lally accompanied Joe to the piers. He hid behind a piling while the boy dropped his line into the water. The silver sinker shimmered and attracted the crabs. Then the boys arrived, ready and eager for another fun-filled encounter with Joe.

"Hey, nigger, ya hungry? Ready for another dinner?" they laughed.

Joe stood up, frightened, but defiant. As they got closer and attempted to grab the pail of crabs, Officer Lally emerged in a long, black cape, stormed towards them, and shoved the four startled teenagers to the ground.

"Look at me!" he shouted, his arms reaching to the sky like some ancient mystical pagan god.

And they did, horrified by the big man with no ears and red scars crisscrossing his face.

"I swear," he bellowed, "by Satan and his army, that if you ever touch this young boy again your faces will look just like mine. And I will see to that! And never call these people niggers again. They are to be called Americans!"

The boys' eyes grew enormous at the sight of the disfigured man and his threat to turn them into monsters. They remembered tales they'd heard in their youth of demons who stole, maimed and killed children, and became terrified of this threatening man. They scrambled to their feet and ran, gasping for breath, to be out of reach of the menacing monster.

When they were out of sight, Lally put his arm around Joe's shoulder and said, "Catch a couple of big ones for me. I think I'm going to be very hungry tonight."

The attackers spread the word throughout the neighborhood that a monster was on the loose protecting Negro boys, and Joe had no trouble from them again when collecting his fish and crabs for Nancy and earning his weekly paycheck. And the customers at Murphy's Bar & Grille enjoyed, and paid top dollar for May's crab cakes and fresh fish. Along with Mr.Grunwald's vegetables and fresh eggs from the chicken coop, Nancy and her family weathered the depression of 1893 quite handily.

Plans for the double wedding ceremony began in earnest in late May. The couples consulted with Father Connolly to set the date, have the banns posted, and conduct the ceremony. When Nancy asked about Father Gannon, to make sure he would not be present, Father Connolly began fiddling with his pen and told them the priest had retired. Bill Peyton questioned him. "But the man couldn't be more than forty-five. How could he retire so young?"

"Well," stammered Father Connolly, "he actually went to a rest home upstate. He suffered from a nervous condition."

With sparks in her eyes, Nancy responded, "That's not all he suffered from!"

The priest, distinctly ill at ease, responded, piously, "He is one of God's children."

"So was Cain!" Nancy shot back. Matthew stood, took her hand and concluded the meeting.

The weddings would take place on the morning of Saturday, June twentieth. There were brides' dresses to be made by Mrs. Lally, a guest list to be drawn up, and a menu to be planned. Then Nancy and Norah dealt with the complexities of moving; Norah to Bill Peyton's apartment, and Matthew to Nancy's home. The transfer of clothing, books and personal items was completed the day before the wedding. Norah's move would be relatively easy, but Matthew had accumulated so many books and medical items during his years living with Dr. Weitz, several trips would be necessary to transfer his belongings.

But the sisters found none of these chores onerous. They delighted in every aspect of arranging the wedding, and would sit at the dining room table, with pads and pencils, making plans and giggling as they did in their youth in Ireland. They eagerly anticipated the arrival of their father, and though they would miss their brothers, Norah felt great relief that her step-mother's weak stomach would keep her in Ireland.

But an unforeseen event lay on the horizon that would make all their plans seem trivial, as reality intruded upon their happiness.

By June sixteenth the wedding plans had been finalized, and Nancy and Norah took a carriage to the West Side piers to greet their father. As they watched him lumber down the gangplank, their hearts fell. He had aged dramatically. Most of his hair was gone, and he appeared quite frail.

"See what that devil Bernadette has done to him?" Norah cried. "She's out to kill him and take the farm. She's been starving him to death, or poisoning his food!"

"Shush now. Don't let Da see you looking worried. Smile and act happy to see him," ordered Nancy.

Nancy grabbed her father's suitcase and threw her arm around his neck, as Norah prattled on about how wonderful he looked.

Her father gave her a puzzled look and said, "Norah, if ye think I'm looking wonderful, it's time ye got yerself some eyeglasses."

Nancy laughed, led him to the waiting carriage, and took him to her apartment. He asked if he could lie down and rest a bit, as the long voyage had left him fatigued. Once he had fallen asleep, the sisters silently put on a pot of tea and exchanged doleful glances.

"He doesn't look at all well," said Norah.

"I can see that!" snapped Nancy, who then apologized to her sister. "Da's sick. I must have Matthew look at him."

"Do you want me to fetch him?"

"Norah, that would be wonderful of you. I have to stay here. Mrs. Lally will be bringing Sean back any minute."

Within the hour, Norah returned with Matthew, who carried his medical bag, and asked Nancy to describe her father's symptoms.

Before she could, they heard moans coming from the bedroom, and they went to the man's side.

"What is it, Da? What's wrong?" asked Nancy.

As Matthew took out his stethoscope, the patient frowned at his daughter. "Now why did ye have to go bring in a doctor?"

"This is Matthew Clarke, the man I'm to marry," said Nancy.

"Hello, Mr. O'Leary," Matthew said, and shook the man's shriveled hand.

The patient looked Matthew up and down, and nodded his approval. "Yer a fine specimen of a man, ye are, Matthew. And I'm going to save ye some trouble. It's me heart."

"How long have you had this problem?"

"Oh, about four years now. But I've stayed on the earth longer than they all predicted I would. And before the Lord sees fit to take me, I was determined to see me girls once again."

Norah began to cry. "Oh, Da, don't talk that way. You're just tired from the trip."

"It's not the trip, lassie. I've been tired for so many years now I'm ready to give up the ghost. But I must meet your man, Mr. Peyton. It's plain to see Nancy's picked well. I must be sure ye have, too."

"Da, you'll be up and about after you've rested a while."

"Norah, Norah," the old man said, gasping for breath. "Stop yer crying and bring Mr. Peyton to me side and grant a dying man his last wish."

"You can't die, Da!" Norah pleaded, bordering on hysteria, while Nancy took her father's hand and firmly told her sister to bring Bill Peyton at once.

"Norah, we all die someday, me girl. Will ye make me death a happy one and do as Nancy tells ya?"

Matthew took Norah's arm and led her out of the room. "You must be brave, Norah, as your father is. I don't think he has much time left. I know what a shock this is to you, and if you don't feel up to getting Bill, I'll fetch him."

"No, you stay with Da, and, can you keep him alive till I come back?"

"I'll do everything in my power. Now go, and be careful. Don't fall in a faint. Take some deep breaths. Show me some of the mettle your father has."

As Norah raced down the stairs, her dark hair flying behind her, she brushed by Mrs. Lally carrying baby Sean, almost bumping into the woman.

Now what's the matter with that one, Mrs. Lally thought. She could have knocked over me and the babe. I'll have to talk to Nancy about that flibbertigibbet!

Nancy let Mrs. Lally into the apartment, told her of the situation, and took the baby in her arms and sat next to her father. "Da, meet your grandson, Sean."

The old man's eyes lit up and he slowly raised his gnarled hand to touch the baby's tiny pink fingers.

"He has your eyes, Da. And your blond hair."

Her father managed a slight smile. "When I had some hair on me head."

The baby squeezed his grandfather's fingers, and Nancy's father's smile broadened. "I think he likes me."

"Of course he does. After all, he was named for you." Nancy, who had kept her emotions in check for so long, could not control the tears now flowing down her cheeks. Watching her dying father touching her little son proved too much for her to bear.

Matthew asked Nancy to bring a glass of water, and mixed it with some powder he drew from his medical bag. "I want you to drink this, sir. It's good for the heart."

The man complied, then lay back down on the pillows. "Promise me, ye will take good care of me Nancy. She's a special person, she is."

"That she is," agreed Matthew. "And you have my word I would die myself before I'd let any harm come to her or Sean."

Nancy's heart broke as she heard that exchange between her father and Matthew, but she also felt a great joy at having these two exceptional men in her life.

Norah and Bill entered the room, short of breath from their race to beat the grim reaper. "Da, this is Bill Peyton, the man I will marry."

Bill took the old man's hand, introduced himself and with all due propriety, asked for his daughter's hand in marriage.

"Ah, Norah, ye've done yerself proud. The man was well brought up I can see. He has manners and respect fer the older generation." His breathing had become more labored. "Will ye promise to take good care of me Norah?"

Bill, having recovered from the initial shock of seeing a man on his death bed, promised he would cherish Norah for as long as he lived.

Matthew took Nancy aside. "I think it's time for the last rites." Sadly resigned to her father's fate, she asked Norah to fetch Father Connelly from the rectory and Aunt May from Murphy's Bar & Grille.

"Da, Aunt May is coming to see you," said Nancy.

"Ah, Nancy. It will be good to see her again. Yer mother, Kathleen, loved her sister May. She longed after her once May left fer America. They wrote to each other all the time, up till a week before yer mother died. And they looked so much alike, that red hair ..."

Nancy watched her father close his eyes, probably seeing the face of his beloved late wife. Then gradually he began to sleep. All that talking and the excitement of meeting his future sons-in-law, had taken their toll.

Matthew checked the old man's heart again, and estimated the end would be soon. Nancy put the tea kettle on the stove, and Matthew held her in his arms and praised the bravery and decorum she'd shown while watching her father slip away.

"But I did get to see him once again. And he met you and baby Sean. And I'm so grateful for that."

Norah returned with May and Father Connelly, and Nancy took them to her father's bedside. His eyes were open, and as he spied May, he cried out, "Kathleen!"

"No, no, Sean, it's me, May. Kathleen's sister."

Hearing her mother's name, Kathleen, inflicted new sorrow upon Nancy. And it brought to mind her father's second wife, Bernadette.

"Da, do you have a message you want me to give to Bernadette?" Nancy asked.

"Aye, I do. Tell her to go to hell! Worst mistake I ever made. The woman was just after me money. But the farm will go to the boys, under Irish law. Then they can throw the witch out and let her find another sucker."

Norah, despite her grief, felt a flush of triumph as her father confirmed her instincts. She had been right about that awful woman.

Father Connolly heard the old man cursing his wife to hell, and resolved to make him retract his statement before giving him the sacraments. He asked everyone to leave the room, then put a scapular around his neck, opened his kit and removed the candles and sacred oil.

"Sean, I'm Father Connolly. Would you like to make a confession and receive communion?"

"Aye, that I would, Father." And the old man recited his sins, few and venial though they were.

"And do you regret cursing your wife to hell?" the priest asked.

"Aye, I guess I do. She'll be in God's hands, and He'll decide where to put her."

The priest could not argue with the man's logic, and a slight smile crossed his lips. He granted Sean absolution, administered communion, made the sign of the cross, and prayed for his soul. He brought the family back into the room, said some prayers in their presence, and left. The family circled the dying man. Nancy and Norah were on either side of his bed and May stood at the foot of it. Sean opened his eyes for one last time and smiled weakly at his two daughters. Then he looked towards May, and mistaking her for his departed wife, made a desperate attempt to rise up, gasping, "Ah, Kathleen, my Kathleen, ye've come home to me!"

The physical effort and emotion proved too much for his damaged heart, and Sean O'Laioghaire fell back on the pillows, his head dropped to his shoulder, and he was gone. Matthew closed the man's eyes, as all about him wept and gave the beloved patriarch one last kiss on his pale, wrinkled cheek.

Matthew took charge of the funeral arrangements. After a Requiem Mass the following day, they buried Sean in a downtown cemetery. The deceased was given no wake, and no after-burial luncheon. The sisters and Aunt May had suffered too much, too soon. Sean died the very day he arrived in America. Norah and Nancy harbored unspoken guilt that maybe, had it not been for his traveling across the Atlantic for their weddings, their father would still be alive. When Matthew and Nancy were alone, she voiced those feelings.

"Nancy, the man was in the last stages of heart failure. Had he not died here, with all his loved ones about him, he would have died a week later, in Ireland, with Bernadette gathering up his money into her purse. It was better this way. And he did see his daughters and grandson. Be thankful. He died in no pain. May God be as merciful to all of us."

Nancy held Matthew close and said a silent prayer, thanking God for the love of this incredibly wise man.

The following day, June eighteenth, Matthew stood at the pier as the ship pulled into New York Harbor. He had not seen his father in six years, and was surprised that the man seemed not to have aged a day. He bounced jauntily down the gang plank, his blond hair blowing in the breeze. He dropped his two suitcases and the men clasped each other, laughingly remarking how well they both looked.

"Well, Da, how was the trip over?"

"It would have been easier, I suppose, if King Neptune had not been in such a bad mood."

"And the meals?"

"Oh, you know, three down and three up."

"So the seasickness got to you?"

"The ocean pulled its rank. But I'm here now, and when Dr. Clarke, do I meet my daughter-in-law to be?"

"We're on our way to see her now." Matthew told his father of the tragic events of the day before and how it might put a damper on their celebrations. He also mentioned what a coincidence it was that Sean was both his father's and Nancy's father's name.

"Matthew. You know what a common name that is. Like John, in America. In every other house in Ireland resides a male named Sean. It's like Pierre in France; Wilhelm in Germany, and Mario in Italy. Now come and show me this great city of New York where all our Irishmen are flourishing."

Matthew picked up his father's bags and, once settled in their carriage, asked him about the health of his wife.

"Oh, Deidre? I suppose she's okay. She ran off with her second cousin, Robert, to Italy last year in a fit of midlife sexual passion. She was all caught up in the romance of it. Robert, the fool, wrote bits of gibberish and called himself a poet. Haven't heard from her since and hope I never do again."

"Da! Why did you not tell me this in your letters?"

"What good would that do? To have you worrying about who was making my dinner? You were right to leave Ireland once I married her. She wanted to be mistress of the house without you around to point out her inadequacies to a lonely widower. But don't let it cause you any grief. I was sick of the sight of her after six months of marriage. And the single ladies of the town see that I eat properly, and bring me stews and jams and pies. But I won't be marrying again. And my estate will go to you, Matthew, though it's not a king's ransom by any means. But it's not the castle that makes the king. It's what's between a man's ears. And you have the brains to make a great success of yourself."

The carriage stopped before Murphy's Bar & Grille as Matthew pondered over the events of his father's life. Just like Nancy's father, he had been taken in by an Irish widow out to insure her future livelihood. A sad, but true fact she and Matthew shared.

Nancy, hearing the clip-clop of the horses, opened the door and welcomed Mr. Clarke. She looked stunning with her auburn hair piled in curls atop her head, and wore an emerald silk shirt which accentuated the vivid green of her eyes.

"Welcome, Mr. Clarke. I'm so glad you could make the trip for our wedding," she smiled.

"No more so than I. But let me offer my sincerest condolences at the loss of your father. I'm sorry I did not get to meet the man."

Nancy cringed at the memory of her father's death, but replied, "Thank you, Mr. Clarke. Now, come, sit down. We have only till tomorrow night to prepare for the ceremony, and we must finalize the plans."

Matthew requested his father to act as his best man, and he proudly accepted. Nancy told them May would be matron of honor for both sisters, and Mr. Murphy had agreed to stand up for Bill Peyton.

"So you see, we're keeping it all in the family," she said.

Sean Clarke hesitated before asking who would give the brides away.

"No one will be giving us away. Our father is gone, so we'll be giving ourselves away, freely, to the men we love dearly."

Sean grinned at the strength of the young women, and said that was as it should be.

Nancy brought the men beers and ham sandwiches and they talked for over an hour, filling each other in on the events since they'd last been together. Then Matthew took his father to May's apartment and helped him settle in.

Although their father's sudden death weighed heavily upon the young women, they knew he would not approve of them postponing the ceremonies. So Friday morning Nancy and Norah visited Mrs. Lally for their final dress fittings, and then it was off to the butcher shop to pick up the roasts Nancy had ordered for the wedding dinner, and the greengrocer's for vegetables. They returned to the Bar, put the meat in the icebox, covered the tables with pale pink linen clothes, shining silverware, wine glasses and candles. The centerpieces were of blooming pink, white and blue petunias Nancy had planted in small pots months ago in anticipation of her wedding.

Peeling of the potatoes came next. "I'm surprised. I don't mind this work at all, as long as my labors won't feed Mrs. Birmingham," said Nancy, looking at the pile of sliced vegetables in the pot of water on the stove .

"And why should you? You're here in your own business establishment," said Norah, wiping her hands on her apron. "There! All's ready for Mrs. Lally to boil and mash these after the wedding tomorrow, and put the roasts in the oven, so all we have to do is look pretty at our party. Are you happy, Nancy?"

She took Norah's hands. "I'm so happy I can't believe I'm not in a daydream. I've waited so long for tomorrow. And you?"

"I'm thanking God that you brought me to America or I never would have met Bill. You were my savior, Nancy. I will try always to make you proud of me. Do you think my English has improved?"

"It's perfect. I knew you could do anything you put your mind to. But you'll have me in tears if you keep this up. Let's finish the carrots and go home."

Saturday morning, June twentieth, had finally arrived. The sisters ate a quick breakfast of tea, toast, and an egg that Nancy insisted they needed to give them strength to walk up the aisle without fainting from hunger.

"Now, we'll sit down and compose ourselves, and go over Father Connolly's instructions. And remember Norah, when the photographer takes pictures of us with our new husbands, do not smile. No matter how happy you feel. The man said if we make a move after he hits the camera shutter, the picture will be ruined."

Then they washed up, did their hair and rouged their lips, just before Mrs. Lally arrived with their dresses.

"Now girls, put on yer corsets," she directed them.

"I will not wear that instrument of torture anymore," Nancy vowed. "Besides, my figure has returned, and I don't need to risk fainting from the tightness of that thing on the most important day of my life."

Norah followed her sister's lead, and Mrs. Lally rolled her eyes, unwilling to argue with the headstrong young women, and helped them into the gowns she had so lovingly created.

"Oh, I forgot about our bridal bouquets!" cried Nancy.

"Well, I didn't," announced Mrs. Lally, very pleased with herself. "They're sitting in water at home to stay fresh, and himself will bring them when he picks us up for the church."

Nancy gave Mrs. Lally a kiss on the cheek. "You're a marvel. You think of everything."

"Now you turn around and I'll button ye up, while ye button Norah's dress," Mrs. Lally ordered.

The sisters praised the woman's workmanship on the similar, but subtly different designs of their floor-length gowns.

"I do wish my dress could be white, like Norah's."

"Well it can't. You've been married before and have a baby. But look how the pale blue flatters your complexion. And don't let me be hearing any complaints out of you." Mrs. Lally treated the girls as the children she never had, and loved them dearly.

"I wish Da could see us today," Norah lamented.

"He does, Norah. He does," Nancy responded.

The organist played "Ave Maria" as the sisters assembled in the foyer of the church. The guests were seated in the pews, and Matthew and Bill stood together at the altar, awaiting their brides.

Abruptly the music changed to Mendelssohn's "Wedding March," and Mr. Grunwald whispered to Dr. Weitz, "Is this not a beautiful thing to hear? Music written by a Jew, played at a Catholic wedding? What a great country is this America."

Dr. Weitz nodded in agreement. His daughter, Rachel, had just become engaged to a rabbinical student, and as she sat beside him, he glanced at her finger and the simple engagement ring she wore. He was a good man, his future son-in-law, and he had cured Rachel of her infatuation with Matthew. No matter how much he loved and respected Matthew, he felt young people had a much better chance of happiness when they married within their own faith.

Joe and his mother, Mrs. Jefferson, sat behind Dr. Weitz and Mr. Grunwald. They were the only colored people in the church, but they did not feel uncomfortable. Nancy, Dr. Clarke, and Officer and Mrs. Lally had become good friends. Mrs. Lally gave Mrs. Jefferson some extra sewing to do whenever she became overloaded. Mrs. Jefferson was an excellent seamstress and could use the extra money. There are some good people in this world, Joe thought. Especially these Irish people who talk so funny.

The sisters walked slowly up the aisle, their timing perfect, and their bearing aristocratic, with just the right touch of innocence. The grooms met the sisters at the altar, and were struck by the women's beauty and their own good fortune.

After the Mass, they exchanged vows and rings, and the two couples strode happily down the aisle smiling to well-wishers on both sides of the church, much like British royalty acknowledging their subjects. Though they hated the English invaders, the Irish did adopt some of their customs, but only those that would be beneficial to themselves.

The luncheon reception at Murphy's Bar & Grille turned into a lively party, with Mr. Murphy playing his bagpipes, guests strumming their fiddles, and the women, except for the two brides, engaging in a lively step dance. Nancy and Norah accepted congratulations and well wishes from their guests, and gracefully mingled with their friends, their new husbands seldom far from their sides, impatiently waiting to be alone with their new wives.

After the couples made the first cuts in Mrs. Feroni's magnificent wedding cake, Mr. Feroni handed out plates to the guests. Nancy sat down at the piano and began playing, while Norah sang the hauntingly beautiful Irish ballad, "Kathleen Mavourneen," as a tribute to their mother, and the guests tried to hold back their tears.

Then, as Nancy played, both sisters sang "Believe, Me If All Those Endearing Young Charms," a song of love continuing as time wreaks havoc on the beauty of youth.

"Let thy loveliness fade as it will; And around the dear ruin, each wish of my heart, would entwine itself verdantly still ..."

At the song's end, the brides took their grooms' arms and waved goodbye to their friends. As they neared the door, Norah, though deliriously happy, still had the presence of mind to whisper to Aunt May to pick up the money envelopes and wrapped gifts the guests had left at the end of the bar.

The temperature registered near eighty degrees, but Norah shivered as she slipped into her new nightgown. Aunt May had instructed the virgin on the wedding night procedure, yet fear of the unknown filled Norah with anxiety. But Bill Peyton gently took his wife to his bed, and her apprehensions dissolved and she responded eagerly to his gentleness.

Chapter 21

REVELATIONS

June 21, 1893

The morning after their wedding, Nancy lay next to her drowsing husband and compared the joy she experienced with Matthew the night before with her first and only sexual encounter with Patrick. How sad and unfulfilling that occasion had been!

Matthew turned towards her and whispered, "Good morning, Mrs. Clarke."

"Oh, how splendid that sounds, Mr. Clarke," and Nancy brushed a strand of hair from his forehead and moved closer to him.

"I almost forgot." He reached for his bag on the floor beside the bed and retrieved a small package.

"This is for you."

Nancy carefully unwrapped her gift.

"Why, it's a book. 'Irish Folk Tales.' Now where did you come across this?"

"My father found it in a store in Galway. I'd told him you were writing short stories, and he asked me to give it to you after we were married. A small gift to remember him by."

315

"What a lovely man your father is. I must thank him for his kindness. I can't wait to start reading the tales of the old country." She clasped the volume to her chest and beamed at Matthew, while he leaned over the bed again and retrieved a thick manila envelope from his bag and gave it to Nancy.

"And what could this be?" she asked, and quickly opened the package and withdrew three magazines.

She furrowed her brow. "Thank you, Matthew, but do you think I need more reading material?"

Matthew laughed, and opened the copy of The Saturday Evening Post magazine to the page where he had placed a book mark. "Does this look familiar?" he asked.

She read the title, 'The Unwanted.' "Matthew! This is my first story. And look! There's my name in print-Nancy O'Leary. How could this have happened? How did they get my story?" Her surprise momentarily overcame her good sense. "Why of course! It was your doing."

"That it was. I took the liberty of sending it to the editor. He liked it and wants another as soon as you can write a new story."

"But I have two more to send him already. This is so wonderful. Thank you so much, darling."

"Unfortunately my dear, you do not have any more to send him. Look at page thirty in The Atlantic Monthly magazine, and page forty-two in Century magazine."

She flipped through the pages and found her second and third stories that she had given Matthew to read. Nancy's heart raced and she felt light-headed.

"But that's not all, darling. Close your eyes and open your hand before me."

After she did as he bid, he said, "One," and something light fell on her hand. "Two," he said, and another paper object brushed her fingers.

Her curiosity overcame her. "What are you doing and how long will you torture me?"

"Just once more." And another paper tickled her palm. "Now, open your eyes."

Nancy stared in disbelief at the three checks bearing her name.

"They're paying me for my stories? All these magazines?"

"Of course they are. Do you think writers give their creative efforts away for free? Every professional gets paid for his work. Do patients not pay me?"

"But I'm not a professional, only a fledgling writer."

"Fledgling. Now that's a good word. Your vocabulary is really improving."

"That it is. Do you know the difference between perspicacity and perspicuity?"

"I don't even know how to spell them!"

"So, you sent my stories to publishers months ago without telling me?"

"Yes, I'm guilty. But if they rejected them, I didn't want you to be hurt or discouraged and give up writing. I thought at least one would be accepted. I knew they were well-written and I liked them, so why wouldn't the magazines want them?"

"You are wonderful!" She threw her arms around him. "You have made me a published writer. I don't know what to say except thank you, I love you, and you are the most clever, most sneaky and best Irishman in the world."

"Well, two out of three compliments I'll accept. But sneaky? Maybe cautious would be a better word," he smiled.

The word sneaky reminded Nancy she had planned to show Matthew the letter Patrick found in the graveyard in Knock, once they were married. She thought now would be a good time to get this task behind her. She felt uneasy keeping it from him, but if her suspicions of the importance of the letter's contents were correct, she knew it would be wiser to wait until after their wedding.

Matthew put on his robe and went to the kitchen to start the tea. She dressed quickly and retrieved the letter from the drawer and placed it in her pocket, then went to the kitchen to scramble some eggs and fry bacon. As they lingered over breakfast, she took the letter from her pocket, and began hesitatingly, "Matthew, you remember the Gaelic words you translated from Patrick's cross that directed him to go to the Knock cemetery in Ireland?"

"Of course, I do."

"And the diamond ring Patrick found at the grave?"

"Yes, he showed it to me. You told me Patrick sold it to buy himself Devlin's Tavern."

"That he did. But I found this letter hidden among his things months after he died. For some reason he never showed it to me. I thought you should read it and tell me what you make of it."

Matthew went over the letter carefully, then reread it. Nancy waited nervously for his assessment of the document. Finally, her impatience got the better of her.

"Well, what do you think?"

His brow had furrowed, and his blue eyes darkened. He spoke very slowly. "The letter is addressed to Patrick. The writer says he is a teacher." Matthew paused between each sentence. "The writer says his clan was once wealthy until the English drove them to the west of Ireland." He took a deep breath. "And the writer uses the phrase 'knowledge is power.'"

Nancy's nervous system teetered on the breaking point, as she waited for Matthew to voice the conclusion she had reached after reading the letter five months ago.

"And the letter is in my father's handwriting." Matthew's face turned stern, and Nancy's heart thumped.

"So this seems to mean," Matthew said menacingly, forming his words carefully. "It seems to mean Patrick was my half-brother."

"Could that possibly be?" Nancy asked.

He threw the letter on the table, stood up and paced the room. "Why didn't you tell me?" He turned to his wife angrily.

"I didn't know for sure. I never saw your father's handwriting." The accusatory glint in his eyes frightened her.

"But it did occur to you that might be the case, didn't it?" He came close to her and slapped the palms of his hands on the table, causing their tea cups to jangle on the saucers.

"Matthew, I'm sorry. I could not be absolutely sure."

"You were sure enough to hide the letter from me for months. Why Nancy, why did you do that?"

Now Nancy became angry and retaliated. "Why did you hide the fact that you sent out my stories without my permission?"

"My actions gave you a happy surprise. What you have kept from me about Patrick and my father was a deliberate deception of a terrible act that disgraced me and my family." Matthew began pacing the room again, running his fingers through his hair.

Nancy had been near tears, but now she became angry, and stood before him, her hands defiantly on her hips.

"I had good reason to hide the letter from you, Mr. Clarke. The Catholic Church forbids a brother to marry his brother's wife, even after his death. And the way the Church makes up new rules all the time, they might have included half-brothers, too. Then where would I be if we could not marry? I might just as well have thrown myself off the Brooklyn Bridge, my heart would be so broken."

Matthew listened patiently to her tirade. "So, you didn't trust me and my love for you."

"It's not that. I just know what a good Catholic you are."

"And you thought the Church would come before you?"

"Well I couldn't take the chance that it might."

Then he broke out in laughter, and took her in his arms.

"Oh, you little fool. Why if I had to, I'd find a minister to marry us, or a judge at City Hall. You must take church laws with a grain of salt, my love. It is God's laws we must obey." He began laughing again, and as Nancy's anger subsided, she too laughed at her groundless fears, and held Matthew close to her.

"Well," said Nancy, "It seems we've had our first quarrel."

"It looks that way. Let's not have any more."

"I understand how you feel, Matthew, but think of the positive side. We have baby Sean. And we'll have children of our own. But Sean's already part of you. Your blood runs through him. He's your nephew. And you'll be his father. You brought him into the world and you will raise him as our son."

Her words made a deep impression on Matthew. "You are right, as usual, my love, and I do love the little tyke. He will be treated as our first child."

Matthew picked up his father and took him to Murphy's Bar & Grille. The weather was atypical for June in New York. Rain poured down and the wind gusts nearly swept the men off their feet. They entered the Bar and Matthew asked Charles Murphy if he and his father could spend some time alone in Callahan's old private room.

"Fer sure. Hang up yer raincoats, and you and yer father can have a good man-to-man talk, without the women hovering over ye both. What can I get you?"

"Two double whiskeys. And don't let anyone interrupt us, please. We have important business to discuss."

Charles Murphy's eyes widened, but he asked no questions and handed the drinks to Matthew, who led his father into the side room and closed the door. The men sat across the table from each other, and Sean lifted his drink. "Here's to you, my son. I wish you many years of happiness with Nancy, and many healthy children."

Matthew did not lift his glass. Instead, he took the letter from his pocket and laid it open before his father.

"What's this you're showing me?" Sean glanced at the paper and the color drained from his face. His hands began to tremble, but he managed to place his drink down before it fell from his grip.

Sean's symptoms alarmed Matthew. "Da, now don't go and have a stroke on me. Let's just discuss this like the grown men we are." He placed the whiskey back in his father's hand. "Have a sip. I didn't mean for the letter to send you into shock." But somewhere, deep in his primeval soul, Matthew felt a slight bit of pleasure witnessing the guilt the letter brought to his father's face.

Sean's voice cracked. "How did you get this?" His father's reaction confirmed Matthew's conclusion that Patrick was indeed, his half-brother.

Matthew then related how Nancy's husband, Patrick, had come to America from Dublin six years before she, and contacted the employment agency in Manhattan, which placed Irish immigrants in positions with the wealthy families in New York, and was sent to Tuxedo Park. Years later Aunt May, who had been working for the Birmingham's as a cook for ten years, brought her niece, Nancy over from Ireland to work with her at the Birmingham's as a scullery maid. Nancy and Patrick met there, were eventually married in Manhattan, and had a child.

After absorbing that startling information, Sean Clarke found his tongue again, and smiled slightly. "If I've followed you correctly, baby Sean is my grandchild?"

"That he is. But he's named after Nancy's father."

"And can you find it in your heart to forgive me?" Sean Clarke asked his son, his eyes watery and his hand shaking as he sipped his drink.

"For what? For leaving my grandmother's ring to your bastard son instead of to me?" Immediately Matthew wished he could withdraw the ugly epithet he uttered out of jealousy and mean-spiritedness.

"Forgive me, Da. I should not have said that. It's not for me to forgive you. The ring belonged to you. It was your property to do with as you wished. But it looked familiar to me. I had the strange feeling when Patrick showed it to me that I'd seen it before. Could that be?"

"You had seen it. I remember you grandmother showing it to you when she told you the story of how the English took our land. You were about six years old then. She never forgave the Brits, and she vowed to keep the ring as a symbol of the Clarkes' once mighty position in Ireland."

"Then you buried it in the cemetery when Patrick was born?"

"I didn't, then. I buried just a short letter, from me to Patrick in a metal box, behind his mother's grave. I told him his parents were young and not able to take care of him. Years later, I married your mother, and when you were about seven, your grandmother died and left me the ring. I was teaching at that time, and knew your mother and I could take good care of you, see to your education, and raise you, and probably leave some sort of inheritance. But the fear I felt for Patrick, not knowing what would become of him, led me to go back to the graveyard and dig up the original letter and replace it with this one," he gestured to the paper on the table. "And I placed the ring in the box for the boy. That was the guilt working on me."

"And who was Patrick's mother?"

"A farm girl named Ellen Flynn. We met at a dance and foolishly thought we were in love. When her parents became aware of her condition, they sent her to a Magdalen House for unwed mothers in Dublin. I went to see her just before Patrick was born. After Ellen died in childbirth, I bought the cross and had it engraved. I gave it to the Mother Superior and made her promise that the adoptive parents would turn it over to Patrick when he came of age. Every year after he reached eighteen I would check his mother's grave to see if he had retrieved the box. I was there six months ago, in the winter. I always carefully replaced the soil so no one would notice the grave had been disturbed. Ten times I dug behind Ellen's grave." He slowly wiped his eyes and continued. "But I'll not have to be going there again now, will I?"

Matthew felt pity for his father, who seemed to have aged dramatically as he confessed his sin to his son.

"Can I ask how the lad turned out?"

Matthew had not anticipated that question, but seeing the anguish on the man's face, he said Patrick had been a hard worker, a good husband, and a brave man who defended Aunt May from the Short-Tail Gang. He explained his involvement with Callahan and Ahern, who eventually had him murdered. Matthew intentionally neglected to mention the word carved into Patrick's forehead.

Sean Clarke shook his head sadly, and sipped his whiskey. "I could say if I had it to do all over again, I would do things differently. But that would not be the truth. If I had married Ellen Flynn, you would not have been born. And you are my greatest joy in life. I'm so proud of the man you've become. I only hope you'll have no hard feelings for baby Sean because he's your half-brother's son."

"I love the lad as my own. And all the more now, knowing that my blood runs through the child's veins." Matthew took a sip of his drink, and looked thoughtfully into the glass. "Da. Now it's my turn to ask your forgiveness. The ring never mattered to me. It was only my pride that was hurt. I'll make my own fortune, and I hope that makes you feel better."

His father smiled. "That it does, son. That it does."

The men sat silently for a few minutes. Then Matthew clasped his father's arm. "Da, drink up. We've finished our business and this is the last we'll talk of it. You'll be going back to Ireland in a few days. We can't waste time. Let's go home to our family."

That night, as Nancy lay in her husband's arms, Matthew became reflective.

"Those letters of mine, that Mrs. Birmingham threw out. They kept us apart and changed our lives. It keeps haunting me, all those wasted years."

"But my love, they weren't wasted. We were so young then. If I had received your letters, nothing on earth could have stopped me from rushing to Johnstown to be with you. Then I might have died in the flood. Or you would have left Johnstown before the flood to be with me, and never have become a doctor. I'd probably have ended up as a maid or cook in a big house in New York and you, as strong and muscular as you are, might have found yourself digging ditches for the new subway."

"You're right," Matthew admitted. "God does His work in ways we mortals cannot understand. It may seem cruel and unjust to us at the time, but looking back, I accept His plan. He knew what would be best for us."

"He just made us wait a bit longer. Gave us time to grow up; to be the people He wanted us to become so we could appreciate the love for each other that He had planned for us."

"Nancy, you are a wise woman, and you make me feel like a fool."

"You are no fool, Mr. Clarke. You're the smartest, most compassionate and patient man God ever put on this earth, if you don't include the old men in the Bible."

"You're talking about the Bible? Does that mean you may someday come back to the Church?"

"Indeed it does. I've been thinking a lot about that lately, and I've come to realize it was childish of me to let one bad apple, it's Father Gannon I'm referring to, take God from me. Look what damage an apple did to Adam and Eve."

He held her tightly. "And now, what do you see ahead for us?"

"A grand life. A wonderful life, loving each other and our children. But only if you promise not to deliver them! You know what embarrassment that caused me. Can you understand?"

He laughed and held her tighter. "Will you never be able to separate the husband from the doctor?"

"No, and I suppose that's the Irish in me."

"Don't ever lose that, my love. It's one of your most endearing qualities."

Nancy disengaged herself from his arms, and looked sternly at Matthew. "And all along I thought it was my beauty, wit and intelligence that drew you to me."

"Well, isn't that what Irish means?"

"Ah, you've redeemed yourself. Now, come back in my arms, my handsome husband, and let's talk about our future."

They pulled the bed sheet over their naked bodies, and Nancy said she thought two more children would suit her fine. He thought he might like three, or four.

"Then you have them! Two more is my limit."

Matthew laughed and squeezed her close to him. "Then two it will be, my love. And I'll instruct you in how that's possible without interfering with our desires."

"You mean there is a way we could be together and not have children for a while?"

Matthew laughed. "There are many ways. And we'll talk about that later. But now, tell me what will happen with the tavern while you're taking care of all our children."

"Aunt May and Mr. Murphy can run the place. I'll still keep the records at home, but there'll be no more cooking or serving drinks at the Bar for me. I'll have my hands full taking care of you and the children."

Matthew gazed quizzically at his beautiful wife, knowing that keeping the accounts of the Bar and caring for the three children they would eventually have, could not satisfy her entrepreneurial spirit. "And would that be enough for you?"

"Of course it will. But also, I'll be writing my stories. And I've been hearing talk that people are moving up to the country, up to the Bronx. They're building houses and opening businesses. It's supposed to be quite beautiful, with lots of open farmland and rivers, and much of it is right on the Long Island Sound. I've some money saved, and I think we should look into buying land there, while the prices are still low, before the real estate investors discover it. Then, in a few years, we'll sell some land for a tidy profit."

"The country is in an economic depression, and I think we should keep our money safe," he warned, but Nancy continued.

"But don't you see? Now's the time to buy if you have the means, when prices are low. And just think, we might even build a house for ourselves by the water. We could spend weekends there with the children and they could grow up playing in the clean countryside, under a clear blue sky, as we did in Galway and Mayo. They'll need a place to restore themselves after spending the week in this crowded city, with its stifling heat in the summer and freezing air and dirty snow all winter. Why they could ice skate on the ponds in December and learn to swim in July in a house in the Bronx."

She turned to her husband and said, "Matthew, are you listening to me? What do you think? Can we?"

He turned his head on the pillow and looked towards his wife, who was now sitting up and mapping out her plans. He smiled up at her and answered, "Yes, my darling, we most definitely can."

He thought about how fortunate he was to have Nancy as his wife. Yes, she was ambitious, but that never came in the way of her fulfilling her obligations to her friends and family, and had not turned her hard or avaricious. His Nancy was just an extraordinary woman, full of love for her family and farsighted enough to ensure their prosperity. He remembered how surprised he was last week, even before they were married, when she had asked him if she could send her brothers some money to put a new roof on the house to replace the worn out thatch they had lived with for years. She hadn't needed his permission to spend her own money. But she thought of them as one, with no secrets between them. He had watched her as she juggled working at the Bar and the Tavern and never let it interfere with her first priorities, her son and Matthew. What could he say? He thought this woman could do anything she put her mind to. He took her hand and said, "And what will your next story be about?"

"Oh, I don't know yet. Something about Ireland as the other three were. It seems publishers like stories set in Europe."

"No, that's not it. They like what you write, and the way you write it, not the location. I knew your father for less than three hours before he died, but I was very taken by the man. And impressed by the way he raised you, to become such an admirable woman, with great charm and strong character. Write about him."

She laughed, and said, "Oh, you do have the Irishman's gift of blarney, and your flattery makes me blush."

"No, I'm serious. Write something inherent to your father's essence, something that reflects his spirit and strength. You never did get seasick, did you? Even on our rocky voyage to America."

329

"No. I told you my father had me out on Galway Bay in his currach for years, fishing with him since I was just six years old. I became used to rough waters."

"That's it! He didn't take your brothers out fishing, did he?"

"They were making hay, and planting, and taking care of the animals."

"But he never took Norah out on the bay, and she was just a year younger than you."

"Norah was more interested in the local boys and didn't like the sea salt spraying on her hair, or wearing overalls and boots. She wanted to be perfectly groomed at all times, just in case she ran into one of the neighboring farmers' sons."

Matthew thought Nancy's whole life up to now had been traveling through turbulent seas. He would make sure that she had smooth sailing from now on. He gently drew his wife back down on the pillows, took her face in his hands, and said, "Name the story for your roots, and what made you the woman you are. And since you're determined to be near the water in the Bronx, it's only fitting you name your next work 'Galway Bay'."

Nancy beamed up at Matthew. "Ah, you've come up with the perfect name. It's decided then. It will be about my father and it will be called 'Galway Bay.' Won't that be grand?"

Matthew smiled down at his wife. "Yes, Nancy, our whole life will be grand."

Chapter 22

LAMENTATIONS

Early December, 1897

The Clarkes' fourth Christmas as man and wife was rapidly approaching, and Matthew had spent an inordinate amount of time deciding on the perfect gift for his wife. His medical knowledge of various birth control methods allowed them years to enjoy each other in the bedroom before they decided the time was right to bring a child into the world. Their Catholicism did not extend to observing all the rules the popes entered into doctrine. Now that Nancy was pregnant, he'd narrowed down the choice to an engraved heart pendant on a silver chain, or gold earrings with three intertwined circles representing them and their new child. He decided on the earrings and ordered them from a local jeweler that afternoon, and now automatically went through the day's mail.

His heart skipped a beat as he opened a letter postmarked Ireland, from his parish priest. This cannot be good news, he thought.

Dear Matthew, I managed to get your address from the postmaster in Knock. I regret to tell you that your father, Sean, is not at all well. The doctor gives him less than two months before the cancer finally gets the better of him. You father is being very brave, and does not know I am writing you. But I felt it my duty to inform you of his condition. He is at peace with the Lord, but you might never forgive me if you were not given the chance to see him one last time.

So, though I have disobeyed your father's wishes, I think I am acting in accordance with my heavenly Father's wishes.

You must now make a decision. And that is what each of us wants: The opportunity to follow our own conscience. If circumstances prevent you visiting your father one last time, God will forgive you. But someday you might not forgive yourself. Should you need to see him once more, you still have the time. I send you all my prayers, and leave the rest to you. God Bless. Father Tom Ryan.

Matthew needed no time to make his decision. "Nancy, come out of the kitchen. We must talk."

His wife waddled towards him, her belly engorged with the baby she would deliver in about four weeks.

"Oh, how my back does ache," she said, pressing her hands on her hips. "I've had a hard day." Sean, now a handful at five years of age, kept Nancy on the run trying to prevent the child from tripping and splitting his head open on a table or grabbing a hot pot off the stove.

"What it is, my love?"

"I've had bad news from Ireland. My father's dying. I have to see him one more time or I'll always regret it. Can you get on without me for about a month? Dr. Weitz will take good care of you."

Nancy was stunned, and her body recoiled from him in anger. How could he even think of leaving her now, just before their first child would be born? She said nothing; just stared at her husband in wide-eyed disbelief.

332

"Now Nancy, you're a strong woman, and I could be home before the child's born. Can't you understand how I must see my father before he dies? You of all people know how much it means to say your last goodbyes to a parent." Matthew pleaded his case as Nancy stood silently before him. "Have you nothing to say?" He questioned her.

Since her well-being was not his top priority, she asked. "But how can you leave your job for a month? Won't the hospital penalize you? Or withhold your salary?"

"I guess I'm more important than you give me credit for. I have no doubt they'll give me leave. Have you forgotten I'm assistant chief of surgery at Bellevue Hospital? And stop your constant worrying about money, please. We have a good bit saved."

"I thought you were indispensible. You work such long hours, and take only one day off a week."

"Nancy. No one is indispensible. People die every day and others take over their tasks."

"I see," she sneered. "And you don't feel you're indispensible to me right now with your baby about to be born?"

"You know I wouldn't leave you if I had the slightest fear for your health."

He took her in his arms and she let him hold her, but her anger prevented her from responding. The idea that he would willingly leave at this most important time of her life appalled her. Patrick had done the same thing when she was pregnant with Sean. Gone to Ireland!

"And you probably won't be back by Christmas, will you?"

"We'll have our celebration when I return. Christ wasn't even born in December. You know that."

"But that's when we celebrate his birth," she spat out.

"Be reasonable, Nancy, please. This is something I must do."

Then she recalled her father's death, and how kind and solicitous Matthew had been to her, and it softened her heart. I must control my selfishness, she thought, and wrapped her arms around Matthew.

"Do what you think is best. For you and all of us."

"That I will. I'll book passage tomorrow."

"You're right, Matthew. You must see your father one more time."

"Ah, that's my girl." He held her tightly and assured her everything would be all right. "I'll have Dr. Weitz stop in everyday to check on you. And Mr. Grunwald, who knows almost as much about medicine as we doctors do. And you have all our friends and Bill and Norah to watch over you."

"A lot of good Norah will be with two toddlers of her own to look after, and Bill Peyton working day and night at the district attorney's office."

"There's also Aunt May and Mrs. Jefferson and her son, Joe. He'll take care of any errands you need done. And he'll come to the house and amuse Sean so you can get some rest and have time to write the novel you're working on. Joe really admires you."

"He is a good young man," she agreed.

"So, there's no need for you to worry. After all, you've decided Dr. Weitz is to deliver our baby, not me."

She jokingly pushed him away. "That he will. You made the baby. You've done enough work."

"And I enjoyed every minute of it."

They laughed, and she led him to the bedroom to pack a bag for his trip. Then she added, "As long as you'll be in Ireland, maybe you could visit my brothers in Galway and see how they're doing. I miss them both so."

"That I'll do, Nancy. That I'll do."

Matthew reached his father's house about two weeks later and was startled to find the man sitting in a chair looking exhausted and emaciated. Mr. Clarke stared at his son in disbelief. "What are you doing here?"

"I came to see you, Da. To see how you were doing."

"Well, I may have the cancer eating me up, but it hasn't gotten to my brain yet. It must have been the doing of that meddling priest, Tom Ryan, who brought you here."

"How do you feel, Da?"

"About as bad as I look. But the locals are taking good care of me. Now tell me all about Nancy and Sean."

Matthew sat beside his father, and while trying to hide his concern at the man's appearance, filled him in on life in America.

"What a pity I'll never get to see your child. Bring him up properly, Matthew, and take good care of Nancy. She's an extraordinary woman."

"That I know, Da. She asked me to visit her brothers in Galway while I'm here. And I'd like to talk to your doctor, if that's all right with you."

"You can talk to him till you're blue in the face and it won't change a thing. But I've had a fairly happy life. Made some mistakes; did some things right. I'm not afraid of dying, but would like to stay around for a bit longer. Let this be the last lesson I teach you. Enjoy your life, live it properly, stay close to God, cherish your family, and be the best doctor you can. And be happy every day because we never know when catastrophe will strike."

At that point Matthew did not realize how wise his father's words were. But within a few days he would understand.

"Now that you're here, Matthew, can you take me to Mass tomorrow and after that visit your mother's grave?"

"Of course, Da. Whatever you wish."

"Well, I'm tired, and now I wish to take a nap. If you want to ride to Galway this would be a good time for it."

"Okay. I'll be back late tonight. Will someone be in to take care of you?"

"It seems the local women are lined up outside the door just waiting to feed me and pray over me. But I have no appetite anymore, and if I haven't prayed enough during my lifetime, their prayers won't help me. So go see Nancy's brothers. It will make her happy. And Matthew," his father sighed, "tis wonderful to see you again."

Matthew saddled his father's horse as tears clouded his eyes. He knew the man had very little time left on earth, and Matthew was already in mourning.

He rode through mist, then cold rain, then sunshine, then rain again and reached the O'Leary farm, wet and shivering, and saw Nancy's brothers out in the field. They looked warily at this stranger rapidly approaching. When Matthew identified himself, they gave him a warm greeting and led him into the house.

"I'm Robert, and he's me younger brother, Phillip. Set yerself down by the fire and warm up. The weather in Ireland is terrible. God should have put a huge umbrella over this whole fecken country!"

Robert's language startled Matthew. He'd rarely heard an Irishman use that word, but he supposed that Robert was tired. The weather had been nasty and the man had been out taking care of the cattle and mending fences most of the day.

Phillip put on the tea kettle while Robert pulled a bottle out of the cupboard.

"Ye'll be needing a bit of whiskey to warm ye up." And he poured himself and Matthew four fingers of the brown brew, and threw his own drink down his throat in one gulp.

"So, how's me sisters?" Robert seemed to be the talkative brother.

"Norah's fine. Has two little children. But I expect you know that."

"I think she did mention that in one of her letters," Robert said. He obviously could not care less.

"And Nancy and I are expecting a baby in a few weeks."

"So ye knocked her up fine, did ya? She's quite a beauty and yer a lucky man."

Matthew, taken aback by Robert's vulgarity, did not have time to respond as Phillip brought in the tea and asked after Norah. "She's a bit of a wild one, but a good girl at heart."

Matthew agreed. "That she is, and her husband works in the district attorney's office in Manhattan."

Robert winked at his brother. "Wonder how much she had to give away to haul in such a great catch."

"Oh, come off it, Robert," said Phillip. "Can't ye never be pleasant? Our brother-in-law's come all the way from America to see us. Be nice, will ya?"

"Actually, I came here to see my dying father in Mayo, and Nancy asked me to stop in to see how you're both doing and tell you she misses you both."

Robert responded, "The sisters seem to be doing much better than we are. One married to a doctor. One married to a lawyer. And here we are digging in the dirt, shoveling shite from the barn, and barely making a few pounds a month."

"Didn't Nancy send us money for the new roof?" Philip reminded his brother. "Ye should show some thanks for her generosity."

"Aye, it's easy to be generous when yer pocket's full," sneered Robert.

Matthew stood up to leave, and Robert pointed to Matthew's untouched whiskey. "Ye've not taken the pledge, have ya? Let's have a toast."

"Yes, let's," said Matthew. "Here's to you, Philip, and thank you for the tea. And Robert, I do take a drink in the proper company. So, to use your favorite word, I think you're a fecken jerk, and I'm sorry to be related to you by marriage. Phillip, I'll tell Nancy how polite and accommodating you were, and how well you look. Robert, you look like shite!"

And Matthew left the house, amazed how different siblings could be though sharing the same family genes. Then it occurred to him that Robert's problem was the bottle. But that did not make Matthew feel any less disgusted by him.

When Matthew reached his boyhood home he found his father sleeping in the chair where he'd left him. He quietly went to his old bedroom, threw off his wet clothes, and fell asleep immediately.

He was awakened the next morning by sounds of dishes clattering in the kitchen. He dressed quickly and went out to find a neighborhood widow cooking and brewing tea.

"Good morning, Matthew. Oh, and haven't you put on some muscle since I saw ye last. I'm Barbara Walsh from the next farm. Though ya probably don't remember me."

"Indeed I do. And how are your boys?"

"They're in England, working fer farmers. It's hard to make a living in Ireland anymore. But they're good boys and send me half their pay every month. Now, set yerself down and eat. Yer father told me you'd be here, so I've made ye some breakfast. He's looking much better today, don't ya think?"

"Good morning, Da. And you do look better. Got some color in your cheeks. How do you feel?"

Sean Clarke gave his son a wary glance."Looks can be deceiving. But I do have more strength than yesterday. It's seeing you again that's got my blood moving."

Sean moved Barbara's plate of food away and asked for just a piece of soda bread with strawberry jam. Matthew's stomach growled from hunger and he dove into his plate of bacon, eggs, and fried tomatoes.

"I've been thinking this morning, son. Would you be up to visiting your mother's grave today in Knock church yard?"

"Of course, Da, but do you feel strong enough?"

"I do. We'll take the horse and cart. Your mother's not far from the road, if you remember, and you and my cane will get me the few yards in."

"We'll go right after breakfast."

Matthew hitched the horse to the cart and helped his father onto the seat. The man was now light as a child, his bones jutting angularly from his clothes.

He walked the horse slowly to avoid jolting the old man, and presently they arrived at the cemetery. They moved slowly to his mother's grave, and Sean removed his cap and blessed himself slowly. The men spent some minutes in prayer and contemplation. Then Sean said, "Goodbye, my love. I'll be with you soon."

Matthew did not know how much of this sadness he could endure, and ushered his father back to the cart. They were silent on the ride home. Sean's emotions caused him a visible setback, and his face once again turned ashen. They pulled up to the house and Matthew helped his father down and walked him to the door. He went back to unhitch the horse and suddenly slipped in the icy Irish mud. He fell against the animal, which then reared up, throwing Matthew to the ground. As he tried to raise himself, the horse's hoof slammed down on Matthew's right hand. Before he felt the pain, he heard the crack of breaking bones. Then the agony set in and he laboriously crawled on one arm back to the open doorway.

"Da, Da, I need help," Matthew cried. Barbara, still cleaning up the breakfast things and settling a blanket over Sean in his chair, rushed out and helped Matthew to his feet.

"Jesus, Mary and Joseph!" she cried. "What's happened?"

"It's my hand," Matthew shouted. "The horse. His hoof got me. I need a doctor!"

Barbara led him to a chair and began trembling as she stared at the mangled mass of blood, flesh and bones protruding from the joints of his right hand. She ran to get a cloth and a pan of water, but Matthew said, "Please, don't touch it. Just give me a whiskey and then get me to a doctor."

Barbara brought him a large glass of rye, and he gulped it down.

"There's no doctor nearby, but the pharmacist right down the road handles these problems. They happen all the time out here. If ye can manage to get to the cart, I'll drive ye there."

"Yes, yes, let's go."

Sean Clarke sat silently watching the goings-on, with tears streaming down his face. Then he said, "Son, it's all my fault. If only I hadn't asked you to take me to the cemetery."

"No, Da, it was the bloody horse's fault. Barbara, bring the whiskey bottle with you," said Matthew, writhing in pain and hoping he would not pass out.

Barbara managed to get Matthew to the pharmacist as quickly as possible, and banged on the door. A middle-aged man came out and did not disguise his concern at seeing Matthew's hand. He brought him into his office as Barbara related the details of the accident to Mr. McNally, who immediately put a tourniquet on Matthew's arm.

"I'm a doctor. I know what to do," Matthew rasped.

"So do I," said Mr. McNally. "We see a lot of this type of injury here. I'll give you something for the pain."

"The whiskey will do. Please, can you try and set the bones?"

"Well, young man, it looks worse than it really is. Only two fingers and one knuckle have been damaged. I'm pouring some alcohol over your hand, so you'd best be having a shot of that whiskey."

Barbara pulled the bottle from her bag and Matthew took a long swig of rye as the pharmacist poured the alcohol over his hand. He winced, gripped the chair, and felt himself falling into unconsciousness.

The pharmacist worked quickly, setting the bones as best he could. He put in a few stitches, closing the gaping wounds in the skin. Barbara had to turn her head. Watching all that bone and blood caused her breakfast to come frighteningly close to expelling itself from her throat.

Mr. McNally removed the tourniquet and brought Matthew back by wafting some concoction under his nose. He then placed the damaged arm in a sling around Matthew's neck and advised him not to unnecessarily move his hand.

"Barbara," groaned Matthew, "Please go into my pocket and get the money to pay Mr. McNally."

"Oh, no. I could not accept a fee for treating Sean Clarke's son. He's a good friend of mine. And I'll be over the house tonight to look in on ye both."

"Thank you for that. And for helping me," said Matthew.

"Can I give you something for the pain?"

"No, thank you," said Matthew. "I have an herb in my bag at my father's house."

"Come at five," Barbara told Mr. McNally. "And I'll have a good dinner waiting for ya."

Barbara, at sixty-five, was still spritely, and helped Matthew into the cart and slowly directed the horse to Sean's house, avoiding any bumps or holes in the road that would jar Matthew's arm. His hand throbbed with pain, and he asked the woman for more of his liquid anesthesia. She opened the bottle and he took another long swallow which deadened the pain slightly. Matthew thought, if only he had a gun he would gladly have shot the damn horse and walked the rest of the way home.

At the house, Barbara opened the door and saw Sean sleeping peacefully in his chair.

"Wait a minute," Matthew cried, and rushed to his father. "Da, Da!" He shook his father and watched the man's head slump to his shoulder. Sean Clarke had died.

Barbara went to fetch Father Ryan and Mr. McNally, while Matthew sat dejectedly across from his father, his mind in turmoil. If they hadn't gone to the cemetery today; if Nancy had refused to let him go to Ireland; if he hadn't had the accident with the bloody horse; if Father Ryan had never written to him; if-if-if! Oh, how the seemingly good things one does can turn out so badly, he thought.

Now he had no father, a destroyed career as a surgeon, and a wife who, though outwardly accepting his leaving her at such an important time in her life, would probably harbor hidden resentment towards him forever.

His hand throbbed, and the whiskey he imbibed helped, but did not make him drunk; a condition he had never experienced, but thought now it might be a blessing. He'd take some of Mr. Grunwald's white willow bark as soon as he could manage to stand up.

Just then the door opened and Father Ryan entered. He went straight to Sean's chair, took out his scapular and sacred oils, and proceeded to administer the last rites. Barbara and Mr. McNally knelt and bowed their heads. The priest and the pharmacist then lifted Sean's body onto the sofa, and the priest addressed Matthew.

"I am so sorry. But it was his time. I'm glad you got to see your father once more."

Matthew stared at the priest stone-facedly, and said not a word.

"I'll put on some tea," said Barbara.

"How's yer hand feeling?" asked Mr. McNally.

Matthew did not reply to any of their questions. He sat dazed, angry and resentful.

"We'll proceed with the wake and funeral whenever you wish," said Father Ryan.

"As soon as possible," Matthew replied, and walked slowly and carefully to his room, calling out "Barbara, can I talk to you?" Even though Matthew was in excruciating pain, his mind was clear.

She followed him and he asked her to sit in the chair next to his bed. "Can you help me? I need a packet from my suit case marked 'white willow bark,' and some water to mix it with."

After he drank the potion he told Barbara, "You're the best person in Ireland I've met since I came home. Can I ask you to be honest with me?"

"Of course. I never lie, if I can help it."

"What do you think of Father Ryan?"

She hesitated a moment, then replied, "He's a meddler. And God forgive me, but I don't like the way he looks at young boys."

"What do you think of Mr. McNally?"

"He's a good man. A very good man and a pretty good surgeon."

"What did you think of my father?"

"Why, I loved the man. My heart's broken by his death." And then she cried. "I had hoped that after a time he might want to marry again. But himself was so above me in station. A brilliant teacher, he was. And me, just a poor, ignorant, farm girl."

"You're neither ignorant nor poor, Barbara. You're wise, and though you might not have much money, you're rich in kindness and spirit. To be honest with you, I thought of bringing my father's

345

body to New York to be buried. But now I think he should stay here in Mayo, with you."

"Oh, thank you, Matthew. I'll take as good care of himself in death as I did while he was alive."

"Can you arrange for the wake and funeral? I don't remember the customs here. Would you do that for me?"

"Fer sure. It will be the grandest funeral they've ever had in Knock."

Matthew asked her again to go in his pocket and take out some money for the funeral. "My hand's in a sling or I'd do it myself."

She did so, and only took a few pounds. "No, Barbara. I want you to have some for yourself. You've been so good to me and my father. Take half of what's in my pocket."

"Oh, that's way too rich fer me."

"The way you've behaved since I met you, nothing's too rich for you."

The wake began the next afternoon, and four days later Matthew boarded a boat back to New York.

Chapter 23

NEW LIVES

December, 1897

As Nancy awaited her husband's return from Ireland, her abdomen grew larger and larger. Sleeping became difficult, as she could not move off her back, and spent most of the day lying on the sofa. Joe came over daily and amused Sean as Nancy caught a few hours of sleep. She thanked God for the young man's help, and occasionally slipped him a few dollars in gratitude, which he never accepted.

Her family and friends heeded Matthew's request to look after his wife until he returned, and they took their responsibilities quite seriously. Too seriously, Nancy thought. Her apartment seemed never to be without at least one caretaker present, and though she was grateful for their help, she longed for some quiet moments of privacy.

But this Sunday afternoon her friends and family arrived en masse. Mr. and Mrs. Feroni stopped in with a tray of Italian pastries. "I made them this morning, right after Mass for you and your family," she said. "Very delicious."

Mrs. Jefferson and her son, Joe, carried in casseroles of chicken and dumplings and sweet potato pies. Dr. Weitz and Mr. Grunwald came bearing a platter of smoked salmon and loaves of pumpernickel bread. Then Norah and Bill appeared, she holding the hands of their two toddlers, while Bill balanced a plate of cookies atop a hefty pot of Irish stew.

They've brought enough to feed an army, Nancy thought, looking at the dining room table laden with her guests' special ethnic dishes. And though she appreciated their efforts, her exhaustion overcame her usual happy disposition. She just wanted to go to bed.

Aunt May and Mr. Murphy came last, bearing a wicker basket full of jars of preserved fruits, vegetables, and jams she'd prepared from the bounty of Mr. Grunwald's harvest from the garden behind the Bar & Grille. "Well, me dear, ye look as if yer about ready to pop," May smiled at Nancy. "How are ya feeling?"

"Like a stuffed pig. And my back is killing me. And Matthew had better be home soon or he'll have hell to pay."

"Now, now, come on, girl, get up and talk to yer friends and stop feeling sorry fer yerself. Where's yer spunk?"

"Aunt May, my spunk has sunk. Just look at Sean running around the room like a little maniac. I spend all of my day trying to keep him from harming himself. Oh, my back's acting up again," she groaned.

"Stop it. Go greet yer guests."

"Hello, Nancy," said Bill Peyton.

Nancy gave him and her sister Norah a kiss on the cheek.

"You look tired," said Norah.

"I am, but I'm glad to see you all. And Bill, how do you like working at the district attorney's office?"

"The work is very different than what I was used to. No more leases to negotiate, or contracts to go over with friendly people. Now I must try and convict the bad guys; murderers, arsonists, burglars and rapists. And I have to try and outwit their defense lawyers who attempt to get their clients acquitted by fast talking the jurors. Nancy, it's a lot more stressful then when I worked with you and Mr. Murphy drawing up your partnership agreement years ago."

"You seem very unhappy," said Mr. Grunwald. "But isn't every accused entitled to a fair trial here in America?"

"Of course they are. But that's not what's bothering me. It's this."

And he held up a document for all to see entitled, 'Plessy v. Ferguson.' "Do you know what this is?"

"Well, no," Nancy hesitated. "But it looks like a court case."

"Yes. It's a case decided by the Supreme Court a year and a half ago. So in my spare time I've been working on an appeal."

"Don't you have enough to do?" said Dr. Weitz.

"Oh, more than enough. But this is important to me. It's a bad decision. It ruled that Negroes and whites have to use separate facilities. They call it 'separate but equal.' But it's just another way to promote segregation. It says Negroes cannot use the same bathrooms as whites, cannot ride in the same railroad carriage cars as whites, and are not allowed in the same restaurants as whites. Or even drink out of the same water fountains as whites."

"Do you intend to work on it here today?" Nancy asked.

"No, but I'm going back to the office after lunch and will give it more thought."

"Why you exhaust yourself? Today is Sunday," said Mrs. Feroni.

None of them had ever seen Bill, usually calm and polite, in such an agitated state. "This decision by Judge Ferguson says Mr. Plessy violated a Louisiana statute that promoted segregation of the races and he was criminally liable for sitting in the same car as whites. Can you believe that?"

The deadly silence was broken by Mr. Grunwald. "Does this law include us Jews, also?"

"Not yet," replied Bill. "But I'm going to do my damnedest to have this ruling overturned before it does."

"It's just like it was in Mississippi," whispered Mrs. Jefferson. "We were separate, but Lord knows, they didn't think us colored folks were equal."

"Exactly," Bill exclaimed, and Norah pulled on his arm indicating he had gone on long enough and overly depressed everyone.

Their attention abruptly turned to Joe when he shouted out, "Get down, Sean," just as the child jumped on a chair and was about to leap off onto the coffee table.

"Watch me, I can fly," the child cried.

The adults gasped as Joe grabbed Sean around his waist in mid-air, seconds before the child would have fallen and surely broken his neck and those of Norah's two toddlers sitting on the floor beneath him.

Nancy jumped up, horrified at the near disaster, and tried to run to Sean, but pain gripped her and she fell back on the sofa.

Dr. Weitz went to her immediately. He watched her water flowing onto the sofa, and heard her groans. The baby would soon be born, he thought.

"Mr. Grunwald," he said, "Help me carry Nancy to the bedroom. Her time has come."

"But I'm not due yet," she moaned.

"Second babies often arrive earlier than first babies. And the labor is shorter, I've observed," said Mr. Grunwald as he helped her into the bedroom.

The guests stood silently, their eyes darting to and fro, not knowing what to do, till Aunt May clapped her hands to attract their attention.

"Now, all of ye, listen to me. Nancy's being well taken care of. Come to the table and enjoy the good food ye've all brought. And no more talk about that Ferguson fellow and Mr. Plessy. We're not going to let them spoil this wonderful day for us."

Nancy's baby struggled to be born, and Mr. Grunwald brought Norah in to help, and as with Nancy's first labor, Norah let her sister grip her hand for almost an hour until she thought it might eventually break. But she continued to whisper encouragement to her sister and mopped her brow with cold, wet towels.

"This baby is coming fast, no?" asked Mr. Grunwald.

"Very soon now," replied Dr. Weitz. "Please get more towels and hot water for me."

Mr. Grunwald brought Aunt May into the room with the supplies, and the baby was born a short while later. But Nancy still writhed in pain.

"Wait!" said Dr. Weitz. "We are not yet finished."

And shortly thereafter he withdrew a second baby from Nancy's body.

"Look! We have twins here," said Dr. Weitz. "A boy and a girl. Is God not great?"

Norah unclasped Nancy's hand from her fingers and wondered if she would ever be able to use them again. She immediately plunged her hand into cold water as Matthew had instructed her when he delivered Sean.

Aunt May tended to Nancy while the doctor cleaned the infants, wrapped them in blankets, and placed them in Nancy's arms. She inhaled deep breaths of air now that the agony was over, then drifted off to sleep, while the guests clapped and cheered at the sounds of wailing from the new-born babies' lungs.

Chapter 24

MATTHEW AND NANCY

Late December, 1897

Nancy stared out her apartment window at the dirty snow piled alongside the road. Though the sun shined, it failed to warm her heart. Where is Matthew? She thought, as she nursed her twins while Sean looked on in awe and resentment at the new arrivals who challenged his supremacy in the household. Christmas had come and gone, and still no sight of her husband. Nancy's emotions see-sawed from fury at having to deliver her children without her husband by her side, to fear that something terrible had happened to him. Life in Ireland had not been easy, but it was dependable. This new life in America presented all kinds of opportunities, but many unforeseen problems; her not knowing enough to purchase fire insurance had cost her the loss of her restaurant; entering into a marriage without loving Patrick had cost her to raise a son alone; Mrs. Birmingham throwing out her letters from Matthew had cost her years of happiness; and now, all this traveling of fathers and husbands between Ireland and America had cost her great grief. Well, she thought, I must remember who I am, and not let these setbacks destroy me. But, she thought, who am I? Well, I'll have to try and remember when I feel stronger.

353

That evening, just as she put the babies down for the night, the apartment door slammed shut and Matthew appeared before her. She rushed to him, but he pulled back to avoid her injuring his hand.

"Oh, Matthew, at last you've come home. But why is your arm in a sling?"

"I had a bit of trouble with a horse in Ireland." He then told her of his father's death and his accident.

"Oh, my poor darling, sit down." Matthew's appearance frightened her. "This is terrible. Can I get you something? You look exhausted."

"Bring me a large drink of whiskey. But not until you give me a kiss and a hug, a very gentle hug, and tell me what have we here?" He pointed to the babies.

"Our children. You are the father of twins, a boy and a girl. Aren't they a beautiful sight?"

He stared in amazement at the two babies lying side by side on the bed. "Yes," he said. "But not as beautiful as you. Can you ever forgive me for not being with you when they were born?"

"You're here now, and that's what matters." She put her arms gently around him and kissed him passionately. She had missed his lips, his touch, his strong body, and had to resist pressing herself against him.

Her embrace brought back the intense feelings he had for his wife and the nights of love they shared in their bedroom before he went to Ireland, and he felt he'd been terribly wrong. "Was it very hard for you?" Matthew's regret at letting his wife go through childbirth without him filled him with guilt. What should have been his primary responsibility, he thought. Was it being with his dying father, or with his wife and unborn children? Had he make the right decision? He would wrestle with the answer for the rest of his life.

"Well, if you want the truth, it was awful. But it's over now. And I have you back and it was all worth it." She kissed him again, gently, avoiding his injured hand. "Now, let me get you that whiskey."

While Nancy was in the kitchen, Matthew walked slowly to answer the knock on the door.

"Matthew! It makes me very happy to see you."

"Dr. Weitz, come in. I need you," said Matthew as he went back to the sofa and slumped down.

"What have you done to your arm?"

Matthew told the doctor of his miseries in Ireland.

"Be at my office at first light tomorrow. I must check out that hand. Now I must look at Nancy and the children."

After examining the babies, he told Nancy that they were thriving. "You are an excellent mother. You do a fine job. But you must also take care of yourself. You seem a little thin. Are you eating?"

"I do when I have the time, but I try to nap whenever the babies are sleeping. They have me up every few hours at night to be fed."

"That is no excuse. You must have three meals a day. You are nursing, and for the sake of the health of you and the babies you must have proper nutrition. Do you understand me?" Dr. Weitz did not hide his concern.

"Yes, doctor," she said. "I will be more careful. Now that Matthew is home, I will make a good dinner every night."

"Now it is late and I must go. But I will see you, Matthew, early tomorrow."

After Dr. Weitz left, Nancy and Matthew lay on the bed and held each other gently. After he told her about his encounter with her brother, Robert, she said, "He's always been a rogue, and his actions were always an embarrassment to me. Phillip's a prince and Robert is a pauper, mentally and financially."

"Well, I gave as good as I got, but it hurt me to talk to your brother that way."

"He deserved it. And I wouldn't blame you if you knocked his block off." Now she began remembering who she really was; that gutsy young girl from Ireland who took no nonsense from anyone.

"Forget about them. Let's talk about more important things. What will we be naming our new babies?"

"I've been thinking they should not have Irish names," she said. "After all, we're Americans now. What do you think of Peter and Madeline?"

"Sounds fine to me. That's what they shall be called."

They then slept soundly for a few hours until the twins began to cry for their two o'clock feeding. Nancy took the babies into the living room and Matthew promptly fell back to sleep.

At seven the next morning Matthew arrived at Dr. Weitz's office. Mr. Grunwald was also present, and that alarmed Matthew. He thought that the doctor must be very concerned with his condition, and he cringed as Dr. Weitz removed the bandage from his hand. The doctor did not mince words.

"I must tell you the truth. This does not look good. The bones were not correctly set, and your hand is infected."

"Damn, I thought that might happen. The man who worked on me was a country pharmacist, or a barber, or a dentist, I don't know. But I couldn't set the bones myself, could I? And the hospital, if you could call it that, was too far away."

The concern on Dr. Weitz's face alarmed Matthew.

"If there is any possibility that you will regain the use of your hand, you may need more than one operation. I don't think it will be necessary, but you must prepare yourself for the possibility of amputation if we cannot destroy the infection."

"Oh, dear God! I hadn't even thought of that." Matthew's heart raced and he silently cursed Father Ryan for sending him that letter. His father could have died in peace, and Matthew could have lived in peace, had that man not meddled in their affairs.

"How could you have thought that far ahead," said Dr. Weitz. "You have a slight fever. You are not able to think clearly. But I will take care of you. Do not be afraid."

"But I am afraid. I could lose my hand, my career, my livelihood."

"Stop now, Matthew. We will proceed one step at a time. Mr. Grunwald, please, give me the iodine and mercury potion you prepared. It's in that cabinet over the sink. I will apply it to the wound."

"And what will happen to me if I, God forbid, if I lose the use of my hand?"

"Matthew, you are a very talented surgeon. Should the worst happen, which I doubt, you can teach, you can diagnose, you can even learn a new specialty." Dr. Weitz reassured him.

"All doctors need two good hands," said Matthew, now quickly sinking into despair.

Mr. Grunwald disagreed. "My friends in Europe have written me about a doctor in Austria who studies the brain. He is also a professor of internal medicine, and a lecturer on neurology. But now he's concentrating on how the mind's energy effects people's actions. He studied with a psychiatrist in Vienna and I am told his ideas are revolutionary and will change all we think about the brain's role in medical conditions. You might want to use your recovery time researching his articles."

"And who might this man be?"

"His name is Sigmund Freud."

"I've never heard of him."

"But you will, Mein Sohn, you will," Mr. Grunwald assured Matthew. "I will give you the material I have about Dr. Freud. He does not have to use his hands to help people. His brain is the only instrument he needs."

"Mr. Grunwald. Please hold Matthew's arm down."

"Well, I will take your advice and read his works. Thank you, Mr. Grunwald. Maybe Dr. Freud can teach me a thing or two. OUCH!" Matthew shouted as Dr. Weitz applied the liquid to the red, puss-filled knuckle, and Matthew grimaced in pain. Mr. Grunwald held down the hand as Dr. Weitz quickly covered the infected area with a clean bandage.

"Now you go home, Matthew, and in three days we will go to the German Hospital up the road and have a look at those bones."

"Why go to the German Hospital?" Matthew was confused. "We work at Bellevue."

"My friend," Dr. Weitz frowned. "Have you not been keeping up with the advances in medicine?"

"I try, but I've been very busy."

"That is no excuse. Do you not know of the brilliant physics professor, Dr. Wilhelm Roentgen in Germany?"

Matthew's pride would not allow him to admit no knowledge of the man. "I think I've heard of him."

"You think? The physicist from Wurzburg University invented a machine that can see into the body. What an achievement, no Mr. Grunwald?"

"Indeed. Yes, it is amazing. Dr. Roentgen calls it the X-ray, and it can look at your bones and show us what must be done to fix your hand. So far the German Hospital is the only institution in New York to have the machine. Dr.Weitz received special permission to try it on you this morning. But he will do the surgery at Bellevue."

"This is incredible news. Thank you so much, Dr. Weitz." Matthew secretly promised himself to become more diligent in his research of current medical innovations, and to let go of his pride brought on by the adulation he had been used to in his village in Ireland as a young man. He was now in his late twenties, and thought he had done very well for himself, but now realized how little he really knew, and how much he must learn to reach the level of knowledge his Jewish mentors possessed.

Three days later, Nancy and Matthew arrived at Bellevue Hospital while Aunt May stayed at their apartment tending their three children. Once in his bed, being prepared for surgery, Matthew and his wife talked.

"Well, now that the infection has cleared up, what did that new X-ray machine show? You know you never told me." Nancy's nerves were at the breaking point, but she did her best to hide her anxiety.

"Dr. Weitz is, as we doctors say, cautiously optimistic. He thinks he can save my hand."

"Oh, thank God!" Nancy relaxed a bit.

"But I might need more than one surgery."

"I don't care how many it takes, as long as you keep your hand."

"He told me the X-ray showed the bones broke clean, and my knuckle hadn't been broken, only badly bruised. Even if all goes well, I'll never be able to perform delicate neurosurgery, but then I never did that anyway. But I will still be able to deliver babies," he winked at her.

"Well, you won't have to worry about delivering any more of mine because I have three. Remember, that was my limit," she smiled. "I'm so happy for you, Matthew. But now I must leave. The babies are waiting to be fed. But I'll be back here before you come back from surgery."

"I know," he said. "But I have to tell you one more thing before you go. And it's very important. If I don't lose my hand, this whole ordeal, bad as it is, will make me a better doctor."

"Why is that my love?"

"I've been operating on people's bodies for years now; just concentrating on where to cut, what to remove, how to suture the wounds. Sometimes I'd never even met the patient before surgery. I'd tell them 'Now, don't worry, you'll be fine.' I never thought much about their emotional condition. Oh, sure, we'd give them some sedation and ether, but the fear! I didn't know how bad that fear could be until today. I'm still very afraid I'll wake up with only one hand."

Nancy held his arm. "You're a wonderful doctor and you've saved many lives. And Dr. Weitz will save your hand."

"Don't you understand? I once amputated a thirty-year-old man's leg and felt so proud of myself for saving his life. And what kind of life did the poor bloke have after that? I was too busy with the next patient to allow myself to consider his future. He might have been happier dying with two legs than living the rest of his life with one. I must change the way I treat patients if I survive this."

Beads of sweat appeared on Matthew's forehead, and Nancy wiped them away. "Have some water."

He took a few gulps and lay back on the pillow.

"I've been praying very hard and I know God hears me. You will be fine and not lose your hand. He gave you this great talent to heal, and would not let a stupid horse rob you of it."

Before the assistants came to take Matthew to the operating room, Nancy kissed her husband's lips and whispered, "God will be with you, my love."

"Keep praying, Nancy. We've come a long way since that day we met on the boat from Ireland. Look at what we've accomplished.

You're a famous writer."

"I am not famous. But someday I may be, after I finish the novel I'm working on, if it's any good."

"And I'm a doctor. Sometimes I can't believe my good luck. We never could have come so far in the old country."

"No Matthew, we could not. If we hadn't had the courage to get on that boat at such a young age, we'd never have found each other. I'd probably be living on a farm and you'd be bored teaching in a one-room country school house, and neither of us would have achieved what we have now."

"Nancy, you're right, as usual."

She kissed him once more, and before leaving said, "We may have some hard times before us, but with the grace of God, we'll get through them."

"Mrs. Clarke, with me at the helm, the wind at our backs, and you at the keel, together we can navigate any rough seas ahead."

~

About the Author

Anne Higgins Petz enjoyed a successful career in advertising and marketing, most recently as Vice President of a large Manhattan advertising agency. She is the author of the novel *The Dream Chaser*, and the creator of the books *Irish Crosswords* and *Bible Crossword Puzzles*. She lives in Cary, North Carolina.

Visit her web site at www.annepetz.weebly.com